LEICESTERSHIRE I SERVICES	
4152866	
Bertrams	05.12.07
f	£10.99
SO	

Fighting for Survival

Carey Brown

Published 2007 by arima publishing

www.arimapublishing.com

ISBN 978 1 84549 227 4

© Carey Brown 2007

All rights reserved

This book is copyright. Subject to statutory exception and to provisions of relevant collective licensing agreements, no part of this publication may be reproduced, stored in a retrieval system, or transmitted in any form or by any means, without the prior written permission of the author.

Printed and bound in the United Kingdom

Typeset in Garamond 11/14

This book is sold subject to the conditions that it shall not, by way of trade or otherwise, be lent, re-sold, hired out, or otherwise circulated without the publisher's prior consent in any form of binding or cover other than that which it is published and without a similar condition including this condition being imposed on the subsequent purchaser.

In this work of fiction, the characters, places and events are either the product of the author's imagination or they are used entirely fictitiously. Any resemblance to actual persons, living or dead, is purely coincidental

Swirl is an imprint of arima publishing.

arima publishing
ASK House, Northgate Avenue
Bury St Edmunds, Suffolk IP32 6BB
t: (+44) 01284 700321

www.arimapublishing.com

PREFACE

THE WAR. Being born in 1975, I missed being alive in the war by a mere generation. Go back another generation, and I would have been a combatant in World War Two. When it began, no one expected World War Two to be over quickly, and the conflict would last for six years, lead to over fifty-five million deaths, and encompass the whole globe. The war left a trail of unprecedented destruction over European soil. In 1940 Britain faced the greatest danger in her history, and threat of invasion, since the Armada in 1588. In 1942 when Hitler was at the peak of his power, four hundred million people were ruled by Nazi Germany. The war would set the pattern of political and military power for the remainder of the Twentieth Century. With hindsight we can view the Second World War (in stark terms) as a conflict between good and evil, but to defeat that evil would demand great sacrifice. On more than one occasion, in the early years of the war, defeat was a very real prospect for Britain. British males were being killed whilst still in their teen's -someone's husband, brother or boyfriend.

Just stop and think for a minute; aged 18 (in the Nineteen Forties), and being sent far away from home to fight, and not knowing whether or not you would be alive tomorrow. *How* would we have fared? Or, how about having discovered that your home has been destroyed by German bombs? Then there was the rationing, queuing, mass evacuation of children, women being conscripted into war work etc. This was the first 'total' war, in which the morale of whole peoples was tested. It's a sobering thought, that, due to the accident of birth, those of us under the age of sixty missed the terrors of World War Two. We can only ever imagine what it was *really* like, only those that lived through those historic six years, know the hardships, suffering, sorrow, comradeship's of 1939-1945. There are ruins, old (deserted) airfields, museums, the cemeteries to remind us of the conflict, and then there are the film reels and accomplished literary works.

Fighting For Survival, the first of two books, represents an authentic best effort as to 'what it was really like' in the war. Experiencing the innocent fun of the teenage children on the one hand, and the horrors of combat —on land and in the air-on the other. We live in a very different world to the 1940's, today, in terms of lifestyle, technological advances and society values. The past seems foreign, although in terms of history the Second World War is very recent. Indeed, cars, aircraft and many other machines were around in abundance in the 1940's, and colour film existed, albeit in it's infancy. We are where we are now, because people were willing to lay down their lives in the past, just sixty years ago. Although very few of them would see themselves as heroes, in my view they were a very remarkable generation, -many ordinary people did exceptional things, and we owe them all a very big debt.

If Britain had been defeated and invaded by Germany, all British males between the ages of seventeen and forty-five would have been deported to continental slave labour camps. The old, the weak, thousands of 'enemies of the state' and 300,000 Jews would have been exterminated. Suitable young British women faced the prospect of being transported to Germany to produce children with Germans.

Thankfully, the outcome of World War Two was a happier one, although it was a close run thing...

Carey Brown
2007

PROLOGUE

At 4:45 a.m. on 1st September 1939, Germany commenced the invasion of her neighbour, Poland. Tanks tore through the border, and over flat Polish countryside, followed by over a million men. From the skies above, the Luftwaffe (German Airforce) pounded Polish airfields, destroying the planes before they could get airborne, as well as attacking bridges and troop concentrations. German Messerschmitt fighters shot those Polish aircraft that did manage to get airborne, out of the sky. Warsaw, the capital of Poland, was bombed, and terrified civilians went scurrying for shelter. The German battleship Schleswig-Holstein bombarded Danzig.

The brave men of the Polish Army, fought with 1918 methods and equipment; they possessed few tanks and were still largely reliant on the cavalry. The desperate Poles launched futile cavalry charges against German tanks, armed with little more than swords and lances. The machine-gun fire from the panzers (tanks) annihilated the horsemen. Within a week, the panzer divisions would advance close to 150 miles. The Poles were victims of German Blitzkrieg tactics, which involved using aircraft as airborne artillery, and fast moving tanks that by-passed strong points, in order to achieve a swift breakthrough. Motorized infantry followed close behind the armoured units, and infantry on foot followed them. Pockets of resistance crumbled, to reveal thousands of dazed Polish prisoners. Some Polish army divisions never completed mobilization.

The much-feared SS quickly rounded up the Polish aristocracy, officer corps and politicians. Jewish areas were torched. Stuka dive-bombers machine-gunned frightened refugees that had clogged up the roads. Each morning, posters would list names of those executed for having spoken ill of Hitler or the Reich.

Four days later, the Polish Government left the capital for Lublin, to the East. The following day, Cracow, the shrine of Polish culture surrendered to the invading Germans.

By 11th September, a jubilant Hitler was able to walk along the banks of the River Vistula, and check that operations were proceeding according to plan.

On 17th September, Poland's fate was sealed, as troops of the "Workers' and Peasants' Red Army" invaded from the East. Behind the Red Army, propagandists brought with them photographs of their leader, Stalin, and distributed Moscow newspapers to Polish citizens.

On 19th September, the mayor of Warsaw broadcast in vain an appeal for assistance to the peoples of the civilized world.

"I have seen women and children being killed in the streets while waiting in queues to buy necessities." He continued. "I have seen the dead lying about unattended." He declared defiantly. "We shall fight to the last man if we have to go down fighting."

On 27th September, after three days of nightmarish bombardment by artillery and bombers, and with its water, food and power supplies down, Warsaw, now a burning wreck surrendered. There were some forty thousand casualties in the city, people had been reduced to living in cellars, and there was an outbreak of typhoid.

On 5th October, the last Polish resistance ceased, and Polish workers were herded together and taken by the lorry-load to an unknown destination and fate. The Nazi jackboot would be brutal, the Poles would be reduced to the status of slaves, and never again would Poland be allowed to rise from the dead. Only Britain and France stood in defiance of Hitler.

At the end of the 1930s, Britain was a nation of contrasts. There had been a slow but continuous economic recovery from the Depression of 1931 and 1932, however, a condition of the prosperity of some groups, was the poverty of others. There were the struggling older industrial regions, but also areas that experienced unprecedented affluence. There were the old inner city tenements, where three generations of the same family would live together, and then there were the comfortable suburban 'semis', with three bedrooms, a proper bathroom, a front *and* a back garden..

At the outbreak of war, there were still two million out of work in Britain, and many people survived on a diet of little more than bread, potatoes and meat. Mothers sometimes went hungry for the sake of their children. In the poorer areas of the cities, head lice, scabies and vermin were prevalent. In some houses, without proper sanitation, it was still the habit to urinate on a newspaper indoors. The 1930s had seen hunger marches, and the poor begging for coins from theatre queues. The unemployed were reduced to backbreaking jobs as collecting pebbles from the seashore. In 1933, forty per cent of miners and a staggering sixty per cent of shipyard workers were unemployed. Large parts of the country were 'depressed areas', such as industrial Scotland, the North East and South Wales. The government attempted to assist these areas through 'special area' schemes.

The growing number of middle classes, however, was richer than ever before. Jobs in management, sales, teaching and clerical desk work all increased. Throughout the (1930s) decade, inflation was low, housing was cheap, and electricity and gas services were extended. They enjoyed radio and the cinema, and smart shopping precincts appeared in the suburbs. The Midlands had enjoyed rapid economic growth, as the motorcar and textile industries boomed.

The railway companies complained of Government restrictions, but new roads popped up everywhere. By the end of the 1930s, car ownership had reached two million. The Model Y, the smallest Ford ever built, appeared in Britain in 1932, for the masses. Motorcycles had been the predominant form of transport until the Depression, so cheaper motorcycles with smaller engines were produced to bolster sales. The working classes took summer holidays by train, whilst the affluent went in their cars on picnics.

People in general were proud of the British Empire and old traditions still held sway. Parliament and the monarchy were still held in high esteem.

Married women were known as 'housewives' and most were totally dependent financially on their husbands. A woman's place was most certainly in the home, and on marriage females in employment were often required to give up their jobs. A man would give his wife a weekly allowance for housekeeping and personal necessities; if she wanted any more money she would have to ask for it.

Children normally left school at 14, and either went straight into unskilled jobs or sought an apprenticeship to learn a skilled trade. Sometimes it was advantageous for an employer to employ unskilled juvenile labour as wages would be lower. The brightest children went to grammar schools at 11: parents might have to pay fees unless a child gained a scholarship. They would have to stay at school until they were 16 but would then get jobs in offices, banks, libraries and the like. A few would stay to 18 and might go on to the universities or colleges.

Meanwhile, in Germany Hitler had become the symbol of all that was dissatisfied and disillusioned in the country. As Hitler grew from strength to strength so too did the German people. Here, at last, was a leader that would make the country great, again.

The desire for peace, with the horrors of World War One still fresh in many memories, ran deep, and calls for re-armament in Britain went unheeded for a long time. There was little stomach in the country for an aggressive foreign policy, despite crises such as the 1935 Italian invasion of Abyssinia, or Germany's entering the Rhineland the following year. The countries of Western Europe saw Hitler as a bulwark against communism in the East, and were prepared, to some extent to turn a blind eye to his excesses. Britain and France reckoned that Hitler's desire to restore German pride could be met by limited concessions. Appeasement seemed to be the sensible course of action −avoid war at all costs.

Neville Chamberlain became Prime Minister in 1937, and he believed that he could contain Hitler's expansionist ambitions. However, the German leader had no respect for peace treaties. Some of the British people were disturbed by stories of the Nazi regime from Jewish refugees fleeing Germany, which seemed to reflect a sinister undertone to Hitler's rule.

In September 1938, the British and French allowed Germany to take control of a large portion of Czechoslovakia, a sovereign country, without consulting the Czechs. Chamberlain was quite taken in by Hitler's willingness to sign a piece of paper guaranteeing peace in return for Britain and France not opposing Germany's occupation of the Czech Sudetenland.

"How horrible, fantastic, incredible, it is that we should be digging trenches and trying on gas masks here because of a quarrel in a far away country between people of whom we know nothing."

So said British Prime Minister Neville Chamberlain on 27th September 1938.

On 30th September 1938, British Prime Minister Neville Chamberlain descended from an aircraft at Heston aerodrome and announced to an enthusiastic crowd that there would be no war over Czechoslovakia.

"There has come back from Germany to Downing Street peace with honour. I believe it is peace for our time."

However, Britain accelerated and expanded her defence programme, with conscription for twenty and twenty-one year old men being announced in early 1939, and £2,000,000 a week being spent on aircraft manufacture by mid-1939. The British Army, although very well trained and disciplined, had fallen behind technically, compared to the German Army. At sea, the Royal Navy ruled the waves.

On 1st September 1939, British Prime Minister Neville Chamberlain addressed the House of Commons, with a last warning to Germany that Britain would honour its treaty obligations to Poland.

"Information which has reached His Majesty's Government in the United Kingdom and the French Government indicates that German troops have crossed the Polish frontier and that attacks on Polish towns are proceeding. Unless the German Government are prepared to give His Majesty's Government satisfactory assurances that the German Government have suspended all aggressive action against Poland, and are prepared to withdraw their forces from Polish territory, His Majesty's Government in the United Kingdom will, without hesitation, fulfil their obligations to Poland."

11:15 a.m. Sunday 3rd September 1939. British Prime Minister Neville Chamberlain broadcasts to the nation.

"I am speaking to you through the Cabinet room at 10 Downing Street.

This morning the British Ambassador in Berlin handed the German Government a final Note stating that unless we heard from them by eleven o'clock that they were prepared at once to withdraw their troops from Poland a state of war would exist between us."

The Prime Minister's voice was slow and solemn,

"I have to tell you now that no such undertaking has been received, and that consequently this country is at war with Germany."

CHAPTER 1 – 3RD SEPTEMBER 1939

In their home in London, George and Mary Baker sat in respectful silence to the chilling words coming from the wireless. The street outside was deserted, and the usual Sunday-morning sound of hand-pushed lawnmowers was absent. The nightmare had come true. The practice blackout in London, on the night 9th-10th August, and recent rehearsals with the queer barrage balloons that looked like silver elephants swaying in the breeze above the capital, really *had* been necessary. And all because the German leader was drunk on power. George leaned in a little closer to the wireless, as the Prime Minister went on.

"You can imagine what a bitter blow it is to me that all my long struggle to win peace has failed. Yet I cannot believe that there is anything more, or anything different that I could have done and that would have been more successful.

The Government have made plans under which it will be possible to carry on the work of the nation in the days of stress and strain that may be ahead. But these plans need your help.

You may be taking your part in the fighting services or as a volunteer in one of the branches of civil defence. If so you will report for duty in accordance with the instructions you have received."

The Prime Minister concluded.

"It is the evil things that we shall be fighting against -brute force, bad faith, injustice, oppression and persecution- and against them I am certain that the right will prevail."

After "God Save the King" was played, George Baker switched off the wireless, and looked thoughtfully at his wife.

Mary Baker sat with a faraway look on her face, trying to take in and accept the consequences of the Prime Minister's words. After all Mr. Chamberlain's efforts to avoid conflict, Britain really was now at war -impossible, but true. The British armed forces were being mobilized. By the end of the day, all men aged between eighteen and forty-one (other than those in reserved occupations), would be liable for conscription. The British would be sending troops across to France within days. The R.A.F. had already landed some bomber squadrons in France. Mary had hoped against hope that 'something' would turn up to prevent war...

George made some sort of prediction that war with Germany would most likely go on for years, just like last time.

Mary thought back to 1918, when she was in her early twenties. Wasn't the Great War meant to be a war 'to end all wars'? It now seemed to Mary that after a mere twenty years of peace, when Europe was taking up arms again, that the Great War had been a waste, and that nothing had been learnt from it. Mary wrestled with her thoughts and tried to convince herself that her brother's death on the Somme in 1916 at the age of twenty-two had not been in vain.

And now, at this very moment her oldest Son John, just twenty years old, of similar age to Mary's Brother when his life was tragically cut short was serving in the army 'somewhere' in Britain, or France even. What would be his fate? He would be required to kill German boys his own age, maybe there would be bayonet charges and gas attacks like in the Great War. Mary shuddered to think.

The room suddenly felt cold.

As if reading his wife's thoughts, George came and put a comforting arm around Mary. George said reassuringly.

"John knows how to look after himself; he'll be alright."

"It wouldn't be so bad," Mary began. "But, what with the little ones being away, too…"

A week ago, Monday 28th August, Mary's younger children, Hannah, almost fifteen, and Richard, thirteen, had gone back to school to take part in a rehearsal for an increasingly likely evacuation. Carrying their gas masks, in small cardboard boxes around their little necks, parcels of clothes and food for the day, Hannah and Richard arrived at school at 6 a.m. Mary had been there too, along with all the other mothers watching the playground evacuation rehearsal. The teachers and voluntary helpers made a careful inspection of gas masks and kit, ensuring that on each child's knapsack there was displayed the child's name, age, address, school number and next of kin. The last act of this mock evacuation was when the children obediently filed onto buses, which waited to transport them to the station.

Four days later it was for real. The same morning that Hitler's troops invaded Poland, Friday 1st September 1939, Mary bid farewell to her teenage children. On this first day of autumn the atmosphere was more subdued, with the realization that the children would not be returning home after school this afternoon.

Britain had been divided up into danger areas (the large industrial cities that people were being evacuated from), reception areas (safely away from likely bombing targets, and receiving evacuees), and neutral areas (neither receiving children nor evacuating them). All around London, police shepherded the moving flocks of children and accompanying adults with the aid of loudspeaker vans. Trains were coming and going, departing from the main stations at nine-minute intervals.

Fighting back the tears, Mary gave Hannah and Richard a final hug on the platform at Victoria station. Armed with no more than spare clothing, nightclothes, a bag of food for the day, soap, towel, a toothbrush, comb, handkerchief and just one toy, her children looked smart in their navy blue school uniforms. Hannah dressed in her neat skirt, blazer, blouse, and tie and felt hat; Richard in his blazer and little shorts and cap, both wore the school badge. Mary felt a sense of pride.

Hannah's best friend, Daisy, would not be joining her. Daisy's father had expressly forbidden that the girl be evacuated, and would rather, in the event of a bombing, the family died together than Daisy survive and be orphaned.

A voice from a loudspeaker requested the children to "Please take your seats quickly, and don't play with the doors and windows on the train." Policemen strode up and down the platform, helping to carry the youngest children. In the chaos, some of them lost food and clothes from their bags, which were then trampled on.

The group of children —two classes from Stone Park School- began to shuffle onto the train. Their faces showed a mixture of emotions —some were smiling, several crying, and others betrayed a fear of the unknown. Towards the back, Hannah boarded, followed by her younger brother. The girl waved. Richard turned round and smiled a nervous smile at his mother.

Hannah was of slim build; she had a longish face and brown eyes and hair. She was a bright girl, who liked reading, and was a worrier. She had the misfortune to be down a year at school, due to an illness earlier in her childhood that had kept her in and out of hospital for nearly a year.

Richard's blonde hair and blue-eyed features endeared him to others. Because he was a small boy, he looked a year or two younger than his true age. He was trusting of others, and, like his sister, he was a polite child.

The magnificent steam engine slowly made it's way out of the station, and the noise, laughter and tears of the departing 'townie' children faded, as the train headed towards a destination in the country. Inside one carriage, brother and sister sat opposite each other, squeezed between the other pupils. Hannah offered Richard a sandwich.

"I don't feel like eating very much," replied the boy. A few moments later, he asked, "I wander what it will be like where we're going?"

"I don't know." his sister bit her lip; she wandered when they would see London again. Their mother had reassured them they'd just be away for a few weeks. Hannah remained unconvinced.

Less than an hour later, the group of fifty plus school pupils disembarked at a quiet rural station. It was Victorian, with quaint old gas lamps, and decorated by a number of flower boxes, and was bordered by a neat white fence. A sign said 'Welcome to Oak Green'. As the train disappeared from view, they caught their first glimpses of the village that would become their home for the foreseeable future.

Wide, sloping, tree-lined fields stretched away into the distance; fields of green and yellow, signifying ripening corn. The sun hung bright and golden in the sky, along with a few slow-moving cumulus clouds. Close by, a rabbit scampered through the grass, and birds descended into a clump of trees. The air was full of the smell of warm grass and corn. Men toiled over the earth, and cattle lazed in the midday sunshine, without a care in the world.

A tall, sombre-faced man in a suit strode up to Mr. Wilson and Mrs. Webb of Stone Park School, and introduced himself as Mr. Henry, a teacher from the village school, and the village-billeting officer. Hannah took an instant disliking to Mr. Henry, and she made a comment that caused some mirth amongst the other pupils.

Mr. Wilson clapped his hands together authoritatively to silence the chattering children, and informed them that there would be a short walk to the Church hall.

The group of teachers and pupils passed through the white wooden gate that was the exit from the station. With Mr. Henry and the two teachers from Stone Park School striding ahead, the children were led up the village main street, passing along the way (amongst other less prominent buildings), a butcher, sweetshop (to the delight of the boys and girls), green grocers, turn-of-the-century post office and a public house.

Richard felt that he and the rest of his classmates were on display, as a number of the villagers had turned out to sight the arrival of the 'townie' children. Richard sensed that a housewife was inspecting the children, one by one, peering through a tiny gap in her washing, neatly hung on the line. Didn't these people have anything better to do? He wandered. His sister, aware of Richard's self-consciousness, clasped his hand as moral support.

A couple of elderly female residents stood talking, outside a cream thatch-roofed cottage. The pair smiled at the children when they came into view, to make them feel welcome. Many of the children waved back.

Within a few minutes, the children found themselves besides a tidy patch of grass in the middle of which stood a monument to the 'Glorious Dead' of the Great War. Most of the children had heard stories —some terrible- from fathers and uncles about the Great War, and the monument served as a poignant reminder of those sons who never made it home just two decades ago. Too many from the village had fallen at Ypres in 1917, when serving in the Royal Sussex Regiment. Here, the road forked. Across the road the other side of the monument, was an attractive pond in which swam the resident ducks. The pond was spoon shaped, with the widest part, some dozen or so yards broad, hugging the road junction; whereas the narrower section of the water ran parallel to the road that led away to the left. To the right, the road led past the village churchyard, church and church hall. Beyond the churchyard lay some woods, above which some birds circled.

The children followed Mr. Henry into the church hall.

Inside, they were met by the Verger and a couple of middle aged bespectacled women from the local Women's Institute. The two ladies began to distribute hot drinks to the grateful children. Mr. Hamilton, the sandy haired Verger, a man of about forty-five years of age, was profoundly apologetic. He explained that the Vicar, Mr. Bailey had dearly wanted to be around for the arrival of the children, but he was unavoidably detained elsewhere. The children did not seem to mind, since they believed that with the absence of the Vicar, they had most likely been saved from a rambling speech.

In the background was a group of approximately a score of women, and a handful of men, dressed in a variety of attire. There were those in pre-War clothes. There was a nurse, a gentleman who looked like the local squire, along with a number of shop workers and labourers.

Richard looked nervously at the adults, as one or two of the women pointed at the blue-clad schoolchildren and made derogatory comments.

"Feel like bloomin' cattle being auctioned off!" complained one of the schoolboys.

"I hope we're not staying with that scary woman!" said a worried schoolgirl to her best friend.

The three teachers began the process of uniting the schoolchildren with their new families. Two sisters had somehow disappeared, and the Stone Park schoolteachers got a right ear bending from Mr. Henry. A well-to-do lady took Dianne, one of Hannah's friends, and it seemed more than just coincidence that a local builder had David, a big strapping lad. An immaculately dressed old colonel was presented with three children, two girls and a boy, and his face had the look that he had taken on a great deal more than he could handle (lamenting the end of a hitherto peaceful retirement). Hannah and Richard were amongst the last to be paired up.

Emily Pavitt warmed immediately to Hannah and Richard, and they to her. Fresh-faced, Emily looked several years younger than her thirty-seven years of age. She was hardworking, intelligent and a caring wife and mother, who had married at a young age. Of slightly above average height, Emily had curly blonde hair, which draped onto the white blouse that she wore with rolled up sleeves. Unlike the other women in the room, Emily was in black trousers, as opposed to skirt, and had a well-worn, but sturdy pair of boots on her feet.

At first, Richard was confused as to why Emily was dressed differently to the other women in the room. But, all was soon to be revealed. The introductions over, Emily received the necessary registration slips from Mr. Henry that would entitle her to money from the Government to pay for the Baker children's food. She then took brother and sister by the hand, and they departed from the Church hall.

"Please, Mrs. Pavitt, where is your house in the village?" Hannah enquired.

"Is it next to the greengrocers?" guessed Richard.

"No, it's not next to the greengrocers," chuckled Emily Pavitt.

"Or is it by the railway station?" Asked Hannah.

Emily Pavitt shook her head.

"Our house is the last house in the village, as far away from the railway station as it could be. We live on the farm."

Those last words filled Richard with excitement.

"The farm!" He exclaimed. "Does that mean —do you have any cows?"

Emily nodded.

"Yes, and chickens, too —more than you can count."

Richard's eyes lit up as he gave out a long slow,

"Coo!"

"We're also not far from the sea, its just a few miles away," added Emily.

"Coo!"

"I think that Richard and I are going to very much enjoy staying with you, Mrs. Pavitt," stated Hannah.

"Oh! I do hope so." Emily Pavitt patted the two youngsters on the head. "And, please call me Emily."

Although Hannah and Richard came from a modest background, they had been properly bought up as children, and it was practically unthinkable for them to address an adult as anything other than Mr. or Mrs. So-and-so. Richard gazed up at Emily as the trio walked along, and thought what fun this evacuation lark was!

Emily explained to the children that there would be no school today for them, although lessons would resume tomorrow.

"When we get to the farm, I'll show you your rooms, and let you both unpack. Perhaps, when the children get home from school, they'll give you a tour of the farm…"

"You've got children, then?" Richard asked, almost indignantly.

"Yes, a girl and a boy. Bethany and Thomas –they're both thirteen years old." Emily replied.

Richard found it hard to believe that Emily was old enough to have children the same age as him. He reckoned that Emily must be at least over the age of thirty!

Emily and the children left the road and walked along a bush lined dirt track that was wide enough to accommodate vehicles. As they progressed, they became aware of the smell of soil and dried manure. A sparrow looked inquisitively at the group as they went past.

After a short walk up the track, they halted in front of a sturdy wooden gate.

"Well, here we are." Emily announced. She looked expectantly at the two children.

From behind the entrance gate, Hannah and Richard surveyed the farmyard. Opposite them, stood an L-shaped white stone farmhouse. To the left, were a walk-in wooden chicken hut and a battered old garage that contained a mechanized farm vehicle. On the right, lay a simple but sizeable building of corrugated iron containing a very high stack of hay.

No sooner had Emily opened the gate, than Richard sprinted into the farmyard.

Hannah shook her head and smiled.

"He's so excited."

Emily (closing the gate behind her), and Hannah followed Richard into the farmyard at a more sedate pace.

As Richard stood in awe, gazing at the two-story farmhouse, an energetic black Labrador dog appeared round the corner of the building, and raced up to the boy.

Surprised, Richard stumbled backwards a couple of steps.

Wagging it's tail furiously, the black dog darted from left to right, almost dancing in front of Richard, in excitement.

"Hello… doggy." Richard outstretched his arm in an attempt to stroke the animal.

"Oscar! Calm down." Emily went up to the dog, and took it firmly by the collar, allowing Hannah and Richard to stroke it.

"He's always this boisterous around visitors." Emily explained.

"Oscar –that's a nice name," said Hannah.

"Yes. Bethany chose the name." Emily continued. "Oscar's two years old now. That's fourteen in human years."

"The same age as me!" Declared Richard, as if he had made an important scientific discovery.

"That explains his behaviour!" Hannah cheekily observed.

Emily, the children and Oscar entered the farmhouse, Richard gripping Oscar tightly by the collar, seemingly inseparable from the dog.

They found themselves in the farm kitchen. The floor was tiled a buff colour, and the walls were tiled to elbow height, then painted gloss above. The kitchen had a modern feel to it, and Hannah noticed a kitchen sink and draining board made of stainless steel, a brick coloured cooker and an electric fridge. The girl could see in an open kitchen cupboard, cans of baked beans, spaghetti and Smedley's Peas, Weston's Biscuits (much to her delight), Bird's Custard, Fry's Cocoa, and more.

Emily placed the children's bags containing their belongings carefully down in a corner of the room. Hannah and Richard sat down at a rectangular wooden kitchen table (that could seat six, if need be), opposite each other, and they began to eagerly tuck into their sandwiches, which their mother had provided.

After the brief meal, Emily showed the children to their rooms. She explained that Bethany was loath to share her bedroom with her brother, therefore Hannah would be in Bethany's room, and the two boys would share Thomas's room.

Emily went downstairs, leaving the children to unpack their few personal items from home. Being a typical boy, Richard had the task completed within a couple of minutes (having 'thrown' most of his belongings out of the bag), whilst Hannah had barely begun. The girl had filled in a postcard to inform their parents of their new address. Richard opted to join his sister in Bethany's room.

The girl's room was wallpapered plain green, and a scatter rug covered the stained floorboards. The neatly hung cotton curtains were stripy —all very Thirties. The bedroom furniture included a mahogany bookcase, a dressing table, and a couple of cupboards. A number of dolls were dotted around the room, and a framed drawing of a dog hung on the wall.

Standing, with hands in the pockets of his shorts, Richard informed his sister.

"Do you know? They've got hot water, here?"

As Hannah continued to unpack, she remarked.

"Hot water? Goodness!"

Richard went over to his sister's bed.

"And look at these sheets…" Richard felt the top sheet, which oozed cleanliness.

"Yes, it certainly is different to home." Hannah reflected. "It sounds awful to say it —rather *better* here," she added guiltily.

Richard could not help but agree. However, he admitted.

"I do wish that Mummy and Daddy could be here with us."

Hannah thought back to home. London, the city of docks, factories, gasworks and warehouses. There were the inner-city tenements, Victorian slums, the suburbs of semi-detached avenues, with tidy gardens and green playing fields, and somewhere in between lay the Baker house, modest but respectable.

Home. Daddy relaxing in quiet contemplation, by the wireless, in his favourite chair, pipe in mouth, dressed in shirt and tie and his green woolen pullover that had seen better days. Occasionally, he would poke the coal on the fire. Mummy sitting opposite him, smartly dressed, doing some embroidery, but thinking about the housework, and worrying…worrying about them.

Her brother's words echoed in Hannah's ears.

"Me too." agreed the girl.

Richard was seated, cross-legged on his new bed gazing out of the window across the farmyard, where some chickens were pacing about. He felt a little apprehensive about meeting Bethany and Thomas. Would they get on well and have similar interests, or would they resent the intruders? This changing house was all because of war with Germany, but it still did not really feel like war, for Richard had not seen a single soldier all day!

The sight of two children, of his age, approaching up the dirt track interrupted Richard's thoughts. Yes, it had to be them!

As the boy and girl paused to open the farm gate, Richard leapt off the bed, and went to fetch his sister. He tapped Hannah on the shoulder, and announced.

"Come on! Thomas and Bethany are here –let's go and meet them!"

Half a minute later, the two pairs of children stood opposite each other in the kitchen, neither pair knowing exactly what to say to the other. Emily turned her attention away from slicing carrots beside the sink, and took the large overcoats off her son and daughter. She remarked.

"Well, you're not usually lost for words, Thomas!" Emily then addressed both of her children. "Go on then, say hello to Hannah and Richard."

As if on cue, Bethany and Thomas said hello to the evacuees simultaneously. Hannah said hello back. Richard, in spite of his eagerness of only a couple of minutes ago, had turned shy, and merely smiled.

Bethany wore a pretty red dress with a couple of white bands around it. She was of average height for her age, and had a good head of curly black hair. The girl was attractive (having inherited her mother's natural beauty), with a perfectly symmetrical face and a dreamy look in her green eyes.

In direct contrast to his sister, Thomas was somewhat scruffy in appearance. Quite a lot shorter than Bethany, he was a freckly, impish-faced boy. His dark blue shirt, shorts and knees were muddied, and his left shin was bloodstained.

Emily noticed the wound to Thomas's leg, and despaired.

"Thomas! How did you do that?" What on earth have you been up to, now?"

Thomas remained silent.

Bethany explained that her brother had received his injury whilst attempting to climb a precarious tree in the school playground.

Thomas glared at his sister, and hissed.

"Snitch!"

"I've lost count of the number of times that I've warned you not to go climbing those playground trees, Thomas! What have you got to say for yourself?" Emily demanded.

"It doesn't hurt, not anymore." Thomas replied. He rubbed his shin and mumbled, "Not much."

Emily let the subject drop.

"Well, tea won't be ready for a couple of hours, yet." Emily declared. She spoke to her own children. "Why don't you two show Hannah and Richard around the farm?"

"We can do that anytime, mum. Let's go blackberry picking!"

Before the words had even left his lips, Thomas had raced out of the farmhouse.

Richard turned to his sister and grinned.

"Blackberry picking –that sounds like fun!"

Hannah nodded in polite agreement.

Emily retrieved a bucket from under the sink. Referring to Thomas, she chuckled.

"As usual, in his haste, he's forgotten a container!" Emily handed the bucket to her daughter. "Here, Bethany, you'd better take this with you."

"Thank you, Mummy."

Bethany, Hannah and Richard left the farmhouse from the rear. They crossed a meadow peppered with buttercups before they crawled through a child-sized gap in some bushes, to find themselves in a field abundant with blackberry bushes.

"Blackberries. Lots of them!" Richard clapped his hands together, gleefully.

Thomas appeared from amongst the bushes, his lips stained with blackberry juice, and emptied his pockets of blackberries into the bucket. The boy remembered when, as a young child of five or six, he first went blackberry picking with his father; how the prickly blackberry bushes dwarfed him, but now they didn't seem so tall and intimidating. He spoke to Richard.

"I'm Tom."

"Richard." Replied the other.

The boys separated from the girls. Thomas informed Richard that his mother always called him Thomas, although he much preferred to be called Tom. It was the same with his sister, Bethany.

"…Her friends all call her Beth."

Richard gingerly picked his first two blackberries off a bush, and placed them carefully in his pocket. Tom picked two, also, and put them straight into his mouth. He declared.

"Mmmn! Pick and eat!"

Richard picked another blackberry; this time he ate it.

"Nice." Richard agreed.

"I thought that people only ate fish and chips in London?"

"No!" Richard laughed.

"But, you are from London, though?" Tom enquired.

"Yes, a couple of miles north of the Thames. We live in a terraced house." Richard replied.

Tom then asked.

"Do you get rats there?"

"No!" said Richard indignantly. "We don't live in a slum."

"We sometimes get rats around the farm." Tom admitted. "Lots of times I've tried to catch them…but, they move too fast."

"Oh!" said a bemused Richard.

"Do you like playing marbles?"

"Yes, and conkers, too." Tom declared.

"Me, too. You and I -We'll get on fine. You'll like it here in the village. There's lots of tasty girls around; some of the boys from the school have actually kissed Victoria Heath-Maxwell, even though she's really posh and lives in a big house with her parents. Then there's Samantha Green —though she always pretends she's not interested. What are the girls like around where you live?" Tom asked his new friend.

"There are one or two nice ones, yes." Richard acknowledged.

"Have you got a favourite film star?" enquired Tom.

"Greta Garbo. I think she's lovely."

Tom screwed his face up.

"Greta Garbo? Ugh! She's German!"

"No she's not, she's from Sweden." Richard correctly informed Tom.

"Well, that's still foreign! I like Gracie Fields —gorgeous!" declared Tom.

"Gracie Fields? She's over forty —that's old!" Richard sneered.

"Well, she's better than Greta Garbo!" stated Tom.

The pair contested this point for some time, before progressing to talk about each other's families. Meanwhile, Beth and Hannah were fast becoming good friends. They discussed their favourite subjects at school.

"I like mathematics and English," declared Hannah.

"Oh! I like English, and also art and P.T.," said Beth. She enquired. "Do you like any sports?"

"Yes, definitely," nodded the other girl, "swimming and hockey." She cast her eyes down gloomily, "although I had to leave my hockey stick at home, as we were not allowed to bring many belongings with us."

"That's a shame." Beth sympathized.

As the girls picked the fruit (and rather more than their Brothers did), Hannah enquired.

"These blackberries, they're not poisonous are they?"

Beth reassured Hannah that the blackberries were safe to eat.

"Thank goodness." Said a relieved Hannah. "You see, I'm afraid that I don't know very much at all about the countryside."

"Not to worry, Hannah, you soon will." predicted Beth. Beth then asked Hannah if she had a boyfriend. Hannah shook her head.

"No. I still feel too young, although I will be fifteen next Birthday, very soon."

"I haven't got a boyfriend, either," declared Beth. "Although I'd like to have one, I find that the boys in my class are too immature."

"Bethany, Thomas, tea's ready!"

The four children bounded noisily down the stairs, excited by the enticing smell of well-cooked food. They had all worked up a good appetite blackberry picking. On entering the kitchen, Tom darted across to take his seat at the table, and the Baker children hushed.

"Let me take a look at those hands of yours, young Thomas, before you sit down."

Tom obediently showed his hands to his Father. The boy's palms were covered in stains of blackberry juice.

"I've told you enough times before, you're not sitting down at this table with dirty hands. To the sink now." Mr. Pavitt ordered.

Ted Pavitt was a dominant presence seated at the head of the table. He had risen through the ranks to lieutenant, and won a medal for gallantry in the Great War. At forty-one years of age, he had still retained much of the handsome features of his youth that had first attracted Emily to him. He had wavy black hair, and a moustache, and bore a striking resemblance to the young Lloyd George. He was smartly dressed with a waistcoat for the evening meal.

The Baker children, felt a little in awe and frightened of Ted, but behind the firm exterior, was a kind heart, and a good father and husband.

Emily led the introductions, and Ted rose from the table, greeted Hannah and Richard with a firm handshake and a smile, before sitting down, once more.

"We've got leek soup to start with. Do you like soup?" Emily asked the Baker children.

"Oh! Yes, please," replied Hannah. Richard also nodded with enthusiasm. Fish served with carrots, green peas and potatoes, with milk to drink, followed the leek soup. The cake for sweet went down well with the two Baker children. The Pavitt family evidently liked to eat well.

Emily engaged Hannah and Richard in conversation, about their home and family background, with frequent interruptions and questions from Tom. Ted only showed passive interest in the two evacuees, enjoying his food. Having been the first to clear his plate, Tom looked across expectantly at his father and asked.

"Please may I get down?"

"Wait a minute, young Thomas, for the rest of us to finish." Ted replied.

After the meal, the four children retreated to their rooms, whilst Ted accompanied his wife to the sink, and took charge of the tea towel. Beyond the kitchen window, dusk was descending, and the sky was purple and motionless.

"Hard to believe we're at war." Ted observed.

His wife nodded her head slowly in agreement.

"It's all the children I feel sorry for." Said Emily. "It can't be easy for poor Hannah and Richard being separated from their parents."

Ted put his arm around his wife.
"No. But, we'll make sure that they'll be well looked after while they're here."

CHAPTER 2 – WAR FOR REAL?

Monday 4th September 1939.

The dawn chorus of songbirds awaked Richard from his sleep. He had had a contented sleep, despite missing his parents. He was finding it all a bit of an adventure, and there was a lot of excitement at being in new surroundings. He sat up in bed, and stretched his arms, before crossing to the window. In the adjacent bed, Tom was still asleep. Richard pulled the curtains apart, and was bathed in rays of hot sunlight. He opened one window, and breathed the fresh air. The soft orange sun sat neatly above a line of distant trees. Chickens paced around in the farmyard below.

The children descended the stairs to the kitchen, for breakfast to find the atmosphere rather subdued, this autumn morning. It had been announced on the wireless that a torpedo fired from a German submarine had sunk a ship in the Atlantic, the previous evening.

As Emily served the four children with cereal, she shook her head resignedly.

"The war's not even twenty-four hours old, and they're already attacking innocent civilians."

Hannah had developed a taste for newspapers the past few months and she read half-aloud from the paper that was lying on the breakfast table.

"The Glasgow liner 'Athenia' (13,500 tons), was sunk without warning at 7:45 p.m. yesterday over 200 miles off the coast of Ireland. The passengers were at dinner when the torpedo struck on the port side, and killed a number of them. The torpedo went right through the liner to the engine room. Those not killed by the explosion took to the boats, and of over 1100 passengers, ships that came to the rescue picked up all but 112."

Hannah paused, and stared at the table with sad eyes.

"How awful…"

"This is what we're fighting against, young Hannah," declared Ted. "Nazi tyranny. Mark my words, we'll see a lot more of this sort of thing –and worse-before this war is out." He added rather depressingly.

"I wish I was older, so I could go and fight these evil Huns!" said Tom, full of hatred.

Richard now took an interest in the newspaper, and peered over his Sister's shoulder.

"Apparently the air raid sirens sounded over London, yesterday –although it was a false alarm."

This mention of air raids prompted Emily to remind the four children to remember to take their gas masks to school. She added.

"When the Nazi bombers come over, Hitler certainly won't give any warning…"

The children walked in pairs, on their way to school, with Beth and Hannah leading, and Richard and Tom following. On their way, they passed the Saint Peter's church, church hall, war memorial and most of the village shops. They got down the main street almost as far as the station, when they turned off down a side road. A hundred or so yards away, the road came to an abrupt halt in front of a gate that led into the woods. To the right, was a row of half a dozen dilapidated nineteenth century terraced cottages; opposite the cottages as the children walked along the road, were two detached houses then the school.

Beth paused for a moment, and announced.

"Here's our school."

"Yippee!" said Tom sarcastically.

The school was not positioned immediately beside the road, for there was a narrow strip of grass, worn by the constant pounding of children's shoes and a modest concrete playground with a few trees dotted around, before the school building itself. In the playground a couple of girls were playing hopscotch.

Tom grabbed Richard by the arm, and proudly pointed to the tree, which, much to his mother's chagrin, he had climbed the previous Friday.

The school was a modern red brick building with a roof consisting of thick grey slates, and dormers at both of the ends. Inside the school, a classroom was sited either side of the central entrance door. Beth explained that the new school was built five years ago, the original school building having been destroyed by fire. Casting a suspicious eye at her brother, she remarked.

"My guess is that the fire was deliberate."

Tom stuck his tongue out.

The children passed through two swing-doors, to enter the right hand classroom. The classroom was square in shape, with approximately thirty little wooden desks with inkwells on, arranged in neat rows facing towards a large blackboard, besides which lay a big open coal fire. Those children who were fortunate enough to occupy desks by the wall that backed onto the playground, each had a window that provided a view of the road and cottages outside. Currently, five children were quietly seated at their desks; without doubt, their numbers would swell as the minutes ticked by. A boy on the back row mumbled a hello to Tom as he passed by. As Beth and Hannah took their seats on the second row from the front, the latter noticed a map of the World with the British Empire in pink, and next to it a map of Poland up on one of the walls. It seemed rather poignant.

Richard went to take a seat beside his sister however, Tom tapped the boy on the arm, and beckoned him over to the fourth row.

The pair sat down. Around thirty more evacuees were expected to join the school that day.

A couple of minutes later, two evacuee children hesitantly entered the room and selected chairs at the desk in front of Richard and Tom. One of the pair, Jack, had been billeted with another of the farmers, who had spent much of the time educating him as to the ways of the countryside. Jack turned to his companion, and recalled how farmer Williamson had informed him of the origins of bacon, bread, eggs and milk, and also how to snare a rabbit. The man had also done his best to warn of the dangers of hedge berries, and how to distinguish between them, as Jack explained.

"Farmer Williamson said that I mustn't eat any red berries, because they're unsafe. Then there's also some sort of dangerous berry that is black, like a blackberry, but is not a blackberry –I think!"

"Black but *not* a blackberry...?" Frowned his confused friend.

As Richard listened in, he could only hope that he had eaten the safe version, the previous day, and not be poisoned.

The doors opened again, and two boys came and took their places next to Tom. They were identical twins, with curly black hair, and slightly mischievous looks on their faces. Tom introduced them as Harry and Henry. The brothers had lived in the village all their lives. Like Tom, both the twins enjoyed football, climbing trees (this slightly worried Richard, in light of the incident on Friday), and being cheeky to most of the girls in the class. Harry immediately spotted the new female seated next to Beth, and made an appropriate wisecrack for the benefit of the other three boys, to which Richard retorted,

"That's my Sister!"

A small bespectacled boy with brown hair who looked like a typical School Swot came and sat down in the vacant seat next to Richard.

"Morning, Edward!" Chorused Harry, Henry and Tom.

The bespectacled Edward glanced at the trio and gave them a wry smile, and then he began to sort through a stack of books that he had been carrying in his school bag. There was also an atlas and geometry set inside. Edward was an only child, a bit of a weakling, and a shy person with few friends. He preferred reading, stamp collecting and chess to active sports.

Richard turned to Edward, and said friendly.

"Hello, my name's Richard. I'm from London"

Edward took his attention away from his books, and with more of a warm smile, said.

"Hello, Richard. I'm Edward. I live above the post office"

The pair shook hands.

"The post office," Richard said thoughtfully. "We passed by that on the way here. Do your parents own the post office, Edward?"

"Yes, they do. My family have run the post office for over fifty years." Came the reply.

"Cool! That means your family have owned the post office since eighteen-," Richard struggled to work back fifty years from 1939.

"Since 1886." Declared Edward with pride.

"Is that a book on aircraft?" asked Richard, changing the subject.

"Yes it is." Edward placed the book in question down on the table, in front of Richard, who looked wide-eyed at the pictures of the aircraft, inside. Edward explained. "That aircraft there is the Junkers Ju87 Stuka dive-bomber, which the Germans are currently, er…using in Poland."

"Have you got any British aircraft in there?"

Edward turned back a couple of pages, and pointed to an aircraft bearing the unmistakable rings of the RAF.

"This one's a Whitley Bomber. It has a range of over a thousand miles, a speed of about 215 m.p.h. and it carries a heavy load of bombs." Edward ran his finger across the page to a picture of a formation of six aircraft flying on patrol. "And, these are called Fairey Battles."

Towards the front of the classroom, Beth had been introducing Hannah to a number of her girlfriends.

Beth had known Clara, Nancy and Samantha since they were all tiny. Clara was the daughter of the village policeman, and knew almost everyone in the village. The tales that her father had told her about some of the more colourful personalities in the village, over the years, could fill a book! Clara was of average height, with medium length chestnut hair, and a round but not unattractive face. She was a very friendly girl, who enjoyed singing in the church choir, and was Beth's best friend.

Nancy was the plain member of the group. She was tall for her age, with a thin face, and wore her brown hair in a ponytail. She was flat chested, almost boyish. Nancy had earned the unfortunate nickname from the twins of 'pencil.' Her father was the local postman, and knew Edward's parents well. Of the boys in the class, Nancy got on best with Edward, although the notion of any romantic attachment between them was unlikely. She was a lover of animals, had a Collie dog called Billy, a couple of rabbits Flopsy and Mopsy, and she dreamed of owning a horse one day.

To Nancy's wallflower, Samantha was the princess. Samantha lived above the greengrocers, which her parents ran. Arguably the most beautiful girl in the class, she had long straight blonde hair, sparkling sapphire eyes, and an engaging smile. A hard working girl, Samantha was more intent on pursuing her studies and being the best voice in the choir than wasting her time on boys. Not that she lacked admirers —a number of the boys in the class had tried their luck with Samantha, and all had failed.

Hannah twiddled her fingers nervously, and stated.

"I didn't very much like the look of that Mr. Henry, I don't think that I'm going to enjoy having him as my new teacher."

Beth gave Hannah a funny look.

"But, Mr. Henry's not our teacher. He takes the other class…"

"Oh! Really?"

"Yes." Beth continued. "Miss Townsend is our teacher."

"You'll like Miss Townsend," added Samantha reassuringly.

"Oh! I do feel relieved, that Mr. Henry so reminds me of an undertaker," declared Hannah.

The other girls chuckled in amusement. Mr. Henry as an undertaker —yes, it seemed quite apt.

As if on cue, Miss Townsend entered the classroom. Armed with a handful of books, she walked rather gracefully across to her desk, smiling at a number of the new arrivals as she did so. Miss Townsend was dressed in a light green blouse and a black medium length skirt. She was twenty-seven years of age, pleasant looking, with an excellent complexion, brown eyes and shoulder length dark brown hair.

Miss Townsend waited a few more minutes for the last of the stragglers to take their seats in the classroom.

Hannah noticed a girl sit down by the aisle on the row behind, who, began to flirt with a couple of boys the other side of the room. The girl was smartly presented, and had a somewhat regal air about her. She was of average build, decent looking, although slightly fat in the face, her hair was fawn in colour, and her eyes were green.

Hannah turned to Beth, and enquired.

"Who's she?"

"*That's* Victoria," replied the other.

"Don't you like her?"

"She shouldn't even be here!" Stated Nancy. She explained, "Victoria's older than us, and attends the grammar school a few miles away."

"What's she doing here, then?" Probed Hannah.

Beth enlightened her friend.

"Oh, she used to go to our school until last term. Her eleven year old brother's in Mr. Henry's class, she's probably just come in today to drop him off and chatter to some of her old classmates." She added with a chuckle, "Can't stay away from the place!"

Clara leaned across the desk in front of Beth, and lowered her voice.

"More like she can't stay away from the boys. She's a bit of a devil for the boys."

Hannah raised her eyebrows.

"Really?"

"Yes. Victoria's had more boyfriends than the rest of us put together!" Clara informed Hannah.

"Goodness!" Exclaimed Hannah.

"What Clara didn't mention was that none of us have ever been out with a boy," declared Beth.

Nancy spoke. "I thought that Samantha kissed that friend of her cousins...?"

"No! I did not!" Said an indignant Samantha. "I didn't kiss Peter —I wasn't even his girlfriend!"

Nancy apologized.

"Sorry."

Beth returned to the subject of Victoria.

"Victoria's alright, really," Beth continued. "She was actually one of the brightest girls in the class, and often has us round to play in the gardens of her big house. I'm sure you'll see plenty more of her during your time at Oak Green" Clara, still leaning awkwardly across the desk concluded.

"The trouble is, Victoria always likes to boast about this boyfriend of hers, that boyfriend of hers, and..."

"Are you sure it's not all in her head? I don't know what the boys see in her; personally I think that she's quite fat!" Hannah declared.

Miss Townsend addressed the older girl.

"Victoria, don't you have a school of your own to go to?"

The girl reluctantly vacated her seat and left the classroom.

Miss Townsend proceeded to speak about the fateful events of the previous few days. She detailed a number of emergency wartime regulations and procedures specific to the school, and checked that all her pupils had their gas masks to hand. In all twelve evacuees had joined the class, this morning. As a result, some pupils had to share corner desks. Miss Townsend expressed her desire that everyone help to make the evacuated children feel at home. In order for the swelled ranks of the class to become familiar with each other, the children went through the exercise of standing up and announcing their name out loud, one at a time.

No sooner had a mathematics lesson started, than Mr. Henry paced into the classroom. Miss Townsend sighed, as her colleague made a beeline for her desk.

"Yes, what is it, Mr. Henry?" She asked very formally.

In a dour voice, Mr. Henry reminded Miss Townsend not to forget that there would be an air raid drill, later in the day.

Miss Townsend stated that she had not forgotten this fact, and, sensing that Mr. Henry had something else to get off his chest, she asked him what else he wanted.

Mr. Henry's eyes scanned the classroom.

"Hmmnn…it's very full up. I didn't know that you were going to have so many pupils, as well…"

Tom whispered to his friends.

"Miserable old custard!"

Mr. Henry continued his voice droning.

"I'm five desks short, I'll have to take all your spares."

"Well, can't you see there aren't any?"

"Oh!"

Miss Townsend put her hands on her hips, and suggested.

"Some of them will have to share. That's what we're doing. I've had to cope with twelve extra pupils."

"I suppose so." Mr. Henry shook his head. "It's such an inconvenience having to take on all these evacuated children…"

"Well, we can't let them stay in their city homes and risk Hitler's bombs fall on them, can we, Mr. Henry?"

On the second row, Beth and Hannah grinned at each other.

Mr. Henry observed that the neighbouring village had received far fewer evacuee children than had been anticipated, and that it wasn't right that his school be swamped with them! He, at last, departed from the room.

Shortly before lunchtime, a small boy burst into the classroom and gave a definitive blow on a whistle before leaving.

Simultaneously, the boys and girls inside, quickly moved their seats back, and delved beneath their desks. Each one revealed a plain box, from which they took their gas mask.

"Quickly, now!" Encouraged Miss Townsend.

Once all the pupils had donned their gas masks, Miss Townsend, armed with a hurricane lamp, led the children out of the room to the rear of the building. From there, the group passed the outside toilets, crossed the playground and descended a brief flight of steps to enter the school air raid shelter.

Mr. Henry and his pupils followed Miss Townsend's class into the shelter. Inside, it was long and narrow, and it was a little bit of a squeeze for all concerned. Miss Townsend revealed a match, and lit the lamp, which gave out a sickly yellow light.

"It's a bit cold in here," grumbled one male pupil.

"It's better than Mr. Henry's boring lessons," said another.

The twins started to make ghost noises until reprimanded by Miss Townsend. A couple of girls sniggered.

Richard sat between the twins, and opposite Samantha and Clara. He took an instant dislike to the corrugated iron shelter, for, despite the lamp, where he was it was still dark, and smelled of damp and earth. Samantha remarked that that it was like being inside a bicycle shed. Richard studied the fair haired girl, a couple of feet away from him —if he did have to suffer this underground bicycle shed, at least he could spend his time looking at this pretty girl, Samantha, opposite him.

Ted shook his head resignedly. He wouldn't mind the blackout so much, if there were the danger of German aircraft flying overhead. However, a couple of weeks into the war, and the Nazi bombers had failed to put in a single appearance over the skies of Britain. Still, Ted's car was prepared as necessary —the vehicle's bumpers and edges of the running boards had been painted matt white, Ted had cleaned the windscreen so that it was spotless, and checked the tyres for the umpteenth time. In addition to this, the headlights were masked so that light only came through a narrow horizontal slit, the side lamps, rear lamps, and indicators were all dimmed, and the inside light and reversing lamps had had to go totally! If all this were not enough, the vehicle had by law to be immobilized whenever left unattended (i.e. most of the time), by taking the rotor arm from the distributor away, or by other means. Petrol would be rationed on 22nd September, although much would be set aside for commercial vehicles, it would be dyed red, so that private motorists could not use it.

In early September, Ted had spent a princely sum on purchasing blackout curtains, drawing pins, and sticky tape, with which, to seal the farmhouse windows, and all at hugely inflated prices. Shopkeepers up and down the country must have been rubbing their hands, for they couldn't flog black stuff, low powered bulbs etc. quick enough! Every night, Emily religiously went through the ten-minute ritual of blacking out their home. Of course, the Government permitted lights to be on *inside* people's houses; it was just the case that no light can be seen from the outside. Blankets had to cover inner doors, in case the front door was opened, and light shone through that way. Husband and wife were obliged to test the blackout materials, by holding an electric bulb against the curtain, and seeing whether any light showed through…all this, and Ted was trying to run a busy farm!

Ted got into the car, and closed the door to the lively voices coming from the farmhouse kitchen, and sounds coming from the cattle sheds. He did not look forward to the journey, for even though it was only a handful of miles to where the farmer's meeting was being held, driving in the blackout, with no street lighting, was absolute murder. Making out and sticking to the road ahead, was one problem, avoiding pedestrians, that had strayed from the pavement, which one might see at the last minute, if at all, was an equal hazard. Even in the cities, there were only very diminished traffic lights. Ted knew a number of people that had been out on foot, and had minor accidents in the dark; Emily had collided with someone else, and only the previous night, one of the farm labourers had walked into a tree. Ted was wary that one old lady in the village placed great faith in waving a rolled up newspaper out in front of her as she crossed the road after dark, but as far as the farmer was concerned, from behind the wheel of the car 'you wouldn't be able to see the bloody thing.'

Danger might lurk behind every bend, and Ted dared not drive much faster than a snail's pace through the village; he might as well have gone out on the tractor at that speed! He passed a solitary spooky figure that was holding a torch dimmed with a double thickness of white tissue paper. The village, with its quaint cottages, and attractive gardens, was normally so cosy, warm and inviting; at this time of year, it would still be warm enough for people to be sitting at tables under the parasols, outside the public house. Now, under wartime conditions, it was morbid and depressing, and the one consolation was that it was like this across the length and breadth of Britain. The farmer prayed that he would not drive into anyone, or anything, and crept away into the country lane with only the crescent moon for company.

The journey dragged, and although Ted's thoughts were never far from the road in front of him, his mind wandered to thoughts of his work. He had learnt about methods of farming from his father, who had in turn been schooled by his father. Ted had been fortunate that due to an inheritance from a rich uncle his family had been able to live comfortably, and he had been able to invest in a tractor. Whereas many of his contemporaries had favoured livestock over cultivation in the Thirties, Ted maintained a mixed farm, he didn't believe in putting all his eggs in one basket. By the start of the war, many farms across the country were both under manned and under cultivated. Now, the nation was crying out to be ploughed, so that it could feed itself. The farmers would each receive a subsidy of £2 for each acre of grassland that was ploughed.

Ted thought of his family and also of the two evacuee children. They were good kids, Hannah and Richard, and they were getting on well with his own children. All of the city and country children were making lots of new friends, and Hannah and Richard wrote home excited letters about the farm and its animals, their new classmates, practice air raid drills and other things. The gossip in the village shops, and the conversation over pints in the pub, had been centred on the evacuee children. "Did you know...?" housewives would begin, in a disapproving manner, and then go on to enlighten the listener with tales (not necessarily from Oak Green) of city urchins covered with dirty septic sores, lice, nits, or children wearing shoes with soles made of cardboard, or children sleeping *under* beds. There were some children who struggled to use a knife and fork, and all the inconvenience for 10/6d a week! There was a narrow element in the village that had never wanted anything to do with the 'townie' children in the first place, and seized upon any opportunity to put them down. However, the village adjusted, and in the main, the children were accepted, and viewed as adding a bit of fun to the area, filling the gap that was left when some of the men folk went off to war. Soon, conversation turned to other topics.

Rather encouragingly, the 4th September, the R.A.F. had launched raids against the German fleet in the Kiel Canal district. In a low level attack, seven out of eight bombers were shot down, and part of the German fleet was put out of action for a few months. However, on 17th September, the Royal Navy had suffered its first serious loss of the war, when a U-boat sank the aircraft carrier H.M.S. Courageous, resulting in the deaths of several hundred crew. Ted hoped that this war with Germany would be over long before Richard and Tom were old enough to fight in it. People were talking about it 'all being over by Christmas', just like last time...Ted remembered back to 1918, after four years of struggle, in the final few months of the last war, when he had stormed an enemy bunker with twenty men. Of the group, only Ted and a corporal made it back. However he never spoke about it.

It was Saturday morning, 23rd September. Beth and Hannah were strolling back to the farm after school sports. They had already paid a visit to the newsagents, to collect the local paper and Tom's weekly copy of his comic, *The Dandy*. Their last stop before the farm would be the sweetshop. Various posters had cropped up over the village. In a shop window, one in red, with white lettering read *Freedom is in peril. Defend it with all your might.* The girls had been intrigued to discover that the top of the village post box had, for some reason, been painted a yellowish colour. One of the villagers informed the pair that the coating was special, and that it would be able to detect gas. They noticed that fewer vehicles were around, since the introduction of petrol rationing the previous day.

Hannah was perusing the morning's news, and was beginning to wish that she had not been so eager to accompany her friend in her trip to the newsagents, and that perhaps she should give up this interest of hers in world events. As she digested the front page, Hannah found it somewhat depressing reading. She thought back to three days ago, and the voice of Mr. Chamberlain, in a statement to the House of Commons, seemingly the perennial bearer of bad news, coming from the wireless.

"On the morning of September 17 Russian troops crossed the Polish frontier at points along its whole length and advanced into Poland." The Soviet Government argued that "Poland had become a suitable field for all manner of hazards and surprises which might constitute a threat to the Soviet Union." The Soviet Government only wanted to protect the population of Western Ukraine and Western White Russia.

Now the Polish capital Warsaw had been surrounded, and yesterday, the two mighty armies of Germany and Russia had linked up at Brest-Litovsk, in the centre of poor little Poland. With Poland all but defeated, might not Hitler turn his attention next to France and England?

Beth and Hannah entered the sweetshop. The smell inside was enticing. The girls' eyes widened as they looked up to the shelves, to peruse the glass jars full of sweets that were all the colours of the rainbow. There were aniseed balls, boiled sweets, cough candy, fruit bonbons, humbugs, sherbets, to name but a few. On other shelves were a variety of Cadbury's chocolate bars. Beth licked her lips in anticipation; she could already feel the taste of the gobstoppers that changed colour in your mouth.

"Yes?" Barked the man behind the counter.

Hannah looked at the confectioner. He appeared beyond retirement age, and had small mean eyes, that had the effect of making the children feel guilty for purchasing sweets. He wore a long white coat that was covered in powder from sweets. Beth had already warned Hannah to use please and thank you at all times in the shop. The girl wondered if this Mr. Micawber-like man didn't like children, and begrudged serving them, why did he choose to work with them? She stood her turn behind Beth with trepidation.

Beth spoke.

"Can I have a quarter of a pound of fruit bonbons, please?"

The man ambled across to the far end of the shelf, apparently unhurried by the fact that two more children, a girl and a boy had entered the shop. He pursed his lips and selected the jar, before he returned to the counter and measured out the girl's allocation to the exact milligram.

"Thank you," said Beth.

However, the shopkeeper was not done with Beth. Casting a suspicious eye at the girl, he enquired.

"You're the sister of that Pavitt boy, aren't you?"

"Yes," she answered with a worried tone in her voice, fearing what was coming.

"Inform your brother that next time I catch him dropping dead squirrels on my doorstep I'll have the law onto him."

"Y-yes."

The confectioner let the matter drop, and turned to Hannah, uttering the one word.

"And?" Hannah spoke at a whimper. The shopkeeper interrupted her mid sentence.

"Pardon? I can't hear you," he put his hand to his ear.

"I'd like a packet of *Smarties*, please."

"At least you know your manners," the confectioner conceded, "You're not from around here, are you?"

"No, I was evacuated…"

The girl handed over her money, and found that the confectioner had no interest in further conversation. He merely glanced past Hannah as if she no longer existed, at the boy standing behind her.

"Next?"

The pair left the shop. Once outside, Hannah declared.

"How rude!"

"Oh!" Beth smiled. "I think that he rather took to you."

The two girls entered the farmhouse. Hannah noticed that Tom, seated, looked as if he had not a care in the world. This was soon to change, when his sister pressed him about the squirrel incident. Beth threw the comic across to Tom.

"I felt a fool in that shop because of you."

"It was only one stupid squirrel, anyway!" The boy protested.

"Yes, well don't do it again."

"Yes, mum!"

Beth enquired of her brother.

"And what are you up to, this afternoon?"

Tom, having began to get engrossed in *The Dandy*, replied, without looking up.

"Read the comic, then me and Richard will probably go and play by the stream. How' bout yourselves?"

Beth turned to Hannah, and asked.

"Do you fancy going on a bicycle ride out to some of the other villages?"

Hannah nodded enthusiastically, before she thought of a potential stumbling block.

"But, I haven't got a bicycle to ride. You see, mine's back at home."

Beth suggested that she borrow Tom's bike.

"Blooming cheek! I'm not having no girl ride my bike!" Exclaimed Tom.

"Alright, Hannah can ride Mummy's bicycle." Beth grinned at her female friend, and added. "Tom's bicycle would probably be much too *small* for her, anyway!"

Tom dropped his comic, and went to hit his sister on the arm. However, Beth moved far too swiftly away from him.

Five minutes later, the two girls were cycling merrily along. The air was warm, and they passed fields of dusty corn that were punctured by the occasional wood or spinney. Hannah couldn't have imagined a month ago, in the confines of London that she would be out doing this!

"I hope that Tom didn't offend you back there; refusing to lend you his bicycle." Said Beth apologetically.

"Oh! No." Hannah shook her head. "No harm done. I do like your brother, even if he is a bit of a scamp."

Beth laughed.

"A *bit* of a scamp? You want to have tried and lived with him for the past fourteen years! He's managed to get himself in trouble with most of the village – poaching trout from the river, scrumping from the apple tree at Victoria's parent's house, scaring old widow Kettle's cat…"

"Say no more."

The girls cycled for a couple of miles, until they arrived at a village of no more than a dozen homes. The air was an aroma of sweet-smelling hay. They dismounted from their bicycles, and proceeded to pay a visit to the peaceful country church.

The churchyard had seen better days. The railings surrounding the churchyard were rusted and barely standing, and many of the gravestones were moss covered and slanting at various angles. Before entering, Beth and Hannah read the few parish notices.

Inside the small church was simple with an air of reverence about it. The two east-facing windows were bathed in slanting rectangles of sunlight. There was a small floral display by the local children. Here, time stood still, the war no longer existed, and it was truly peaceful.

A while later, the pair resumed their journey down a winding country lane. In the sky above, seagulls circled overhead, and a short while later, the sea revealed itself in the distance. Hannah could just make out soldiers laying out barbed wire besides the coast. Somehow it made her feel a little more secure.

On the return journey, the girls picked some rose hips from the fields, so that Beth's mother could make rose hip syrup.

As Beth and Hannah neared the farm, they came across Richard and a bedraggled looking Tom.

Referring to her brother, Beth asked aloud.

"What's happened to him?"

"Yes. He's all wet." Hannah observed.

As the girls drew level with Richard, they slowed down, and listened as the boy explained, giggling.

"Tom was trying to build a dam made out of twigs across the stream, when the twins -Harry and Henry, appeared and pushed him face down into the water!!!"

"You wet, Tom!" Said Beth cheekily.

Hannah could not resist being rude to the hapless Tom.

"Yes. You wet!" She mocked.

The two girls pedalled off at speed.

Richard placed a hand over his mouth in an attempt to stifle his sniggering.

"It's not funny!" Declared Tom.

Sunday 1st October 1939, Emily and Ted at the farm, and George and Mary in London, gathered round the wireless, to listen to a broadcast by Winston Churchill, the First Lord of the Admiralty, on a review of Britain's position.

"The British Empire and the French Republic have been at war with Nazi Germany for a month tonight. We have not yet come at all to the severity of fighting which is to be expected.

…Poland has been again overrun by two of the great powers, which held her in bondage for 150 years, but were unable to quench the spirit of the Polish nation. The heroic defence of Warsaw shows that the soul of Poland is indestructible, and that she will rise again like a rock, which may for a spell be submerged by a tidal wave, but which remains a rock."

Mr. Churchill spoke about the actions of Russia, and the U-boat menace that had so far been kept in check. He went on.

"To sum up the results of the first month, let us say that Poland has been overrun, but will rise again; that Russia has warned Hitler off his Eastern dreams; and that the U-boats may be safely left to the care and constant attention of the British Navy.

Now I wish to speak about what is happening in our own island.

…A large army has already gone to France. British armies upon the scale of the effort of the Great War are in preparation.

…It may be that great ordeals are coming to us in this island from the air. We shall do our best to give a good account of ourselves.

…Directions have been given by the Government to prepare for a war of at least three years. That does not mean that victory may not be gained in a shorter time.

…It was for Hitler to say when the war would begin, but it is not for him or his successors to say when it will end.

…No doubt at the beginning we shall have to suffer because of having too long wished to lead a peaceful life. Our reluctance to fight was mocked at as cowardice. Our desire to see an unarmed world was proclaimed as the proof of our decay.

Now we have begun: now we are going on; now with the help of God, and with the conviction that we are the defenders of civilization and freedom, we are going on, and we are going to go on to the end."

CHAPTER 3 – FRANCE

It was close to midnight at the port, at an unspecific location in Southeast England. Trains from Scotland, the East of England and from the West poured into the docks in a regular unbroken stream.

From the trains, the men, dressed in their khaki battle dress, passed onto the ships. Unlike 1914, there were no marches through cheering crowds; the troops slipped away practically unnoticed, each one wondering if it would be like the last war.

The German enemy were already proving themselves, having overrun much Polish territory. Blitzkrieg determined that tanks and airpower would play a significant part in this war. How would the Tommies fare against this modern German fighting machine? Only time would tell.

The whirlwind of events of the past few days had still to sink in. Drawing water bottles, mess tins, knives, forks and spoons from the stores, then ammunition, gas capes, groundsheets and other equipment. The confinement to the drill hall of the barracks, for a couple of days, with regular kit inspections by sergeants, sergeant-majors, captains and other officers, with lights out at ten p.m., and a morning wake up call by the blast of a bugle. A final morale boosting talk by the colonel, and promises that it 'would all be over by Christmas'…just like last time.

John Baker, son of George and Mary, six feet tall, sporty, in the prime of his youth, boarded one such ship. He, along with the other men, packed like sardines, would have a mere 18 inches of deck board on which to sleep. John settled down for the Channel crossing, with all that he currently had in his possession. He wore the two-piece garment that was battle dress; with its heavy serge fastening at the wrists. The uniform contained a large patch pocket on the front of the left trouser leg, which held maps and message pads. Fitted onto a belt on his left side, was a haversack containing a mess tin, water bottle and emergency rations. Just above the waist, a couple of pouches on either side contained ammunition. He also carried an anti-gas cape and respirator, plus rifle, bayonet and scabbard.

Before long, the vessel was full, and John Baker, one man amongst 1100 or so troops –but a fraction of a British army that numbered in excess of 860,000 men, set sail for France. Beside him, lay his friends, men from a cross section of backgrounds in twentieth century Britain. They were sons of farmers, labourers, coal miners, office workers, and some for whom the army had been a family tradition.

For those from working class backgrounds, army life offered escape from boring, repetitive, thankless work that bordered on exploitation. But, once they had taken the oath of allegiance to the King, there was no turning back, seven years service lay ahead.

John remembered how barracks had had to be kept spotlessly clean, from the floor, to the cast iron stove, to every piece of equipment. You really could see your reflection in your boots. The regular kit inspections involved laying all one's equipment neatly on the bed in a set order. If it were not laid out properly, the inspecting officer would tip it up and make you lay it all out again. There had been lots of PT and drill to instill discipline and obedience in battle. At mealtimes, food was plain but plentiful. Life had been Spartan, but the men developed a strong sense of camaraderie.

The Lee Enfield rifle the soldiers were armed with, was extremely accurate, had a reasonable rate of fire, and the recoil was not too severe. In training, they had done range and sighting practice. In addition to this, there was bayonet practice, during which the men would charge at straw filled sacks, and also training with the Mills hand grenade.

Initially, 160,000 Tommies would be going to France. The British force would be stationed along the border with Belgium, since France's defensive fortification, the Maginot Line did not extend along the Belgium border.

It was necessary for the sea crossing to take place at night, with the threat of attack from the air ever present. The crossing would be long and tiresome, certainly no pleasure-boat cruise up a river. The virtually airless decks were completely blacked out, and the smoking of cigarettes was strictly forbidden. To provide a little cheer, songs were struck up from time to time during the night.

As the gloom gave way to the dawn of a new day, many of the men stretched their legs and went up to the bulwarks to catch, what was for most of them, their first glimpse of the French coast. It was Saturday 9th September, and many of the men wondered when they would see Blighty again.

The disembarkation was orderly and efficient. Under the watchful eye of the French Navy, the ship drew alongside the quay, and the gangways were lowered. The troops calmly filed down these, as if preparing for a normal day in peacetime, to enjoy hot tea and sandwiches on the dockside. John and a number of his friends bought pretty souvenirs from stalls at the docks, for the mother or girl at home. Despite the welcoming smiles of the French, behind the façade John detected that these people were fearful of what war with Germany would bring.

Before long, the British soldiers were dispersed into small groups, and led to troop trains, which would then transport them to their places of assembly "Somewhere in France". John could not help but smile as he boarded a weather-beaten wagon, upon which some Tommy had scribbled *First Class*!

An hour and a half later, the men would be obliged to continue their journey on foot. As John and his column marched three abreast, passing through one village after another, the crowds flocked around the new arrivals, cheering them on their way, often providing them with biscuits and other gifts. Along the route, notices in English marked the way. A British military policeman stood at virtually every crossroads to direct the column of marching men.

A day later, in a hamlet deep inside Northern France, John and the rest of the Tommies were allocated their quarters in some farmhouse stables. They were assured that this would be temporary accommodation, however, most of the group were unconvinced about this. A manure pit nearby and an over aggressive farm dog did not look too promising. An orchard was tantalizingly close, although a notice on the entrance gate said in English *Keep out!* As the men began to unpack their equipment, a couple of Tommies appeared with a large Dixie of tea, and before long, a few tubs and pails were rounded up, and pressed into service as baths!

"Not exactly the Ritz here, is it Sarge?" Complained one of the men.

"What did you expect, satin sheets and a private bath?" Came the reply.

Another Tommy remarked that it was the first time that he had been abroad. John realized that he too, had never before set foot outside of England's shores.

"Mind you keep away from those apples," warned another man, "the captain wants them all for himself!"

The barn erupted into howls of laughter.

John reflected upon the life that he had left behind. There were his parents, younger brother and sister. His sweet girlfriend of six months, Molly, from the village near to the barracks, had decided to end their relationship. The war would make their courtship unworkable, she had argued. But, also she was eighteen, too young to face the prospect of a letter arriving announcing that her boyfriend was dead. She hadn't even turned up at the station to see him off, didn't want to make it any harder for him, told him to forget her. Like the closing of a chapter, gone were the days of trips to the cinema under starry skies. They'd kissed countless times, but never slept together. It did not seem so long ago when he had turned up, nervous, at the recruiting office, to succumb to the discipline of army life. Further back in the recesses of his memory was his schooling, where he achieved average grades, apart from in history at which he excelled. A few years back John had developed an interest in motorbikes, although he had to borrow his friend's machine, as he couldn't afford one of his own. Now soldiering was his passion.

John looked across at Bill Gardner who had become his best pal in the army. A tall, stocky dark haired lad, the son of a builder, the soldiers called him Builder Gardner. He was the same age as John, and had joined up at the same time as John; together they had gone through the highs and lows of army training. The rat faced corporal with a cruel streak, whose head Bill had felt like shoving in the shit, the marathon route marches, the cheerful nights spent knocking back the pints. Bill was a bit of a Romeo, having juggled two or three girlfriends whilst back in England, or so he led them to believe. A real spit and polish man, he was checking his rifle for the second time since their arrival, handling it as tenderly as he would one of his women.

In the still late afternoon, the other men, now that things had quietened down, were deep in their own thoughts, contemplating what life in France would be like, thinking of families back in England, reflecting on an uncertain future.

John wandered outside for some brief solitude. He crossed the dirt and straw covered farmyard and rested against a gate, behind which lay the splendid apple trees, at which he gazed longingly. The air was warm although light was beginning to fade, the sun casting ever-longer shadows. In the distance, men continued to toil the French fields. *War, what war?* He thought of Molly, his parents and his brother and sister. If there were any fighting to be done, he reflected, then it would be for them.

The silence was broken by the shrill calls of birds. The noise was ominous, and as the chorus went on unceasingly, it became tortuous, almost frightening, and John became filled with a deep sense of foreboding. Any idea of further contemplation totally disappeared, as John detected the sound of footsteps behind him. He barely heard the voice or felt the reassuring hand that Builder Gardener laid on his shoulder. John was no longer at peace. The earth and trees in front of him turned to blood, as John had a vision of the dead and dying from the last war.

Over the coming days, the platoon of thirty men got to know the local area. They rehearsed attacks across open fields, where French peasant women harvested the crops. Occasionally, an allied aeroplane flew overhead, artillery fire was noticeable by its absence, and there was not even the slightest sign of the enemy. It was curiously calm. Within days of his arrival in the French village, John wrote home.

"We have plenty of work in the day, digging trenches and practising short rushes amongst the cabbages. The locals keep to themselves, although they are amiable people. Our food is plentiful and varied, meals being prepared by field kitchens in a courtyard. There are apples, grapes, peas, and peaches growing all around. At night we sleep in warm straw and blankets. The weather has been fair, and the other men and myself are in good health and good spirits.

We have yet to hear from Jerry, although I suppose that it is early days yet. Predictions of the duration of the war range from six months to eight years! Choose your pick! I suppose that it shall probably lie somewhere in the middle. Word has it that our French allies are giving the Germans what-for along their part of the front. Here, it doesn't yet feel like war but when Jerry comes we'll be ready for him!

XXXXX - John."

One day in October, Mary Baker's thoughts turned once again to her son who was still serving in France, as she listened intently to the B.B.C. correspondent, Richard Dimbleby broadcasting from across the Channel.

"We had driven along those roads, splashing through puddles and seeing through the foggy windows of the car the villages and hamlets, and even the towns, which have been built up from the wreckage (of the First World War). We had with us in our car an Air Force officer who bombed many of these districts during the last war."

Richard Dimbleby recalled how the driver and his fellow passengers recognized various villages, hills and valleys from the last war, and he said in summary.

"It was the modern army that I could see around us that night. But even as that Air Force officer told how when he flew over France today he could see the marks of trenches stretching for miles over fields and meadows, so I had seen the marks, the signs and the graves which make up the ghostly pattern of that other Army in that other war."

Mary silently switched off the wireless, and wiped a tear from her eye. She prayed that John's war would not be a rerun of the Somme in July 1916.

John sat lazily in a French field, a comfortable distance away from the front line; for he had recently been enjoying a spell in reserve. In a couple of days it would be November, and his company would once again return to the front.

John observed the French peasant girls toiling away. It had been a funny old war so far; neither he nor those French had probably yet felt *really* touched by the war. In recent weeks, the French Air Force had bombed the Ruhr and the Rhineland, and her soldiers had tentatively advanced 5 miles into Germany on a 15-mile front; rumour had it that the entire civilian population of Saarbruecken had been evacuated. The Germans then launched a counter-offensive in mid-October, only to find that most of the French had withdrawn two weeks before! General Gamelin, the commander of the Allied forces, had no intention of attacking the Germans. In the event that the Germans attacked the French, then Gamelin would order his troops to retreat behind the Maginot Line. After virtually two months of war, the British, French and Germans occupied the same positions as on 1st September 1939 —and that was it. On a darker note, Germany however had overrun Poland...

John looked forward to one last night out on the town, tomorrow evening. He closed his eyes for a moment and thought of the taste of lemonade and grenadine on his lips. He would be tempted to eat the steak and chips again —a bargain at 5.50 francs. The French liked the Tommies to sing all the old First World War songs, such as 'Tipperary' and 'Keep the Home Fires Burning'. He wandered if Kenneth Faulkner would be the source of amusement with his dreadful singing, and whether Bill Gardner would end the evening with another different French girl on his arm. John smiled. He had taken rather a fancy to one of the locals from the village, himself. Her name was Claudette, and John believed her to be eighteen years of age. Claudette had golden flowing hair, and a happy, bubbly face. John had spotted her at work, harvesting the crops one day. John sighed. The girl probably did not even know who he was; just another one amongst the faceless crowd of uniformed British boys.

Mary Baker sieved through the morning's post, and turned her attention to the envelope that had arrived from France. She eagerly took out the letter that was inside; it was dated 20th November.

"Dear Mother & Father,

It is now however many weeks since we arrived in France, and does it seem far longer?! There is a growing sense of impatience amongst us all at Jerry's inactivity.

There is a constant need to be on the alert, but for *what?* The only invasion we have had to deal with so far has been that by a platoon of French Poilus, who were armed only then with a football! It was a rather unconventional game of football that we had against our French comrades; there were twenty on each team, and the match lasted for close to three hours! There was no damage to our pride, as we ended the game 2 apiece. Bill Gardner scored our second goal. The other men and myself rather took to the French soldiers, although (and it does sound a bit cruel to say this), they did stink of garlic!

Time is spent holding the front line in forward positions, followed by a spell in reserve. Typically, when at the rear, one spends the day overhauling the weapons, collecting water from a river and washing. It is all getting rather tedious, there is *little* to do, and to keep us occupied we often end up helping local farmers with their work! We have three, often four meals a day —tea, sugar, bread, butter, cheese, jam and vegetables are very much in abundance, and there is a daily portion of fresh meat, occasionally there is bully beef, and quite often fish (herrings or sardines). There is no danger that your son will starve to death! The French drinks taste different to ours. Their beer tastes a bit vinegary, and wine is a little bitter, although one gets used to it.

Thankfully, (if a little ironic), there is more to do at the Front; building and manning shelters with corrugated iron, tree trunks and boards. Beyond our front line (and an anti-tank ditch), the fields are criss-crossed with barbed wire. I think I'm correct in believing that, on a ridge, four miles away, are the Germans...biding their time.

At night time we routinely venture out into No-mans-land on patrol. I shall now describe to you one such patrol, last week.

Shortly after 11p.m. having arranged passwords for our return with the section commander, four of us went out on patrol, armed with rifles and hand grenades. Crossing through a gap in our own barbed wire defences, the moonlight glinted off our weapons, and provided good visibility for fifty yards, maybe sixty. Our objective was a couple of farm buildings three-quarters mile away out in No-mans-land. Once we had reached the buildings, we were to keep an eye out for signs of any enemy activity in the vicinity, and intercept any Jerry patrols.

A radium-illuminated compass acted as our guide, as we silently moved forward, crouching, so as to present a smaller target. Every so often, we would have to cut through barbed wire; progress was slow.

I had noticed that high above clouds were increasingly obscuring the moon. We had almost reached the nearest building, and hence, our first objective —the cattle stalls- when it started raining. Visibility was reduced.

We crept up to the cattle stalls, and halted beside the entrance, which was doorless. Corporal Smith and Private Jameson stepped tentatively inside to investigate the building, whilst Kenneth Faulkner and myself kept watch, at the entrance.

A couple of minutes later, Corporal Smith and Private Jameson reappeared. They reported the cattle stalls empty, and had found no sign of any recent enemy activity there. I think we breathed a collective sigh of relief, and pressed on towards the farmhouse.

We must have been within twenty yards or so of the building, when the unmistakable sound of some object being toppled over came from inside.

Hearts pounding, we checked our weapons. I could feel myself breaking out into a sweat, despite the driving wind and rain on this cold November night. There was a distinct possibility that Germans were inside that building, perhaps even a patrol just passing through, like ours. How many Germans might there be? We had heard them, but had they been made aware of our presence? A thousand and one such thoughts raced through my mind, as we approached the farmhouse.

Corporal Smith put his hand to the farmhouse door; alas it was locked. He nodded to me, and so I raised my rifle, then gave the door an almighty kick, to force it open.

Inside was pitch black. Thankfully I was greeted by silence, and the other three men followed me in. For a few moments, we all stood motionless, our eyes adjusting to the darkness all too slowly.

Corporal Smith turned to me and grinned, as the source of the disturbance a couple of minutes ago revealed itself —a thin half-starved cat that had been scavenging for food. The situation could easily have been very different, and much more serious. We proceeded to check out the remainder of the building (and with more confidence), before commencing the return journey back to the safety of our lines. This passed uneventfully, save Kenneth Faulkner carelessly muddying his uniform in a deep puddle!

I almost forgot to mention that we received a visit from the Church Army, two days ago. They had a mobile canteen with luxuries such as chocolate, sweets, lemonade and cigarettes all available. Mind you, we were still obliged to pay for these luxuries! At least it shows that the good people back home are still thinking of us.

XXXXX – John."

John Baker's last letter home from 1939 was written at the very end of December.

"Dear Mother & Father,

For many days now, the landscape has been covered in a heavy frost. Snow looks set to fall, imminently; it is bitterly cold. One day is much the same as the other. They say that we are at war, but where is the fighting? The French are content to sit in the Maginot Line, wearing badges displaying a fortress and the words *On ne passe pas*.

A couple of weeks ago, we were visited by a team of the Entertainments National Service Association (E.N.S.A). They put on a play, there was a magician and also a comedian. The comedian was a bit corny, and I think that a number of the chaps dearly wished that they had some rotten fruit to hand, but at least it broke the daily monotony!

Christmas day arrived, and there was ready-cooked turkey, shared between thirty-two of us! In keeping with army tradition, the officers served the men their food. I especially enjoyed opening your parcels. A large group of us sung songs, late into the evening. I am sure that you will recognize this song, which we have been singing rather a lot, recently.

We're gonna hang out the washing on the Siegfried Line,
Have you any dirty washing, Mother dear?
We're gonna hang out the washing on the Siegfried Line,
'Cos the washing day is here.
A happy and peaceful New Year to yourselves, Hannah and Richard.
XXXXX – John."

By the end of January 1940, the British Expeditionary Force in France had suffered in excess of 700 casualties. The fighting proper had *still* not started, yet daily life for the Tommies in France had not been getting any easier, on the fringes of No-mans-land, a wilderness of wire, shell holes and abandoned farms. As John Baker wrote on 31st January 1940.

"Dear Mother & Father,

The weather has got even worse. It has surely been the coldest winter in living memory. Some nights, the temperature has fallen to minus ten degrees. When I was a child, I used to love the snow, but now I *hate* it. Much of the time is spent digging out equipment, only for it to be covered again, with fresh snowfalls. If one touches a piece of cold metal with the bare hand, then one receives a burning sensation. Streams are frozen solid, the earth is like rock and there is a biting wind, which makes it a danger to expose one's ears for very long. Someone had the bright idea of filling sandbags with straw, which we then wrapped round our legs for warmth. Sounds silly, but it works!

A few days ago, we had 48 hours of alternative thaws and frosts. Next came the rain –turning the roads into ice rinks. Traffic movement is non-existent. Apologies for my being so British, and talking about the weather all the time, although it is the weather that governs our daily life at the moment. We are currently manning the outposts, and by the time that food reaches Private Jameson, and myself it has gone cold. I do feel thoroughly fed up; for us lads over in France, the Spring cannot come soon enough.
XXXXX – John."

CHAPTER 4 – THE WAR CREEPS SILENTLY CLOSER

The morning of Tuesday, 17th October 1939 saw talk and speculation more excited than normal in Miss Townsend's classroom.

Whilst waiting for their teacher to arrive, Beth, Clara and Hannah were having a discussion about the previous days air raid on the Firth of Forth by the Germans; the first time that Germany had launched a raid on Britain. A few nights before, a U-boat had audaciously sailed into the harbour at Scapa Flow and sunk the 29,000-ton battleship "Royal Oak", with the loss of 810 lives.

"None of us are safe, now that the German planes have started to attack Britain," declared a worried Hannah, as she twiddled nervously with her pencil.

"My Dad says that we're not to panic, for Hitler's aircraft were bound to bomb Britain, *sometime*." Clara said reassuringly.

Beth added.

"Clara's right. It was only one small raid by a handful of aircraft. I'm sure that the main target of the German planes is going be the Maginot Line." Pointing to the lead article in Hannah's newspaper, she added. "Look! It says here that passengers on a train travelling from Edinburgh were warned that a raid was in progress, as they neared the bridge. However, most of the passengers preferred to continue the journey! How's that for British defiance?"

Hannah's mood perked up.

"And we did manage to bring down four German bombers."

Nancy appeared. The girl was very red around the eyes, and had clearly been crying. She took her seat, without looking at or saying a word to any of her friends.

Beth turned to Nancy.

"Nancy, what's the matter?"

Nancy explained that her parents were taking her pet dog to the vets, that morning, to put it to sleep, for fear that the animal might bark hysterically in the event of an air raid.

"But, how awful!" Hannah exclaimed.

Beth spoke, lowering her voice as she did so.

"I didn't want to tell you this, Hannah…When Daddy went into town, a few weeks ago, he said that all the people were queuing outside the vets with their cats and dogs, to put them down. The worst bit was seeing all these unhappy people leave, carrying the dead animals home in little brown sacks. It bought tears to my Daddy's eyes."

"That raid on Scotland was what made my parents finally decide that it was best to put poor Billy to sleep," sobbed Nancy. "I hate Hitler!"

Beth put a comforting arm around her friend.

Miss Townsend duly arrived, and handed each of the children two sheets of paper, stressing that this was to last them all day.

At the rear of the class, Tom held one of his sheets of paper up to the window, and gave it a look of disgust.

"Yuck! I can't write on this; it's full of little wood-chips!"

"Look how thin this new pencil of mine is? I won't be able to write without the damn thing breaking!" Harry stated.

Miss Townsend had heard the boy's grumbling.

"Tom and Harry, stop moaning. There is a war on, you know?"

Dinnertime brought more dissent. As Tom queued up with Richard and the twins, he was aghast to find that the entire selection of available food had been reduced to mincemeat, potato and a limited range of vegetables. He screwed his face up, and observed.

"That's rubbish!"

Receiving a disapproving look from one of the dinner ladies.*

For the meal, the boys joined Beth, Hannah and their girlfriends at the table. Tom deliberately placed himself down beside Samantha. Tom winked at her.

"Hello, Samantha!"

Unimpressed, Samantha sighed, before turning her head away, to ignore Tom.

Tom turned his attention to his meal. Again, he screwed his face up, as he unenthusiastically placed his fork into a potato.

Hannah, opposite Tom, noted with irony.

"Poor Thomas, this meal is probably the most healthy one he's had for ages…"

"True. He never eats his greens at home." Beth added.

Tom grunted an incomprehensible reply.

Richard said that he and Hannah did not mind vegetables too much, and Nancy declared that she thrived on them.

"Then no wander you're so thin, Pencil!" Harry said spitefully.

Tired with his meal, already, Tom opted to become a nuisance. He selected a potato from his plate, and pushed it gently onto the end of his fork so that the potato only just hung on.

Richard watched his friend with bemusement. Harry and Henry both smirked.

Tom flicked the fork so that the potato broke loose, and catapulted through the air towards his sister. However, the boy's aim was poor, and the potato flew between Beth and Hannah to land harmlessly on the floor.

The girls had not missed this assault, and were determined to get their own back.

Suddenly, Tom was under attack with peas, which Beth and Hannah joyfully launched at him.

"Oh! Come on you two, that's enough!" He protested.

One of the peas hit Tom in the eye, and he let out a loud.

"Ouch! That really hurt!"

The whole table of boys and girls found this highly amusing.

---

* School dinners were not actually introduced for a couple more years.

"What a weed!" Samantha chuckled.

The whistle signifying an air raid or drill interrupted the merriment.

"That is typical –right in the middle of dinner." Hannah lamented.

All the school made their way to the air raid shelter. In their haste, everyone got mixed up, and Richard, Samantha and Tom found themselves away from Miss Townsend and the rest of the class, to be graced by the company of Mr. Philpot, the caretaker. Mr. Philpot, was about sixty years of age, and was a veteran of the Great War. He leant forwards, and with a wistful look in his eyes, he addressed the children.

"Let me share with you a couple of stories about my experiences during the last war…" He began.

Most of the children, in wide-eyed anticipation of his memories, huddled closer to the caretaker. Tom, however, folded his arms disinterestedly, and stared vacantly up at the roof of the shelter. Richard, turned to Samantha, and referring to Tom, said.

"It just isn't his day."

Samantha smiled.

"Poor little pea-brain."

Eight days later, 25th October 1939, Clara's father, David, was patrolling the main street of the village, when he came across Nancy's father, Kenneth, finishing off his post round. Kenneth, a tall rugged faced man with jet-black hair said a cheery hello. The autumn wind swept red and yellow leaves across the road.

"Morning, Ken." The village Bobby nodded in reply. He walked across to Kenneth, and then stood with his hands clasped behind his back. David was a portly but amiable man with a round face, who knew everyone in the village.

"That's the end of Mister Hitler's peace offensive, then." The postman began.

The Constable gave his greying moustache a tickle.

"Well, after Czechoslovakia and Poland, you can't believe a word that Bavarian Corporal ever says, again. He insists he won't withdraw his troops from Poland, so how can there be peace?"

"That speech of *von* Ribbentrop's last night?" The postman said the German Foreign Minister's name in a sarcastic manner. "All that rubbish about Britain being to blame; and Britain secretly preparing for war against Germany for years!"

"It's Germany that wants war alright. Remember a million young British men died last time. I myself lost a cousin at Ypres." The Constable shook his head. "No one in their right mind wants to go through that, again."

"What with Blitzkrieg, panzers and war planes, where will it all end?" Asked the postman.

"I don't know, Ken, I don't know. But, we'll see it through."

A short while later, the Constable was confronted by Mrs. Stafford, one of the more well to do women in the village, who was in a quite a flap. Mrs. Stafford, was fifty years of age, but looked older, of slim build, and dressed in immaculate rather old-fashioned clothes and wearing lots of jewelry. She tended to look down upon most people in the village, and liked everything in her life to be orderly, neat and tidy. She was refined, and a perfectionist to the point of obsession. Mrs. Stafford had a daughter at school in Mr. Henry's class, who, like her Mother had few real friends in the village. Back in September, the Staffords had been obliged to take an evacuee under their wing; a shy city girl called Ethel. Mrs. Stafford had always had a prejudice against the 'townie' people, viewing them as dirty and of lower social class. The idea of housing such an evacuee for an indefinite period had filled Mrs. Stafford with horror, although she could do little but to accept the fact. She had taken every opportunity during the past few weeks, to complain to unwilling villagers about Ethel's standard of hygiene, labeling the poor child as 'insanitary' and 'verminous'. It transpired that, this morning the girl had absconded.

"The wretched child's nowhere to be seen, Constable!" Mrs. Stafford stated.

The policeman leant a sympathetic ear, as Mrs. Stafford continued.

"I went to wake her at 7:15 a.m. as usual, only to find that her bed had not been slept in! I've looked everywhere for her; goodness knows where she's gone. I mean, the bed wetting was bad enough, but, *this* is the final straw!" Mrs. Stafford cupped her head in her hands. She despaired, "Wretched City children!"

The Constable gave Mrs. Stafford a tap on the arm, and said reassuringly.

"Now you calm down. I'll find her."

The twins, Harry and Henry, arrived on the scene.

"Morning Mrs. Staffs!" They chorused.

Mrs. Stafford did not exchange the pleasantries.

Noticing the distressed look on the woman's face, Henry turned to the policeman, and enquired.

"Anything the matter?"

"Nothing that I can't deal with. Now why don't you two lads hop along to school?" the Constable replied authoritatively.

"Well...I suppose that these boys might be able to help, Constable." Mrs. Stafford conceded. She addressed the twins. "I don't suppose that you have seen *that* Ethel anywhere, this morning? The wretched child's gone missing!"

The twins replied that they had not seen the girl since the day before.

"Let's return to your house, Mrs. Stafford, and make an attempt at retracing the girl's steps." The Constable proposed.

The two adults, with the twins in tow, headed towards Mrs. Stafford's house. Harry confidently predicted.

"Me and Henry —we'll help you find Ethel."

The Constable cast a suspicious eye at the curly-haired boys.

"Looks like you two just want to bunk off school."

Before the party reached Mrs. Stafford's house, Beth and Hannah came up the road cycling away furiously on their bicycles. They dismounted in front of the Constable, and, breathless, pointing behind her, Beth explained.

"We've got young Ethel back in the farmhouse, Mummy's looking after her."

Hannah added.

"Ethel ran away from that awful woman that she has been living with. She said that…" Hannah broke off in mid flow, as she suddenly realized the presence of Mrs. Stafford, and quickly put two and two together.

"Is that so?" Mrs. Stafford frowned.

Behind Mrs. Stafford's back, the mischievous twins sniggered.

"So, the girl's safe, then." The Constable nodded in conclusion.

Everyone followed the two girls back to the farm.

Inside the farmhouse, they found Ethel sitting at the kitchen table tucking into a hearty breakfast, which Emily had prepared. In the corner of the room a concerned looking Richard stood quietly. Ethel, a small child with curly brown hair, was eating her food as if she had not a care in the world. However, on seeing Mrs. Stafford enter the room, the girl became withdrawn, and slid a little under the table, so that only her head was now visible.

"Oh! Morning, David." Emily said warmly.

"Morning, Emily," smiled Clara's father, as he removed his helmet. He then turned to look at Ethel. How sad her eyes were, he thought.

Emily explained that Jack, one of the farm labourers, had been going round the farm doing the early morning feed, when he had been disturbed by a noise coming from one of the small wooden storage sheds. He went to investigate, and was surprised to find a little girl scratching around inside! He had handed Ethel over to Emily, who promptly sent Beth and Hannah off out in search of the policeman, with the news that they had gained an extra child.

"I hope you realize little girl, what trouble you have caused to all these people…wasting the Constable's time!" Mrs. Stafford spoke to the child with measured hostility.

The girl sobbed.

"I'm not going back home with her. I hate her, I hate her!"

Emily went over to comfort Ethel. She stroked the girl's hair, and said soothingly.

"The poor dear, she only ran away from Mrs. Stafford's house because she felt so desperate…"

"I don't want the wretched child anywhere near my house, ever again!" Mrs. Stafford declared. "I totally wash my hands of her –and any other filthy evacuee children!" She threw her hands up into the air, before storming out.

The Constable sighed, and tickled his moustache.

"Well, that's certainly cleared the air. Our Mrs. Stafford's clearly one of these people who can't adapt to the city children. I suppose she's not the only one. But, where does that leave little Ethel? She hasn't got anywhere to stay, now."

"I could let her stay here." Emily began. "Although widow Kettle's been making noises that she would like to take an evacuee child under her wing. She's been very lonely since her husband died in thirty-five, and she has got four Grandchildren."

"Could be the ideal solution. But, how does that sound to Ethel?"

The girl nodded her head enthusiastically. Widow Kettle had always taken the trouble to speak to the children, and the old woman did have such a lovely black cat.

"Well, that's that." The Constable put on his helmet, and was ready to leave, when Emily offered.

"Would you care to stay for a cup of tea?"

The Constable did not take any persuading.

"Yes, I believe I would."

The drama over, the twins had departed for school. As they passed the two detached houses just before the school, Henry observed.

"You know, that Hannah looked nice when she got off her bike earlier? I quite like her."

Harry said indignantly.

"You keep your eyes off Hannah, I spotted her first!"

"She's too old for you."

"So, she's too old for you, too!"

October turned to November, and there was a taste of things to come on the Home Front, as the Government announced that butter and bacon would be rationed from mid-December 1939, the price of petrol went up, and a shopping 'curfew' was introduced. Shops would close at 6:30 p.m. on ordinary days, and at 7 p.m. on Saturdays.

In the air, German planes dropped bombs on the Shetlands, and mines on the Thames estuary, and at sea, on 14th November, the British destroyer 'Blanche' was sunk.

In Germany, Hitler had survived an assassination attempt. Minutes after Hitler made a speech to Nazis in a Munich beer cellar, a bomb exploded wrecking the building. Eight people were killed, and a further sixty injured. A cabinetmaker with Communist sympathies and two British intelligence officers kidnapped from the Dutch border were among those accused of planting the bomb.

The train pulled up at the Oak Green station with a final hiss of steam. Hannah and Richard looked at the engine expectantly. Behind the Baker children, stood Emily, with her hands resting supportively on their shoulders. A solitary porter, a W.A.A.F., and an elderly gentleman were waiting on the platform otherwise the station was deserted. The trees had by now shed most of their leaves, and in the distance a lone tractor meandered its way across an otherwise empty field.

"There's someone special coming to visit you two," said Emily.

"I wonder who it is, do you think it's the King?" Suggested Richard.

Hannah shook her head and smiled, she knew that there would be police and guards present if the King were coming to Oak Green.

The carriage doors opened, and the travelers spilled out. On sighting one female passenger, Richard broke into a sprint, and shouted.

"Mummy!"

The boy's mother threw her hands around him.

Emily and Hannah joined them. Emily winked at the girl.

"I knew you wouldn't be disappointed."

Mary Baker addressed Emily.

"So, you managed to keep it a surprise, then?"

"Yes, somehow," replied the other.

Mary extended a warm hand over the top of Richard's head.

"I'm pleased to meet you at last." She added. "I'm so grateful for your taking these two on."

"Oh! They're no trouble, really."

Mary Baker fiddled momentarily with her curly dark brown hair. She was a little slimmer than average build. She was forty-three years of age. Her brown eyes betrayed a slightly worried look on her face.

"Where's Daddy?" Her children fired other such questions at her; how long was she going to stay, how was London, was there any news on John.

"All in good time, when we're back at Mrs. Pavitt's house," replied Mary.

"I bet you're in need of a good cup of tea," said Emily.

A short while later, they went through the gate into the farmyard. There they found Tom and his father immersed in a pile of wood and junk. As Ted raised a hammer, the group realized that he was constructing something. Closer inspection revealed that he was joining a wheel to a plank of wood. Tom watched throughout with keen-eyed interest.

"I knew her old pram would come in useful one day," Ted declared with satisfaction, whilst shooing away a nosey chicken, "Making the boys a cart," he explained to the on looking group.

"But what about if there's any grandchildren?" Asked Emily.

Ted looked at Tom, and shook his head. Tom smirked, and then addressed his friend.

"I bet you want to be the first to come and race with me on my new cart, Richard? We'll be faster than Jack the delivery boy on his bike!"

Emily spoke, once more.

"May I introduce Mrs. Baker, Hannah and Richard's mother, you two hadn't forgotten that she was coming to visit today, have you?" she added, "Anyway, Thomas, you can't race with only one cart."

"Oh!"

Ted scratched his head.

"Didn't think of that, son."

Hannah glanced at her mother and laughed.

They sat down for dinner, rabbit stew and dumplings followed by steam pudding. The children had water to drink, whilst the ladies enjoyed a glass of tonic wine each, and Ted a beer, on this special occasion. Mary spoke about London, and how it had changed, the blackout, the sharp reduction in the number of vehicles on the streets, how you couldn't go anywhere without seeing someone in uniform. They'd had a practice gas attack the other day, as Mary explained.

"The rescue workers have to wear special clothing –yellow oilskin trousers and coats, Wellington boots, gloves and masks…"

"I bet they look like aliens from a movie!"

"Yes, they probably do, Tom." Mary continued. "A number of the neighbours had to pretend to be casualties, and the man in charge of the rehearsal went around assessing the wounded. However, when pressed he wasn't able to answer the question whether to treat wounds or gas first!"

Mary asked the Pavitt children about their schooling.

"Beth did well in a Latin test last week, mummy," said Hannah.

"Hannah got good marks, too," added Beth. She went on "We've been on a couple of nice nature walks with the class, and Hannah and myself try and get out on a cycle ride to the surrounding villages, if the weather's fine."

"That sounds nice," smiled Mary.

"Yes, we enjoy it," nodded Beth.

Mary turned to the girl's brother.

"And how about you, Tom?"

"I'm not a Swot like the others, but the class all liked it when I put a frog on rotten Mr. Henry's desk!" Smirked the boy.

"Oh!" Mary raised her eyebrows, and began to worry about the kind of company that her son was keeping.

Hannah spoke up.

"Yes, but Tom forgot to mention that he got fifty lines when Mr. Henry discovered who the culprit was!!!"

The group erupted into laughter.

They spoke at length about the new friends that Hannah and Richard had made. There was Beth's nice group of girls that included Clara, Nancy and Samantha. Richard had of course, made friends with Edward, and the mischievous Harry and Henry. Tom went on about the twin's antics, and mentioned, half-jokingly, that one or even both of them had a crush on Hannah. Beth suggested that Hannah liked Jack the deliver boy, to which Hannah retorted.

"He's awful!"

They all stayed up later than normal that night, and Ted treated Mary to a glass of sweet sherry. Further discussion included air raid practices and time spent with creepy crawlies in the school air raid shelter, the meanness of the confectioner and the incident with little Ethel. Tom unashamedly recalled incidents of trespass and general mischief making with the twins, all of which apparently occurred before the arrival of the Baker children, whose appearance seemed to have had a taming influence on the boy. Throughout, Mary sat with an expression of mild horror on her face, whilst Ted shook his head despairingly.

The next day, was a Sunday. The Bakers and Pavitts attended the morning church service. Clara and Samantha sung their hearts out in the choir. Hannah jested that Tom would look very angelic in the choirboy's whites. It was noticeable that more prayers were said than before the war started. After dinner, the boys took the new cart to an outlying field and got to ride the cart down a rutted farm track. Later on, with the exception of Ted, who was currently working a seven-day week, they all saw Mary off at the station. Richard hung on tight to his mother's coat. He didn't want her to go, it was like when they departed from her at Victoria station two months ago, except that this time the two children would be standing waving on the platform. Mary gently explained that she must go and get George's tea, and after a final embrace, closed the carriage door behind her.

On 11th November, the Queen made a broadcast to the women of Britain and the Empire. Separated by some sixty or so miles, Mary Baker in her city home, and Emily Pavitt in her farmhouse, listened to the speech, bound by a common cause, in a battle against a formidable enemy.

"For twenty years we have kept this day of remembrance as one consecrated to the memory of the past and never-to-be-forgotten sacrifice, and now the peace which that sacrifice made possible has been broken, and once again we have been forced into war.

I know that you would wish me to voice, in the name of the women of the British Empire, our deep and abiding sympathy with those on whom the first cruel and shattering blows have fallen –the women of Poland. Nor do we forget the gallant womanhood of France, who are called on to share with us again the hardships and sorrows of war.

War has at all times called for the fortitude of women."

The Queen continued by saying.

"We, no less than men, have real and vital work to do. To us also is given the proud privilege of serving our country in her hour of need.

The call has come, and from my heart I thank you, the women of our great Empire, for the way that you have answered it."

Indeed, 45,000 women had already been recruited as volunteers for the women's services, and another 25,000 had enrolled in the Women's Land Army.

The Queen paid tribute to the unselfish help provided by so many women in a variety of fields, then went on to speak about the separation of families.

"Many of you have had to see your family life broken up –your husband going off to his allotted task- your children evacuated to places of greater safety. The King and I know what it means to be parted from our children, and we can sympathize with those of you who have bravely consented to this separation for the sake of your little ones.

Equally do we appreciate the hospitality shown by those of you who have opened your homes to strangers and to children sent from places of special danger."

The Queen concluded.

"We all have a part to play and I know you will not fail in yours…"

It hadn't been a bad start to the day for the Constable that crisp late autumn morning. He'd first passed several members of the Women's Land Army, armed with pitchforks, on their way to toil in the fields, in their uniform of khaki corduroy breeches; green pullovers and khaki felt hats. The girls had been singing merrily away.

Back to the land, we must all lend a hand,
To the farms and fields we go.
There's a job to be done,
Though we can't fire a gun,
We can still do our bit with a hoe.

The girls were mostly city dwellers in normal life. The work on the land was physically demanding, they were out in all weathers; the working week was fifty hours, and the pay modest. The girls performed tasks such as driving tractors, harvesting crops, milking cows and caring for livestock. They were proving as good as their male counterparts at tending poultry and pulling peas, however, they found more strenuous jobs such as turning hay and milking, harder.

One of them, a freckly-faced redhead had winked cheekily at the Constable. The group had marched on, continuing their song. Clara's father thought them far too cheerful for that time of the morning; they must have been drinking the night before.

The children had then started to appear, in two's and three's on their way to school, with their cardboard boxes, which contained their gas masks slung around their necks. A couple of girls teasingly tried to knock the delivery boy, Jack off his bike, as he cycled past, leaning into the wind, his face red with effort. Jack nodded a hello to the Constable.

A black and white cat strolled across the road; the Constable watched as it carefully picked its way over some dirty leaves. A starling danced on the yellow topped post box, until it sighted the cat and wisely flew off. The last few blackout curtains were being drawn; yet again it had been a quiet night free from disturbance by German bombers. David reflected for a moment or two on this image of the village at war, tickled his moustache and popped into the post office.

The day had gone downhill after that. The policeman found that there were mumblings of discontent in the food queue, outside the butchers, as he strolled past that morning.

"They're paid more than the army!" Came one woman's voice.

A second woman, wearing a headscarf, caught the Constable's eye.

"Isn't it a disgrace, Constable?"

"What is, Mrs. Taylor?"

"The Air Raid Wardens' annual wages bill." Mrs. Taylor explained, her eyes widening, hypnotically. "It comes to ten million pounds more than that of the Navy, thirteen million pounds more than that of the Army…"

"-And twenty-seven million pounds more than that of the R.A.F.!" Interrupted Mrs. Lee. "It's in the papers."

The Constable had a newspaper waved menacingly at him, and rubbed his eye.

"But that doesn't necessarily mean that each individual warden is paid more than each soldier."

"Well there's obviously too many of them!" Snapped Mrs. Taylor.

"Three pounds a week!" Shouted another dissenting voice.

"They're getting paid for nothing, whilst my sister's lost her job after fifteen years as a housekeeper." Said Mrs. Lee.

"And my cousin's lost her job as a secretary, with only a week's pay…and she's still faced with paying the rent!" Shouted another.

David wished that he had now given the queue a wide berth. He would dearly have rather handled naughty children or cheeky Land Girls. Everyone certainly seemed to regard the wardens as the lowest of the low. He declared.

"Yes, but when the German bombs start falling, we might need all those wardens."

"Hmmnn…" Went a couple of women.

The Constable went on his way. He came across a newspaper seller, who said, with irony.

"Germans in Berlin, French in Paris"

David let out a deep sigh. That just about summed it up –the phony war, or bore war, no real fighting, and the British preoccupied with moaning.

CHAPTER 5 – DECEMBER 1939

Where would it all end?

Mary Baker sat, blank sheet of paper in front of her, ready to pen a reply to the latest letter that she had received from her two children. *They* seemed to be enjoying themselves, she knew that from her recent visit, but Mary could think of few inspirational things to write to Hannah and Richard about. Two more European countries were now at war with each other. Russia had wanted strategic Finnish territory, in exchange for some useless Russian land, to protect its naval bases at Leningrad and Murmansk from possible future German attack. Finland refused, so three days ago, 30th November 1939, Russia had invaded Finland at eight points along Finland's frontier, and Helsinki, the Finnish capital had been bombed, killing some eighty civilians. Did the politicians not know any other ways of settling their disputes?

Mary re-read the letter –a joint effort between her son and daughter. They really were having a whale of a time at the farm. Both the children loved the farm animals; Richard especially liked Oscar, the black Labrador. Countless happy hours had been spent playing in the fields and in the woods and down by the river, with Beth and Tom, with whom they got on so well, which was nice. Now that it was winter, indoor activities became popular, and the children enjoyed playing Ludo and Postman's Knock. A concert had recently been held at the village school, and the children had dressed up as characters from King Arthur. Hannah was proud to write that she had played Morgan le Faye.

London. Mary reflected on city life the past few months. Thankfully, the much-feared air raids had failed to materialize; instead the population had been bombarded by petty officialdom and regulations. Just across the writing desk beside her, lay her food ration book, containing numerous little square coupons with the words butter, sugar, bacon and ham, and various numbers inscribed on them. The ration books had been issued last month, and the food-rationing scheme would come into operation on the 8th January. A person would be permitted four ounces of every rationed foodstuff per week, except sugar (twelve ounces).

Soon, Mary's letter to her children began to flow…

"I'm glad that you are both enjoying fresh milk and eggs, remember to eat you greens and to say please and thank you at the Pavitts. I'm glad to hear that you are keeping up your reading Hannah, and that you Richard, have got addicted to *The Dandy*. Don't neglect your studies, especially your arithmetic, Richard! I can see that you have got back into your hockey, again, Hannah, and are enjoying playing it with Beth and her classmates.

Here, the roads are almost totally empty of cars, and there has been a surge in the use of buses and trains, due to petrol rationing. On the crowded buses, children often have to sit on someone's lap. Many of the tiny shops are really suffering, due to the exodus of evacuees to the countryside. It has been common for most retailers to increase their prices by at least ten percent; for example, milk prices have increased by ½d. per pint because 'they were now selling to fewer customers.' Mr. Robinson has been forced to sell up and retire, as he says that business is no longer viable. I suppose that your country shops are enjoying a boom!

With the men folk having gone away to war, there is now the odd sight of women working as bus conductors and porters, and women replacing men in delivering the mail. And a good job they are doing of it, too! I wander what the men will think, when they return home (whenever that is), to find that all these women have adequately performed their jobs with little complaint! Still, I feel that the 17 shillings a week paid to (private) servicemen's wives is rather paltry, and they probably have little choice but to work. So your village still has a postman? If Nancy's father were a few years younger, then he would be liable for call up.

Night time is a very strange experience. With the blackout, it must resemble what London was like a century or so ago. There is <u>no</u> street lighting at all, and vehicles have only dimmed-out headlights, the interior lighting of buses is very restricted, and the conductors struggle to tell the coins apart. Mrs. Woodrow says that she comes over all queasy when using public transport, during the hours of darkness. Old Mrs. Briggs is in hospital after having been knocked down by a car in the blackout. Air raid wardens patrol the streets, and shout 'Put that light out' at the slightest chink of light coming through the curtains, and threaten heavy fines. It is all very worrying. When I read in your letter about that lady who waves a newspaper in front of her when crossing the road at night, I did chuckle, although I shouldn't, as it's a serious matter.

Percy King has volunteered for the army, in his words, to 'escape a boring job and a dull marriage!' Herbert Williamson on our road has joined the Auxiliary Fire Service, with one of the schools currently doubling up as the 'fire station'. From what I gather, he and his fellow auxiliaries are unpopular *both* with the regular firemen, and the general public. I feel that the criticism is unfair, as Herbert is only trying to do his bit to help out, and all for quite a low wage. In my mind, it's the bossy wardens that are the biggest nuisance! Incidentally, as a precaution against incendiary bombs, every house in our street has been issued with a hand-operated stirrup-pump and long handled shovel.

We had a little bit of drama, when a barrage balloon came bumping over the rooftops. The balloon had evidently needed to be cut free in strong winds, and its trailing wires broke a number of chimney pots, and cut a nearby trolley-bus cable!

Daisy says 'hello', Hannah. With most of the teachers having departed for the countryside with their pupils, she has had to move to another school, and is having trouble settling in. She misses you, and wishes that you were there to talk to. Daisy's father says that he has been vindicated now that the bombings have failed to materialize. I suppose we shall see who is right there.

Anyway, I don't want to make you two worry yourselves silly about us. I expect that you both have now been thinking about Christmas. If I keep on hearing reports from Emily about what good children you have been, then I am sure that 'Father Christmas' will reward you both. Look after your brother, Hannah.

Write to me again, soon.

Your loving Mother. XXXXXX"

Hannah had spent an enjoyable evening with an American lady who had just come to Britain after having spent some time in Germany. Hannah had interviewed the lady as part of a school study on life in Europe under Nazi rule, and how the Germans were themselves coping after over three months of war.

During the 1930's they had all seen the newsreels of stage-managed Nazi rallies of growing German military might, with Hitler whipping his mass audiences up into frenzy with his oratory. The 1936 Berlin Olympic Games fly pasts of warplanes, torch lit processions and powerful searchlights conveyed to the world a Germany that was powerful, unified and had a sense of purpose. With the destruction of the Reichstag by fire in 1933, came the end of democracy in Germany. Buildings were taken over by the National Socialists, newspapers banned, and opponents of the regime were arrested and often murdered by Hitler's uniformed brown shirts. Trade Unions were replaced by a government controlled Labour Front. Racism and anti-Semitism were at the centre of Hitler's beliefs. Two years later, anti-Jewish legislation was fully in place in Germany. The manner of Germany's defeat and the harshness of the 1919 Treaty of Versailles left a permanent legacy of bitterness in Germany, which Hitler embodied. Ominously Hitler had called more and more loudly for *lebensraum* (living space) outside Germany. War had followed.

The girl sat on her bed, thoughtfully watching the minute hand of the wall clock, before turning her attention to the tiny handwriting, necessary to conserve paper, and starting to write up the interview notes.

"Is food being rationed in Germany as well as in Britain?"

"Yes. The German people see it as a necessary evil. At the end of the Great War, many Germans died of starvation, and to avoid a repeat of that situation, virtually all foods have been rationed since the beginning of the war. Strangely, cakes are not on ration! The people have different coloured ration cards for different types of food. Farmers are exempt from rationing, and miners, due to their hard work, are allowed larger rations. Food rationing for pets has recently been introduced."

"Pets!"

Then there was an interesting comparison to Britain.

"Germany is the most heavily taxed country in Europe. Can you believe that the average German worker pays four times the tax paid by the average British worker! The Germans have to pay compulsory taxes in the form of contributions to the Hitler Youth, the Winter Help Fund and other such organizations."

"So, the war is proving expensive for Germany?"

"Yes, economically, Germany isn't ready for a long war; they really need it to be over quickly, like the blitzkrieg in Poland."

"Are the Germans supporting Hitler in his war?"

"Most of the German people do seem to think that Hitler is a very good leader. They think it is unfair that England, a smaller country than Germany, has her Empire, and see Hitler as being able to restore the balance of power in Europe, and even the whole world, in Germany's favour."

"Do they think they can win the war?"

"Yes, although they realize that Britain and France together are strong. They think that the Royal Navy is a formidable force, however, they have great faith in their own U-boats. The German air force is also very large…"

"Do you think that the Germans will start bombing England, soon?"

"No, I think that they will have to bomb France, first, maybe defeat them, and then turn towards England."

Hannah put her pen and paper away. The girl thought *the Germans aren't that much different from ourselves*, there being some similarities and some differences between the two warring nations. Although *the Germans are foolish to slavishly follow Hitler.*

"The news which has come from Montevideo has been received with thankfulness in our islands and with unconcealed satisfaction throughout the greater part of the world.

The "Graf Spee," which has been for many weeks preying upon the trade of the South Atlantic, has met her doom, and throughout the vast expanse of water the peaceful shipping of all nations may for a spell at least enjoy the freedom of the seas."

The words of Mr. Churchill, First Lord of the Admiralty, bought some much-needed pre-Christmas cheer to the British people. Later that day, Monday 18th December 1939, as she lay in bed, comforted by the bedside lamp (for Beth was already sound asleep), Hannah reflected on recent events. The 10,000-ton battleship, the "Graf Spee," pride of the German fleet, had gone down. Good news at last! Of course, they had all so very closely been following the news reports, the past few days.

The battleship had been terrorizing shipping in the South Atlantic for weeks, when three British cruisers, the "Achilles," "Ajax" and "Exeter", attacked, causing the "Graf Spee" to limp into Montevideo harbour, Uruguay. However, the Uruguayan authorities had denied the battleship time to make essential repairs, providing the ship's captain, Hans Lansdorf, with a considerable dilemma.

It was not until the children were at school, this morning, when an excited Mr. Philpot suddenly burst into the classroom to announce that the "Graf Spee" had been scuttled by her crew. Shaking with excitement, and making wild arm gestures, the school caretaker had explained.

"They blew her up in the middle of the river off Montevideo –there was this huge explosion, and vast sheets of flame raced up into the air!"

The children cheered.

Mr. Philpot added. "The Jerry captain shot himself."

"Thank you for sharing that last bit of information with us, Mr. Philpot," frowned Miss Townsend. The teacher then smiled. "Well, that really is good news, children." Miss Townsend surveyed the classroom with a glint in her eyes. "The loss of a German battleship –a British victory."

Afterwards, Miss Townsend had got out a wind-up gramophone, and the children proudly sung along to 'Land of Hope and Glory' and 'There'll Always be an England.'

Hannah turned out the light, ready to go to sleep. Outside, it was still and windless, and the frost glistened under the night sky. Yes -a British victory. After the events of Poland and the losses of British shipping, maybe the German's were not so invincible after all. Happy Christmas Herr Hitler!

The children had an enjoyable Christmas at the farm. For both Hannah and Richard, it had been their first spent away from their London home. Far from the festival faring badly when compared to those of the pre-war years, this Christmas was the most exciting, yet; or so it seemed from what the children had wrote. In a letter dated 27th December, Hannah and Richard described to their parents how the farm was decorated with paper-chains, which hung from the walls and ceilings, and how coloured electric bulbs brightened practically every room.

"Our tree went up a week before Christmas Day. It was a very pretty tree, and was very much taller than me. Richard and myself helped Beth and Tom decorate the tree, with glass balls, pine cones and apples, after Beth's father made sure that it was properly secured in the pot." Hannah wrote. She recalled how the hapless Tom had been hit on the head by a loose bauble as it fell from the tree, and then continued, "Our last day at school, Father Christmas paid us a visit, and handed out sweets to every child in the class. The twins, Harry and Henry say that Santa does not really exist, and I must admit that our Santa did bear a close likeness to Clara's father. Of course, we had all already written to the real Santa, and Ted went off and posted our lists of requests in the postbox. We went carol singing, along with Beth, Samantha and Tom, a couple of evenings, singing "Silent Night," "O' Little Town of Bethlehem" and many more. Most of the Christmas cards that we have received have pictures to do with the Nativity or Britannia.

On Christmas Day, I wore my party frock, and we sat round the big kitchen table, with all of Beth's family and had goose, Christmas pudding, cakes, sweets (not all at the same time –please do not think me greedy!), and pulled crackers. To drink, Beth's father made up for us a strange cocktail that included carrot, orange and strawberry! All of us stayed up very late, that night.

On New Year's Eve, all of us children will be attending a party at posh Victoria's house. Apparently, her parents hold a children's party there every year, and nearly all of the girls and boys in the village attend. I am really looking forward to it, as Victoria's house is massive, and there is going to be lots of dancing and games to play.

It really has been a very nice Christmas, and it is not yet over! If only we could have had you and Daddy here with us, then it would have been perfect. Richard and myself do miss you both...XXXXXX"

As the final few hours of 1939 slipped away, Mary Baker reflected upon a year that had seen her children be separated from her. John, her eldest son, serving for King and country in France, and Hannah and Richard evacuated to the perceived safety of the country. With war had come Public Information Leaflets, national identity cards, price increases and the blackout.

Over Christmas, the Pope had appealed for a peace conference, and the King thanked the Empire for its sacrifices in coming to Britain's aid in the war. Hitler, for his part, had spoken of his dream of a Europe liberated from "British tyranny". In Poland, there was continued misery, with public executions, forced labour, arrests of prominent Poles and looting. Churches had been befouled, and forced to close for six and a half days of the week, Polish art treasures and historic buildings were looted. Attractive girls in their late teens had been deported to Germany. Worst to suffer were the Jews and gypsies. Life had indeed got tougher, and in a weeks time there would be the need to adjust to rationing. No doubt 1940 would throw up fresh surprises and challenges.

CHAPTER 6 – THE NEW YEAR

On the Western Front, the Allied and Axis soldiers still observed each other from their fortified positions along the two hundred mile front. The British and French, separated from the Germans by the barbed wire-covered fields of no-mans-land, watched and waited. So too did the neutral countries of Europe, with growing apprehension.

Tom gobbled up the last piece of his food at the breakfast table; the other three children were barely half way through their meal. Tom ran over to the window, pulled back the curtains, and peered anxiously through the glass. Outside, in the grey-blue half-light, day had not yet fully broken through. Tom smiled. The farmyard was white -everything was white.

"Don't worry, Thomas, the snow's not going to disappear that quickly," came Emily's voice.

It was Saturday 20th January 1940.

Tom looked across to the table. The look in his eyes begged the boy and two girls to hurry up with their breakfasts. Slowcoaches!

Emily spoke, again. She warned.

"And you're not going anywhere outside, unless you wrap up warm, Thomas."

Tom sprinted up the stairs, two steps at a time, for his coat, hat and gloves. He shouted after him.

"Hurry up, you lot!"

Not long later, Tom was searching around frantically, in one of the farm outbuildings, for his cherished sledge. Beth, Hannah and Richard watched in amazement.

"Where is it?"

Spare bicycle wheels, pieces of wood, an old tennis racket and various other bits and pieces, went sprawling around everywhere.

"Oh! Tom! Look at the mess you're making." Beth shook her head despairingly. She grabbed her brother's arm, and moved him to one side. "Here, let me look."

The girl duly found the sledge. It was wooden, and a little old and battered, but still had a good few years' use left in it, yet. Beth and Hannah returned the pile of equipment to some sort of order.

The two girls and two boys tramped across the farmyard, and out through the gate, along the track to the main road, Tom making heavy weather of pulling the sledge. Initially, they took great fun in exaggerating their footprints, seeing whose could go the deepest, or who could make the biggest strides. Hannah shook an overhanging branch, as Tom drew near, with the result that snow came showering down onto the boy's head.

The girls both wore boots, woolen scarves and long coats, which came down almost to their milky white knees. Richard, like Tom, wore long trousers, coat, wooly hat and boots. All their cheeks glowed red.

The fields, covered in a thick blanket of snow, looked majestic, they were bathed in yellow and orange, from the sun. The air was cold, crisp and silent. Sheep huddled together on a distant hilltop, like a giant mass of cotton wool. The trees, draped in white, resembled snowmen, their numerous arms pointing in many different directions.

They made their way up the road, to the top of the hill. Hannah pulled her scarf tighter around her neck, as a chill wind blew across the peak of the wintry landscape. Tom put the sledge into position, and climbed onto the front of it. Beth sat down, to occupy the vacant space behind her brother, and put her arms tightly around him.

They had a good panoramic view for miles around, of distant farms, cottages, woods and streams. It was a long way down the slope, and Beth had a feeling of slight apprehension. Hannah and Richard placed their hands on the back of the sledge, ready to push, when Tom gave them the nod. Beth looked down the hill, and took in a deep breath of air. Tom glanced round.

"Ready, go!"

The sledge was away, carrying its two occupants. Beth gave out a squeal, as the sledge, meandering a little, gathered pace. The girl felt her eyes watering, the cold air brushed past her cheeks, and her hair flailed behind her. At the front, Tom, grinned from ear to ear. The freedom, the thrill, the danger, the fear!

Above, Hannah and Richard watched in awe; soon it would be their turn.

As the slope became gentler, the sledge began to slow and veered off, whether by Tom's design or by accident, towards the roadside ditch. Fearing the worst, Beth clenched her eyes shut. The sledge came to a halt, almost teetering onto its side, and throwing up clumps of snow. Tom rolled over headfirst into the soft snow. Beth caught her breath, and the pair simultaneously broke into laughter.

Richard and his sister, ran excitedly down the hill, and met the Pavitt children, part way up. They climbed swiftly up the hill, in eager anticipation of the next speedy descent. The Baker children took their turn on the sledge, then Tom insisted on riding with Hannah. After a couple more rides, Tom left the group, and began to build a snowman at the foot of the hill. He became totally engrossed in his project. The snowman was nearly destroyed within minutes, before it was barely underway, by the two girls, tearing past, on the sledge.

"Careful!" Shouted Tom.

Tom's snowman had achieved shoulder height, and they boy was meticulously adding a couple of twigs for arms, when he received a sharp blow to his back. Momentarily stunned he then spun round, half-crouching, to find the twins, Harry and Henry, standing mischievously, armed with snowballs.

"Harry! Henry! You..."

Tom delved into the snow, to make his own spherical weapon, alas, before he could launch it, the twins had each struck him, again, with more snow.

When Richard appeared, Tom roped him into the battle, on his side. Richard got Henry on the ear, only to receive some snow in the mouth himself.

The girls appeared, speeding down the hill on the sledge, and pelted the unsuspecting boys with snow. The males then got their revenge, by pinning down the outnumbered females, and shoving cold snow down their necks.

"Look at them shivering!" Laughed Tom.

Before long, the group was rolling around in fits of giggles, in the snow. Harry suggested that they go and lark around doing a bit of skating on the village pond, which was iced over. Henry spoke up.

"All the other children in the village are there." He cast an eye at Tom and Richard, and added. "Including Samantha."

Tom shot up.

"Let's go!"

It was an anti-climax, for the group reached the edge of the pond, but got no further. One of the villagers had deemed the surface of the pond to be unsafe, and there were indeed, some cracks beginning to appear in the ice. The last of the group of young skaters, that included amongst others, Clara, Nancy, Samantha and Victoria, were quitting the ice, and going home. The villager, a big, strapping man, not to be argued with, scolded the girls and boys.

"Bloody idiots!"

The boys could only admire from a distance, Samantha, as she walked gracefully down the road, a slender figure, in a beautiful white coat, and disappeared from view.

A silence descended upon the village that cold, clear Monday morning. Steven Granger, a cheery-faced and popular lad was known to most people in the village. He used to play football in the street as a boy, and had gone out with a nice girl from the village. He had been serving on H.M. destroyer "Exmouth," when a U-boat had sunk it, a week ago, the 21st January, with considerable loss of life. "Exmouth" had been lost only two days after the destroyer "Grenville" was sunk by a mine. Steven Granger, nineteen years of age, was among the dead; the whole village was in mourning.

As a mark of respect, the schoolchildren noiselessly lined the main street, awaiting the arrival of the funeral cortege. Beth, standing in a dark overcoat, between Hannah and Richard, shivered in reaction to the biting wind. Her father, had been a good friend with Steven's father, and Ted would be attending the funeral service itself. Beth looked at the sad faces all around her. There was Clara's father, the village Constable, Nancy's mother and father, Samantha's parents, posh Victoria's family, Miss Townsend, Mr. Henry, the casual farm labourers, workers from the railway station, two immaculately dressed ratings, and many more.

Shortly before 10:30a.m, a simple horse-drawn carriage bearing a coffin draped in the red, white and blue of the Union Jack appeared. The black clothed undertaker guided the horse, and close relatives of Steven and half a dozen naval ratings followed the carriage.

As the procession passed by the children, Richard could see that most of the ratings, who were all about twenty years of age, were fighting back the tears. The younger children could not really understand what was going on. Next to him, Richard noticed that Beth's hand was trembling slightly, and her hand was clutching a handkerchief. The boy took the girl's hand gently, to give her support. It wasn't meant to be like this. In the books and movies the good guys didn't get killed. Hannah and Richard had never met with Steven, yet both were still gripped by a horrible feeling of loss.

Later on, as Steven's coffin was lowered into a grave in a quiet corner of the churchyard, Ted's gaze moved from the ground to the woods opposite. It being the middle of winter, the trees had lost all their leaves, and were mere skeletons of their usual selves. But, in a couple of month's time, those trees would come to life again, unlike poor Steven. The group that surrounded the grave —sobbing relatives, friends, neighbours and ratings, consisted primarily of people in their forties, fifties, sixties and even seventies, however, the youngster that they had come to bury was but a fraction of their age. Fate had delivered him a cruel hand.

It was Tuesday 8th February 1940. Before lessons began that morning, the girls were discussing how they were helping the waste recycling campaign.

"We're putting all our newspapers and cardboard beside the dustbin." Samantha proudly announced.

"Beth's Father donated an old plough and a couple of old milk pails," said Hannah.

"Have you donated your brother as waste?" Nancy cheekily asked Beth.

"I heard that, Pencil!" Came an indignant voice from the back of the classroom. Harry joined in the banter.

"You girls shouldn't go upsetting Tom, or he'll put chalk in your inkwells!"

Nancy turned round and glared at Beth's brother.

"So it *was* you who did it last time, Tom? I knew it!"

Miss Townsend entered, and started off the morning by speaking for a short while about developments in the Russo-Finnish war, which was now over two months old. She followed this by asking the class to write a story from the point of view of a Finnish civilian or Russian soldier involved in the conflict.

Beth liked story writing. The girl chewed thoughtfully on her pencil, and stared at her solitary sheet of paper, with its wood-chip mosaic. She would have dearly wished that she could have written gaily over several sheets, however, in these times of hardship, one had to adhere to the paper shortage. Beth would have to write as small as possible.

Miss Townsend distributed a collection of newspaper cuttings detailing the war in Finland, so as to provide the children with food for thought. The children began eagerly to discuss the articles among themselves.

The Finns had had their homes bombed by the Russians, and the fighting men of both sides had been enduring conditions of intense cold. The picture that emerged was that Finland was successfully blocking the advance of the huge Russian army. In late December, the Finns had even pushed the Russians back over their own border. The Russians had so far suffered some 150,000 casualties, to the Finns 10,000. The Russians called the Finns, on their skis and camouflaged in white, the White Death. But the Russians wanted this war; had they not got what they deserved?

Beth was discussing the Russo-Finnish conflict with Hannah.

"What the Russians have done is awful." Hannah declared. "Their pilots have been dropping incendiary bombs, high explosive bombs and then they machine-gun the fire-fighters! Worse still, they even attacked a Finnish field hospital, which was prominently marked with a Red Cross." Hannah, with a very worried look on her face, enquired of Beth. "Do you think that's what Hitler and his planes will do to us?"

"You mustn't worry yourself silly, Hannah. We've got a good army to defend us —plus the French," came Beth's reassuring reply.

"No I mustn't worry." Hannah conceded. "The German soldiers have got to get past my older brother John, in France, first."

Beth asked Hannah if she had decided what she was going to write about.

"I will imagine myself to be a Finnish civilian trying to survive the terror created by the bombing from Russian planes. How about yourself, Beth?"

"I'm going to write about a Russian soldier who, had initial high hopes of an easy victory, and has been taken prisoner by the Finns, after narrowly surviving the Arctic weather. I think it will take the form of a diary that the young soldier keeps, for the benefit of his sweetheart, should he fail to survive the conflict. I've been reading some interesting articles, here…"

Beth started to put pen to paper. She backed the outnumbered Finns one hundred per cent in this war against the Red Army, for the Soviet leader Stalin seemed to be just as wicked as Hitler. However, in spite of this, she deeply sympathized with the ordinary Russian soldier. She re-read the newspaper cuttings detailing the appalling military reverses that the Russians had suffered. There were tales of Finnish soldiers, during the night penetrating thick forests to the rear of the Russians, where the Finns would machine-gun their enemy. The Finns would then disappear, leaving two bodies of Russian troops fighting each other in the darkness, thinking they were Finns. Powerful Finnish anti-tank guns, hand grenades and inflammatory explosives would disable dozens of Russian tanks, which were left abandoned in ditches beside the roads. One correspondent wrote.

"Inside one of these tanks were the charred remains of its Russian occupants —all four in ghastly postures which somehow resembled Polynesian dancers. We counted more than forty such tanks, and several more were said to have plunged off bridges and disappeared beneath the waters of the lake."

And then there was the severe cold...

There were instances where Russian troops became cut off where the Finns knew the terrain created natural traps. The Russians, totally surrounded, dared not to light fires, for fear of attracting Finnish snipers. The Russians had been so confident of a quick, easy victory that they had never been issued with winter clothing. Flimsy shelters built from spruce branches proved to be woefully inadequate against the cold. The Russians could hardly walk or sight a gun, so cold were the men's fingertips. A lack of food forced men to resort to consuming horseflesh, whilst some even gnawed at the bark of trees. Soon, in temperatures of minus twenty degrees centigrade they began to freeze to death by the thousand, newly fallen snow forming a shroud over the bodies of the dead. What hell!

Edward, being an aviation enthusiast, told the story of a Russian pilot, and how his character continually wrestled with his conscience, as his bombs rained down on the Finnish civilian population.

"Nikolai was not trained for night flying, so he was obliged to attack his targets by day." Edward wrote. "His most cunning tactic was to cut out his engine, and glide silently over a target before releasing the bomb load. However, much to his annoyance, sometimes Nikolai would miss his target. For example, during one raid over Helsinki, his bombs fell harmlessly into the sea! Nikolai's greatest fear was being shot down. The Finns had augmented their defences with foreign planes, and it was rumoured that, after two months of war over two hundred Russian aircraft had been brought down. Nikolai had also heard the stories of the alleged atrocities committed by Russian pilots against the Finnish civilians. Personally, he disapproved of the deliberate targeting of old folk, women and children, although he accepted that sometimes there would be innocent victims during a bombing raid. That was war..."

A month later, 13th March 1940, Finland surrendered. The Finns had been hugely outnumbered, and had latterly suffered unsustainable casualties, as their front line collapsed. A large part of its territory was ceded to the Russians, and 400,000 Finns living in the Karelian Isthmus were forced to leave their homes under the terms of the Finnish-Soviet peace treaty. Britain, France, the U.S.A. and even Italy condemned the Soviet position.

George and Mary Baker sat watching the newsreels in the cinema, as the defeated Finns evacuated their homes. In pitiful scenes, the people, wearing thick coats, hats and scarves to protect against the cold, were piling their belongings onto hand-sledges and sledges pulled by reindeer. Many of the women were crying, as prosperous farmsteads were abandoned. An old lady broke down on her doorstep as she left the home that she had most likely occupied for half a century. Signposts were being dismantled before the arrival of the Russians. The final images were of Helsinki, where the Finnish flag was flown at half-mast, in honour of Finland's dead.

The question praying on Mary's mind was *who next?* In a world where dictators and military aggression seemed to rule, how soon before the Germans, under their power-hungry leader Adolf Hitler, made their move into Western Europe? Would scenes such as those witnessed in Finland, soon be repeated in Belgium, France or Holland, or maybe in all three countries? And if so, then what hope would there be for Britain..?

Britain herself was to a large extent detached from the war. Six months into the conflict, the mass bombings by the Luftwaffe had failed to materialize; British Army losses could still be measured in the hundreds, and the people's biggest concern seemed to be petty officialdom. The first civilian to be killed in an air raid occurred at Scapa Flow in mid March. Many hundreds of thousands of evacuees had returned home and hardly anyone bothered to carry their gas masks around with them. In London, the construction of cinemas and office blocks continued, and the roads were still surprisingly busy. In the theatre, an ironic sketch called 'Awfully Quiet on the Western Front', in which the Tommies were depicted as knitting and drinking endless cups of tea, was proving popular. Couples danced "The Blackout Stroll", during which the lights went out and everyone changed partners. The Disney film "Pinocchio" opened in London. The Allies appeared content to let the Germans make the first move. The remainder of March passed by uneventfully, save a woman being fined £75 for buying sugar for 140 weeks' rations, which she transported home in her Rolls Royce. Crowds besieged restaurants and bars, and people went to the coast in large numbers, for a few days at the end of March, for Easter, which fell on the 24th…

"It's Easter Sunday!"

The boy's loud, excited voice was like an unwelcome foghorn in his sister's ears. Beth turned over on the soft pillow, and pulled the blanket protectively over her head. She wished for the boy to disappear.

Her brother went over to Hannah's bed.

"It's Easter Sunday!" Come-on you pair of lazy bones', GET UP!" Tom glanced at Hannah. "I know you're not really asleep…"

Hannah rubbed her bleary eyes, and glanced at her watch.

"Is that all it is?"

"Don't you know it's considered rude to enter girl's bedrooms without knocking first," came Beth's voice from under the blanket.

Tom ignored the remark. He marched across to the window, and opened the curtains wide, casting a curious eye at a dripping spider's web on the outside of the pane. A slanting rectangle of bright sunlight entered the room.

"Tom! You rotter!" Shouted Hannah.

"You've *got* to get up." Tom was wide eyed with excitement. "Don't you two want your Easter Eggs?"

Beth sighed.

"Oh! Yes. The annual Easter egg hunt. I'd almost forgotten about it." Her voice was less than enthusiastic.

Hannah sat up in bed, and glanced across at the other girl.

"I suppose we'd better get up," she conceded.

"Good." Satisfied, Tom joined Richard, who was loitering by the doorway. Grinning, Tom declared. "Nice pyjamas, Hannah."

"Tom!" Beth scowled.

The boys returned to their own room, and Beth remarked, with a smile on her face.

"Anyway, he's forgotten that he's got to go to church, first."

They came out of the church, the Baker children, all of the Pavitt family, and practically the whole village. The service had been somber, and there was reference to those serving overseas. Hannah's mind inevitably wandered to thoughts of her brother, John, 'Somewhere in France'. What sort of Easter would he be having? The early morning dew was evaporating under an orange sun that was growing more powerful. Hannah's group said a cheery goodbye to Clara's family, and made their way along the road, past cows which stood lazily in the fields, to the farm.

No sooner had they entered the farm kitchen, than Tom uttered the words 'Easter egg hunt'.

"Let me take my hat and coat off, first," complained Ted. "Don't be so impatient, son."

"Boys versus girls." Tom winked at Richard.

"No, actually there'll be a change this year," declared his father. "I'm putting you with Hannah, and then Beth and Richard together."

"Oh!" Tom's face dropped.

Hannah didn't look too pleased, either.

After a few seconds pause, Tom grabbed Hannah by the arm.

"Come-on, let's get going, then!"

"Wait a minute before you go racing off, Thomas, you haven't got the clues, yet!" Said Emily.

The children dispersed into two pairs, in the farmyard, clutching pieces of scrap paper that had faded slightly brown, paper was getting very scarce now. Whilst Beth and Richard went gaily off into the fields over the back, Tom led Hannah into the chicken hut. The chickens were pacing around everywhere, inside the straw lined hut, and on entering, in the semi-darkness, Hannah nearly trod on one. Tom went to rummage in a darkened corner. Hannah held her hand to her nose, for the smell was fetid. She enquired.

"Why have we come in here, Tom? We should…"

Tom turned round, and put his hands on his hips. He had gained a few strands of straw on his person. He explained.

"Because this is the chicken hut, and if the Easter eggs are going to be anywhere, then it's going to be in here!"

Hannah looked at the boy disbelievingly. The word 'idiot' came to her mind. She bit her lip, and pointing to the sheet of paper she said.

"We're meant to be following the clues. Look, here's the first one. *Follow your nose to above where water flows.*"

Tom looked confused, and shrugged his shoulders.

"It's impossible."

"No it's not. It must be referring to the brook that cuts past the south meadow, and 'above' must mean the little footbridge across it."

"Yes, that's what I thought, but didn't want to say, and look stupid."

The girl stroked her chin, viewing the boy with suspicion.

"Hmnn…"

They crossed the fields towards the brook. Hannah asked Tom why he kept on glancing behind them, as they walked. He informed her.

"Just making sure that Beth and Richard aren't following us."

They're most likely ahead of us, thought Hannah. *Poor, silly Tom.*

They reached the brook. Tom stood on the footbridge that spanned it, which in reality was just a solitary plank of wood. Beneath him the brook sparkled. He rubbed his forehead.

"Can't see no eggs, here."

Hannah bent down on one knee.

"Here. There's a sheet of paper stuck to the side of the bridge."

"A sheet of paper?" Tom frowned.

"Obviously another clue," declared Hannah.

Tom groaned. Hannah read from the sheet.

"*Don't fall to pieces by this wall.*" The girl frowned and repeated the words. "*Don't fall to pieces by this wall…*"

"I know where that is," the boy declared, pointing across the field. "Not far from here, where the wall's fallen apart…"

Hannah followed the boy, impressed.

Meanwhile, Beth and Richard were emerging from a clump of trees, at the top of a slope. The branches hissed in the breeze, and above them, birds circled. Richard took Beth's hand, to help her in the descent, and the girl thought this sweet. As the ground became gentler, Beth ran a hand through her dark hair, and asked.

"So, what do you want to do when you're older?"

After a moment's pause, Richard replied.

"Be a policeman." He laughed. "I don't know why; it looks a good job."

"I'd like to be a nurse," the girl volunteered. "It would be nice to do something that really helps people."

"I think you'd make a very good nurse."

"Thank you." She smiled.

He smiled bashfully. He realized that he was still holding her hand.

Hannah and Tom arrived at the broken wall. All that the rubble had to offer was another clue. Tom's face dropped, as Hannah read aloud.

"*Take a dip along with the sheep.*"

"This will take all day at this rate!" Tom complained.

The sheep dip revealed a fourth clue. *Hollow at this log.* The pair crossed two fields to a hollow log, which had lain at the farm since Tom's Grandfather's time.

Tom stood with his hands in his pockets, and kicked the ground, disinterestedly, as Hannah dirtied her hands, searching inside the log. She squinted in the darkness.

"I think there's something in here…"

"Another clue?"

"No. It feels like…an egg."

Tom regained interest, as Hannah's dirt covered hand revealed an egg wrapped in old newspaper.

"Let me have it!" Tom rudely snatched the egg from her.

Hannah rested her back against the log, as Tom eagerly unwrapped the goody.

"What a swizz! What a bloomin' swizz!" The boy threw the newspaper down to the ground in anger, and repeated the words over and over.

"What is it?" Asked his bemused companion.

"This!" Tom held the egg out in disgust –a chicken's egg.

"Oh!"

"A swizz! No chocolate."

"Maybe there are more of them in there."

"So what if there is? I'm off!"

The disconsolate pair returned to the farmhouse. They did not care to think how Beth and Richard were getting on. They came across Emily in the kitchen. Hannah said awkwardly.

"We, er, we found this, Emily."

"Well done, you pair, you've returned before the other two." Looking at Tom, she observed, "What's the matter with droopy face, here?"

Hannah answered.

"I think he-we- were hoping for a chocolate one."

"But, there's a war on. We can't get chocolate eggs any more, it's called rationing." Emily's face and tone were serious.*

"Some bloomin' Easter we're having!" Tom grumbled.

"You should think of the poor children in Poland, who have lost their homes," said the boy's mother.

Tom fidgeted on the spot.

After a few seconds, Emily let her son suffer no longer. She opened a cupboard door.

"Although we have got this rather nice Easter cake, instead."

"Thank you, Emily." Said an appreciative Hannah.

"Coo!" Said the boy.

At that moment, Beth and Richard came through the door.

"What kept you?" Remarked Tom mockingly.

---

*Chocolate and sweet rationing was actually only introduced in 1942

On Tuesday 2nd April 1940, Neville Chamberlain boasted to Parliament that Germany's economic life was being strangled by allied strategy. War trade agreements had been made with Belgium, Denmark, Holland, Iceland, Norway and Sweden, to limit their trade with Germany. The Prime Minister was ten times as confident of victory than at the start of the war, and claimed that.

"Hitler has missed the bus."

But, Germany desired control of Norway, so that it could use its sea power effectively against the Allies, rather than being bottled up in the Baltic Sea.

A week later, just as the Royal Navy began laying mines in Norwegian waters, to hinder ore exports to Germany, Nazi warships were sailing up towards the fjords from the South. The axis invasion of Denmark and Norway had begun.

Tiny Denmark was overrun in a matter of hours. In the morning dawn, German motorized and armoured columns, tore through the Danish frontier at Schleswig, and had reached the northernmost part of the country by the afternoon. The Danish capital, Copenhagen, was in German hands by eight in the morning, after a non-existent resistance. After a thousand years of independence, Denmark had ceased to exist as a free democracy. It was small mercy that the Danish King Christian was permitted to keep his title and his palace.

Early afternoon, that same day, the 9th April 1940, Nazi aircraft roared above the rooftops of the Norwegian capital Oslo, whilst down below, the heavily armed advance-guard of German troops entered the city. The Osloans were curious and surprised; there was neither tears nor jeering, and Nazi sympathizers saluted. The atmosphere was almost surreal, as German military bands played martial and jolly music to keep the Norwegian civilians in good humour.

On the day of the Nazi invasion of Scandinavia, Neville Chamberlain addressed Parliament.

"It is asserted by the German Government that their invasion of Norway was a reprisal for the action of the Allies in Norwegian territorial waters. This statement will, of course, deceive no one. So elaborate an operation, involving simultaneous landings at a number of ports of troops accompanied by naval forces, requires planning long in advance.

…We at once assured the Norwegian Government that in view of the German invasion of their territory, His Majesty's Government have decided forthwith to extend their full aid to Norway."

The following day, reality sunk in. A new government had been installed in Oslo, which was headed by a Norwegian Nazi, Major Vidkun Quisling. His name instantly became a synonym for traitor. The rapidly reinforced German soldiers pushed further North, sweeping aside Norwegian opposition. General mobilization in Norway was only announced *after* the invasion had started, and the Norwegian Commander in Chief had to be replaced, as he was unfit for service! The British were caught off balance, and were confused about how to deal with the invasion.

On 14th April, the British and French began landing men along the Norwegian coast, as part of an expeditionary force. However, many of the allied troops were without artillery or aircraft support. The biggest success for the allies came at the port of Narvik. The German surface fleet was crippled, with them losing ten destroyers (to the loss of just two British).

On 2nd May 1940, the Prime Minister made the sobering announcement to the House of Commons, that allied troops were being withdrawn from Norway. He stressed.

" It is far too soon to strike the Norwegian balance sheet yet, for the campaign has merely concluded a single phase, in which it is safe to say that if we have not achieved our objective, neither have the Germans achieved theirs, while their losses are far greater than ours."

The Prime Minister was trying to put a gloss on events, but the reality was that Allied troops were seriously outnumbered, and German local air superiority meant that it would be impossible to land the necessary artillery and tanks in Norway. The Norwegian campaign had been a disaster, and on 7th May 1940, Admiral Sir Roger Keyes declared in the House of Commons.

"It is a shocking story of ineptitude which ought never to have happened."

The Germans could now launch a determined U-boat campaign against British shipping convoys.

On the night 30th April / 1st May 1940, a German mine-laying aircraft crashed at Clacton-on-Sea, the explosion killing the crew and three others, and injuring 150 others. These were the first civilian deaths of the war on mainland Britain. Pictures of destroyed and severely damaged semi-detached houses appeared in the newspapers. The war was coming closer to Britain.

CHAPTER 7 – BLITZKRIEG

In the early hours of Friday 10th May 1940, German parachute troops were dropped into Belgium and Holland. Everywhere there was the noise of battle, as German guns thundered into action, along 150 miles of the Western front. Over the next few hours, Nazi warplanes bombed allied airfields, communications and military strong points. Most of the Belgian and Dutch Air Forces had been destroyed on the ground. Five great German armies began their march into Belgium, Holland and Luxembourg. Here and there, the invading Huns were checked for a moment, but before long the fighting columns renewed their advance.

The French Army made up the bulk of the Allied land forces. Britain had ten army divisions in mainland Europe, compared to the ninety-four French. But, the quality of many of the French troops was sadly questionable. Most of Britain's Air Force still remained at home (awaiting an attack on Britain), and many of the aircraft that were in France, compared poorly to those of the Luftwaffe. Roadblocks and a lack of Belgian locomotives held up the Allied troops crossing into Belgium.

The German attack could not have come at a worse time and later that same day, Neville Chamberlain resigned as Prime Minister, to be replaced by Winston Churchill. He was seen by some as a maverick but swiftly established his leadership. Churchill's government would be an all-party coalition with Conservative, Labour and Liberal seated together at the cabinet table. In Britain, and in France, Belgium, Holland and Luxembourg, life had suddenly become very uncertain.

Over the next few days, John Baker confided his thoughts to his diary…

"11th May 1940.

Yesterday (10th May), the German swine violated the neutrality of Belgium (and also Holland and Luxembourg). In response to this action, this morning, we were given the order to move into Belgium, to come to the defence of our tiny ally, and take up positions by the River Dyle. Marching along cobbled, poplar-lined highways, we have so far received an enthusiastic welcome from the Belgians. Such is the response that one feels as if one has already won a war! Everywhere, we have been cheered along the way. Local girls pluck lilac from the roadside bushes for us, and in *every* village we are presented with mugs of beer! What marvellous people these Belgians are. Morale is good, we sing 'Tipperary' and other songs as we march, and there is a feeling that we can take anything that Jerry throws at us. The fighting currently taking place to the East, between the German invaders and the defiant Belgians seems very distant."

The platoon spent the next night in a barn. To lie in the straw was luxury after the long tramp. John took out his diary before he fell asleep.

"12th May 1940.

Our march Northwards continued. The atmosphere seems so much different from that of yesterday. Word got round that a column of Tommies, advancing up the road just a few miles ahead of us has been dive-bombed by Nazi planes. There were rumoured to be a number of casualties, some fatal (where was the R.A.F?). Although I have yet to engage in battle, this sort of incident brings the bloodshed, which, for us must now be inevitable, that much closer.

We are now seeing far fewer civilians on our journey. Those that we do come across are fleeing from the German invader, abandoning their homes for an indefinite period. I have seen pitiful sights of small groups of people washing and cooking meals in the fields. There are farms where in the pasture sheep still graze, in the courtyard hens run about and the dogs still lie in their kennels. Yet, despite this appearance of normality, inside the farmhouses, beds are unmade and meals are left on the table, uneaten. Every home tells the same story –the inhabitants have gone. In the fields stands corn, which, will never be harvested. At one point, Tom Walker found a tatty doll lying in the road, which, must have fallen from a refugee cart. The doll will never be reunited with its owner. Tom remarked that it probably meant the world to some little girl.

At nightfall, we reached the River Dyle and dug in, weary after two days solid of marching, but thankfully still in one piece."

There had not been a good start to the next day. As John penned his diary entry, he observed the men around him; there was an ever-growing sense of anticipation.

"13th May 1940.

I was awoken by a ferocious artillery duel between British and German batteries, somewhere to the East. As breakfast commenced, low flying Jerry planes could be seen attacking our positions a handful of miles away. From across the fields, plumes of smoke rose from a clump of trees. Not long later, British casualties –the first that I have seen in this campaign- passed through our positions on their way to field hospitals. The men in our platoon became silent for some time afterwards those casualties could just have easily been us. Orders came neither to withdraw nor to attack. I knew that it would not be the easiest of days. The engineers are destroying the bridges over the River Dyle, and in the sky there are frequent dogfights between Hurricanes and Messerschmitts. Suddenly, one finds oneself welcoming nighttime, and a little respite."

Also on the 13th May, Winston Churchill addressed the House of Commons for the first time as Prime Minister. Churchill had long believed that he was destined to lead Britain in her hour of need. Back home in the peaceful village of Oak Green, they read his speech in the next morning's paper.

"I have nothing to offer but blood, toil, tears, and sweat. We have before us an ordeal of the most grievous kind. We have before us many, many long months of struggle and of suffering."

He continued defiantly. "You ask what is our aim? I can answer in one word: It is victory –victory at all costs- victory in spite of all terrors- victory, however long and hard the road may be; for without victory there is no survival –let that be realized-no survival for the British Empire.

…I take up my task with buoyancy and hope, and I feel sure that our cause will not be suffered to fail among men. At this time I feel entitled to claim the aid of all, and I say: Come, then, let us go forward together with our united strength."

"Do you think Daddy will join up?"

Hannah did not know the answer to her brother's question.

Events in the war were unfolding rapidly day by day, the situation in the Low Countries was perilous. The group in the farmhouse, consisting of the Pavitt family and the two evacuee children, sat huddled around the wireless, like millions of others across the country. It was shortly after 9:15 p.m. on Tuesday 14th May 1940, and the Secretary for War, Anthony Eden, had just made an important appeal over the radio, which had come not a moment too soon.

"We are going to ask you to help us in a manner which I know will be welcome to thousands of you." He went on. "We want large numbers of men in Great Britain who are British subjects, between the ages of fifteen and sixty-five, to come forward now and offer their services…The name of the new force which is now to be raised will be the Local Defence Volunteers."

Ted declared that he would enroll the very next morning, and expressed his sincere hope that many more men in the village would do the same.

Ted's two children looked at him, feeling pride, and at the same time, a little fear. Could it be possible that their Father would soon be fighting the Germans on British soil?

Within a day, a quarter of a million loyal British subjects had gone to their local police stations, in order to volunteer. However, for the time being, the men would have neither weapons nor uniform, and it would be a while before they began to resemble a proper army.

14th May 1940. John wrote:

"Our Belgian allies are beating a chaotic retreat. Sadly, today there seemed to be more Belgian soldiers fleeing to the west, than civilians! The desperate, broken men of the Belgian Army are retreating, often weaponless, and a few do not even possess boots!"

John Baker outstretched his arms lazily, and yawned. He wiped the sleep out of his eyes, and with it the semi-real night time images, a blurry mix of strolling through the cornfields with the French girl Claudette, refugee columns and Nazi dive-bombers. He went to have a wash and a shave in a basin. A couple of minutes later, he enjoyed some bread and tea, with a dozen other men from his platoon, in the riverside cottage that they were occupying. The remainder of the platoon had taken up positions in a similar cottage fifty yards or so away. Next to John, Keith Johnson was reading about the progress of his young child, Richard, in a letter he had received from his wife. Bill Gardner lamented the unavoidable separation from a French girl with whom he had struck up a particularly close friendship over recent months.

"Stop thinking about her, Builder. She's probably long since forgotten you!" One of the other men joked.

"I've never even had a proper girlfriend." Said another, the boyish faced Charlie Lawrence.

"Don't waste your time with women!" Chirped up an older member of the platoon. "Once you marry them, they'll have you wrapped around their little fingers." He gestured with his hand, making the other men laugh.

John finished his cup of tea, and stepped outside into the rear of the garden of the cottage with Keith Johnson. The sun shone down, and the birds were singing their early morning chorus, and the wind whistled through the long grass. It seemed incredible that anyone could be fighting a war on such a fine Spring morning. Together, John and Private Johnson settled down besides the stone garden wall, and peered out across the tranquil River Dyle, focusing on the trees opposite. They could determine no sign of enemy activity, although, they both fully understood that the Germans were *somewhere* over the far side of the river...exactly how far away was anyone's guess.

The Tommies knew that the Germans were good soldiers, well organized and equipped, for they had overrun Poland so quickly. They'd heard reports as to what the Germans had done when they'd occupied first Czechoslovakia and then Poland. In Czechoslovakia, students parading through Prague, the capital had been charged by Nazi armoured cars. Nineteen Polish officers who had surrendered were murdered outside a village. Many more civilians had been lined up against walls and shot...early examples of Nazi brutality in World War Two. In the cities, Jews had been herded into ghettos surrounded by barbed wire and guards, and allowed no contact with the rest of the Polish population. Hans Frank, the Nazi governor of Poland, had openly stated his aim to make the Poles the slaves of the German Reich. In January, the Polish government in exile announced that the Germans had killed 18,000 prominent Poles. No, the Tommies were not prepared to give up Belgian and French soil easily.

"Silent as the grave. I doubt that Jerry will bother us, today," Private Johnson observed confidently. He mused that if it were peacetime then maybe there would be children playing and people fishing along the riverbank.

A few moments had passed when John realized that the birds had stopped singing. Private Johnson looked at John searchingly, but said nothing. The latter's eyes moved slowly to look skywards. To his horror, John could see in the distance, high up in the air, numerous tiny black dots, growing ever larger, as they approached.

The aircraft filled the sky; there was wave after wave of them. Private Johnson's mouth gaped open. Coming from that direction, the planes could only be German.

Sergeant Fell darted out of the cottage, in order to investigate the droning sound that had broken the silence on this clear Spring morning. Seeing the Nazi bombers, he exclaimed.

"F***ing hell! Now we're truly in for it!"

Sergeant Fell shouted for everyone to take cover.

Large groups of the German bombers peeled off to the left and right, to strike at numerous other British strong points along the River Dyle. There remained at least a dozen aircraft heading towards the positions of John's company of 120 plus men. As John and Private Johnson descended into a prepared slit trench, the latter suggested that, perhaps, the bombers were going to make an attack on targets further to the rear. It was wishful thinking.

The first German plane deposited it's cargo to the right, and at least one bomb scored a direct hit on the cottage occupied by Corporal Smith's section of the platoon. The plane flew so low that it's neat black cross marking was clearly visible. If any of the Tommies had remained inside the cottage, it seemed highly unlikely that anyone could have survived that.

The most almighty sound came from within a few yards of John's slit trench. He had not even sighted the aircraft, which had delivered the bomb that took out half the garden wall to the left. A few pieces of rubble fell harmlessly into the trench. Seconds later, another aircraft screamed overhead, although its bombs slightly overshot its target, missing the cottage, and causing a crater in the road at the front of the house. John began to wander if he could take much more of this.

Within a couple of minutes, the aircraft had gone. No doubt they had progressed to attack the British positions in depth (to the rear). A little shaken, John and Private Johnson slowly clambered out of the slit trench. The Sergeant appeared, to check that the pair was still in one piece. His particular section had suffered no casualties, however, as for the chaps in the devastated neighbouring cottage, who could say?

Movement was evident from across the river. A frontal assault by the Germans could be but a matter of minutes away. In preparation, the Sergeant promptly posted four men to the upstairs of the cottage, sent another couple to bridge the gap between that building and the other, and dispatched two more to cover the flank on the extreme left (under the cover of a scattering of bushes). Private Charlie Lawrence would remain downstairs in the cottage, and act as runner to keep constant the supply of ammunition. The Sergeant and Private Hancock joined John and Private Johnson, at the garden wall, to face the enemy.

"I only joined the army to get three square meals a day, and a decent bed for the night," said Private Hancock. "Never thought it would come to this."

Sergeant Fell spoke, confident and reassuring.

"You're good soldiers, all of you. Just make sure that every shot counts".

John had spotted a grey-clad figure crawling through the long grass, on the far riverbank, and knew that this had to be a German. The figure temporarily disappeared from view, before his helmet became visible; this time distinctly closer to the water.

John raised his rifle, bit his lip, and concentrated on his target. The German must have been under the misapprehension that the British soldiers could not see him. How wrong! Now John, could even make out the man's face…just a little closer.

A gun cracked, and a single shot rung out, instantly killing the German.

John glanced to his left, and noticed a look of satisfaction on the face of the Sergeant, as if he had just shot some game (he had not been as hesitant as John had). Yes, it took quite a lot to actually kill a man; flesh and blood, not some target comprised of paper and wood. John trained his eyes on the river, once again.

German mortars —at least two of them- burst into action. A dull pumping sound, came from the enemy positions, and was followed by an explosion, at the edge of the river, directly in front of John. A jet of water went shooting up into the air.

Less than two seconds later, another explosion, this time behind John, demolished part of the roof. John was horrified to see the chimney of the cottage come crashing to the ground.

"Christ! They certainly mean business!" Private Johnson remarked.

Two more explosions, in rapid succession, occurred in the garden, somehow missing all four men positioned there.

"Hold your positions," ordered the Sergeant.

Bullets skimmed along the top of the garden wall, from some German automatic weapon. Two Germans sat camouflaged at the edge of the woods, on the opposite bank. However, the four British, hugged against the garden wall, dare not raise their heads to return fire. Also, the Tommies upstairs in the cottage could do little by means of assistance, for the German mortar teams were concentrating all their firepower on that building.

John, the Sergeant, Privates Hancock and Johnson, decided to throw caution to the wind, and risk momentarily raising their heads above the parapet, to take occasional potshots at the German positions. However, their shots were wild with the urgency to quickly take cover, again, and the enemy was still largely invisible.

A blast completely took out one of the upstairs windows of the cottage, and there was a gaping hole above it, where that part of the roof should have been. Agonizing screams came from inside the building.

Crouching, Private Lawrence (the ammunition runner) ran out of the cottage, shaking and breathless, he informed the Sergeant, half-mumbling.

"Pete Sturgess killed, sir —direct hit; enemy mortar. George Williamson still alive, but, in a serious condition; three pieces of shrapnel sticking out of his chest, sir. I tried to pull a bit out of his flesh, but I couldn't. It was red-hot, you see, sir…I think he's had it!"

The moaning from inside the cottage had by now ceased. The Sergeant put a reassuring hand on the shoulder of a tearful Private Lawrence, and slowly nodded his head in grim acknowledgement.

Yet another mortar bomb landed upon the fated cottage, quite close to the position of the remaining two men upstairs.

"Tell Privates Gardner and Wright to get the hell out of there!" The Sergeant barked to Private Lawrence.

Private Lawrence raced back into the cottage to deliver this order.

The Germans had launched a rubber assault boat, onto the river, which was now already almost half way across the water. The boat contained eight enemy soldiers, armed with rifles, although four of them were occupied with steering the boat, using wooden oars.

The Sergeant reckoned that the Germans on the far bank (with the automatic weapon) would for the moment refrain from firing on the British positions, for fear of hitting their own men in the boat. Hence, he asked of his men to take out as many of the German boat crew as possible, once he gave the signal.

The boat was over half way across the river, when the Sergeant signaled for his men to open fire. As one, John, Hancock and Johnson raised their heads, and took aim.

Two Germans were hit, and both slumped lifeless into the river. There was disorder in the boat, as one of the men made clear his preference to turn back, by gesticulating. However, his superior ordered for the crossing to continue, and three of the remaining Germans lost no time in returning fire at the British.

By the time the boat made contact with the bank, a little further downstream, the British had picked off another two of its German occupants.

Alas, the Tommies in the garden had suffered their first casualty. Next to John, Private Keith Johnson lay lifeless; he had been shot in the head by a German bullet.

The Germans scrambled ashore. The last to leave the boat stumbled, and this error cost him his life, as a shot from the Sergeant's gun finished him off.

Another German, revealed himself from the cover of a bush, and was shot by the Sergeant, although not before the German was able to launch a stick grenade over the wall, which killed Private Hancock. He had paid a very high price for his three square meals a day.

Of the remaining two Germans, one was severely wounded by a couple of Tommies holding the left flank. The last made a suicidal sprint into the rear cottage garden. John, who this time took no delay in pulling the trigger of his rifle, at almost point-blank range, spotted him.

The German attack had petered out, and they would attempt no more crossings at this point of the river, today. John sunk to his knees, half closed his eyes, and gave a sigh of relief. The Sergeant praised his men for preventing the Germans from taking this side of the river. John thought of the fatalities —four of the men that had occupied the same cottage with him at breakfast, earlier that day, were now dead, amongst them Keith Johnson, leaving behind a young widow and a small Son that would grow up never to know his Father. Of the other section of the platoon he would later learn that they had lost half their number. It did not seem very much like a victory; it felt like a bloody stalemate, and the Germans would be back again, tomorrow, the sixteenth, without a doubt.

The German *panzers* had advanced over seventy miles in three days, reaching the River Meuse. On 14th May, the tanks crossed the Meuse at Sedan in northern France, in force, pushing the French defenders ever further back. The French counterattacked, but were mauled by aircraft and tanks. Meanwhile in Holland, a hundred Heinkel bombers attacked Rotterdam; nearly a thousand people were killed in the bombing. A day later, the Dutch surrendered.

The main force of the German attack had fallen on the hilly, forested Ardennes region of Belgium, supposedly impassable, where the French forces were weakest. Since a large part of the British and French troops were now positioned along the River Dyle, further north, the Germans had begun to drive a dangerous wedge between the allied armies.

Shortly before midnight, on Friday 17th May, the War Office announced that the British had withdrawn West of Brussels. That same day, the Germans entered the Belgian capital. The long retreat by the British army had began...

The column of British troops that included John would march six miles, before having a short rest, then march another six miles, the whole time, desperately tired, with Jerry hot on their tails. Men were marching half-asleep. Those that fell asleep (totally) received a rude awakening when the man marching behind bumped into them. They had to resort to taking water out of the ditches, and boil it to drink. They could hear intermittent bursts of small arms fire in the distance; the fighting was not too far away.

The planes in the sky were *always* German. The only British or French aircraft that John ever saw were burnt-out shells on abandoned allied airfields. He had heard the stories of how useless the 'Boys' anti-tank rifle was against enemy *panzers*, the shells it fired simply rebounded off the tanks. The Germans always seemed to have close artillery support, whereas the British artillery was conspicuous by its absence.

The few German prisoners that they came across were as youthful as John was. Although smart and soldierly, the Germans appeared bewildered that they had actually been captured! There were stories of Belgian Fifth Columnists who had assisted the Germans by, for instance, put arrows in corn and wheat fields pointing to Allied targets.

At night, the Germans would, at intervals, send up a star shell, which would linger in the sky, and throw out a blinding light. The enemy would then shell any British positions that had the misfortune to be illuminated by the light. Each evening, as John and the other Tommies bedded down in stables or abandoned cottages, bought the dread of discovery by this artificial light. Even during nighttime, the battle was ever present in one's mind.

There had been hold ups caused by bottlenecks at river crossings, and slow-moving French horse-drawn artillery. The men's nerves were strained, and tempers ran close to the surface. John recalled an incident earlier on in the day, when the

Tommies had to force themselves past some Poilus* who were crawling along the road with a couple of heavy guns at a snail's pace, apparently leaderless.

"Bloody French, abandoning the front, leaving us in the shit!" Cursed Bill Gardner.

"Bet they haven't even fired a shot in anger," sneered another.

The French soldiers looked at the British impassively as they pushed past.

The road narrowed, with the result that half the line of Tommies remained stuck behind the procession of French with their horses and guns. Sergeant Fell was at the end of his tether; at this rate the Germans would overtake them. Brandishing his gun, he strode up to an unsuspecting Frenchman, and, not caring whether or not the man understood him, declared.

"If you don't get that f***ing thing off the road out of the way, my men will bloody well do it for you!"

The Frenchman, embarrassed and apologetic, tried to explain, in broken English, that the gun was a very valuable piece of equipment.

"Its no bloody good to anyone, now, is it?" Shouted the Sergeant.

A handful of the Tommies and Poilus hurled insults at each other.

Somehow, the situation had calmed down, as the French gave way, and let the British file past before continuing themselves. Just another rotten, regrettable part of the long retreat.

Every town and village that they passed told the same old story. In the streets there were fires and smoke. Cars that had run out of petrol were left abandoned, and dogs were running about. As for the damaged buildings, smashed furniture protruded through the splintered windows. In the surrounding fields were cows, which had not been milked, and in the woods most of the trees had been uprooted by falling shells.

Then there were the refugees...

The Belgian civilians, young and old had put together their meagre belongings into every type of transport, horses and carts, large and small. Some had their possessions rolled in red blankets slung around their necks. These poor people shuffled along the road looking frightened and tired, the wide-eyed children, some riding on the handlebars of their parent's bicycles, did not yet fully understand everything that was happening to them. Occasionally, one of the elderly people would collapse due to exhaustion, and would have to be rescued by their younger relatives. Belgian civilians were continually going up to the British troops, and asking what they (the civilians) should do.

"Stay at home," the Tommies would reply. "Don't leave, and clog up the roads..."

But, it was too late.

John became aware of a distant drone. Two Stuka dive-bombers appeared in the sky, coming up fast behind the long line of people, on the road. The soldiers immediately dispersed into the ditches and fields. The Belgian civilians, exhausted,

---

*French soldiers

did not move so quickly. As the Stukas swooped down, sirens on their wheels made a horrific screaming noise, adding to the sense of panic. As the five hundred pound bombs left their racks, they wobbled hesitantly, and then straightened up as they gained speed. The bombs landed, one impacting on a cart, fairly close to John, who was lying spread-eagled in a ditch.

The skies became empty, again. Trembling, John rose from the ditch, and surveyed the scene of carnage that surrounded him. There were a number of bodies lying in the road; those closest to the blast were too mutilated to determine whether they were male or female. A little girl, no more than six years of age stood dazed, crying out for her Mother. A horse had had its guts ripped open, and to end its misery, the British soldiers shot it. All the casualties were refugees. It was heartbreaking that the Tommies could spare no time to help clear the road, for the Germans would probably then encircle them, if they delayed. As John resumed his march, he realized that this war of Hitler's did not discriminate between soldiers and civilians. A number of John's comrades remarked what bastards the Germans were.

CHAPTER 8 – CORNERED

The German trap had closed. German troops had reached the coast at the mouth of the Somme on 20th May 1940. The allied armies were now split in two, with *panzers*, infantry and artillery in between them. An armoured counterattack by the British near Arras, on 21st May, shook the Germans, but could not halt the enemy offensive.

Desperate times called for desperate measures. Over in Britain, Parliament passed an extension of the Emergency Powers Act on 22nd May, the most drastic legislation in British history. The Government would have complete control over all persons, rich and poor, all property, and the munitions industry would come under state control. Ernest Bevin, the Minister of Labour, was handed dictatorial power to direct anyone to do anything needed in the struggle for national survival. In addition to this, Excess Profits Tax i.e. on industries which had benefited financially because of the war was raised to one hundred per cent.

There was now no coherent front line, and 'fight and fall back', became the daily norm for the men of the B.E.F., as they retreated towards the coast.

About forty men, including John had drawn the short straw, and they were to stay behind and take up 'rear guard' defensive positions along a railway embankment, under the command of an officer (captain) from D-company. They were armed only with light weapons, including a couple of Bren guns. Here, a secondary road crossed the railway line, and it was almost certain that the Germans would make use of this road in their relentless drive towards the coast. Behind the British men, was a field of mature corn, and to the left, hugging the railway line, lay a small wood. The Tommies lying in wait anxiously atop the embankment, had a good view, and were able to see across the level fields that lay astride the road up which the enemy would come, for a good mile or so, before the land climbed to a distant line of trees.

The Germans were not long in coming. A German spotting plane had already flown over earlier, as a prelude. However, instead of the anticipated dreaded sighting of tanks or armoured cars, it was a group of foot soldiers that appeared. John was amazed to see that, as the Germans came closer, they were quite bizarrely casual in manner, as if on a summertime stroll in peacetime. Stupidly so, it would soon prove.

There were approximately thirty Germans in all, marching three-abreast, up that single, exposed road. As they came within the range of the British rifles, the Sergeant (NCO nearest to John), nodded to the half-dozen men closest to him, and within seconds, the British guns cracked into action.

The Germans, after the initial surprise, dispersed into the surrounding fields. Eight of them already lay dead or wounded in the road. The Tommies then picked off those of the enemy, who were closest to the railway embankment.

Taking what scant cover was afforded from roadside ditches, and from behind bushes, the Germans, now only at half strength, began to return fire. However, their fire was erratic, and was no match for the British, well protected, and who outnumbered the Germans by over two to one. The Germans beat a hasty retreat, a couple more of their number being felled as they did so. A wave of confidence swept along the British line.

We'll show them! After that display, we can hold this line forever! Thought John.

Incredibly, the British had suffered no fatalities, and only one minor casualty —a shoulder wound to one of the Corporals. The Tommies all enjoyed a celebratory biscuit. But, then, thoughts started to creep in to some of the men's minds…when would the enemy be back?

It was sooner than expected, and the attack was not in the manner expected.

As John peered, almost entranced out over the railway line, the fast rattle of small-arms fire suddenly disturbed him. This was followed by the agonized screams of a number of the Tommies to the extreme right of the British line. With a growing sense of urgency, John's eyes darted from left to right. Exactly *where* was the source of this enemy activity?

There was still no sign of any German soldiers in the fields immediately in front of John, and it dawned on John with grim realization that the enemy had somehow outflanked the British positions, to attack them from the rear!

To a man, the Tommies dived into the corn for cover. At least a dozen Khaki figures already lay dead. The Germans, still invisible to the British, started to rake the cornfield with a ferocious level of gunfire. The British were obliged to keep their heads so low that it was virtually impossible to fire back.

As John lay with his chin in the soil, he turned his head, searching desperately for his comrades. He could only make out the form of Private Wilson, who lay equally still, scared and frightened, a few meters away. The pair may as well have been the only British in the cornfield, and it really felt as if all the German guns were focusing on their respective patches of ground.

Next, the German mortars opened up.

Inevitably, several of the British began to be hit. It was mass murder, and John felt like a sitting duck. A continuous stream of enemy mortar bombs was being lobbed into the corn. John knew that they simply *had* to escape this mayhem; although in which direction dare they crawl?

From somewhere a voice bellowed.

"Head for the woods, lads!"

The defiant Sergeant appeared from the corn, half-crouching. He fired a couple of shots from his gun, into where he perceived the Germans to be.

The Tommies crawled and slithered through the corn as quickly as they could, towards the woods. All the time, the mortaring and small-arms fire was relentless.

There was certainly a sizeable Jerry force out there. John locked his focus onto those trees. Only another fifty yards to crawl, forty yards, thirty…

Then, disaster! The first couple of Tommies had just reached the trees, when a number of grey-clad figures appeared atop the railway embankment. This group of twenty-plus Germans had a fine view of the Khaki-clad men wriggling desperately through the field down below.

A third Tommy now sprung up from the relative cover of the corn, at the extremity of the wood, only to receive a deadly bullet in the back. The two Tommies inside the woods, fired at the Germans, wounding one in the leg, and causing them to retire back along the railway line, but, only a little.

The Sergeant's voice boomed, once again.

"C-mon, lads, it's either them or us!"

He was right -it was a simple choice. If the British stayed where they were, a combination of German mortar bombs and small-arms fire would annihilate them. If they raised their heads above the corn, true, they would be even more visible, although at least they could make some attempt at fighting back, and keep alive a small hope of survival. The Sergeant, bold as ever, stood up first, to be followed by a score British.

He was the first to be struck, as dozens and dozens of bullets raced across the field, into the corn one way, and into the embankment, the other. Casualties were equal to both sides, however, the Germans, somewhat rattled by the courage of their foe, retreated down the other side of the embankment, losing two more men, in the process. Sixteen (out of the original forty-plus) British finally made it into the relative safety of the woods. There was time to pause only very briefly, and to take stock of the situation.

A Corporal was the only NCO now left to take charge. He reported that, with regret, the Captain had been killed when the German bullets first hurtled into the British held embankment from the rear. British ammunition was now running low, and the Corporal put his men under no illusions that their outlook was bad; they were surrounded by a strong enemy, which most likely numbered hundreds of men, yet, there was no talk of surrender. On the plus side, there appeared to be no enemy tanks in the vicinity. The order was simple —hold out in the woods until dusk, if possible, before making a risky attempt at escape towards the British line to the West —however far that may be. The Tommies scattered into pairs, to take up defensive positions along the perimeter of the wood.

The German response came almost immediately.

The peace was broken by a piercing shriek, which grew louder and ended with the ground shaking and chunks of earth being thrown up into the air. The German artillery was setting about their work on the British held wood.

"Christ! What next?" The man beside John wondered aloud.

More and more shells landed in the wood, upturning trees, and showering the men with mud. The noise that heralded the arrival of each shell was akin to an express train, hurtling at full pelt through a tunnel. One Tommy was killed outright –the mutilated body a horrid sight, but at least he would have known nothing about it.

As suddenly as it began, the artillery barrage ceased abruptly. The British gathered their senses, and watched and waited; it was late afternoon, though darkness was still several hours away.

A wave of German infantry, guns raised, strode through the corn. They were to attack the wood from two opposite sides, in a pincer movement. Forward they stepped, steel helmeted figures in their unblemished grey uniforms, supremely confident.

Despite now the close proximity of the Germans to the woods, not a shot had been fired in anger. One of the German infantry glanced across at his officer, and looked at his face searchingly. Maybe the officer thought the same as him that the British, realizing that they were finished, might still surrender –*that* would be the sensible option. The woods were a mere twenty yards away, it was almost as if both sides were afraid to fire the first shot; the British needing to conserve ammunition, the Germans showing a grudging respect to their enemy.

Then the Germans halted. All eyes were on the German officer. The officer calmly raised his arm, and then signaled his men forward.

In a split second, all hell let loose, as those Germans who moved swiftest, and hence, closest to the trees were cut down by an unseen enemy. However, the Germans were numerous, and many remained, crouched, tucked away just inside the corn. A group of four proceeded to infiltrate the British positions by skirting round the side of the woods.

John had had enough trouble fending off the equally forceful attack from the other end of the wood. The Germans had again rushed forward through the corn, but with the chance loss of their officer, they had shied away from the trees, and took to frequent sniping into the woods, from the perceived safety of the corn. Sadly, the Tommies had lost another of their number.

John chanced on sighting those Germans creeping into the trees, less than ten yards away to the left of him. Noiselessly, John shifted deeper into the woods, then stealthily followed the Germans on their journey. It became apparent to John that the enemy daringly planned to attack his fellow Tommies from behind.

John had his rifle trained on the man bringing up the rear. He could easily hit him, and probably take out a second man, although John very much doubted that he could strike all four of them. He did reckon that the ensuing commotion from *inside* the woods would alert the other Tommies to the danger, however.

From close by, a gun crackled. The leading German stumbled lifeless to the ground. Some other Tommy had also detected the Germans!

John pulled the trigger on his weapon, and the German at the rear fell. Startled, the remaining two Germans attempted to make a run for it. One, clutched his stomach and collapsed, having been shot by the other Tommy. The other German, managed to successfully get away through the trees, but in his haste, had discarded his weapon in the process.

With the danger having passed, a voice called out from amongst the trees. John grinned; it was Charlie Lawrence, who John had given up for dead back in the cornfield. Charlie, who was nursing a nasty wound to his thigh, recalled that he had managed to crawl into the wood during the lull in the German activity. The boy had become a man.

The noise of gunfire gradually abated, and the Corporal appeared, announcing that, by good fortune, the battle weary Tommies had beaten off the two-pronged German attack, with relatively few casualties.

The Germans would make no further attempt to take the wood that day. The British men were tired and hungry however, and darkness would provide problems of a different nature. For now, the British would have to risk a breakout attempt from the woods.

Shortly after 10 p.m. the British made their move. Ten men led by the Corporal moved to the edge of the woods. A second wounded Tommy, who had played dead, had struggled back into the woods from the cornfield, after the German attack had fizzled out, boosting the number of British to fourteen. However, four of the men were to stay behind in the woods to cover the escape of the others, as they were too badly injured to meet the demands of the journey that would face them. The Corporal peered out from the trees; outside the woods it all seemed quiet. He beckoned his men closer.

One of the Privates had suggested that they leave the woods from the Eastern perimeter, which bordered the railway embankment. Wrongly or rightly, this man believed that the side nearest to the (distant) British line to the West would have been the most obvious exit to the Germans. The Corporal took on board this idea, and in single file, the British carefully began to filter out of the Eastern edge of the woods. They would skirt round to the West in a roundabout way, and cover as much distance towards the coast as they damned well could, before first light.

John was fourth in the line, and he picked his way tentatively through the grass up the embankment to the railway track. The man in front had already descended down the other side of the embankment. Crouching, with one hand resting on the cold metal of the railway line, John glanced to the left and to the right along the long straight tracks, before he darted across, and slid down the far embankment.

The remaining six men followed.

The first obstacle cleared, the men followed the Corporal along a route, which hugged the railway embankment. The ever-distant woods that they had recently left remained mercifully silent.

A quarter of a mile or so further on, the Corporal halted, and raised his arm. The men behind him also stopped. Word passed down the anxious line of men, that Jerry was approaching, and the order was to lie flat against the embankment in silence.

John strained his eyes. Fifty yards or so away, he was just beginning to make out four figures heading along the railway line towards the position of the British men.

Although the British could easily deal with this handful of Germans, the Corporal did not want to prematurely create any unnecessary commotion. In all probability, the enemy still believed the British to be inside the woods. It was obviously not in the interests of the British to indicate otherwise to the Germans.

The British lay still. John could hear his heart race, as the voices of the Germans became clearly audible. The Germans drew level, a mere handful of yards away. Every passing second felt like minutes. Despite it being a cold night, John was sweating.

The Germans paused. Why, of all places, did they have to stop *here*? John thought. Had the British been spotted?

John swallowed. He could only see two of the Germans, and dare not turn his neck in order to get a view of the others.

One of the Germans lit a cigarette, and discarded the match, so that it landed beside the man in front of John. All four Germans became visible again, as they made an about turn, and slowly headed back the way they came. The Germans could be heard to be laughing and joking amongst themselves as they disappeared.

Stupid Jerries! Thought John. He wiped his brow, not wishing to repeat too many of such instances.

Then the German voices could no longer be heard any more. After sufficient time interval, the British pressed on.

Some fifteen minutes later, the Corporal deemed it safe to traverse back over the railway line, and begin the long journey to the West, guided by a radium-illuminated compass. The soldiers crossed a couple of fields, before moving tentatively past a farm outbuilding, to which the darkness gave a haunting look. They had not got far when, to the South came a booming sound, and the outline of trees were silhouetted against the dark night sky in a momentary flash of light. The woods still occupied by four Tommies was under renewed attack by the German artillery. John really felt for those brave chaps left amongst the trees; their fate would never be known.

The ten fugitives, hungry and tired, continued through the farmland, which appeared to be endless.

Incredible though it seemed, it was now midnight, and it had been some two hours since the British had left the stricken woods. Keeping to the fields, and avoiding the roads, their progress was slow to steady. The wind had gradually picked up, and it started to rain. John felt utterly miserable. However, to a man, the British believed it preferable to force their exhausted bodies ever forwards, rather than to surrender and endure (most likely) years of tedious captivity at the hands of the Germans.

The men were in the process of negotiating a jagged stone wall, when one man pointed and could swear (at a whisper, of course), that he could make out a number of shadowy figures moving a short distance away. The Corporal ordered his men to prime their rifles, crouch down, and focus on this illusory target.

John was unsure as to whether there was anyone there in the shadows, or not. It was wishful thinking to believe that they were anywhere near the front line, and this, a remote area far away from the lights of a village, also seemed an unlikely place for the Germans to assemble en masse.

Then John too, *definitely* saw something move. But, how many of these figures were there in total? It looked as if there were at least three. The British had noticed them, but had *they* detected the presence of the British? They were heading in the direction of the Tommies, for certain.

The figures were now very close to the British soldiers. A couple of John's comrades were poised to shoot without asking questions.

Suddenly, the tension lifted, and the man next to John broke into laughter.

"It's just a bunch of bloody cattle!" He announced.

The rest of the men stood up, ready to move, however, the Corporal permitted a ten-minute break. They all needed it, for that was two scares already that night. Despite the terrain being sodden, the Tommies gratefully collapsed to the ground. If only they could tuck into a little food…

As the miles passed slowly by, dawn crept ever closer. John lost count of the numerous hedges, streams and other natural obstacles that he and the other nine men had encountered. Fairly soon, they would have to find some kind of shelter in which to spend the daylight hours.

As the men emerged from a copse, they sighted a hamlet of about twenty buildings, up ahead. Crouching, they followed a wall that ran alongside a country road, towards the hamlet.

"Any sign of Jerry activity in the village, Corporal, sir?" Asked the man in front of John.

"Hard to tell." Came the answer. "Wait here a minute, I'll just go and take a closer 'recce'."

No sooner had he scurried up the road a bit, than the Corporal, returned, panting.

"Whole place is crawling with Nazis. I reckon we've stumbled upon an entire panzer division. Parked against the roadside buildings, they've got tanks, motorbikes and half-tracks. They've even got vehicles scattered about the other end of this blasted field!"

A number of the men sighed.

"Well, the road to that village lies dead to the West." The Corporal summarized. He asked aloud. "Ideas anybody?"

It was a bold plan, but in the absence of alternative ideas, certainly worth a try. It was still ninety per cent dark, and in the foul rain, who could tell one group of marching men from another?

The Corporal ordered the small band of Tommies to look lively, and to march tall and proud; they were going to walk straight up that street, and through the hamlet to the other side, posing as German infantry.

The British crept onto the puddle-laden road, one hundred yards from the hamlet, and marched towards it two-abreast, not as a sleep-deprived disheveled rabble, but as a proud ten-man army.

As they reached the first building, they passed a couple of members of German tank crews, beginning to warm up their vehicles for the day ahead. The British hardly dare to glance sideways, and John felt the hairs on the back of his neck stand up.

As the penultimate pair of Tommies drew level with the Germans, one of the tank crew, looked directly at the marching men, and shouted.

"Heil Hitler!"

In synchrony, the Tommies automatically replied.

"Heil Hitler!"

As the Tommies continued, they noticed the lights were on in some of the buildings, as the Germans stirred, to begin the day with breakfast.

Before they knew it, the British found themselves at the far side of the village, and then beyond. They now walked along the road with a renewed air of confidence. After a short distance, they noticed in the half-light, a track, which led up to a bombed-out farm building. This appeared to offer the best form of shelter for the day, since a hefty tree that had been toppled by bomb blast was blocking the entrance to the track to enemy vehicles. It would be most unlikely that the Germans would occupy such a ruin.

The weary Tommies ventured up the farm track, and on finding the cottage deserted, after a quick check of the vicinity, they settled down. They would remain there, undetected until dusk.

John and the nine other British men spent the following night dodging enemy soldiers. Although the group of Tommies had traveled a fair distance, so too had the Germans. Intermittently, bright flares streaked the darkness, as artillery guns fired, signifying that (the) battle was close. However, the next morning, the small band of weary men stumbled upon a British position. They were provided with a first rate army breakfast, and, their sprits boosted, they pressed on towards the coast. Then followed a few more days consisting of hours of long marches, and nights spent snatching a few hours sleep in stables or other basic accommodation. Constantly, and all around, glowing red splodges denoted burning towns and villages.

Brave actions by men thirty or forty miles inland, had bought the Allies precious time, and enabled men to reach the coast. At one town, a couple of British guns whose crew included a cook and a mechanic, fired until they ran out of ammunition, seeing off three enemy tanks. At another town, the defenders fought with mounting casualties, until their positions were surrounded, and engulfed in flame.

The British desperately held on to Calais until the 27th May, in order to draw the German tanks away from Dunkirk. Elsewhere on that day, the SS had executed nearly a hundred men of the Royal Norfolk Regiment who had surrendered, at a farm outside a French village. On the 28th May Belgium had surrendered. Belgian field hospitals were overflowing, guns were low on ammunition, and food was running short. This left the retreating British Army even more exposed.

By the closing days of May 1940, the French Army in the north, trapped alongside the British, had lost all their armoured fighting vehicles and all their heavy artillery. Levels of ammunition were low. The situation was desperate.

Back at home the government had put out an urgent appeal for assistance from all varieties of little ship.

"The admiralty wants men experienced in marine internal-combustion engines, for service as engine men in yachts or motor boats."

The British army was going to be evacuated from the French coast.

However, it would be a big risk, being the first time that a large-scale evacuation by sea, under aerial bombardment would be attempted. Some in the government talked of the possibility of a negotiated peace. If the evacuation failed, then that, and Nazi victory, may be the only option available.

Mary drew back the blackout curtains, and noticed that something rather odd was going on, some workmen were removing the railings from the garden wall of a house at the end of the road. All over London, and, indeed, the entire country, old bandstands were being demolished, and railings from parks and gardens were being taken down for scrap, to assist the war effort.

In the rural depths of the neighbouring county that Saturday morning, 1st June, Mary's children, along with the Pavitt children were going through the village, methodically knocking on door to door, in a drive to obtain precious scrap metal.

As they dragged an old farm cart along, they passed a few of the village boys playing football, and the men of the Local Defence Volunteers went by on drill, without uniform, and armed only with broomsticks. The group halted the cart outside the old cottages opposite the village school. The woods at the end of the street were alive with the sound of birds. Tom, full of initial enthusiasm, ran up the garden path, past fragrant flowers and a lawn that buzzed with insects, and knocked forcefully on the rotting front door of the first cottage. Richard followed. Hannah wiped her brow, and stood watching from the road, with Beth.

A raggedly dressed lady, in her early sixties, but who looked much older, opened the door to the boys. She blinked in the bright sunlight, and looked inquisitively at the impish-faced boy in long grey shorts.

"Morning, Mrs. F." Tom gave a toothy grin. "We're collecting aluminium for Spitfires."

"And iron, too, for tanks." Added Richard.

Mrs. F. stroked her chin.

"Well…"

Tom spoke, once more.

"My cousin, he's a Spitfire pilot; we need scrap metal to build more of them, for him and his mates, so that they can beat the Germans. Have you got any scrap for us, Mrs. F.?"

Mrs. F. shuffled back into the house. She returned a few minutes later, armed with a German helmet from the First World War, complete with spike on top.

"Wow!" Tom's eyes lit up.

Mrs. F. presented it to the boy, explaining.

"My late husband picked it up in the last war. I don't need it anymore. He died back in thirty-two. It was being gassed in the trenches that killed him, it made his lungs weak, you see."

"I'm sorry," said Richard sympathetically.

"Well, I'm sure you two boys will put it to good use."

The pair thanked Mrs. F., before returning to the two girls at the cart. Tom showed off the helmet triumphantly.

"Look at this!"

"Yes, well just remember that you can't keep it," warned Beth.

"Couldn't you get a British one?" Enquired Hannah.

Tom ignored the girl's remarks, and proudly put the helmet on his head. It was clearly too big for him, and he had to constantly adjust the helmet so that he could see from beneath it. The girls could barely contain their giggles.

At the neighbouring cottage, they obtained an old kettle and rake. The occupier wondered if she would receive any payment for the scrap, but the boys informed her that this would not be the case.

Harry and Henry appeared from the woods, where they had been playing. They looked a state, their knees and clothes were muddied; no doubt their mother would have a fit when she saw them.

"Hello, Hannah!" Chorused the pair of boys.

"Here comes trouble," observed Beth.

"What's in that cart of yours?" Enquired Henry.

"Nothing that would interest you," said Beth.

Harry delved inside the cart, his arm purposely brushing against Hannah's. His face lit up as he retrieved a metal toy soldier.

"You can't have it," said Beth firmly. "It's for the war effort."

"Oh!" The boy's face dropped.

Richard and Tom emerged from a cottage garden to rejoin the group. Henry tapped his brother on the arm.

"Look! What's that on Tom's head?"

"Heil Tom!" Said Harry sarcastically.

Tom pulled a face.

"You're only jealous."

"Haven't you two boys got anything better to do?" Asked a despairing Beth.

Whilst Richard and Tom set about knocking on doors, once more, the twins loitered in the street much to the chagrin of the two girls with the cart.

The next door was opened by a raven-haired woman in her forties, wearing a headscarf, and an apron over her clothes. She greeted the boys with a warm smile.

"Morning, we're collecting aluminium for Spitfires…" Tom began with his well-rehearsed phrase.

"Oh! Yes, I've heard over the wireless about the appeal for scrap metal."

The woman went into the house and retrieved an old aluminium saucepan, which Tom duly placed on Richard's head.

"Now you've got a helmet of your own!"

Richard was not amused, and wrestled away from Tom when he tried to keep the saucepan on his head.

"Come on Fritz! Stop clowning around, we haven't got all day!" Beth shouted to her brother.

The boys, still tussling, retreated down the garden path. They passed Kenneth, heading towards the cottage. He did not look his usual cheery self, on this morning's post round. The children lingered by the garden gate as Kenneth handed the woman a solitary envelope.

The woman held the postman's gaze, as she opened the envelope. From a distance, the four boys and two girls watched with mild curiosity.

"Oh!"

The woman exclaimed, and put her hand to her mouth, as she slowly collapsed to her knees. The first words that leapt out at her from the letter were *Killed in Action.*

Kenneth put a comforting hand on her shoulder.

"I'm so sorry, about George, Elizabeth."

"It c-can't be true. My…my only son…it happened over in France." She sobbed.

The last thing that the grieving mother required was an audience. Hannah, becoming tearful herself, addressed the other children.

"Come on, we'd better go."

The Germans had dropped leaflets showing the Allied pocket pinned to the coast, encouraging the Tommies to surrender.

British soldiers! Look at this map: it gives your true situation! Your troops are entirely surrounded-stop fighting! Put down your arms!

The men with John saw the leaflets as a handy supply of toilet paper.
John and his fellow soldiers (their ranks swelled by numerous other stragglers) reached the outskirts of the French port of Dunkirk. Earlier, they had known that they were nearing Dunkirk, since a huge column of smoke billowed, evidently betraying a giant fire at the port. They headed there with trepidation. Just outside Dunkirk, lorries lay on their sides, and some were upturned, dumped in ditches and fields, many blackened after bombing by the Luftwaffe. In the fields, lay mountains of abandoned blankets, gas capes, shoes and even typewriters, which were being set

alight. He thanked his lucky stars that he had made it there at all, for they had run into some trouble a few miles back along the road on the approach to the town.

An hour ago, another of the feared Stuka dive-bombers had appeared. The shrieking noise of the plane as it made its steep descent, was like those made by the whirly rides at a fairground. Predictably, the bomber was making straight for the road, so John threw himself into a hedge. Initially it looked as if the Stuka was out of control and would hit the ground; however, as it delivered its payload the plane pulled up again, before quickly disappearing over the horizon. John had survived the attack, but several of the men around him had not.

Inside Dunkirk, the scene was one of devastation, and Tom Walker observed that the town resembled a junkyard. As the column of men crossed a canal, they noticed big guns —more than could be counted- dumped in the canal – such a waste! Further along drivers were abandoning then torching their own vehicles. They passed buildings that were riddled with bomb splinters and bullets. The entire place reeked of petrol, and smoke hung over everything. It seemed like madness, thought John.

A military policeman directed the group of men onto the sand dunes, where they promptly collapsed besides countless other weary Tommies. Now came the wait...

The beach stretched for further than the eye could see. The sand was black with large groups of soldiers, who queued right out to sea. It was almost like Margate on a Bank Holiday. However, closer inspection revealed the depressing sight of dead Khaki-clad men scattered around, here and there. All the seafront buildings had been bombed, all the cranes were half-standing, leaning at angles, and in the distance, thick black smoke came from a coastal oil installation. There were beach chairs, carousels, and push-pedal cycles littered around. Some men played cards, some read, others were plainly drunk. There came the smell of salt and seaweed.

John had only been on the beach a few minutes, when a mile or so away, he witnessed the horrifying sight of a couple of German fighter planes strafing the sand with machine gun fire. The men on the beach were sitting ducks.

In the water, there were all varieties of boat, from destroyers and passenger ferries, to barges, lifeboats and tiny motorboats. They had names such as Swallow, Duchess of York, Resolute, Our Lizzie and Auntie Gus. Army trucks had been put into the water at low tide and lashed together to make improvised jetties. The beach shelved so gradually that, unfortunately, the destroyers could not get in very close at all. Many of the larger ships were lined up against the long narrow East Mole, made of concrete piling topped by a wooden walkway that stretched out into the sea. Men were being collected from there, and were also being picked up directly from the beach by the smaller boats. *Lucky devils!* Thought John.

They got chatting to some of the other Tommies, and traded stories of the hell that they had collectively been through. They spoke to a sandy-haired signalman, who despaired that the French had rejected the wireless for security reasons, in favour of telephones and motorcycle dispatch riders. However, the fast-moving Germans overran some telephone lines, and others were cut as the Allies kept retreating. The motorcyclists often got lost, or failed to locate a unit that had suddenly moved.

After a number of hours of inactivity and boredom, Bill Gardner tapped John on the shoulder. Bill reasoned that they had no chance of any immediate rescue from the beach, so they might as well kill some time by searching the ruins of the seafront buildings. The men were all hungry and good fortune might well lead them to some food.

John, Bill and a third man walked to the top of the beach. As they investigated one building after another, there was nothing to be found; other Tommies just as desperate as John had looted all the French cafes, shops and dwellings. In a side street, the dejected men came across an army supply lorry, and Bill eagerly tore open the back doors of the vehicle. From inside, came the most almighty stench. Bill covered his nose with his hand, and backed off. John cautiously stepped inside the back of the lorry. He noticed a gaping hole in the roof, and discovered the badly mutilated body of a British soldier, which had its legs missing. The supplies inside the lorry had disintegrated from the force of the bomb blast.

"Let's get out of here." Said John, as he clambered out of the lorry.

The trio sat down amongst the other men. They heard that a Tommy they'd befriended from a different unit had attempted to queue-jump and board a ship alongside the Mole, but he had been held back at gunpoint by an officer, who, on checking his regiment, told him bluntly that it "was not his turn."

The group saw the heart-rending sight of two casualties on stretchers being denied access to the boats, as each stretcher would take the places of four men. The stretcher-bearers resignedly took them from the beaches, back into the town. Not only had the men lost limbs but also they now had to face the double-blow of becoming prisoners of the Germans.

As nighttime came to the beach, the evacuation continued, and some soldiers, desperate not to lose their places in the queue, stood in line with their eyes closed. The tops of the waves were a mauvy-fluorescent colour from the oil, and bodies that were in the water were touchingly surrounded by a fluorescent halo. They could hear the occasional clank of oarlocks. It was chilly, and to boost morale, some of the soldiers sung.

During that day, 31st May, German shells had begun to fall on one of the evacuation beaches. Around the Dunkirk defensive perimeter, which ran five or six miles inland, many Tommies were feeling the pressure, and some had to be ordered to stand firm and hold their positions, by officers at gun-point. Fortunately, the marshland and dogged resistance of the defenders prevented the Germans from breaking through.

Across the Channel, seamen were feeling the strain. They were snatching little sleep, the little ships were virtually unarmed, and civilian crewmen were dying. There were some instances where crews had to be forced to return to Dunkirk at bayonet-point by the navy.

John, just one man amongst thousands on the sand dunes, wandered *how did it all come to this?* The Allied and German armies were roughly equal in number, yet the Germans had smashed through the British and French defences in no time at all, perhaps the enemy had superior equipment, or more tanks. John had seen countless men be killed, and realized that each man's life was expendable, of insignificance in an army a million strong. But, to the grieving relatives -the parents, the wives, the children-each young man's death was devastating. He thought back to his arrival in France the previous September, when he had had his vision of hell at the gate to the orchard. The hell had come true; terror had predominantly rained down from the air on soldiers and civilians. It was hard to take it all in, for there was so much to make sense of. As he thought of the carnage around him, John found himself questioning God. He also became resolute that the British *had* to beat the Germans...somehow. John would soon be leaving France, he tried to sleep; yes, May had been hell, what horrors would June bring?

As the sun rose in the sky, at the start of a hazy dawn, it gave the sea a copper colour. That morning (1st June), John and his comrades found themselves being arranged into a "series." This consisted of a group of two to three hundred men.

Mid-afternoon, the series adjacent to Johns were given the go-ahead to make their way down to the water's edge. Slowly, that group of men was reduced in number, as all sorts of small boats collected them off the beach. John watched enviously.

At long last it was the turn of John's group. The captain of a pretty little motorboat, which may, at a push, take twenty men, beckoned the troops over.

"Over here, boys!" He said encouragingly.

As the men raced forwards, half a dozen German bombers dominated the skyline. These Jerry pilots certainly picked their moments! On sighting the approaching aircraft, the captain of the motorboat shouted.

"No! Go back!"

Frustrated, John and the others raced back to the sand dunes for cover. Fortunately, the bombers did not come very close to their position, choosing instead to target the larger boats further out to sea.

Most of the bombs dropped exploded harmlessly in the water, sending spouts of it up into the air. One, however, struck a trawler, and it was a horrifying sight, as a number of the men on board were blown over the side. The boat started to lurch, and more men began to jump into the cold water. Worse was to come when German fighter aircraft appeared. Three Messerschmitt 109's tore over the water, strafing the survivors. Those poor chaps were so helpless.

John was able to board his motorboat with seventeen other men. On board, they learnt that the captain, an accountant by profession, had been asked for his boat at a moment's notice, and had never been out at sea before! Furthermore, the boat had no compass, and the captain thanked God that the Admiralty had issued him with a navigational chart. The boat was not armed. The motorboat efficiently ferried them across to a waiting destroyer, a little distance out to sea. The men of the navy threw rope ladders down to the tiny boat, in order to help them up the side of the mighty warship.

"Hurry up, lads!" Shouted the sailors. "Let's get you away from here as quickly as we can!"

On board the destroyer, the marvelous fellows of the navy distributed cocoa, tins of beef and loaves of bread –*fresh* bread. Ironically, most of the Tommies had fallen asleep immediately as they had boarded the vessel! The destroyer began the journey home, away from Dunkirk, where minutes felt like hours, through a sea littered with floating debris, foundered ships, and countless corpses. Worryingly, there were too few life jackets. John noticed how dangerously overloaded *all* the ships were. Men were crammed in everywhere- down the stoke hole, in the engine room, mess deck and on the upper deck. Behind them, Dunkirk burned, whilst the Luftwaffe continued their reign of terror in the skies above the town.

John caught up on a bit of sleep, and awoke to find that they were now sailing towards Britain in the dark. All that was visible was the glow of the wake at the rear of the ship. They could not be far away from Dover; it felt reassuring. Half asleep, John afforded himself a faint smile, for it would be nice to see Blighty again. But, what would the people back at home think of him and the other men? Trounced by a superior enemy, had they not just run away from battle?

At Dover, the men dirty and unshaven staggered down the gangplanks, and were surprised to be treated like heroes. Some, in various state of undress, wore little more than oil stained blankets and tin hats. After a welcome cup of tea, they were quickly shepherded onto awaiting trains, which would take them North.

They moved into a countryside as yet unspoiled by war. John's train passed through station after station, and crowds on the platforms showered the men with chocolates and cigarettes. Children waved Union Jacks, and someone held up a banner saying 'Well done, Boys!'

A broadcaster from the B.B.C. observed.

"At the station I watched the men climbing into the long waiting trains. It was astounding to walk along carriage after carriage, and to find in each one –silence."

The last troop ship left Dunkirk in the early hours of 4th June. The British Army had suffered 68,000 men killed, wounded or taken prisoner in Belgium and France. Close to 2,500 artillery guns, 90,000 rifles and 63,000 vehicles had been abandoned. The number of ships sunk at Dunkirk was 243, and the number of aircraft lost during the campaign on the Continent was 474. However, of great importance was the fact that 338,000 Allied troops had been safely evacuated back to Britain.

Mary Baker was deeply concerned about recent military developments across the English Channel. What with the Dutch then the Belgian armed forces surrendering, and the outnumbered British having to retreat to the coast, the German army seemed to be invincible. On 3rd June, the first large-scale air raid against Paris had caused the deaths of 254 civilians. The photographs in the newspapers of the exhausted allied troops at the docks and on the trains were quite disheartening. Mary had heard the rumours that many of the returning soldiers felt bitter and resentment towards their senior officers, over events in France. It was said that the fighting men detested Chamberlain and the Conservative Party, and the R.A.F. also came in for criticism. There was still no news as to the whereabouts of (her Son), John. Was he alive, even?

It was under this sort of atmosphere that a tense and anxious British population listened to the words of Winston Churchill on the 4th June 1940. The Prime Minister had delivered his speech to the House of Commons in the afternoon, and it was broadcast to the nation a few hours later.

The Prime Minister began by detailing the fateful course of events, which had led to the withdrawal to Dunkirk, such as the German breakthrough at Sedan, and the capitulation of the Belgians and Dutch. He proceeded to speak about the evacuation at Dunkirk.

"The enemy attacked in great strength on all sides, and their main power —the power of their far more numerous air force-was thrown into the battle or concentrated upon Dunkirk and the beaches…

For four or five days an intense struggle raged. Their armoured divisions, or what was left of them, together with great masses of German artillery and infantry, hurled themselves in vain upon the ever-narrowing and contracting appendix upon which the French and British armies fought.

Meanwhile, the Royal Navy, with the willing help of countless merchant seamen and a host of volunteers, strained every nerve to embark the British and allied troops. Over 220 light warships and more than 650 other vessels were engaged. They had to operate upon a difficult coast, and often under adverse weather conditions and under an almost ceaseless hail of bombs and increasing concentrations of artillery fire. Nor were the seas themselves free from mines or torpedoes.

It was in conditions such as these that our men carried on with little or no rest for days and nights, making trip after trip across the dangerous waters. The numbers they have bought back are the measure of their devotion and courage…

The enemy was hurled back by the retreating British and French troops. He was so roughly handled that he did not dare molest the departing armies. The Air Force decisively defeated the main strength of the German Air Force and inflicted upon them a loss of at least four to one. The Navy, using nearly a thousand ships of all kinds, took over 335,000 men, French and British, out of the jaws of death and shame back to their native land and to the tasks which lie immediately before them.

We must be careful not to assign to this deliverance the attributes of a victory. Wars are not won by evacuations. But there *was* a victory inside this deliverance, which should be noted. It was gained by the Air Force.

Many of our soldiers coming back have not seen the Air Force at work. They only saw the German bombers, which escaped their protective attack. They underrate the achievements of the British Air Force. This was a great trial of strength between the British and the German airforces...

Every day formations of German aeroplanes –and we know this is a very brave race- have turned on several occasions from an attack of one-fourth of their number of the Royal Air Force and dispersed in different directions. Twelve aeroplanes have been hunted by two. One aeroplane was driven into the water and cast away by the mere charge of a British aeroplane which had no more ammunition...

When we consider how much greater would be our advantages in defending the air above this island against an overseas attack, I must say that I find these facts a sure basis upon which practical and reassuring thoughts may rest...

May it not also be that the cause of civilization itself will be defended by the skill and vision of a few thousand airmen?"

The Prime Minister spoke in stark terms.

"Nevertheless, our thankfulness at the escape of our Army, and of many men whose loved ones have passed through an agonizing week, must not blind us to the fact that what has happened in France and Belgium is a colossal military disaster. The French Army has been weakened. The Belgian Army has been lost...We must expect another blow to be struck almost immediately at us or the French. We are told that Herr Hitler has a plan for invading the British Isles...

We must put our defences in this island into such a high state of organization that fewest possible numbers will be required to give effective security, and that the largest possible potential of offensive effort may be realized. On this we are now engaged...

I have myself full confidence that if all do their duty and nothing is neglected and if the best arrangements are made, as they are being made, we shall prove ourselves once again able to defend our island home, ride out the storms of war, and outlive the menace of tyranny if necessary for years, if necessary alone."

The end of the Prime Minister's speech was Shakespearean. His defiance in the face of probable military defeat roused the nation.

"We cannot flag or fail. We shall go on to the end. We shall fight in France, we shall fight on the seas and oceans, we shall fight with growing confidence and growing strength in the air. We shall defend our island whatever the cost may be. We shall fight on the beaches, we shall fight on the landing grounds, in the fields, in the streets, and in the hills; we shall never surrender. And even if, which I do not for a moment believe, this island or a large part of it were subjugated and starving, then our Empire beyond the seas, armed and guarded by the British Fleet, will carry on the struggle until in God's good time the New World, with all its power and might, sets forth to the liberation and rescue of the Old."

As Mary and George Baker sat listening to the stirring words, Mary felt a mixture of fear, apprehension and pride. Many miles away, her children, at the farm with Emily, Ted and their children were equally enthused by the speech. Ted cheered and remarked that the Prime Minister had given the country the confidence that it required to believe in itself.

CHAPTER 9 – ALONE

"The 4th June", announced the German victors, "the Wermacht can report to its supreme commander that a gigantic task has been accomplished…Dunkirk has fallen after a furious battle…the first phase of the campaign is over."

As Operation Dynamo (the evacuation of the B.E.F. from Dunkirk), drew to a close, at the beginning of June 1940, the main French armies, commanded by General Weygand, were establishing themselves on a line that ran along the River Somme in Northern France. Many of the French troops defending the line were poorly trained reservists.

In the early hours of Wednesday 5th June, the guns of the German artillery opened up along a 120-mile front. The German dive-bombers launched concentrated attacks on French positions, followed by infantry and tanks. The Battle of the Somme had begun.

The next day, Thursday 6th June, the British civilian population learned that the latest German offensive was under way. At the breakfast table, before going to school, Beth and Hannah, buoyed up by Mr. Churchill's speech two days ago, read the front page of the newspaper optimistically, as they digested the previous day's news. Richard and Tom eagerly leaned across the table to peer at the paper. Beth then read aloud for the benefit of the two boys, for whom the paper was upside-down.

"The heroic French defences are faring well in the battle raged thus far. The French have designated fortified villages, which are spaced in depth. Even when German tanks have penetrated the forward zone, French resistance continues behind them, against German supply columns bringing forward ammunition and petrol."

As the children departed for school, each crossed their fingers that the German army could be kept at bay. Richard had fanciful thoughts that the gallant French might even force the Germans all the way back into Germany!

On the third day of the offensive, Friday 7th June, General Weygand proclaimed.

"The battle for France has begun." He asked of his soldiers. "Hang on to the soil of France."

The Germans had launched two thousand tanks against their foe. Although slowed by the fighting spirit of their opponents, the German forces were grinding ever deeper into French territory.

Sunday 9th June, Hannah was dismayed to learn from the paper of a "slight strategic withdrawal" by the French allies. Hannah thought about this, and remembered Mr. Churchill's warning that wars are won neither by evacuations nor withdrawals.

A day later, the news from mainland Europe became very bleak. Mr. Duff Cooper, Minister of Information, announced in an evening broadcast over the wireless.

"Mussolini, Dictator of Italy, has declared war upon the Allies, by whose side Italy fought in the last Great War, and who then, by their efforts, saved Italy from destruction. He has timed the blow with characteristic cowardice and treachery. He has waited for more than nine months. He has waited until France has fought desperately against great odds. At last the opportunity to stab an old friend in the back, in the hour of that friend's greatest peril, has proved too strong a temptation for Mussolini to resist. It will be remembered for generations as one of the vilest acts in history."

Britain's response to Italy's declaration of war was to bomb Milan and Genoa on 12th June. Four days later, the Italians sunk two British submarines in the Mediterranean.

Italian troops were poised to launch an attack on France through the Alps, at any moment. Rouen, the old Norman capital now lay in German hands, and the River Seine, had been crossed in many places by the German armoured units. The invading Hun was just thirty miles away from Paris.

In Miss Townsend's class, the children had taken great interest in plotting the progress of the battle for France on a sizeable map, which was pinned to the wall. It proved to be a good way of teaching Geography; there was not a child in the class that did not know the location of places such as Compiegne, Rheims or the River Marne. However, by Thursday 13th June, the map had been discreetly put away. It was evident which way the tide of battle was going. All the talk was now of Paris. The school children discussed whether or not the French would make a stand in their beloved capital. But, that would almost certainly reduce the city to rubble...

The French government had already departed South to Tours, a few days ago. The streets of Paris, the café terraces, the great squares, were all deserted, and there were by now, no newspapers. Less than twenty percent of the population remained, as hundreds of thousands of Parisians were retreating on foot, on bicycles, in cars and by train, to Southern and Western France, away from the advancing Nazis. Smoke from the ever-closer battle zone blackened the sky. That night, under the instructions of the French government, armament factories on the outskirts of the city were destroyed.

The next day, Friday 14th June 1940, the German troop columns goose-stepped into Paris, and the swastika flag was raised above the Eiffel Tower. The French capital had been declared an open city, the French being unable to defend it. Signs sprung up, declaring *Germany conquers on all fronts*.

Millions had left other cities, towns and villages in Northern France, in what became known as the 'Exode' or Exodus to the South. The population of Chartres, for instance, fell from 23,000 to 800. The Exode caused great trauma, as five million people took to the roads, and members of families became separated, and many personal possessions were abandoned. Those fleeing by car, pots and pans hanging from their doors, ran out of petrol, or became caught in queues.

Elsewhere in France, the fighting continued, as the Germans threw 150 divisions into the battle. On Sunday 16th June, the French began to evacuate the Maginot Line, since the Germans had outflanked it.

The British Prime Minister surveyed the war situation in Parliament, on Tuesday 18th June. The speech was relayed to the country, later that day.

"We do not yet know what will happen in France, or whether French resistance will be prolonged both in France and in the French Empire oversea. The French Government will be throwing away great opportunities and casting away their future if they do not continue the war in accordance with their treaty obligations, from which we have not felt able to release them."

Mr. Churchill spoke of the prospect of imminent invasion.

"We have in arms at the present time in this island over 1,250,000 men. Behind these we have the Local Defence Volunteers, numbering 500,000, only a portion of whom, however, are yet armed with rifles or other firearms. We have incorporated into our defence forces every man for whom we have a weapon. We expect a very large addition to our weapons in the near future, and in preparation for this we intend to call up, drill, and train further large numbers at once."

The Prime Minister turned to the subject of a German invasion fleet.

"The efficacy of sea-power, especially in modern conditions, depends upon the invading force being of large size. It has got to be of large size, in view of our military strength, to be of any use. If it is of large size the Navy have something they can meet and bite on...

We also have a great system of minefields, recently largely reinforced, through which we alone know the channels."

Mr. Churchill continued.

"It seems quite clear that no invasion on a scale beyond the capacity of our land forces to crush speedily is likely to take place from the air until our Air Force has been definitely overpowered...

The great question is, can we break Hitler's air weapon? It is a very great pity we have not got an air force at least equal to that of the most powerful enemy within reach of our shores, but we have a very powerful Air Force which has proved itself far superior, in quality, both of men and of many types of machines, to what we have met so far in the numerous fierce air battles which have been fought...

I look forward confidently to the exploits of our fighter pilots, who will have the glory of saving their island home and all they love from the most deadly of all attacks."

As the Prime Minister came to a conclusion, his words were masterful and moving.

"What General Weygand called the 'Battle of France' is over. I expect that the 'Battle of Britain' is about to begin. Upon this battle depends the survival of the Christian civilization. Upon it depends our own British life and the long-continued history of our institutions and our Empire.

The whole fury and might of the enemy must very soon be turned on us. Hitler knows that he will have to break us on this island or lose the war. If we can stand up to him all Europe may be free and the life of the world may move forward into broad and sunlit uplands. If we fail, then the whole world, including the United States, and all that we have known and cared for, will sink into the abyss of a new dark age made more sinister and perhaps more prolonged by the light of a perverted science.

Let us, therefore, do our duty and so bear ourselves that if the British Commonwealth and Empire lasts a thousand years men will still say, 'This was their finest hour'."

Four days later, 22nd June, the French signed an armistice at the forest of Compiegne, in the railway coach used for the 1918 German surrender. Panzers had been roaming at will in central France, and hundreds of thousands of French troops had surrendered. Marshal Petain headed a new French government, based in Vichy, which was allowed to administer the country south of the River Loire. Petain's regime would be authoritarian and anti-Semitic. For four bleak years the Vichy government would veer between tacit endorsement of Nazi policies, and active collaboration.

From England, a little known French general, Charles de Gaulle, appealed to his countrymen to keep the flame of French resistance alive. By the end of the month, Britain recognized him as the leader in exile of France.

A report by the German High Command declared.

"After this greatest victory in German history over an opponent who was regarded as the most powerful land power in the world, who fought both skillfully and bravely, there are no longer Allies. Only one foe remains: England."

On a clear day, the Germans could see the white cliffs of Dover, from Calais, across the twenty-mile wide stretch of water. One German commander called for an immediate invasion of Britain led by paratroopers.

In Britain, during the past month, factories were working seven-day weeks, strikes were outlawed, and the government advised people not to have holidays. In a bid to 'Dig for Victory', and avoid starvation, land all over Britain was being turned over to the plough. Allotments were appearing in parks, and vegetables were replacing flowers in gardens. The butter and bacon rations had been cut to four ounces, and the sugar ration reduced to eight ounces. In order to curb profiteering, the government announced that clothing would be controlled in price. In the "Second great trek", many children over the past few weeks had been evacuated from London, and vulnerable coastal (likely invasion) areas of Norfolk, Suffolk, Essex, Kent, Sussex and Hampshire. The Luftwaffe, flying from airfields in France, could focus its attention on Britain. Plans had even been drawn up to *completely* evacuate Brighton, Canterbury, Dover and other threatened towns.

A couple of weeks ago, the schoolchildren had, under the watchful eye of Mr. Henry spent the afternoon on a Sussex beach gaily filling sandbags. Richard was proud since between them he and Edward had filled two-dozen bags with sand- the joint highest total for the class. At the end of the afternoon, an army lorry had transported the load away to London.

Now, Saturday 6th July, with the threat of invasion greatly increased, they were not allowed anywhere near the beach, let alone on it. You needed a permit to visit the (Southeast) coast, which had been declared a 'Defence Area'. They knew through Hannah and Richard's parents that at the London stations there were lists of hundreds of little stations on the coast that could no longer be visited for 'holiday, recreation or pleasure'.

Their brother, John's depleted battalion had received a couple of hundred replacements from conscripts who had just completed six months basic training. They also had new inexperienced N.C.O.s, some of whom faced a steep learning curve, and earned less respect from the men than others. John, and the other soldiers, undertook further training in weapons, tactical exercises, rapid deployment and anti-parachutist exercises. They went on route marches in burdensome full service marching order, most days on ten miles, although sometimes twenty or thirty miles. At night they frequented the local pubs, drinking, singing and playing darts. Sometimes, they had to investigate reports of enemy spies, such as lights flickering from bushes (always false alarms!). Some of the men thought that Britain was finished and was only playing for time; there were barely any anti-tank guns, armoured cars or tanks on mainland Britain. Others believed that the country could hold firm against the Germans and that it was perhaps a blessing to have rid of the French.

Hannah and Richard, sat with the Pavitt children on a hillside, bordered with hedgerows that were busy with sparrows, and bright green grasshoppers, overlooking the English Channel, which lay a mile or so away. A copper sun shone down upon the fragrant meadows. Richard thought wistfully of the last family holiday he had spent at the seaside the previous year. He had busied himself for countless hours, building sandcastles, as all little boys did. Richard smiled to himself as he remembered how his sister, assisted with enthusiasm by his mother, had buried him in the sand, until some got up his nose and made him sneeze! But, that had

105

been in peacetime. War had deprived the boys and girls of any frolicking on the beach for the foreseeable future.

The golden beaches were covered with masses of barbed wire, and at frequent intervals stood gun emplacements and also blockhouses made of concrete and steel, which could cover every possible line of approach by the German enemy. The sea itself was continually patrolled by ships of the Royal Navy and by aircraft.

In the surrounding countryside, the army and the Local Defence Volunteers had been hard at work. Roads leading inland were barred with ingenious tank obstacles, and deep ditches had been dug across fields. Everywhere, destinations had been removed from buses, trains and trams, and place names had been obliterated on signposts and milestones; even the village name on the war memorial had been erased. Outside Mr. Bailey's church, a notice had gone up politely informing people that services would go on as usual, although the church bells would no longer be used, since they would only be rung as an invasion warning.

A few miles away to the right, half a dozen white whiffs of smoke denoted field guns practising for battle. The children could not fail to be impressed by England's defences. However, a mere score miles across the Channel (from Dover, at least), the mighty German army sat waiting.

In Germany, the Nazis proposed moving the Jews living under German rule to Madagascar, to make them easier to control. Meanwhile, the SS had prepared a Black Book with the names of almost three thousand Britons to be rounded up as dangerous adversaries, including Noel Coward, J.B. Priestly and Virginia Woolf, in the event of an invasion.

There was a great fear of the unknown amongst the English population. Many more people were carrying their gas masks around with them, again. The thought of German soldiers marching up the road below sent shivers down Hannah's spine. Staring at the blue waters of the Channel, with both her hands resting on her knees, Hannah asked aloud.

"Do you think that Hitler really will invade?"

After a couple of seconds, Beth replied.

"Who knows…"

Tom, who was occupying himself pulling blades of grass in half, spoke, his eyes wide with excitement.

"Henry's heard that German parachutists dressed as vicars are going to land all around us, to create confusion!"

"Now you're just being silly!" Beth retorted. "Anyway, if they do land, then they'll come for you first, Tom!"

Hannah spoke up.

"We shall have to start calling him *Miss Leaky Mouth*!"

The two girls grinned at each other, and chorused.

"You should join the silent column!"*

Tom picked up an earthworm, and threw it at the girls, but missed.

Beth suggested that they purchase her brother an "anti-gossip handkerchief."

The children zigzagged down the hill, chasing each other. Hannah had almost caught up with Tom when she slipped and fell on her backside. For their part, Beth and Richard pulled each other to the ground, and rolled along through the grass laughing.

The group strolled towards home at more of a sedate pace, passing hedges full of murmuring bees. Whilst walking along one peaceful lane, they came across a big wide field that was eerily silent, and full of row after row of derelict cars and clapped out hay-wains.

Tom climbed over the perimeter fence, and hurried across the field, over to the nearest vehicle.

"Look at this!" The boy waved his arms aloft.

The other three children followed Tom into the field.

The vehicles, mostly shells of cars from the 1920's, with black paint that was peeling off and deflated tyres, were strategically placed in this field, to counter against a possible landing by enemy aircraft. In other parts of England, all around fields, golf course and recreation grounds in the South and East coasts, were similar obstacles —cars, hay rakes, old bedsteads.

An eager Tom opened the door of one, and climbed into the driver's seat. He gripped the large, stiff steering wheel, and moved his hands up and down it, as if driving the car.

"Come on! Get in!" He beckoned to the other three.

Hannah had her reservations about the idea.

"I don't know if we should…"

Beth and Richard looked at Hannah imploringly. The three of them climbed into the spacious back seat of the car. What a lark! From the driver's seat, Tom turned round and, adopting a hoity-toity voice, he asked "Where to?"

"Oh! London, Piccadilly." Beth requested.

"Do drive carefully," added Hannah.

Tom attempted to move the gear stick, but it was stuck fast. To his chagrin, he also discovered that the foot pedals were gone.

"Bloomin' vandals!" He muttered.

Beth and Hannah sniggered.

Tom pretended to drive, and mimicked the noises of a car's engine, puffing his cheeks out as he did so. *Brruummm, brruummm…*

The other three children, sprawled over the back seat, could not contain their laughter, as Tom took his role as chauffeur to the extreme.

"Look out! Cow on road ahead," joked Beth.

---

*The 'Silent Column' was a campaign to discourage gossip that consisted of drawings of people who should be regarded as unpatriotic. Miss Leaky Mouth was depicted as going on like a leaky tap about the war.

"Police car behind," smiled Hannah. "Better stop that speeding," she warned.

After a while, true to character, Tom became 'bored', and he jumped out of the car, as quickly as he had scrambled into it.

The children left the field.

On returning to the village, the foursome noticed that the Local Defence Volunteers were training in the fields behind the village pond. Along with Edward's, Nancy's and Samantha's Fathers, Beth's Father had enrolled in this civilian army.

Beth smiled. For ten days ago, only two of the men had uniforms, and Ted had been drilling in his farm clothes, but today the men of the village stood proud in their khaki army uniforms. Whereas, last week the Local Defence Volunteers were obliged to drill with broomsticks and pitchforks, now they were armed with rifles. The twenty or so mostly middle- aged men in that sun-kissed field looked like proper soldiers. Beth felt proud.

From the edge of the field, the children keenly observed the Local Defence Volunteers practice, in threes, a short bayonet charge against sacks suspended from a crude metal frame. Then, they heard the officer in charge, an army regular, explain that, if the charge was for real against enemy soldiers, the ideal spot in which to stick the bayonet was the lungs, stomach or throat. The officer added.

"Give the bayonet a good twist before pulling it out."

It all sounded a little gruesome to the two girls.

"I think we've seen enough." Hannah hinted, whilst clutching her stomach.

Back at the farmhouse, Emily was engrossed in a pamphlet. It was very official looking, and was ominously titled *If the invader comes. What to do —And how to do it.*

The two girls nosed at the leaflet.

"It's from the Ministry of Information." Hannah observed.

"So what *should* we do if the invader comes, Mummy?" Beth enquired.

With all four children listening intently, Emily read direct from the pamphlet.

"The Germans threaten to invade Great Britain. If they do so they will be driven out by our Navy, our Army and our Air Force. Yet the ordinary men and women of the civilian population will also have their part to play. Hitler's invasions of Poland, Holland and Belgium were greatly helped by the fact that the civilian population was taken by surprise. They did not know what to do when the moment came. YOU MUST NOT BE TAKEN BY SURPRISE. This leaflet tells you what general line you should take...

When Holland and Belgium were invaded, the civilian population fled from their homes. They crowded on the roads, in cars, in carts, on bicycles and on foot, and so helped the enemy by preventing their own armies from advancing against the invaders. You must not allow that to happen here. Your first rule, therefore, is: -

    (1)   If the Germans come, by parachute, aeroplane or ship, you must remain where you are. The order is STAY PUT."

The pamphlet went on to warn about the danger of rumours. One should not believe them, and not spread them. If people saw anything suspicious, they were to go at once to the nearest policeman or military officer and inform them what they had seen. Emily continued, quoting from the leaflet.

"The sort of report which a military or police officer wants from you is something like this —At 5:30p.m. tonight I saw twenty cyclists come into Little Squashborough from the direction of Great Mudtown"-

Tom, doubled up with laughter, remarked.

"Little Squashborough? Great Mudtown? What silly place-names. Ha! Ha!"

Emily reprimanded her Son.

"Be quiet, Thomas! This is a very, very serious business. Any more cheek from you, and you'll be having heart and liver for dinner…they're not on ration."*

Beth screwed her face up.

"Ugh!"

Emily explained that if the German parachutists came down, civilians were not to give them anything to assist them, such as food, transport or maps. However, if requested to by British Army or Air Force officers, civilians were to help the military in any way. This might include blocking roads, for example. The leaflet ended.

"Remember always that the best defence of Great Britain is the courage of her men and women. Here is rule 7 —Think before you act. But think always of your country before you think of yourself."

---

*Not being on ration these sorts of offal actually gained in popularity during the war

CHAPTER 10 – THE BATTLE IN THE SKIES

"There are about ten German machines dive bombing a British convoy which is just out to sea in the Channel. There's one coming down in flames –somebody's hit a German, and he's coming down...there's a long streak. He's coming down completely out of control, a long streak of smoke...a man's bailed out by parachute-the pilot's bailed out by parachute-he's a Junkers 87, and he's going slap into the sea. And there he goes –Smash!"

BBC live broadcast on the air battles over the sea, July 1940.

In order to invade and defeat Great Britain, Hitler needed to secure mastery of the skies over the English Channel and the North Sea. The German dictator would therefore have to defeat the Royal Air Force using the Luftwaffe.

Hundreds of Luftwaffe pilots had gained valuable combat experience in the Spanish Civil War, when they had been rotated through the Condor Legion, aiding Franco's nationalists. In Spain, the Germans had developed and refined tactics, and returned to their units to pass on their knowledge. By the middle of 1940 the Luftwaffe could boast a hundred flying schools that were producing up to fifteen thousand pilots a year. Although the Luftwaffe had lost thirty per cent of its fighter aircraft in the campaigns in Poland and France, the British were viewed as already half beaten, and morale in the Luftwaffe was high.

The RAF, for their part, needed to deprive the Luftwaffe of air supremacy. By the fall of Dunkirk in early June 1940 Fighter Command had been reduced to 330 single-engined aircraft. However, Britain's factories were churning out new aircraft, and many planes that would be damaged in the coming weeks would be repaired and returned to service. By early July 1940, Fighter Command could field fifty-eight squadrons against the enemy, six more than was believed to be the minimum number required to successfully defend the British Isles. These squadrons were actually currently over-manned, although numbers of pilots would inevitably dwindle as the battle of attrition went on.

The groundbreaking technology of radar gave Fighter Command advanced warning of German attacks. This was important because it took a Spitfire thirteen minutes to scramble and climb to twenty thousand feet, and a Hurricane took sixteen minutes.

Pilot Officer Peter Stone (cousin of the Pavitt children) was nineteen years of age. He was of medium build with brown hair. His looks were boyish, betraying the fact that despite his outward show of confidence, he appeared too young to be a fighter pilot. Since that day in his early teens when he was taken up briefly in an old biplane from a flying circus that was touring the country, Peter was instantly hooked, and knew his destiny lay with aircraft. In the summer of 1939, he had left school, and had entered the R.A.F. through the Training College at Cranwell. After just under a year's instruction, on 1st July 1940, he graduated from Cranwell, and joined his squadron. He was part of Eleven Group, which was based in the South East of England.

They were a good bunch; a couple of the other lads were new arrivals like Peter, and even the old hands were barely out of their teens. A number of the pilots had fought in France, and they felt a little sorry for the new recruits, since the coming months would see the air battles reach their greatest intensity. The new inexperienced pilots were most likely to be shot down, once they met the Messerschmitt 109's, unless luck was on their side. The pilots who returned from Dunkirk had conquered fear, and came back older mature men. In order to prepare for the onslaught, the squadron practised methods, which had been tried and tested over in France. They rehearsed scrambles, flying in formation and dogfights. They got to know landmarks, and looked for suitable fields in which to land in an emergency. Days were long, and the hardest thing to get used to was the requirement to be at readiness from half an hour before first light, right through till after dusk. Any leisure time was spent playing cards, reading or writing letters. The odd evening, the pilots visited the bar, and indulged in a few pints.

Peter flew a Spitfire. The aircraft had a long shapely nose, and thirty-seven feet wingspan. Its graceful wings had curved leading and trailing edges. It was armed with eight machine guns; four on each wing, which carried sufficient bullets for fourteen seconds firing. Of the eight guns, two were loaded with armour-piercing ammunition, two with incendiary and four with ball. The controls were sensitive, the gun platform steady, and the plane manoeuvrable, being capable of very tight turns. The Spitfire was far superior to the planes that Peter had flown in training, and with a top speed of 365 mph he felt confident that it would outperform any aircraft, which the Germans could throw at him. A ground crew of three, a rigger, fitter and armourer serviced it.

It was mid-July, and the Luftwaffe had been attacking British shipping convoys in the Channel, for a number of days. Stuka dive-bombers were the main weapons at this stage of the German offensive. Fighter Command faced a dilemma, since aircraft would be lost if the R.A.F. responded to the German attacks, whereas shipping loses would be severe if Fighter Command stood idly by. Some R.A.F. squadrons had already been severely depleted, and their remaining pilots were physically and mentally exhausted. However, the R.A.F. was giving a good account of itself, with fifteen enemy aircraft destroyed, for the loss of just six fighters, on 11th July alone.

The invaluable ground crew had already started up the Spitfire's Merlin engine, by means of a lead connected to a twenty-four volt starter battery, which was on a wheeled trolley. Peter trotted up to the aircraft, placed a foot in the step set into the side of the fuselage, hoisted himself up, and clambered in, placing his parachute down on the seat first, and the ground crew strapped him in. Peter's mouth was dry, and he felt a mild nausea, not uncommon for a first combat mission. He proceeded to rev the plane's engine, in order to warm it up whilst another member of the ground crew sat on the tailplane to hold it down. Behind the Spitfire, the slipstream flattened the grass.

Inside the tiny cockpit, it smelled of engine oil and leather. Peter checked the oxygen and instruments. Peter signaled that he was ready to go, and a ground crew member promptly disconnected the battery lead. The ground crew guided the wingtips of the aircraft, for it's long nose permitted virtually no forward vision when taxiing. Peter opened up the throttle then waved the men clear, no turning back now, stick close to the Yellow Section leader.

The squadron was divided into two flights, A and B, which were further divided into two sections (Red and Yellow, Blue and Green). Of the three airplanes in a section, two 'wingmen' flew either side, a little to the rear of the leader.

Peter opened up more throttle, and the aircraft bumped over the ground at increasing speed. Power surged through the Spitfire, and the next moment, it was airborne.

"A flight airborne." announced Squadron Leader Archie North over the RT.

A voice came back.

"Roger. Patrol Dover and await instructions."

In the air, with the propeller spinning easily in front, the sun felt hot through the aircraft's Perspex hood. Peter kept his eyes peeled for enemy aircraft; continuously checking the air all around him. Flying in formation bought a sense of collective security. The voice of Archie North came over the RT, exuding confidence, and bolstering the mood of his pilots. Flying up to approximately twenty thousand feet, it was remarkable that the fifty or so miles between London and the coast down below looked little distance at all, and the English Channel was like a mere river. Everything was normal on the instrument panel; the needles in the dials quivered slightly, oil temperature and pressure and manifold pressure were fine. Peter had already put his oxygen mask on, and could feel the gas flowing against his cheeks.

Down below, plots had been passed from the radar stations to Fighter Command headquarters, foretelling where the enemy planes would be in fifteen minutes. Indeed, the pilots had great support from people on the ground. They were at the top of a pyramid that included the ground crew, WAAFs (Women's Auxiliary Air Force), anti-aircraft gunners, the Observer Corps, aircraft factory workers and many thousands more.

Suddenly, the voice of the controller came over the RT.

"Control to Red leader. Dover, Angels 14." That meant the German bombers were flying at fourteen thousand feet. They should come into view, very soon. Now, where were they?

The voice of Archie North came over the RT. Excited, he had spotted the enemy aircraft, and he informed his fellow pilots.

"Red leader to all sections. Bandits at ten o' clock!" He ordered the Spitfires into attack.

"Tally-ho! Let's get the bastards!"

Down below, a number of Stukas were attacking a convoy of ships. A fountain of spray erupted high into the air close to one large ship that was lumbering its way through the blue. No time to lose!

Peter felt his pulse quicken. This was it, the moment he had been trained for. He promptly lowered his seat, so as to obtain maximum protection from the engine block in front and the armour plate behind, tightened his straps, and switched the gun button into the firing position. He was ready. The waiting was over, and along with the other Spitfires, his plane dived down into battle.

He remembered Archie North telling him and the other new arrivals when he joined the squadron, that he would come up against Messerschmitt pilots who had hundreds of hours' flying under their belts. If each airman were to be able to destroy one enemy plane that would be good, to destroy a couple would be magnificent and help to win the war for Britain.

Red leader goes into attack a suitable target —an unsuspecting Stuka dive-bomber. Within seconds, the German plane spins down, out of control, thick black smoke pouring out of it.

Peter selects his own Stuka to attack. He comes within three hundred or so feet of the enemy aircraft, and fires a short burst into it; his Spitfire shudders as he does so. However, the Stuka remains undamaged, and, aware of the presence of the British plane, it begins to dodge and weave. Peter's head is pushed down on his chest —a result of the heavy G force. Peter, becoming the hunter, closes in, grinds his teeth together, concentrates on the yellow circle and dot of the reflector sight in front of him and thinks *I'll get you this time you bloody arrogant German!* This time! He remembers what Sandy Rose, the leader of Yellow Section had told him about deflection shooting —aiming just ahead of his prey by the (rather imprecise) deflection angle, rather than shooting in a straight line at a fast-moving target.

Had he been hit? Smoke begins to appear from the Stuka's engine. Next moment, the Stuka turns onto its back and spirals down, entering the sea with a tremendous splash!

Peter felt exhilaration. He had passed the test —such a feeling of relief. From nowhere, a body, legs and arms flailing, with an unopened parachute pack attached, fell past his Spitfire-not pleasant.

Sighting another German aircraft, Peter gave chase, and opened up his guns, however, in his haste, he had started to fire too early, the bullets wobbled and wavered away from the enemy plane. He was dismayed to find that as he closed in on the enemy plane he was now out of ammunition. He had no choice but to return to base.

Only now, with the excitement over, Peter became aware of the physical discomforts and demands of aerial combat. His oxygen mask felt wet, and his whole face was perspiring, his eyes irritating, and he felt sore all over. As he headed home, flying above the Channel, patches of fluorescence indicated pilots that had ended up in the drink. Peter crossed the chalk cliffs of Kent and flew over hop fields and orchards.

The Spitfires returned to the airfield in dribs and drabs. It had been a good outing for the squadron; Red leader had one definite 'kill' and another 'probable', three of the other lads had each downed a Stuka. Two Spitfires were lost, although, mercifully both the pilots had managed to bail out, and were back unharmed with the squadron by nightfall.

As Peter taxied across the grass, seemingly every available man descended upon the Spitfire, to check for bullet holes and service it. Peter's armourer, Neville, an amiable lad of eighteen, looked at Peter expectantly, and, after having confirmed that the aircraft had performed reliably, he asked, with slight hesitation.

"Did you shoot any down?"

"Yes. A Stuka."

Neville's face broadened into a grin.

On Sunday 14th July 1940, Winston Churchill broadcast to the British Empire and America. He declared.

"Should the invader come to Britain there will be no placid lying down of the people, no submission before him as we have seen, alas in other countries. We shall defend every village, every town and every city. The vast mass of London itself, fought street by street, could easily devour an entire hostile army. We would rather see London laid in ashes and ruins than it should tamely and abjectly enslaved.

…There are vast numbers, who will render faithful service but whose names will never be known, whose deeds will never be recorded. This is the war of the Unknown Warriors."

They were interrupted half way through breakfast, as they had been scrambled to meet incoming German raiders but had failed to make contact with the enemy. It was 8:30 a.m. As Peter's Spitfire descended, he was able to see labourers starting work in the fields, milk floats going from house to house, the chimneys were smoking, and steam trains snaking their way across the countryside taking workers to the towns and cities.

He taxied across the grass, and threw back the hood of his aircraft. He heard a voice say.

"Time to finish breakfast!"

They duly finished their meal and decided to walk across to dispersal, it was turning out to be a fine morning. The sun was rising ever higher in the sky, and the mid-summer air felt clean and fresh. They walked unhurriedly; hands in pockets, one or two of the pilots were smoking cigarettes, one of them winked cheekily as they passed a couple of WAAF's.

Squadron Leader Archie North was their C.O. Tall, and exceptionally fit, Archie was always positive, seldom had a bad word for anyone, and able to motivate the whole squadron. He had a natural air of authority, yet such was his character that he had no personal enemies. He had had several 'kills' in France, and was already considered by some to be an 'ace'. He was not so many years older than Peter.

The pilots in the squadron were typical of most of those who flew Spitfires and Hurricanes. They were the men with the quickest wits and fastest reactions, the adventurers.

Percy Green was the same age as Peter, and had joined the squadron at the same time as him. This helped the pair to form a natural attachment to each other, and they quickly became firm friends. Percy's hair was as black as night, and his mischievous eyes were green in colour. The son of a solicitor, he had a school boyish sense of fun, though took flying and defeating the enemy with deadly seriousness.

Sandy Rose came across as reserved to those who did not know him very well. Twenty-one years of age, everyone called him Sandy because of the colour of his hair. Newly promoted to Flight Lieutenant after his exploits in France, he had taken Percy and Peter under his wing, and developed a strong bond with the pair, who he treated as his equals. He loved music and the gramophone, and had a girlfriend as a WAAF serving at another base. He had apparently been made a fighter pilot (rather than bombers) because he was very good at flying upside down!

As they approached the dispersal hut for the second time that morning, Percy was pulling the leg of one of the other pilots, something to do with a phobia of frogs and toads. The group settled down into the deckchairs that were scattered around in front of the hut. There was the smell of high-octane fuel and the buzz of insects in the air. How long would it be before the dreaded ring of that telephone?

Sandy took a neatly folded letter out of his pocket, and smiled. It was from his WAAF girlfriend confirming a dinner date in the West End of London. Peter engrossed himself in The Daily Express, and was pestered by one of the other pilots, asking him each and every cricket score. The others busied themselves reading and writing.

Before long, Percy had challenged Sandy to a game of draughts, which might easily develop into a dozen games. Sandy accepted, but warned.

"OK. As long as you don't cheat like last time."

Percy's face was a picture of innocence.

"How can one cheat at draughts?" He looked across to Peter for support.

"You did last time!" Sandy was indignant.

"Did not!"

"Did too!" Sandy blinked in the bright sunlight, "It was when I had my back turned."

"Well, it wasn't my fault that you had a fly in your eye!"

"You took advantage of the situation, and removed one of my pieces from the board."

Peter spoke up.

"It was two pieces, actually."

"You knew, as well?" Sandy looked at him accusingly.

Peter maintained Sandy's gaze. The Flight Lieutenant glanced across at Percy then back to Peter, his face broadened into a grin, as he said.

"You young pair of tykes!"

All three airmen burst out into spontaneous laughter. Seconds later, the telephone rang and the call to scramble came.

The twelve Spitfires flew in neat formation, having got up in the air a shade inside four minutes. That was good – they were getting faster. In Yellow section, Peter's aircraft was close behind Sandy's. The date was Thursday 25th July.

As Peter flew along, almost effortlessly, the engine purring smoothly, on checking his instrument panel, everything looked fine. Peter felt powerful, a hunter, although he would not yet admit to having nerves of steel, for his mouth felt dry. Indeed, it was hot under the summer sun. He constantly twisted his head, left and right, and up and down, scouring the blue for enemy aircraft. From now on, Peter would always fly with an open neck shirt and a silk scarf. For, Harold Fowler from Blue section had complained that when he had recently bailed out over the Channel, his shirt collar had shrunk in the water, and nearly strangled him!

The squadron hurried towards enemy aircraft that were harassing another Channel convoy. Below, the pilots could make out clusters of towns and villages and the wakes of large ships cutting through the blue sea.

Peter tore into attack a German bomber, however, he overshot the enemy aircraft, to find that his Spitfire was now coming under direct fire from a Messerschmitt 109, which was in hot pursuit, the sun glinting on its wings, and the smoke trails of its guns converging on Peter's aircraft. Glowing white tracer began to appear, hurrying past the cockpit. Although frailer-looking and with a narrower wingspan than the Spitfire, the ME 109 was a vicious fighter. It was fast, and armed with two machine guns and a 20mm cannon in each wing. The ME 109 could out-dive a Spitfire but on the other hand, the British fighter was the more agile of the two aircraft.

This was fear at it's most extreme. A real and determined enemy was shooting at Peter in his aircraft with *real* bullets. He was momentarily paralyzed. Much as he tried to duck and weave Peter failed to lose the 109. There were a number of bangs, and numerous bullet holes suddenly appeared in his wing, the Spitfire staggered, and began to lose height; the needle on the altimeter was dropping like a stone.

None of the Spitfire's controls would now work. Peter had no option but to get out of his disabled aircraft. First he unplugged his oxygen and pulled the pin to release his restraining harness. Next, he slid back the canopy and climbed out of the cockpit, and attempted to jump. However, the force of the wind threw him back in again. Not a good start!

Peter rolled the stricken plane onto its back, and pushed himself out of the cockpit. He began to experience the sensation of free-fall. He tumbled head over heels; first the sea came into view, then the sky, followed by the sea, again. The air was cold, and Peter kept his eye on his stopwatch. After 40 seconds, he pulled the ripcord, and to his immense relief, the silken canopy opened.

The Spitfire pilot drifted down at a more sedate pace. It was then that he noticed how far away the English coastline was –at least three or four miles. The sea below was deserted, and he dearly wished that rescue by an English boat would be swift.

Peter crashed into the English Channel, and was nearly choked by a mouthful of salt water. He promptly turned a metal disc on a small box ninety degrees to free himself from the parachute. Whilst treading water, he inflated his Mae West life jacket, continually harassed by the waves, which half-blinded him. He started to shout for help, realizing that he could be stranded alone in this water for some time…

The relentless heat of the summer sun gave Peter's face a pounding. He intensely disliked being stranded in this watery no-mans-land between the German enemy and home. With only the seagulls for company, Peter suddenly felt very lonely, and thought of family back home, in order to take his mind off his helpless situation.

He tried to put to the back of his mind thoughts of other pilots who had ended up in the Channel and spent in solitude their final few hours on the Earth there. If he were going to die, he would prefer the end come sooner rather than later.

After three-quarters of an hour, although it seemed infinitely longer, a boat came into view.

"British! British!" Peter cried.

The boat came up close, and a burly tattooed sailor hauled an exhausted, but eternally grateful Peter aboard. The seaman commented that if he had been a Nazi bastard, they'd have happily left him to drown in the sea.

The boat returned to port, during which time, Peter enjoyed a mug of hot drink on board. A small crowd had gathered at the harbour. They had seen what had gone on, and cheered as the pilot got off the boat and walked up the harbour steps. Someone gave Peter a packet of cigarettes. He caught a lift back to base with a lorry driver, and received some initial stick from the other chaps, who thought that he had 'bought it', and were just relieved to see him, again. The pilots later enjoyed some well-deserved drinks in the bar.

Despite his ordeal of baling out, Peter was keen to get airborne again, and have another crack at the enemy. That was his duty.

On the first day of August, across the Channel, the following directive was issued from Hitler's headquarters.

"Directive No. 17.

For prosecuting air and sea war against England.

I have decided to carry on and intensify air and naval warfare against England in order to bring about her final defeat. For this purpose I am issuing the following orders.

1. The German air force with all available forces will destroy the English air force as soon as possible."

And the Germans planned to intensify the air war in a few days.

The children at the farm heard from Hitler the next day. The morning of 2nd August 1940, Richard had pulled back the bedroom curtains, to discover a large sheet of paper dancing across the farmyard on the wind. Thinking this curious, since paper was on ration, the boy had hared down the stairs, and out into the farmyard, to investigate further. He retrieved the sheet, and frowned, for it was headed *A Last Appeal To Reason by Adolf Hitler*. The leaflet was one of many that had been dropped by German aircraft over Britain the previous night, as propaganda. Richard entered the farmhouse, once more, and returned to the bedroom. The boy woke Tom, who was still slumbering in his bed.

"Look at this!" Richard waved the sheet in front of his friend.

Tom wiped the mist out of his eyes.

"What is it?"

"It's from Hitler."

"How did it get here?"

"I don't know."

"Let me look at it!" Tom made an attempt to snatch the paper out of the other's hand, but Richard kept a firm hold on it. Hearing the commotion, Beth and Hannah appeared at the door.

Richard announced.

"Its from a speech by Hitler on 19th July."

The children listened intently, as Richard read aloud.

"A great empire will be destroyed –an empire which it was never my intention to destroy or even to harm. I do, however, realize that this struggle, if it continues, can end only with the complete annihilation of one or the other of the two adversaries - Mr. Churchill may believe that this will be Germany. I know it will be Britain…I see no reason why this war must go on. I am grieved to think of the sacrifices which it will claim."

"What a load of rot!" Scoffed Tom.

"There's more." Said Richard.

"I don't think we want to hear any more of that, Richard." Beth firmly declared.

Half an hour later, Tom had gobbled down his breakfast, and disappeared upstairs to his bedroom whilst he waited for Richard to finish his meal. When Tom re-entered the kitchen he was proudly carrying a toy gun. He said.

"Come-on Richard, we've got a whole village to patrol."

Hannah glanced across cheekily at her brother.

"Looks like Tom's got you organized for the day, Richard," she turned to Beth. "What are we going to do today?"

"I've got to work on my sketch for the young artist's competition. It'll take me all morning. Sorry, Hannah," replied the other girl.

Emily spoke.

"Never mind, Hannah, I don't suppose that the boys will mind you tagging along with them."

"Yes," nodded Richard enthusiastically, "We can do with more soldiers, can't we Tom…?"

The two boys and Hannah left the farmhouse, Tom swinging the gun along at his side cockily. They sidestepped Oscar who was circling the farmyard energetically.

In the distance they could hear the sound of sheep bleating. It was another gloriously sunny day.

They headed into the village, passing Kenneth on their way outside the church. Tom led the group down a side road past tearooms, a quiet garage, and a handful of houses set back some distance from the road so that open country now lay in front of them. They halted next to a red phone box with the words GR on it, which was positioned outside the last houses. On the other side of the road, lay a cricket field, with a whitewashed wooden pavilion and a sunscreen standing on the neatly cut grass, a picture of serenity. The road ahead followed the contours of the land, and dipped then climbed away into the distance, where a cluster of buildings from a neighbouring village rested on a hilltop a mile or so away. Hannah and Richard looked at Tom with expectation.

"Richard," he began, his voice authoritative and bossy. "Now, you stand guard here and let me know as soon as you see any Germans."

"But, how will I know what they look like?" Richard asked.

After a moment's pause his friend replied.

"You won't really see any Germans —well, I hope not- it's just pretend!"

"Right." Richard nodded.

"Then, what's the point of him standing here?" Questioned Hannah.

Tom sighed.

"Look! We've got to be seen to do our bit for the village."

Tom left them for a few moments to go searching in the roadside undergrowth. With his back turned, Hannah remarked to her brother.

"He does take this rather seriously, doesn't he?"

Tom paced up to the boy and girl, and thrust something solid into Richard's hand.

"You'll need this!"

Richard peered down.

"It's a stick."

"I haven't got any more guns, Richard, you'll just have to patrol with this instead." Explained the other boy.

"Why have I got to stand by this silly phone box?"

"Questions, questions!" Tom shook his head.

"It's an important communication point. Can't you see that when —if- the Germans land, they'll come straight for here?"

"Oh!"

"Tom's not trying to worry you," said Hannah disdainfully.

Tom put his hands on his hips.

"Any more mumbling from you two, and I'll have you peeling potatoes in the guardhouse for the next week! Have you got that Privates Baker and Baker?"

"Yes sir," chorused the pair.

It did not go unnoticed to Tom that Hannah was struggling to suppress laughter. Tom stroked his chin and addressed the girl. "In fact, for your cheek, Hannah, you can stand guard here too with Richard. Right, I'm off to rope the twins into patrolling the village." As he stomped off, he added, "And you can find your own stick!"

The two siblings were left alone. They watched with mild fascination a bird as it paced atop the sunscreen, like a tightrope dancer. They caught a glimpse of a fox, which disappeared back into a hedge as quickly as it had emerged. During the following twenty minutes, whilst the pair stood resignedly by the phone box, the only sign of activity was that of a farmer leading a horse into a distant field. As time dragged on, and with the German Army's failure to put in an appearance, any thoughts that Richard entertained of his bravely fending off the enemy in the little streets of England, soon disappeared. He kicked the ground a couple of times.

"I'm fed up of standing here! Nothing's happening at all."

"I'm beginning to wish that I'd stayed at home with my French book," lamented Hannah.

"I'd rather be playing with Tom's toy soldiers."

"I wander what mummy and daddy are up to at the moment," the girl thought aloud. Through half-closed eyes she let her thoughts wander back to home, and for a few blissful moments she enjoyed being back in the living room with their parents. She said.

"I wander if daddy's still smoking that filthy pipe?"

Richard smiled back at her, only half-listening. He was thinking back to the days when he would play football in the city streets, with his mates Billy and Johnny and gain a few cuts and bruises in the rough and tumble. Still, despite changing circumstances, Richard had enjoyed a number of games in the village, as well. His sister spoke, once more.

"Do you realize that we've been here nearly a year, Richard?"

"Yes," the boy nodded. "I like it here though. Don't you?"

"Yes, I do." She smiled. "I really like Beth and Tom, all the Pavitt family are nice."

Richard sat down cross-legged on the ground, and the boredom began to set in once more. At that timely moment, one of the villagers, a smartly dressed lady in her mid-thirties appeared, to make use of the phone box. She gave the pair, who she had not met before, a warm smile, and asked kindly.

"What are you two children up to?"

"We're protecting this phone box from the Germans," explained Richard in a very innocent way.

"Really?" The lady raised her eyebrows; she was an attractive looking brunette with her hair arranged on top of her head restrained with a ribbon, and an excellent complexion. She continued. "Well, I think I can safely say that you won't see any Germans today, they would have appeared by now."

"Yes, I think so too," agreed Hannah. She suggested to Richard that they go. He readily agreed, and they left the friendly lady to make her phone call.

They caught up with Tom, again, who was marching badly along the main street with a reluctant Edward in tow. Hannah wandered what happened to the twins that

Tom had supposed to be recruiting. Tom expressed his disappointment that brother and sister had deserted their post. Edward, nursing a nasty bruise on his arm, complained that Tom had struck him with his toy gun, something about him joking that he was a Fifth Columnist.

"Oh! Tom!" Hannah gave the boy a parental look of disapproval.

"So I got a bit carried away!" He confessed.

"Well, I'm off now that you two are here, I'm needed at the post office." With that, Edward straightened his glasses, and walked away.

"See you tomorrow. Edward." Richard called after him.

They came to the far end of the village, near the station. The sun, a powerful golden orb in the sky was nearing its zenith, and the road on the outskirts of the village was hot and dusty. Hannah wiped her brow.

"I could do with a drink."

Something, or rather someone had caught Tom's attention.

"What's going on here, then?" He pounded the gun against the palm of his hand, like a schoolmaster ready to use the cane, as he viewed a detached house further up the road with narrow eyed suspicion.

"Tom, I hope this isn't just another wild goose chase," declared Hannah.

"No, wait," said Tom, before he made off in the direction of the house he had in his sights. Walking at first, he then broke into a sprint, with Hannah and Richard following a little distance behind, grumbling about overexerting themselves, probably for some stray cat, in the heat. Tom went into a driveway and out of view.

Panting, Richard reached the driveway just before his sister and halted besides a bush. Hannah appeared next to him, and rested a hand on his shoulder. The sight that greeted them took them by surprise.

"Oh!" Exclaimed Richard.

"Tom! What are you doing?" Shouted the girl.

There was a bit of a kafuffle going on in the garden. Tom had a boy of similar age pinned down to the ground, and was thumping him as the other struggled to get free. As Richard and Hannah edged cautiously closer, Tom explained in broken sentences, as he caught his breath, that he had caught a flamin' German red handed as he tried to burgle a house.

"Tom, are you sure?" Asked Hannah. "I mean he's not wearing any uniform?"

With an accent that was clearly not English, the boy on the ground protested.

"H-help, pleazzee...!"

"Quiet, you German!" Ordered Tom, showing no mercy. "Hannah or Richard, go and get the policeman!"

Brother and sister looked at each other, neither quite knowing what to do. For, whomever Tom had apprehended, he was only a lad. The expression on Tom's face was becoming more strained, due to the physical effort needed to hold the boy down.

"What are you waiting for?" He pleaded.

Suddenly Clara entered the driveway. She was horrified at the scene, and demanded that Tom release the boy at once. Hannah was amazed at how resolute the other girl had now become.

"Tom, let him go, I can deal with this."

Tom gazed inquisitively at the girl; he was not totally convinced. But, when Clara walked up to the two boys, her strength of character was such it put paid to Tom's remaining doubts, and instead he began to feel a twinge of guilt. He slowly released his grip on the boy.

Clara helped the foreign boy to his feet, put her face close to his, and asked in a soft voice if he was all right after his ordeal. He nodded as he blew into a hanky, a little dazed. The figure before them wore dark shorts and a grey pullover. He had straight black hair, which was swept across the front of his round face, and brown eyes. The girl smoothed his clothes, frowning at the grass stains that had been caused by the village boy.

"Tom! You idiot!" Clara reprimanded him. She addressed all three of her friends. "This is David, he's a Jewish refugee from France. He fled to England a couple of months ago, fearing for his life when the Nazis were overrunning his country."

Tom avoided Clara's gaze, and stared dejectedly at the ground.

"Oh! I'm sorry." He uttered the words barely louder than a whisper.

Clara went on.

"David's father's missing, believed to be in a German prisoner of war camp. His mother had to stay behind in France."

"How awful," said a sympathetic Hannah.

"Why was he sneaking about, trying to climb in through that window, though?" Asked Tom.

"David's only just arrived in the village. Although this is where he now lives, I expect that he got locked out, as he doesn't yet have a key."

David nodded in agreement.

"It's a good job I came round to check on him," concluded Clara. The girl informed them that David had a fairly good grasp of the English language, and would be joining them at school next term. As she led the introductions, she said to Tom.

"I think you owe David an apology."

It took Richard longer than normal to get to sleep that night. As he lay semi-conscious he clutched the copy of Hitler's speech in his hand that was the first exciting discovery of that eventful day. He carefully placed the paper on the bedside table, like a piece of treasure. His thoughts wandered from Hitler's curious peace offer to the new arrival in the village. Poor David, what a pity that the French boy's first encounter with them should see Tom, in typical Tom manner getting the wrong end of the stick.

Across Britain, the population was equally unconvinced by the German leader's speech, which had fallen on deaf ears. Copies of Hitler's speech ended up being auctioned off in aid of the Red Cross. Hitler thought that the war was probably already won. His had been a sincere peace offensive, as he appreciated that further continuation of the war could be costly for both countries. If Britain and her Empire fell, then others, such as America and Japan would be the main beneficiaries. The 19ᵗʰ July speech was widely advertised throughout the world as 'Hitler's last appeal to reason', although it's essential tone was *make peace with Germany, or else face the consequences of the Luftwaffe!* . Hitler was baffled and disappointed that the British would not come to the peace table.

Air Chief Marshal Hugh Dowding, head of Fighter Command, was experienced, organized, and had led the R.A.F. forward technically since the mid 1930's. What he lacked in numbers, he would make up for in quality of aircraft. Also, he would only commit one or two squadrons against each enemy raid, so as not to gamble large numbers of precious fighters in one battle.

Production of British fighter aircraft was increasing month on month, although pilots were proving harder to replace. The R.A.F. had performed well against the Luftwaffe in July, however, eighty regular R.A.F. squadron and Flight Commanders had been killed or wounded during the month. Their experience could never be replaced, and the new replacement pilots needed time to train, time that the Luftwaffe would deny them. To help make up the shortfall, pilots from Poland and the Empire, including Australia, Canada, New Zealand and Rhodesia were helping to defend Britain.

On the German side, the Stuka dive-bombers had been shot down in large numbers. However, the Germans believed that the British must be close to defeat.

On 5ᵗʰ August 1940, Italy marched into British Somaliland, in the Horn of Africa. The defending British force numbered just a few thousand, and could only play for time. Two weeks later, the capital, Berbera, fell, and the British left the country. Elsewhere, in Africa, the Italians occupied a few border towns in British held Kenya and Sudan.

On Thursday 8ᵗʰ August 1940, the Luftwaffe began to attack Britain in force. The German aircraft first attacked at nine a.m., then at half-past nine, at half-past eleven, and again at half-past four in the afternoon. The enemy dive-bombers had attacked a shipping convoy off the Isle of Wight, and later, Bournemouth. A third of the ships in the convoy were sunk, and others were damaged. However, the Germans received a hammering by the R.A.F., losing twice as many aircraft shot down and also put out of action than the R.A.F., which lost eighteen. These sorts of successes would have to continue, for the R.A.F. had seven hundred serviceable fighters with which to defend Britain, against four times that number of German bombers and fighters. Since Dowding's planes were widely dispersed across Britain, the Luftwaffe might enjoy a local advantage of ten to one!

Days earlier, Hermann Goering, head of the German Air Force, had announced to his senior commanders that the R.A.F. would be destroyed in two phases. He boasted that the first, the destruction of R.A.F. Fighter Command in the south of England, would take just four days. The second phase, moving north across England to destroy the remainder of the R.A.F. would be completed in four weeks.

The next two days had been quiet, and in the village of Oak Green, there seemed to be more trouble with petty officialdom and the Home Guard (renamed from the Local Defence Volunteers), than with the German Airforce.

On their way to church, that Sunday (11th), Emily and the four children met up with Ethel Taylor, a raven-haired woman of forty-ish. Emily was acquainted with Ethel, as she had a daughter in the same class as Emily's children. Ethel, looking somewhat harassed, recalled that, the other day, she had been quietly going about the business of doing her shopping, when, seemingly from nowhere a member of the Home Guard appeared, and demanded to see her identity card.

"It was at the Hastings street junction. I found his manner quite abrasive." Ethel said. "I felt even more uncomfortable when I noticed that there were two more tin hatted figures, armed with a Bren gun, tucked behind a circular parapet of sandbags."

The four children looked at Ethel Taylor inquisitively. She went on.

"I suddenly recognized him as that retired Captain from Blackthorn lane. Well, he *must* have known who I was, but he would insist on verifying my identity."

Emily raised her eyebrows.

"Really?"

Ethel gripped Emily by the arm.

"Catherine Fayers was stopped by a patrol next to the station. It's as if we're being watched ninety-nine per cent of the time…I feel quite on edge."

Unseen, Tom smirked at Richard. Ethel Taylor was overreacting, and the farmer's wife did her best to prevent her from worrying unnecessarily.

"I'm sure that most of us will be stopped by the Home Guard sometime or another. It's to guard against Fifth Columnists." Emily said reassuringly. She hastily added, "Not that there's likely to be any spies around here."

"I do hope not."

At that timely moment, they passed a poster of a man telling his wife at breakfast, "Of course there's no harm in your knowing…" with Hitler eavesdropping under the table. At the bottom of the poster were the words "Careless talk costs lives".

The group entered the village church.

As had been the case over recent weeks, the place of worship had become increasingly full. Events on the Continent in June had dictated that. However, many parishioners also regarded this as an opportunity to socialize, and gain strength from a feeling of togetherness during these unsettling times. Mr. Bailey certainly cherished the size of the congregation, whistling away to himself as he prepared his papers at the pulpit.

Wearing her Sunday best, Hannah sat between her brother and Beth. Hannah found the atmosphere inside the church one of contrasts. The older members of the congregation always had a subdued and reflective air. They had lost husbands and sons in the Great War, and the current conflict must bring all that back to them. Most of the middle-aged people had sons serving in the army, navy or air force. Every week, parents would exchange news and ask after so-and-so serving on H.M.S. such-and-such. Often the news was bad, and Hannah would overhear the fateful words 'killed,' 'wounded' or 'missing in action.' At the opposite end of the age spectrum, the children –more so, those pre-teens- tended to be carefree and cheerful. Many did not truly understand the significance of what was going on around them. Perhaps, mused Hannah, ignorance was bliss.

"Hannah!" A voice from the back of the church caught the girl's attention. It was a silly giggly voice, and when Hannah turned round she spotted the twins seated several rows behind, with mischievous looks on their faces; they were obviously discussing girls, again. These were two admirers she could do without. Hannah glared at them, signaling her disapproval. Elsewhere, she noticed Clara and Nancy, who were deep in conversation. Nancy was saying how she was dreading mathematics when they returned to school. At the front of the church, Samantha, the princess, pretty as ever, was sorting through her hymn sheets ready to sing with the choir.

The service commenced. Mr. Bailey was an above average orator, and his war-dominated theme was moving. Now that German air attacks were becoming increasingly intense, British civilians were also in the front line. It was a time to be brave, and hold onto the belief of ultimate victory and a world free from Nazism and tyranny. Prayers were said for those men and women in the fighting services, with special mention of the pilots in the R.A.F. Mr. Bailey stressed that the German pilots, too, which had been shot down and killed, were also somebody's sons. The Germans believed in their cause, even though it was a misguided one.

A number of hymns were sung. The boys and girls enjoyed singing, and, Beth, Hannah, Richard, Tom and the other children all sang with fervour.

As the congregation poured out of the church, Richard's ears alerted him to the distinct roar of aircraft. As he blinked in the bright sunlight, his arm pointed skywards, for the benefit of the other children, to the distant sight of Hurricanes taking off. The crowd of people cheered.

To the West, the Hurricanes were racing to engage German aircraft that were attacking a coastal convoy. By the end of the day, the tally of German aircraft shot down would be twice the losses of British planes.

Monday 12th August, it was the turn of Dover, Portsmouth and the Isle of Wight. The Germans called the 13th August Eagle Day, as over 1,400 aircraft were launched against Britain. That day, Portsmouth and the Thames Estuary were hit. But, again, twice as many German planes were lost as British. Several hundred German aircraft were attacking each day. On 15th August, the German bombers penetrated far inland, to attack aerodromes.

Beth, Hannah, Richard and Tom were larking about in one of the fields. Tom was acting the goat with a stick of corn in his mouth, whilst the girls were taking delight in seeing how ticklish Richard was.

Up above, the aircraft twinkled like diamonds in the brilliant sunlight. There were patterns of white vapour trails all over the sky. Today, the aircraft were more numerous in number and a lot closer to the village. Maybe a quarter of a mile away, an enemy fighter aircraft tore past, at only a few hundred feet. The German plane was closely followed by a Spitfire, which was moving in for the kill.

The children became transfixed. Tom shouted.

"He'll get him!"

The two planes headed over some trees, then, as quickly as they appeared, passed out of sight.

"Coo!" went Richard.

The children excitedly sprinted home to report what they had seen to Beth and Tom's parents. They regretted that they did not know the ultimate outcome of the duel, but sensed that the Spitfire pilot would emerge the victor.

Late that night, a loud knock on the door announced that Ted had returned home during a spell on Home Guard duty. A bleary eyed Emily let her husband in, and as he entered the kitchen, there was more than a hint of excitement in his voice, and he evidently had some news to tell. The children, in their pyjamas, poured down the stairs and into the kitchen, eager to listen to Ted's story. Ted sat down at the kitchen table, whilst Emily hurriedly put the kettle on.

"We were patrolling along the road by old Skinner's fields near to the station." Ted recalled. "The twins' father, Joe, heard a rustling noise in one of the hedges, and, with his gun at the ready, challenged, rather dramatically, *Who goes there, friend or foe?* Well, this figure then emerges from the hedge, and starts speaking in broken English."

"What happened next?" Asked Emily.

"I shone the torch on him, and Joe then goes, *it's a bloody German!*"

"Really?"

Ted nodded, and gratefully took the mug of tea from his wife.

"He gave himself up without a fuss. He'd been shot down that day, and had managed to evade capture. However, he realized that he had no chance of getting back to Germany, and he'd probably broken his arm on landing. He was only a young lad of about twenty, and looked in a right bedraggled state. He must have been a reasonable pilot himself, though, as he'd shot down a couple of our planes the past month. He spoke briefly about his parents, showed us a picture of his younger sister, and expressed his surprise that, at this stage, England was still willing to fight the war. He offered us his cigarettes before the authorities came along and took him away."

The children looked admiringly at the man in khaki uniform. Beth and Tom's Dad had captured a real life German! Maybe it was even the pilot from 'their' plane that they had seen from the field earlier on that day. Everyone in the room felt proud of Ted; wait till the other kids at school heard about this!

The farmer went back outside, to conclude his spell of duty, and the children drifted back to their bedrooms. Suddenly, the war was becoming thrilling!

The newspaper headlines on 16th August claimed that 144 German aircraft had been shot down the previous day*. To the Luftwaffe, the 15th August became known as 'Black Thursday'. Luftflotte 5 operating from Norway had lost twenty per cent of their aircraft in one day. Losses of British aircraft had been put in the eighties. Britain had endured an unprecedented attack from the air, and sixty-two lives had been lost when Croydon Airport was bombed.

As she digested the news, Hannah felt the most optimistic she had been for months. The British were faring better in this air battle than the Germans. She reckoned that the Germans had had too much of an easy ride over the skies of Poland and France, now they were meeting their match over the British countryside.

Hannah considered herself fortunate to witness an epic air battle later that day. She was playing with her brother and Emily's children in the fields surrounding the farm.

High up in the air, there were two formations of enemy aircraft crossing the coast (several miles away). The first formation consisted of in excess of forty German bombers, the second, to the rear and approximately a mile higher up, comprised double that number of fighters.

Down on the ground, the children had never seen so many aircraft together at the same time. Richard observed the enemy formation, open-mouthed.

"Over a hundred aircraft. Coo!"

The German planes had passed by and were almost out of view, when two squadrons of British fighters charged up at right angles, to confront the menace.

The Spitfires and Hurricanes started to break up the bomber formation, and aircraft dispersed in every direction. A German Dornier spun down vertically out of control, and must have hit the ground with the most tremendous impact. Another bomber fell down to earth in a ball of flames. The German fighters screamed down to join the battle, and within moments, a Spitfire was shot down, an inferno of red-hot metal, emitting clouds of smoke.

The children turned their heads in every direction, so not to miss any of the action that was taking place at any height between a mile and five miles above them. The aircraft farthest away darted and twisted like little silver dots in the brilliant sunshine. They saw one stricken German plane jettison its bombs in a wood, in order to make its escape more quickly.

When the sky eventually became clear again, the children were bemused by what looked like dozens of pieces of brown paper descending down into a far corner of

---

* The true figure was actually 76 German and 35 British.

the field. The two boys hared across to retrieve these. Tom stood staring at one such piece, and as his sister appeared behind him, he declared.

"It's bits of aeroplane!"

Part of the black cross from a German plane was evident on one piece of metal. It all seemed rather gruesome to Beth and Hannah and they forbade Tom from taking a piece home as a trophy.

It was the third scramble of the day. The pilots were already fatigued from the earlier battles, and the aircraft had barely been rearmed and refuelled. One Spitfire had to remain on the ground, men swarming all over it like insects, patching up countless bullet holes.

Peter already had one kill, several hours ago –a Dornier bomber, and was now attempting to finish off a Heinkel 111 bomber, which just would not die. The aircraft had a crew of five, a speed of 275m.p.h., and was armed only with three machine-guns. Aeroplanes were zipping all over the place –British and German, although, as usual, the attackers heavily outnumbered the defenders.

An excited voice came over the RT.

"Crikey! That's Blue one going down!"

Blue one, Leslie Walker a damned good pilot, with two confirmed kills, and another two probables, Spitfire trailing smoke, no parachute; an experienced and valuable pilot lost for good.

Peter cursed, as he ran out of ammunition. The Heinkel had numerous bullet holes, but it did not appear to have suffered mortal damage, and would most likely limp back across the Channel to France.

A few miles below, the burning wrecks of other, less fortunate Heinkels glowed orange and red across the English countryside.

Suddenly, Peter sighted a Messerschmitt 109 in his rear-view mirror. The German plane was in hot pursuit of the Spitfire, and Peter could see tracer flash by his wings. He took evasive action; sky and earth, left and right, up and down, alternated at fractions of a second. He violently pulled the Spitfire round in a tight circle. The 109's guns flashed, as it followed the Spitfire into a tight merry-go-round.

As the Spitfire turned, so too did the Messerschmitt in hot pursuit. Three bullet holes appeared in the glass around the cockpit, somehow missing Peter. Holding the plane in such a tight turn was extremely demanding; he could not take too much more of this punishment.

More daylight began to appear between the two aircraft, and finally the 109 gave up the chase, unable to compete with a Spitfire on a turn that tight. The sky was now curiously empty of aircraft, so Peter dropped down almost to ground level, in order to fly home undisturbed.

Back on the ground, there was the usual excited talk with the other pilots.

"Did you see 'my' Heinkel go down?" Grinned Percy. Very animated, he then added. "Exploded-BOOM!"

Sometime afterwards, Harold Fowler's Spitfire loomed into view above the tops of trees bordering the airfield. Smoke was trailing from the aircraft, and the personnel on the ground watched with apprehension, as it swooped in a few meters above the field. The Spitfire landed unevenly, bumping along the ground, and came to a halt enveloped in smoke.

A staggering figure emerged from the grey cloud, and ground crew rushed across to assist him. It emerged that the pilot had been shot up. His injuries had been that serious that he had had to land semi-conscious and one handed, juggling throttle control, control column, flap control, under-carriage control! With good humour, Harold swore that he had left the German aircraft in a worse state.

That day (16th August), the first Victoria Cross to be won by a fighter pilot had been gained by Flight-lieutenant James Nicolson, who continued to engage and shoot down an enemy fighter, whilst his cockpit was on fire. With complete disregard for his own safety, he sustained serious burns to his hands, face, neck and legs.

CHAPTER 11 – THE HARDEST FEW WEEKS

In front of the dispersal hut, the pilots sat, some in deckchairs, some on the dry yellow-green grass. A short distance away, at the perimeter of the airfield, the Spitfires stood proud. A couple of the men were reading, two more were playing a game of draughts, some were dozing under the hot rays of the sun. They were all in their late teens or early twenties, a magnificent group of men, brave and dutiful. They were all strained and tired, waiting for that sound…waiting for the telephone to ring. Peter thought of a 'normal day'…

Being woken at 4 a.m. by his batman, armed with a cup of tea. Then snatching a bit of breakfast in the dining room, each man silent, in quiet contemplation. Next, clambering into a vehicle and being driven round the perimeter track in the semi-darkness, to dispersal. At the locker, collecting the helmet, parachute and life jacket. Out there, at that early hour, it is very still and peaceful –the calm before the storm and the killing that will inevitably come later. The silence is broken; as the ground crew has the starter trolleys wired up to the aircraft, and quietly go about the task of starting up the Spitfires. One by one they roar into life, and blue flame comes out of the exhausts. The ground shudders. The engines of the magnificent aircraft are kept running for a further few minutes to warm them up, an impressive sight. Then comes the waiting.

He was doing it for Britain. First the British sailors had been bombed, followed by the people in coastal towns, and now their very own R.A.F. personnel were being targeted. If the Germans were to be allowed to continue this madness, then *who next*…the milk floats? Buses? Schools? Peter knew one pilot who had seen a Jerry aircraft jettison its bombs over the village where his parents lived, and of the resulting hatred that had boiled inside him.

The call to scramble came, cards, books, magazines and chairs went flying, and the pilots were sprinting out to their aircraft, rubbing bleary eyes, in the race to get airborne.

Peter watched as the propeller turned slowly at first, then it blazed into life with a cough and a cloud of smoke. Voices came over the radio, and one of the ground crew unplugged the starter battery.

The previous day, the German aircrews took some respite, and so no enemy aircraft had appeared in the skies above Great Britain. However, the lull in German activity only lasted twenty-four hours, for today, the 18th August, the Luftwaffe unleashed what they hoped would be the killer blow.

How many of the attacking bastards would they have to fend off today? Which Spitfires wouldn't return? Peter shut such thoughts out of his mind. The Spitfire was airborne.

Ever confident, Archie North talked to the pilots over the RT.

Peter searched the sky for aircraft.

There was no time to relax. Sandy's voice came over the RT.

"Bandits at one o'clock!"

The German aircraft still some distance away, were a few thousand feet above the British. Typical! The Spitfires would have to attack from below, which was less favourable.

Initially, Peter could only make out a handful of aircraft. However, a mass of dots quickly began to fill the sky. Swarms of bees. *Crikey!* Thought Peter. *How many Jerry aircraft in total were there? Never mind, just get on with the job old chap, and take down as many of them with you as you can.*

There were over thirty German Dornier bombers approaching in such a tight formation that they might as well be glued together. Meanwhile, up above in the sun, spots of twinkling lights ominously signified roughly the same number of Jerry fighter aircraft. Against this was pitted a squadron of just twelve Spitfires.

The British tactic was to break up the neat formation of enemy bombers, so that in smaller groups they no longer had the benefit of strength in numbers. Ideally, the leader (bomber) would be shot down, since he was the pathfinder for the raid.

Both Peter's feet were on the rudder bar, his left hand on the throttle and his right on the firing button. Peter maintained his gaze on the approaching enemy aircraft. His lips set in a thin line, he switched his gun button from 'safe' to 'fire'. Amid cries of 'Tally-ho!' the British tore into the bomber formation.

As he went into his attack, Peter took a quick glance above, to check for the position of the German fighters. Thankfully, they seemed content to remain circling higher up. Teeth clenched, Peter got a Dornier in his gun-sights and pressed the firing button. The tracer initially floated into the sky, then moved faster and faster towards the German aircraft. He kept his thumb on the button for three seconds. He felt the Spitfire nose dip slightly under the recoil.

"Take that, you bloody German!" He muttered, as the plane with the black crosses on it became peppered with holes.

Coolant began to stream out of the Dornier. The gun barrels poking out of the rear of the aircraft slanted upwards, signifying that the gunner had been neutralized. Peter closed in, and fired a short, rapid burst into it. The Dornier staggered. The Spitfire closed right in, and finished the enemy plane off, as it dropped down out of formation. Moments later, there were three puffs of white, indicating that the rest of the crew had survived and they would parachute down to certain captivity.

"Watch out for the snappers!"* An excited voice came over the RT.

Peter could not afford even a momentary lapse in concentration. A glance in his rear-view mirror revealed that the fighters –ME 109's had now descended from above. The sky was raining German aircraft, and two of them were hot on Peter's tail!

The ME 109's were firing away furiously, yet they were still too far behind to hit the Spitfire with any accuracy. The Germans were wasting their ammunition prematurely, however, they were gaining fast on Peter's Spitfire. Peter could feel his heart pounding away. Suddenly, two holes appeared in the Spitfire's wing.

---

* ME 109s

Sandy's Spitfire tore across the sky, and fired a deadly burst at a right angle into one of the 109's, which immediately fell away. Its dive became ever steeper until it was plunging away to its doom at terrific speed in a vertical dive.

Seizing his chance, Peter turned his aircraft as hard to the left as he possibly could. The second ME 109, its pilot unnerved by the appearance of Sandy's Spitfire, overshot Peter's plane.

Peter laughed. It was an automatic reaction; had it not been for the intervention of Sandy's aircraft, Peter knew that he would most likely have been shot down, maybe killed. He was still in one piece in his killing machine -the German was not. One day, perhaps, the German would be the luckier of the two. It all seemed too unreal.

Fighters were rolling, zooming, banking and firing through a network of tracer bullets all over the sky. The Spitfires were still heavily outnumbered –the odds were against them, but they were defending their country. * Peter was transformed from the hunted into the hunter. He chased the ME 109, and fired a short burst, as the target became bigger and bigger. The pilot of the ME 109 took evasive action.

Peter emptied his guns into the Jerry aircraft, which slowly began to lose height. The enemy pilot would perhaps make it back to France. That ME 109 would have to be declared as a 'probable.'

Slightly frustrated at the uncertain fate of that second ME 109, Peter took his aircraft down almost to ground level, and headed home. He overheard excited voices and much shouting over the RT, indicating that elsewhere the battle was still raging. The pilot wondered who would have gained the upper hand –the Spitfires or the German enemy.

Back at the airfield, he learnt that three Spitfires had gone down. Two of the pilots had managed to make it home safely, but the third, Johnny Turner had 'bought it'…plane went down, no parachute. He had only joined the squadron six days ago –the poor bugger.

Percy's Spitfire was last to return to the airfield. As the plane came to a halt, the hood flew back, and the pilot's head appeared over the side. He theatrically wiped his brow. Peter and Sandy trotted over to the aircraft along with a couple of ground crew. Peter asked.

"Where the devil have you been?"

"What kept you?" Enquired Sandy, he added, "The C.O. was getting worried."

"The Spit's taken a bit of damage," Peter observed.

Percy revealed all.

"Had a spot of trouble throwing off a 109 that was fixed on my tail."

"So, what happened?" Probed Sandy.

"I flew down to treetop height, to find myself confronted by a set of power lines. I just managed to get under them in time, the 109 wasn't so lucky, his propeller cut right through the cables and he hit the ground."

"That's a hell of a lot of volts!" Said Peter.

"It sure was, and it was a damn close call for myself..." as Percy went on to tell them twice more later on that night in the bar.

Hundreds of German aircraft had attacked Southeast England. The sky was filled with a maze of white vapour trails, as aircraft, droning, roaring and screaming did battle. In the middle of the day, the Luftwaffe attacked Biggin Hill and Kenley airfields. Coastal air bases such as Gosport and Thorney Island were bombed, and even a passenger train came under fire.

The following day, Beth and Hannah set out for an early morning cycle ride. As they came up to the newsagents, Hannah beckoned to her friend to slow down. The newspaper headlines had caught her attention.

ANOTHER 115 DOWN -heralded The Daily Express.

NAZI'S WORST DEFEAT: 140 RAIDERS DOWN! The News Chronicle proclaimed.

Losses of British aircraft were put at a fraction of these figures.

Hannah cycled off with a big grin on her face. With quiet confidence, she thought *we'll beat them!*

Tuesday 20th August 1940, the Prime Minister paid tribute to the R.A.F. pilot's performance in the Battle of Britain. He said to Parliament, and the nation.

"Never in the field of human conflict was so much owed by so many to so few."

In buoyant mood, Winston Churchill detailed that two million soldiers protected Britain against invasion.

"...Rifles and bayonets in their hands."

The House of Commons cheered.

Beth and Hannah were returning from an afternoon cycle ride. They perspired under the fiercely burning sun, and every time they breathed in they inhaled warm air. The girls decided to dismount, and walk the remaining distance back to the farm, at a leisurely pace. The sky was blue and cloudless, and yellow corn stood tall in the fields, and trees, in full bloom were alive with the sound of birds.

In the air battles the previous day, Saturday 24th August, the Luftwaffe had lost forty aircraft to the R.A.F.'s nineteen. The Germans had bombed a number of airfields in Kent. On Thursday, the German gun batteries on the French coast had shelled Dover, sending its inhabitants scurrying for shelter.

As the girls came round a bend in the road, Hannah observed.

"Isn't that Tom, up ahead, by the pond?"

Beth strained her eyes at the crouching figure in grey shorts.

"Yes, it certainly looks like my brother. I wander what he's doing?" The girl hastened her step.

The pair approached Tom, who had his back to them, unseen. They were now right behind the boy. Hannah opened her mouth to speak, when Tom spun his arm round twice like a windmill, bent down on one knee, and released what looked like a cricket ball.

"Tom?" Beth addressed her brother.

The two girls watched in fascination, the path of the ball, as it bumped along the road surface. The ball rolled between three curious metal objects standing upright at the edge of the road, adjacent to the pond, then slowed and came to a halt. A couple of ducks sat in the parched grass between the pond and road, uninterested in the boy's antics.

Tom turned round and scowled at the girls.

"Look what you did! You made me miss!"

"No I didn't." Beth retorted. "I spoke after you released the ball!"

Hannah nodded in agreement.

The boy was evidently playing a game of skittles, of sorts. But, what were those strange metal objects that he was using as bowling pins?

The girls lay their bicycles down gently at the roadside. Beth walked across to inspect the peculiar cylindrical objects; she picked one up, and frowned at it, before replacing it on the ground.

"Where did you find these?" She asked her brother.

Tom strolled across, with his hands in his pockets, and an air of nonchalance.

"Nowhere in particular, just down the lane," he added. "If you want one, it'll cost you."

Beth turned to her friend.

"Hannah, come and have a look at these. Are they what I think they are?"

Hannah examined the metal objects. She confirmed, as Beth suspected, that they were the tails of German one-kilogram incendiary bombs. Normally eighteen inches in length, all that remained of the stick bombs, which were in Tom's possession, were just a fraction of that size.

Beth looked at Tom accusingly.

"They're parts of incendiaries."

"I know that," said Tom indignantly. "There's probably lots more in the fields near where I found them."

Hannah spoke.

"A German raider must have jettisoned them in panic over open country."

Tom retrieved the ball, and chucked it repeatedly up and down in the air, impatiently.

"Well, these bits aren't going to do anybody any harm, now…"

The girls had to agree.

"So, do you two want to play skittles, then?"

Hannah looked at Beth for an answer.

"Oh! Go on then, just a quick game." Said the latter. The girl snatched the ball off Tom, took up position, and wiped her brow. She released the ball, and it struck one 'skittle'.

"Oh! Well done, Beth." Hannah applauded her friend.

"Not bad," said Tom.

The twins, Harry and Henry appeared. Harry nudged his brother in the side.

"There's that Hannah…Cor! Look at those legs!"

"I wouldn't mind a bit of her." Said Henry, cheekily."

"You can dream!" Scoffed Harry. "You stick to tubby Clara."

"Harry, Henry!" Tom welcomed the twins with an impish grin. Pointing at the skittles, he asked. "Wanna play?"

As one, the twins cast a sly glance at Hannah, and nodded enthusiastically-anything to be near to her.

"Now, whose turn is it?" Enquired Tom, taking charge.

"It must be Hannah's?" Suggested Beth.

Hannah smiled bashfully.

"Oh! No. I want to let Tom have another go —see how the expert does it."

Tom aligned the pins then walked back to the group. He took aim, with a concentrated frown on his face. He let go of the ball with a powerful release of energy, so that it bounced along the ground, initially. The ball hit home with one of the rear pieces of incendiary, and sent the metal rolling into the middle of the road, just as a car rounded the bend, by the war memorial.

"Oh!" Gasped Hannah.

The twins sniggered in amusement.

The vehicle swerved, although the metal rolled under the car, and the vehicle came to an abrupt halt.

Tom bit his lip, guilt written all over his face.

A middle-aged man, with an angry look on his face, got out of the car. He strode over to Tom, and scolded the boy. Worse was to come, as before he departed, the man collected the pins, declaring that they were vital scrap metals that could be put towards aircraft manufacture. He drove off; leaving Tom red faced, and deprived of his game.

There remained four days left in August 1940. Peter, on a day's leave, was paying a visit to the farm. After having enjoyed tea consisting of cold meat and salad, followed by home made cake, the pilot sat in the lounge, talking to his two young cousins, and Hannah and Richard about his exploits…

Peter explained that the typical German aircraft that he was fighting against, at the moment, were the Dornier Bomber, nicknamed the 'flying pencil', because of its long, slender fuselage, and the ME 109 single-seater fighter plane.

"The Spitfire, which I fly, can go at speeds in excess of three-hundred and sixty miles per hour." Peter continued. "My plane is armed with eight machine-guns, and can fire over a thousand rounds each minute."

"Coo!" Said Richard.

The children sat listening at Peter's feet with wide-eyed interest.

"Is it true that the reason why the Germans are losing more aircraft than us, is because we've got the best pilots?" Hannah asked.

"No! Harry says the Germans can't train their pilots very well, 'cos they've got no petrol!" Laughed Tom.

Peter smiled.

"The Royal Air Force has got a splendid organization behind us pilots, to provide support. Ground crew, the observer Corps, aircraft factory workers, Women's Auxiliary Air Force…they all provide marvellous assistance. The Spitfire itself is more manoeuvrable than either the ME109 or ME110, and can out-turn both of them." The pilot added. "Although, yes, the R.A.F. do also have the best pilots!"

The group looked at Peter with admiration. The R.A.F. officer was their hero, sitting right there in the Pavitt's very own living room!

"How many German pilots have you killed?" Tom enquired.

Emily, who had just entered the room, rebuked her son.

"Thomas! Don't ask questions like that."

After a momentary silence, Peter began his reply.

"It's alright. I wouldn't like to say it's a case of how many Germans one can *kill*." Peter placed particular emphasis on the last word. He paused, as he gathered his thoughts. "It's hard to explain what it's like when one is up there, doing battle – machine against machine. It's vital to spot the enemy before he spots you."

The children leaned in closer. Peter continued, his tone of voice matter of fact rather than boastful, but also showing no hint of regret.

"I myself, have shot down three enemy aircraft for definite, and another three 'probables', which means that the German plane might or might not have staggered back across the sea to France. Often the enemy crew survive; they parachute out of the plane to safety." He chuckled. "Although, then they end up in one of our prisoner of war camps!

The children laughed with the pilot. He studied their faces, and hoped sincerely that the war would be over before they too (or the boys, at least), would be old enough to fight, in a few years. The two girls and two boys were clearly fascinated by his experiences, and he felt no compulsion to stop; he would refrain from going into any particular gruesome details. The conversation was such that Peter talked freely, with interruptions from the children only when they asked questions.

"When I have my thumb on the firing button, it's more a case of shooting at an aircraft with black crosses on it, rather than firing at the individual men inside it." Peter added, his eyes narrowing, his voice unfaltering. "I do intensely dislike those German pilots –dropping their huge bloody bombs on innocent English civilians down below. I've also lost a number of my friends from the squadron –all of them good men, not many years older than you- one can not easily forgive them for that."

Peter's eyes met with Hannah's. As if feeling obliged to offer some sort of response, the girl said.

"How awful that must be for you…"

"It isn't easy. But, one mustn't dwell, that makes it harder. You have to maintain a grip on yourself."

"The sort of British stiff upper lip?" Suggested Beth.

"Yes. I suppose so."

Peter thought back to the easier days of July, when they had had rich pickings with the Stukas. Then, the British aircraft had become more and more outnumbered, as July turned to August, and losses of British airmen mounted.

Peter then posed the children a question. "I've never really thought of it, until now. I don't know what you make of these air battles from down below in the streets and houses. But, can you see much of the fighting from the ground?"

It was Hannah that replied.

"Yes. We –I find it all very exciting."

The boys nodded.

"It's brilliant." Richard added.

Tom recalled the time they witnessed the tiny pieces of aeroplane fall to earth, and Beth detailed her father's accounts of the captured German airmen. The R.A.F. officer listened with interest.

Peter enlightened them with a recent amusing incident.

"One day Archie North –that's our Commanding Officer- was about to reprimand us for breaking RT silence, when he realized that he was listening not to British but German voices! By chance, both the Germans and ourselves were using the same frequency! Well, we soon surprised the blighters, and the next thing we heard over the RT was *Achtung Spitfuern!*"

Beth asked her cousin if he had a girlfriend.

Peter shook his head.

"No. It's rather difficult at the moment, what with each day being so intense. It would also be a little irresponsible, if one got too involved with a girl, and then one got killed in action… Saying that, a couple of the chaps at the base have got lady friends." Peter's eyes misted over, "I can dream about the famous actresses. I adore Greta Garbo."

Richard chirped up.

"Oh! I like her."

Tom pulled a face.

It came time for the pilot to leave. Emily, Peter and the children made their way to the kitchen. They lingered by the outside door for a few minutes.

Peter smiled and cast his eyes down to the children.

"Well, Cousins Beth and Tom, it's been good to see you two, again. How you've both grown." Peter turned his attention to the Baker children. "It's been a pleasure to meet you, Hannah and Richard."

The children beamed back. They had both instantly liked Peter, and found his stories captivating.

Peter addressed Tom.

"I expect you to look after your sister and Hannah"-

137

Hannah interrupted the pilot.

"Tom look after us!" She laughed. "It's more the other way round —he's the one that needs looking after!"

Tom looked at Hannah indignantly. The girl suddenly found that all eyes were on her, and she began to feel embarrassed by her outburst, even though it had a ring of truth to it. Peter spoke.

"Yes, you're probably right, there."

Tom shrugged his shoulders. His sister rubbed his hair playfully.

Peter held his gaze on Hannah, and the girl's cheeks started to redden. The pilot was nice. No, *very* nice. Hannah could only describe herself as mesmerized by him. She had never regarded any of the boys at school in this way; he looked so handsome. Those few moments, she felt dizzy, ecstatic, but also ashamed. If the others found out —they would just think of her as a silly schoolgirl with a hopeless crush!

Emily put her arms around the pilot.

Peter hugged his aunt tenderly, and as he released his grip, she said.

"Please, do be careful."

Peter hugged both his cousins in turn, and then patted Richard on the shoulder, like an older brother. Lastly, he came to Hannah.

Hannah thought that she was going to die. She held her mouth slightly open, and her eyes flickered across Peter's as he gently placed his right arm around her back and leaned into her. Peter kissed the side of Hannah's face, and the girl momentarily closed her eyes; she felt electrified.

Peter promised Emily that he would pay the family a visit, again, soon, before the farmhouse door closed shut behind him, and he departed into the night.

They'd been up since dawn, ensuring that the Spitfires were airworthy, and would work through to dusk, with only half a day off in ten. The previous night, he'd cleaned and oiled each of the eight machine gun barrels on Peter's aircraft. Between sorties, he would remove empty boxes of ammunition from the aircraft and re-load the guns in just three or four minutes. The 30th August, Neville was out in the open field, along with Andy, the airframe fitter, and Bob, the engine fitter, servicing a Spitfire. The planes could no longer be kept in the hangars, because then they could all be destroyed together in a raid.

For Neville, the Spitfire was a difficult aircraft to service, as most of his work was done on his knees under the wing, causing his arms and neck to ache. He'd also cut his hands on the sharp edges of the gun panels. The ground crew was full of admiration for the pilots, and was always anxious when the Spitfires were up in action. When a pilot died, his ground crew felt it deeply.

During the frenzied summer months, once they'd finished working, the ground crew walked just over a mile to the nearest village for a couple of pints each before closing time. The Red Lion was a good place to unwind, being cosy and the atmosphere friendly and noisy. If the young men were lucky, a few of the local girls might be there to talk to. Indeed, Andy had struck up a blossoming friendship with an eighteen year old farmer's daughter, and had started to see her on his half day off.

The air raid siren had barely sounded when the German bombers appeared. The R.A.F. personnel hoped that they would not receive the same treatment as Manston. That Fighter Command airfield had been bombed repeatedly since 13th August. One hundred and fifty high explosive and fragmentation bombs had been dropped on Manston creating a mushroom cloud that had climbed up thousands of feet into the air. The workshops and two hangars had been hit. Morale had plummeted, and some ground crew had refused to leave the shelters.

Neville, Andy and Bob worked up to the last possible moment. As the enemy aircraft thundered into view, Neville and the rest of the ground crew broke away from the Spitfire, before lying down on the grass, some distance away. Closer to the hangars, terminal and other buildings, other R.A.F. personnel threw themselves into slit trenches. It was a terrifying ordeal for the men pinned down out in the open. A man too close to the parked aircraft would be blown up, whereas someone too far away risked being machine gunned; they were sitting ducks.

Some pilots managed to get their Spitfires into the air in the nick of time, others were not so fast moving. In blind panic, Richard Speares, the newest pilot to the squadron, careered his plane into a parked Spitfire.

The German bombers flew terrifyingly low over the airfield, with their bomb doors visibly open. Chin resting hard on the ground, Neville could make out an enemy aircraft strafing with machine gun fire first one parked Spitfire, then another. A couple more German planes roared over the buildings, dropping bombs. Several explosions came from that area, causing large amounts of concrete and masonry to come crashing down to earth. Thick black smoke began to climb up into the sky, from the buildings.

A couple of brave ground crew tried firing at the enemy aircraft with their Lee Enfield rifles, however they discovered it was difficult to hit a target moving at such speed. A corporal, half-standing, fired once, and cursing as he struggled to reload in the mayhem, was struck by an unseen enemy bullet. He collapsed to the ground. A man nearby wriggled over to the body and, his face ashen, said to no one in particular.

"Bloody hell! They've got old Sid!"

Ack-ack guns, located near to the airfield, to defend it, were going ten to the dozen, chattering away. Neville was somewhat concerned to find that chunks of shrapnel from these guns were descending down on the field all around him! Ammunition had been set off in burning Spitfires, causing a staccato sound as bullets flew around in every direction, creating added terror.

Concrete was being thrown up into the air as one aircraft deposited its bombs on the airfield's entrance road, leaving behind a nasty crater. Vehicles bounced up and down on their wheels from the force of the explosions. A few fields away, a German bomber crashed to the ground, a smouldering wreck. Neville wandered when the hell would end.

When, at last, it was all over, everyone rallied round to clear up the devastation. Craters needed to be filled in, unexploded bombs had to be located and human casualties given prompt medical assistance. The entire airbase looked a mess.

As he walked over to the buildings, Neville passed dazed R.A.F. personnel, climbing out of the slit trenches. Their uniforms were dirtied and bloodied, some were clearly injured, but they put a brave face on it. An officer staggered out of an office, fighting for breath in a blue cloud of smoke; where maps had fallen from the walls, files had been blown from cabinets and debris covered everything. At the edge of a bomb crater, lay two bodies; they looked a grim sight, but at least their deaths must have been instantaneous. It made it no easier for the survivors, a rigger, a young lad of about twenty collapsed kneeling beside one corpse and said, distraught.

"My...my...girlfriend!"

Three aircraft on the ground had been damaged beyond repair, half the buildings lay in ruins, the mains electricity and gas supplies were both down and bullets or shrapnel had damaged every vehicle on the airbase.

Neville noticed a WAAF in some distress. In earlier days, the airmen disliked the WAAF's for wearing "their" uniform, but now they were all in it together. During air raids at this, and other airfields, WAAF plotters, switchboard operators, anti-gas squads and first aid workers had all been on duty, ensuring that the base continued to run smoothly, keeping their nerve during the crisis. WAAF's had had the courage to continue working despite plotting tables being semi-destroyed by bombs and masonry. Neville gently placed his arm around the sobbing girl to comfort her, and shook his head mournfully.

In the skies above, Sandy was having his own personal battle. His Spitfire was in serious difficulty, having been bounced by a couple of 109s. A bullet followed by several more in quick succession entered his side. He unwillingly loosened his grip on the controls. Then things began to happen in slow motion. He became oblivious to the melee around him, the enemy fighters swooping in for the kill, all wanting a piece of him this easy prey. There was little blood, no pain, a drowsiness, a feeling of floating, a vision of a young boy stroking a playful dog, he was in a thick white cloud so dense that he could no longer see the Spitfire's nose or wings, he lost all sensation of speed. He was no longer afraid, and there were his Grandparents waiting to meet him...and then nothing.

...Peter picked up the receiver, and viewed the dial with a hollow empty expression. Outside, it was throwing it down and in darkness, which summed up his mood, as he dialed the number. He was dreading breaking this news. A female voice that of the widow answered the phone.

"Rose, it's Peter," he said in monotone voice.

"Oh! Hi, Peter."

"Rose, I'm so sorry..."

Sandy had married her just days before. The pilot was close to breaking down himself.

As the first anniversary of the outbreak of war approached, bombs were inadvertently dropped on Central London, on the evening of 24th August (Hitler had declared the capital out of bounds). In response, the next night, the R.A.F. bombed Berlin. An enraged Hitler ordered that the Luftwaffe set about destroying London and other British cities. On 27th August, the Germans launched night raids against twenty-one British towns and cities. Worryingly, the defending Blenheim night fighters did not get a single contact with the enemy. A major air attack on London was inevitable and imminent.

September 1940 would bring terror to an even greater number of British civilians.

As September approached, British losses were mounting. On 31st August forty British fighters were destroyed, nine pilots killed and eighteen badly wounded, the heaviest losses so far. However, not one important Fighter Command airfield had been closed, despite the bombing. Until lately, Luftwaffe target recognition and navigation had been surprisingly bad, although now the Germans were beginning to carry out their attacks with greater skill and better tactics. It was ominous that hundreds of self-propelled barges had recently been moving down from Dutch and German harbours to ports of Northern France.

On 4th September, Hitler spoke at a rally in Berlin, and raised the prospect of an invasion of Great Britain.

"In England they're filled with curiosity and keep asking, *Why doesn't he come?* Be calm." Hitler declared. "He's coming! He's coming!"

The Messerschmitt loomed large, guns blazing, moving head-on towards Peter's Spitfire, at well over three hundred miles an hour. Peter quickly reacted by pressing the firing button, however, his guns fired only for a mere half second –he was out of ammunition. A sitting duck, bullets from the 109 poured into his Spitfire in abundance. A couple tore through his flying jacket, and into his upper arm. Peter winced with pain. The two fighter planes were now that close, and moving so fast, that collision seemed all but inevitable.

At the very last moment, the 109 swooped overhead, so near that Peter caught a brief glance of the German pilot. All that remained of the 109 was a white vapour trail.

Inside his cockpit, Peter's problems were just beginning. Flames emerged at his feet. He vainly attempted to put them out, but the fire demon took hold of the Spitfire, and very soon the whole cockpit (with Peter trapped inside), would be engulfed in flame. With escape from the plane offering the sole chance of survival, Peter tried desperately to open the canopy, but failed. His oxygen mask had become displaced and the escaping gas helped to feed the flames. His clothing was now on fire; this looked like the end. Peter, his skin blistering, began to scream in pain, the smell of burning flesh made him throw up, as the stricken aircraft plummeted to earth, rapidly, and belching out smoke; the most horrible way imaginable to die…

Peter sat bolt upright in the bed. His breathing was fast, and he was drenched with sweat. He blinked back a watery blur. The nightmare had been so vivid. The room was dark and melancholy. It was not yet five a.m. His sleep had become more disturbed of late. Nighttime invariably followed the pattern of nightmares about being trapped in the cockpit, or losing limbs and living out his remaining days as a cripple or the whole squadron being wiped out and him being the sole survivor. Trembling, his hand reached for the comfort of the light on the bedside table. It was a strain —indeed for every pilot- day after day, worse so during those long days of the summer, being woken before first light, and driven out in the pre-dawn to dispersal. Then, the anxious hours spent at dispersal, killing time, waiting for the fateful ring of the telephone. It became impossible to relax. There were often three or four sorties a day, the Spitfire squadron always seriously outnumbered. Then afterwards filling in the 'F form' combat report. Replacement pilots arriving more often than not, surviving only a handful of days, having spent pitifully few hours flying a Spitfire, prior to entering battle. Across Britain, some were even having to be trained with the squadrons, who themselves were short of both aircraft and time. Many of the surviving veterans had had more than one crash, and bore scars and burns. As squadrons had been rotated out of the main combat area, Fighter Command had actually lost four more aircraft than the Luftwaffe on 3rd September, although the R.A.F. won the air battles on the 4th and 5th September.

Since mid-July, six of the chaps had 'bought it' —that was six too many- good men. The deaths were never discussed, the remaining pilots detached themselves from it —they *had* to. But the deceased pilots were always toasted the evening of their death. An empty room containing the few earthly possessions, such as uniform, shaving kit, cigarette case and lighter, sporting equipment, photos served as a poignant reminder of a lost pal. Poor old Arthur Birch was the most recent to get 'the chop'. Slightly eccentric, in a very English sort of way, charming, a real ladies man -poor old Arthur. But one didn't talk about it or dwell…

When he had calmed down, Peter tugged the blanket protectively over his neck and shoulders, and struggled against the odds to snatch a little more sleep. He dared not think what 6th September would bring, or whether he would get to see the dawn of the 7th.

The afternoon of Saturday 7th September 1940, Mary was in her suburban garden enjoying the autumn sunshine. The war was now a year old, and it seemed incredible to believe that the children had been away that long. Mary knew that Hannah and Richard were in good hands, but she still worried about them, as a mother it was only natural. She thought of John doing his bit in the army, and then her thoughts turned to those brave British airmen racing up daily into the sky to do battle with the attacking German hordes. Despite the privations of rationing and the blackout, sometimes the war felt very distant to Mary, the dutiful hardworking housewife.

Mary was distracted from her thoughts, and was alerted to the sound of aircraft engines. As she looked to the sky, she watched with incredulity, the largest formation of aircraft that she had ever seen. From the direction that they came (up the Thames estuary), the planes had to be hostile. Between 16,000 and 20,000 feet up in the air, over 350 German bombers, and almost double that number of fighters, Dorniers, Heinkels and Junkers, virtually unopposed by the R.A.F. were now directly over the East End of London –the centre of the British Empire. They moved through the sky across a front twenty miles wide. An armada. At 4:43 p.m. the sirens sounded.

When the vast group of planes did not split up as they usually did, she overheard a neighbour say.

"This doesn't look good…"

What Mary could not see –she would only read about it in the following morning's papers- were bombs falling down by the hundred, whistling, flashing and thudding, on the docks, Woolwich Arsenal, Bermondsey, Limehouse, West Ham, and the crammed back-to-back houses of Canning Town and Silvertown. In an instant, houses were transformed into rubble, factories were set ablaze, and people were dying. Solid embers descended into the roads, creating terror, the heat was intensely fierce, and everywhere there was the smell of burning. Unfortunately, the buildings in the docks area were clustered tightly together, with narrow roadways between them, facilitating the spread of fire. A thick cloud of black smoke darkened the streets, making it hard to see. People's faces, hands, bare arms and legs, were dirtied by greasy dust, and bomb-blast even whipped the clothes off the very unfortunate. In and around the factories, everything burned –grain, paint, pepper, rubber, tea. A rubber warehouse, when burning, produced black clouds of smoke that were so asphyxiating, that the fire could only safely be fought from a distance. Paint, rum and sugar floated on the Thames, burning away. To combat the fires, was a fire service, which mainly consisted of volunteers, most of which had no experience of fire fighting. Such was the heat firemen put their faces against the nozzles of their hoses, to feel the draught of cold air, which dwelt around the water jet. The glow from the flames from burning oil and petrol dumps was visible from twenty miles away. The Germans were tightening the screw, and the capital of Britain was well and truly being put to the test.

The German bombers returned, again, that night, free from any real interference from the R.A.F. (which could only muster one squadron of night fighters), guided to their target by the red glows that signified blazing London. More fires were created, and many people in the city became surrounded by walls of flame, praying that their rescue would be swift.

The raids that day had left 430 dead, 1600 injured and many more homeless, in three square miles of Silvertown, hardly any houses had remained standing; over 650 tons of high explosive and incendiary bombs had been dropped on London.

However, this was just the beginning, there would be further suffering. The German bombers further targeted the East End for four more days in a row.

The Baker and Pavitt children had been spending the autumn evening of 12ᵗʰ September out blackberrying. Although Tom had consumed a sizeable portion of their pickings, he thought that his mother would be proud that they had collected sufficient fruit to make several scrumptious pies.

The other three children threw themselves into the task of picking blackberries. Hannah seemed to be doing so in a rather detached manner. This had not gone unnoticed to Beth, who asked, when the pair was alone.

"Are you alright, Hannah? Is there something troubling you?"

Hannah took a few seconds before answering, as if it took her a while to realize that Beth had spoken to her. She replied by throwing a question back at Beth.

"Why do you ask that?"

"You've been acting strangely lately. Evenings, weekends, at the farm, even tonight, out here. You play with your food at breakfast. It's as if you're in a dream world!"

Hannah tried to avoid Beth's gaze, and stretched into the bush for a blackberry.

"No I'm not."

Beth looked the other girl straight in the eye.

"I've been your friend for long enough now, Hannah Baker, to know that something is on your mind," she said encouragingly. "What's up?"

"Well, you see...Oh! No! You'll laugh..." Hannah became increasingly flustered.

"No, I won't."

"You see, I think I'm in love!" Confessed Hannah.

Beth looked at her friend with incredulity.

"Who...? Is it anyone I know? One of the twins?"

Hannah shook her head.

"No. It's Peter."

It took a couple of seconds for it to register with Beth, before it became her turn to be lost for words.

"You mean my cousin?"

Hannah nodded sheepishly.

"I can't stop thinking about him."

There had been quieter moments, when Hannah, alone, had thought about the pilot so much that it pained her and the thought that she may never even meet him again had brought her close to tears, depressed like she'd been bereaved. Despite him being constantly in her thoughts, she often struggled to picture his face in her mind. She felt powerless over controlling her feelings and powerless about if she could see him again.

Beth smiled and went to speak, but the untimely appearance of Richard and Tom silenced her. Hannah grabbed Beth by the arm.

"You won't tell them, will you?" She pleaded.

"No. Don't worry, Hannah, your secret's safe with me."

There was an awkward silence as the four children began their journey back to the farm. Daylight was fading fast, and they had really stayed out for longer than they should have. Tom did not help matters, by repeatedly swinging from the branches of trees, slowing them down.

They returned via the cemetery. By now it was pitch black and very spooky, and Hannah held Beth's hand tightly, for comfort. They passed by the imposing winged figure of a stone angel.

"I don't like it here," shivered Hannah.

"Me neither," said Beth.

The distant, but unmistakable droning of enemy bombers broke the silence.

"London, again?" Tom wandered aloud.

"I expect so." Hannah predicted.

The noise of the aircraft became closer. Nearby ack-ack guns thundered into action, and orange flashes appeared in the sky. The presence of the artillery was comforting, but Beth had learned that they never hit anything.

Led by a panicky Tom, the children scrambled over the cemetery gates, and sprinted the short distance home. The German aircraft must have been directly overhead, for the noise they caused was indescribable. Heaven knows how many of them there were. In the distance, a dog was barking, and at the farm, the cows were mooing a somber chorus. The children put their fingers in their ears as they approached the farmhouse.

Ted literally threw the children into the shelter.

"Where have you been?" Emily demanded. "The air raid siren went ages ago!"

"We didn't even hear it." Beth confessed.

Emily shook her head in despair. Richard had never seen her this angry, she must have felt it very serious that the children were absent when the siren sounded.

The air raid shelter was sited a reasonable distance away from the farm buildings. Ted had constructed the shelter a few months back, when the threat of invasion first became very serious. It had taken him a little under a week, and lots of expletives to dig the five feet deep hole, and erect the corrugated iron structure. The shelter fitted six persons, although it was a bit of a squeeze. Oscar was in there too, with cotton wool over his ears, in case the noise panicked him. Anyone in the shelter had to share it with earthworms and snails.

Ted revealed a dilapidated rectangular box.

"I don't know how long it will be before the all clear. Looks like we might be needing this."

Richard's eyes lit up.

"Oh! Ludo!"

The air raid sirens wailed into action, once again. Next came the ominous droning sound of approaching enemy aircraft.

Mary Baker was alone in the London house, her husband having being hastily put on the roster to do fire watching duty at his office. Mary unhurriedly put the novel that she had been reading to one side, and switched off the bedside lamp. She found herself being drawn towards the bedroom window, where she carefully pulled the blackout curtains apart a little. Mary felt reasonably safe, since, none of the local ack-ack guns were firing, which they undoubtedly would have been, if the raid had been nearby (then Mary would have sought immediate shelter).

On 9th September, the South London suburbs had been bombed, and 370 were killed, while on the 11th September, it was the turn of the Docks. Each night, the bombers had returned without fail. Little did the Londoners suspect that they would continue to do so for two more months.

In the distance, several searchlights began to finger the night sky, stabbing at the darkness, in their search for the German bombers, and the anti-aircraft guns opened up. It was another night clear of clouds; good bombing weather.

Amid the explosions, a fire appeared on the horizon, quickly followed by a succession of others. Soon, individual fires merged into each other, before all that area of London seemed to be ablaze. From the window, Mary stared transfixed at the scene.

Somehow, the red glow a handful of miles away was perversely beautiful. The area covered by the red glow became ever larger, as more buildings were engulfed in flame. Church spires became illuminated. Nothing was safe from the destructive path of the fire.

The staccato sound of the capital's anti-aircraft guns was unceasing throughout the raid. It was almost like a fireworks display, as shells burst, producing star-like flashes high up in the sky. Tracer too, was frequently fired up into the darkness.

Mary shook her head. She thought *those poor, poor people in central London-Her city*. Mary thanked God that her own dear children had been safely evacuated to the countryside, and found herself saying a prayer for London's citizens.

The public house was heaving with airmen. There were also a good number of the local villagers, young and old, relaxing after another testing day, of long working hours. The pub had a homely feel to it, and inside the atmosphere was cheery. Pictures of turn of the century street scenes covered the walls, and various ornamental plates hung above the bar, in one corner there was a dusty old bookcase. The smell of smoke filled the air. Peter, in conversation with Percy was trying to make himself heard above the noise. They had talked about cars, sport and family.

"I had a fun time at the farm, the other week." Peter began. "Auntie Emily seems to be keeping well, although she worries that Uncle Ted's overdoing it."

"How about your cousins, are they OK?"

"Beth and Tom? Yes, they're fine." The pilot took a sip from his drink. "Met the two evacuees staying at the farm, whilst I was there —a teenage boy and a girl."

"Oh?"

"Yes, Hannah and Richard."

"And, what's she like, then, this Hannah?"

"Likeable girl, slim brunette, intelligent."

"How old is she?"

"Sixteen, I believe." Peter could tell from the knowing look on Percy's face, that this was a leading question. "Oh! For heaven's sake, Percy, she'd be too young!"

Percy nudged Peter.

"But, you like her, don't you?"

Three more of their group, who were propping up the bar, interrupted the pair. Brian Page, who had replaced Sandy as the leader of Yellow section, at twenty-six was a few years older than the rest of the pilots in the room. He was a good pilot, liked his drink, was outspoken, and was as much anti-communist as he was anti-Nazi. Brian, who was getting a little boisterous, and had a distinct glow in his cheeks, leant across the bar, and, spilling his drink in the process, spoke, his voice slow and loud.

"We were having a discussion, Douglas, Harold and me..."

Harold Fowler, the quiet member of the group, shook his head. He felt embarrassed and would rather have been elsewhere. After that tough landing in his bruised, smoking Spitfire on 16th August, he'd spent two weeks in hospital, and only returned to ops days ago. Douglas Lamb grinned, treating it as a bit of light hearted fun. It could be said that he was as bad as Brian. Brian continued.

"We shoot down the Germans, and they shoot down us, killing each other...what's the bloody point? I mean, before long there won't be any of us left! Hitler won't invade, and seriously we can't hop across the Channel to France."

"What exactly are you getting at?" Asked Peter.

"It's the drink talking." Harold sighed.

Brian went on.

"We should be worrying about the Russians; we fight ourselves to exhaustion, and the Reds take over!"

Percy groaned.

"Oh! This isn't about your anti-Communist crusade, again?"

"I see, he wants yet *another* enemy to fight!" Douglas observed with irony.

"The Russians are no better than the Germans. The German pilots are only doing their job, just like ourselves." Said Brian.

Douglas Lamb disagreed.

"The German pilots are bastards. Flattening cities, dropping their bombs on innocent civilians."

"I'm just saying you can't tarnish them all with the same brush," stressed Brian.

The pilot received a black look from a couple of other drinkers.

"I think you should lower your voice," advised Peter.

Percy promptly changed the subject.

A trio of local girls, in their early twenties, and wearing colourful frocks entered the bar. After ordering their drinks, they remained, hovering by the group of pilots, exchanging frequent glances.

Brian winked at the other four men.

"Decent looking broads over there."

The pilots smiled and mumbled in general agreement. The airmen were always the centre of attention in the bar, they were the glamour boys, who basked in the adulation of the locals, especially the females. The villagers might treat the pilots to a pint, or get them to join in a game of darts. The locals loved the little West Highland terrier that Douglas had started to bring into the bar recently, even though the animal was a little partial to beer! They missed Sandy Rose, a good sport, who had once entertained them on the piano.

Brian rubbed his hands together.

"We'll join you chaps, again, in a few minutes." He declared, before, a little unsteady on his feet, heading towards the girls, dragging an unwilling Harold along with him. He was beginning to pine for the pretty nurses; these girls seemed cheap by comparison.

"Phew. At last, some peace." Sighed Douglas; even he was getting worn down.

"I think Brian's been over doing it, lately. Can't he remember why we're fighting this war?" Lamented Percy.

The break was short-lived, for, as promised, Brian (and Harold) returned within a few minutes.

"Their names are Annie, Charlotte and Janet. They're all Land Girls." He announced, merrily.

"Really?" Percy was taking a keen interest.

"Yes." Nodded Brian. "Annie fancies you, Percy, you lucky chap."

Percy's face lit up.

Brian addressed Peter.

"That popsy Charlotte's got her eye on you, Peter."

"Oh?" Peter felt awkward. The blonde-haired girl was not unattractive, but was noisy and confident, she looked like a woman of the world, too tarted up, and he feared that she was probably the local bike!

Brian egged him on.

"They know where to get cheap double rooms for the night at a local guesthouse, no questions asked. What you need Peter, is a good woman."

"Go for it, old chap. If you're not interested, then I'll have second claim!" Encouraged Douglas.

"Well, what are you two waiting for? Come over and talk to them." Said Brian.

Percy was ready to move.

"You say her name's Annie?"

Brian nodded.

"I think I'll just stay here, and turn in early," declared Peter, as he turned to the barman to order a final pint. He fixed his eyes to the floor.

"What's the matter with him?" Brian asked aloud, before leaving the group.

Percy raised his eyebrows.

"Cold feet, Peter old chap?"

Peter gestured his head towards the girls.

"You go over and join them, Percy."

On 13th September, six bombs fell on Buckingham Palace. The German bombers now started to move around London, attacking the City and the West End, as well as the East End. Most Londoners were getting by on only four hours' sleep.

The Germans aimed to launch operation "Sea Lion", and invade Great Britain in the latter half of September. It was intended that the invasion force would consist of around twenty-five divisions, which would land between Dover and Portsmouth (the first wave appearing in fast moving landing craft, and protected by strings of U-boats and minefields). Hundreds of tanks had been modified as amphibious assault vehicles. Over three thousand converted barges were made available from the Rhine to be used in the invasion. The three German armies, that included panzer and motorised formations, planned to advance north, establishing themselves on a line eastward from Gloucester to south of Colchester. London would be surrounded from the north, by troops advancing west of the city, and isolated from the rest of Britain, precipitating the collapse of the country. Against the enemy, the British could only field around a hundred tanks.

The British were on invasion alert. Three-quarters of the army were confined to barracks, and kept in a state of alert. The daylight attacks by the Luftwaffe on Southern England, on 14th September, met with comparatively weak resistance, only thirteen German aircraft being lost. The London Docks, a sprawling mass of warehouses, packed with combustibles was set ablaze, once more. Hitler's invasion fleet was ready, and the invasion of Britain was set to take place on the 21st September.

The next day, Sunday 15th September 1940, Hermann Goering, head of the German Airforce, sent in excess of five hundred aircraft over the skies of London, in an all-out offensive. The climatic battle, which followed saw Hurricanes and Spitfires engaged in a running fight with the Luftwaffe over a huge battlefield that extended from West London to the coast of Northern France. This was going to be the day that the Luftwaffe knocked out the R.A.F. once and for all.

The order to scramble had come a quarter of an hour ago. After a slightly misty start early in the morning, the weather was warm, sunny and clear. It was set to be a busy day, since Peter's squadron, along with numerous others, was to meet a large German bomber force head on over London.

The attacking force had already been reduced in number, when it was intercepted by other Hurricane and Spitfire squadrons, over the coast. A sizeable number of the German fighter escort had already had to turn for home, as their petrol reserves ran low, due to having been forced to fend off the earlier British attacks. However, bombs had already fallen on parts of South London. During the earlier skirmishes, a downed Dornier had crashed by Victoria Station. In another incident one German pilot who parachuted from a stricken aircraft, on landing in London, was attacked and killed by enraged civilians armed with pokers and kitchen knives.

As he prepared to do battle with the enemy aircraft that had broken through to the Nation's capital, Peter thought *how dare they arrogantly fly over Big Ben, Buckingham Palace, Trafalgar Square, Docklands, the Royal Parks... Today, you'll get a nasty surprise, you Nazi bastards!*

Below, an unseen army of rescue workers, ARP, firemen, nurses and many more, toiled amongst burning and smoking houses, factories and railway lines.

Forty or so Heinkel Bombers supported by roughly the same number of 109's came into view. Tiny dots to begin with, the shapes changed into a pack of vultures, before revealing themselves as planes flying in lines of five aircraft-abreast. The fighters were positioned protectively some distance above the bombers.

Peter glanced around at the other Spitfires, and felt a sense of pride.

The British aircraft commenced attack. Peter tore in through friendly anti-aircraft fire from London's defences.

Somewhere to the left of his plane, a ME 109 spun down out of control. *Curses! One of the other lads had already bagged a kill!*

The gunner in the German aircraft opened fire.

You won't hit a thing from that far away-amateurs! Thought Peter. He closed in behind the Heinkel to within forty yards, and gave the enemy plane a three-second burst, before breaking away, again. A piece of debris from the German plane went spinning by. It didn't do to hang around. He knew –if he wanted to stay alive- to resist the temptation to follow a stricken enemy plane down to its doom.

Peter twisted and turned in the cockpit, ever vigilant for any enemy planes, which could, at any moment swoop down on him. He sighted the crippled Heinkel fall away out of formation.

The sky was chaos. The RT was alive with excited voices. Peter saw a propeller on one Heinkel jerk to a halt, as one of its engines gave out. Elsewhere, a Hurricane flopped uselessly onto its back. Inside doomed aircraft, pieces of metal flew off, and men screamed.

"I've got two of the bastards on my tail!" Came an unknown voice from another squadron. "I can't shake them off…!"

A little way below his aircraft, Peter spied a ME 109 empty its payload into a Spitfire. Incensed, Peter dived down, with the sole purpose of destroying this old enemy.

The ME 109 had a reasonable head start on Peter, and noticing the Spitfire, the Jerry pilot took evasive action. In no time at all, the two aircraft had flown out across the suburbs, and were in the skies above the open Surrey countryside. Below was a patchwork of green and yellow fields that were divided by roads that resembled pieces of string.

The main body of the attacking German bombers flew on remorselessly. *So much for the R.A.F. being finished! There seemed to be more British aircraft in the sky today than ever!* Thought grim faced bomber crews. The range of the ME 109's protecting the Heinkels was too limited over London, and on some days the German fighters had failed to rendezvous on time, or lost their way, with costly results for the bombers. The German fighter pilots themselves were increasingly frustrated that, under

Goering's orders, they had to fly straight and level with the bomber formations, surrendering the advantages of height and speed to the British. This (the English) was an enemy that was not prepared to keel over on his back and die! The past few weeks had shown that. If Germany couldn't invade Britain in September, the worsening weather would destroy any further prospect until the spring.

The ME 109 did not stand a chance. Peter had established himself as a good pilot, and he was getting better all the time. He timed his moment with perfection, and went in for the kill. The pilot of the 109 did not know what had hit him. Peter felt euphoric, as if he had just shot some game.

At first there was only a little flame on the fuselage of the enemy plane, then it grew larger, and, the 109, black smoke pouring from it, fell into an ever-steeper dive, and hit the ground in a ball of fire. There had been no parachute.

What a horrible way to die, thought Peter. The German pilot was most probably a young lad, like himself. For a few moments, Peter felt ashamed. Then he realized that British pilots, too, had suffered similar fates, and had also been badly burned. The Germans had chosen to attack this country —they must be prepared to suffer the consequences. But, for how much longer would —could- the Germans attack…?

The attacking German force, now widely dispersed, limped home, their crews (among them many dead and wounded), numbed by the ferocity of the British defenders, and their aircraft strewn with bullet holes. The young idealists of the Luftwaffe who had been spellbound by the words of their leader just a year or two before, had met their match.

The skies above London calmed, and the sirens sounded the 'all clear'. The city's inhabitants emerged from their shelters, blinking in the sunlight, whilst rescue workers toiled among the rubble, searching for the dead and wounded.

Out in the countryside, villagers had stared in awe up into the blue over rooftops and treetops. They had witnessed German aircraft come crashing down to earth in a blaze of glory, or saw enemy bombers riddled with bullets descend ever lower to make forced landings, and slide to an undignified standstill in an English field, under the watchful eyes of farm workers.

At the Fighter Command airfields, ground crews stood on the tarmac in front of the hangars patiently waiting for the Hurricanes and Spitfires to return. They stared anxiously into the sky, wandering how many of those hangars would be empty that night.

Later on, the BBC summed up the day's events.

"Here is the midnight news. Up to ten o'clock (tonight) 175 German aircraft had been destroyed in today's raids over this country.* Today was the most costly for the German Airforce for nearly a month. In daylight raids, between 350 and 400 enemy aircraft were launched in two attacks against London and Southeast England. About half of them were shot down."

---

* The true figure was 61 German to 29 British.

The Luftwaffe returned to London in daylight on 18th September 1940, however, it could only muster seventy heavily escorted bombers, which achieved little.

20th September 1940.

George and Mary were rudely awakened from their sleep by the wail of the air raid sirens. Mary let out a groan, before she reluctantly clambered out of bed, and quickly changed out of her nightdress, and into her (all-in-one) zip-up siren suit. Meanwhile, George hurried downstairs, and placed their ID cards and ration books into a suitcase by the back door. The case already contained their insurance policies, some magazines, a couple of books and a pack of cards. He also picked up two rugs, and quietly waited for his wife to appear. Mary, having turned off the gas, joined her husband, and they went into the back garden.

Outside, white pillars from the searchlights swept the sky, and the thundering sound of the ack-ack guns was all pervading. Agitated voices could be heard, as neighbours hurried down damp lawns to the bottom of their gardens and into their own shelters. One husband had to retrace his steps into the house, cursing his wife for leaving a light on. The occasional dog was barking.

Mary followed George into the shelter. By now the noise of the German bombers was clearly audible, and she felt glad to be inside the Anderson, even though if there were a direct hit on the shelter, it *–they–* would not survive. They made themselves as comfortable as possible; George picked up a book, and Mary selected a *Woman* magazine. She perused articles about how to make soap last longer, and making gifts from scrap. Both of them strained their ears to listen out for and interpret the slightest sound. It was amazing how the mind worked overtime in such circumstances. Only now, Mary noticed that the shelter light was overbearing, and also a cold draft coming through under the door of the shelter began to annoy her. As London boomed overhead, George gave his wife an encouraging smile. Mary tried to concentrate on her magazine, in an attempt to settle down and endure another night of restless anxiety.

In the shelters in neighbouring gardens, such scenes were being replayed over and over. A wife would ask her husband if that noise close by had been a falling bomb, and he would reply reassuringly that it was an ack-ack gun. Others would stay indoors, seeking shelter under tables, and drinking endless cups of tea. The bravest would stand outside and watch the flames spurting into the air, the red and yellow looking all the more striking against the black background. Some people sincerely believed that this night it was going to be 'curtains' or 'the end' for them all. They could but pray that, if and when they emerged, red-eyed, tired, their nerves tested that their home would still be standing in the morning.

CHAPTER 12 – AUTUMN TERROR

Hannah was helping out one evening in late September alongside Wendy, a middle-aged lady, in a mobile canteen van, as the regular helper was off sick. Wendy was a member of the Women's Voluntary Service (W.V.S.) and wore a uniform green tweed suit with grey woven into it, a beetroot red jumper and a felt hat. The W.V.S. provided care and support; they assisted evacuees on their arrival, knitted socks and other clothes for soldiers, and did lots and lots of cooking.

Wendy wove the canteen van through dark country lanes to an anti-aircraft site. Earlier, the pair had paid a visit to two men of the Royal Observer Corps, who were responsible for estimating the size, weight and direction of enemy raiders. Theirs was a lonely sandbagged hilltop emplacement, whose only normal link to the outside world was a landline, and they were grateful for the food and all-too-brief company.

"How are you finding it living on a farm, then?"

Hannah turned her thoughts away from the window and the dark fields and bottomless black ocean of sky beyond.

"It's good fun. Very different from London."

"How are your parents coping with the raids?"

"I don't think they've been hit too badly…so far," she continued, "They've got a shelter in the garden, anyway."

"That's good."

Hannah nodded.

Wendy then asked.

"And you Hannah, do you have a gentleman friend?"

"No." Hannah decided to let Wendy in on her secret. "I've got a crush on my friend's cousin, he's a pilot."

"Very nice. What's the young man's name?"

Hannah could feel the colour rushing to her cheeks.

"Peter."

They arrived at the battery, a flat, wide-open field, which could well and truly be said to be out in the sticks. There were a few huts dotted around, containing living quarters, telephones and plotting devices, and two guns surrounded by sandbags. A single pipe and tap provided the water supply. Among the team of men, there were cooks, a medical orderly, height finders and telephonists.

A steel-helmeted uniformed man emerged from the command post, and Wendy informed Hannah that this was the Gun Position Officer (G.P.O.) who was in overall charge. The two females got out of the van. The air was cold, and the ground damp. Hannah rubbed her hands together for warmth. Wendy smiled at the officer.

"Evening, Harold."

"Evening, Wendy. Whose this young lady, then?"

Wendy introduced the G.P.O. to Hannah. Harold was an affable man of fifty; he had kindly eyes, graying hair and a moustache. He turned to Hannah.

"Have you seen these sort of guns before?"

"No." Hannah shook her head.

Harold led the girl gently by the arm, over to one of the groups, whilst Wendy opened up the serving-hatch ready for the men. Harold explained.

"Our gun is a 4.5 inch one. The high explosive shell it fires, weighs almost half a hundredweight. Did you know the shell is hurled to a height of eight miles in the space of just fifty seconds?

"Fifty seconds, goodness!" Hannah listened with intent.

"But, it's not easy trying to hit a Jerry plane that's moving at two to three hundred miles an hour. To destroy the plane, the shell needs to burst within about eighty feet of the target. And we generally have to aim about two miles in front of a plane flying at great height."

"What type of planes do you shoot at?" The girl enquired.

"Dorniers, Heinkels, you name it…Messerschmitts even. If we can put the fear of God into some of the more fainthearted Jerry pilots, and disturb their aim, or even get them to jettison their bombs in fields rather than cities, preventing accurate bombing, then that's satisfying."

"Do you have to live out here? What's it like?"

Harold was enjoying educating the girl.

"We spend time reading and writing letters. We've had a couple of visits from E.N.S.A. –they put on a little concert party. In the day, the men keep themselves busy with cleaning, maintenance, arms drill, P.T. etc. That last winter was tough; snow and then frost right through to February."

The G.P.O. asked after Hannah, and she informed him a little about what she did, and life at the farm. The girl returned to the van, and assisted Wendy in serving hot food to the men of the battery, who came across in one's and two's. The men joked that Wendy's usual assistant was renowned for giving each man the precise amount of everything –the exact amount of sugar, the correct amount of milk in a mug of tea. Woe betides anyone who tried to scrounge an extra slice of cake! One cheeky young lad asked if Hannah would mend his socks for him, another wanted the girl to stay and play cards with the men.

Suddenly, there was the ringing of a telephone from inside the command post. Harold could be seen talking excitedly to his assistant, an N.C.O., who was responsible for relaying Harold's orders to the guns. It was clear what was happening –enemy aircraft were approaching!

The N.C.O. bellowed various bearings and angles, the men positioned their guns, and then they erupted into action. As they fired, flashes of flame over twenty feet high came from the guns, along with an almighty explosion.

Hannah covered her ears, and felt her heart in her mouth. It was all very exciting and impressive –this was where the war was happening. She caught a glimpse of an enemy plane silhouetted in the moonlight. Wait till the others heard about it!

High up in the air the shells exploded. Searchlights were sweeping the sky, and neighbouring gun sites were going into action, also.

Up above, two German aircraft stood steadfastly to their course, guided by radio signals of dots and dashes crackling over the earphones of their crew. *Why didn't the stupid British surrender? They had proven to be so stubborn.* Orange balls of flame came racing up past them in the dark night sky. The aircraft shook alarmingly. *Best to take evasive action. Those bloody searchlights!*

Down on the ground, they watched one bomber dodge and weave, as it got caught in a searchlight. Soon after, there appeared two distant orange flashes, in quick succession, as bombs met the ground.

"That scared him, alright." Harold nodded with a grin of satisfaction.

They hadn't got the bomber, but they'd rattled him, and made him take an early turn for home.

"But, what about the bombs?" Asked a concerned Hannah. "Where have they fallen?"

"Nowhere in particular." The G.P.O. laid a reassuring hand on the girl's shoulder.

Jack, the delivery boy, swung his bike into the entrance to the long driveway, startling a couple of birds in a nearby tree. The largest house in the village, was to him more a palace than a house, with its countless rooms, turrets and massive bay windows, loomed into view, imposing; the last house on his round. He afforded himself a faint smile. That 'posh family' lived here, with their popular daughter, Victoria. Well, they weren't that posh really, just well spoken, and with pots more money than anyone else in the village. He'd got to know Victoria a little, as she'd been flirting with him, lately. Kept asking him when he was going to take her out. Why him? Him, a seventeen year old with barely two ha'pennies to rub together leading a humdrum life, take *her* out. She was decent looking enough, perhaps a bit young. It was all harmless fun.

He got off his bike, and knocked on the door to the big house. It was late afternoon, and the sky behind him had turned red. A squirrel scuttled along the branches of an oak tree, and fallen leaves drifted by on the wind. Victoria's mother answered the door to the figure in beige jacket, trousers and cap, making an observation about the fine weather. The brown haired boy passed her the bag of goods, as she fished in her purse for the correct money. Within a minute or so, the weekly ritual was over, and Jack was cycling back down the driveway…home.

Just before he got out onto the road, a figure popped out from behind a large tree; it was her, Victoria. As the girl was effectively blocking the path, he came to a halt.

"Oh! Hello," he smiled.

He did not know it, but the girl's appearance was planned. She had had her eye on him for weeks. Here was a boy a little bit older and mature than her peers at school. She stood there in a white flowery dress, bright red shoes, with her hands clasped behind her back, her chest sticking out more than usual, and the sun reflecting off her face. Was he imagining it, or did she appear more attractive today? She had dressed up especially for him.

"Hello." She smiled.

"I didn't see you there on the way in, Miss Victoria."

She dropped her head onto one shoulder, and lowered her eyelids.

"I've been out in the garden the whole time."

He gave a vexed laugh. She continued, telling him, rather than asking.

"It's alright if I join you?"

"Well, I've finished, now, I'm just on my way home." He was a little unsure of himself. "But, it's OK, Miss."

The pair walked along, the road, unhurriedly, him pushing his bike. The girl walked close to him, so that their hands occasionally brushed, and they made light conversation about each other's day. Before long, they came to Jack's house, an old cottage its walls draped in honeysuckle, in which he lived with his parents.

"Home sweet home." Jack went and parked his bike down the side, then returned to his female companion. They stood together in the porch.

"Let's go for a walk." She grinned.

"It's nearly time for my dinner, Miss…"

Before Jack could make any further protestations, the girl, without warning, pressed her body against his forcing him against the front door. He stared into her green eyes, just inches away, transfixed. *Kiss me* they pleaded. Both their hearts were beating faster, and as one, they slipped their arms around each other, and their lips met.

He didn't know if she'd been teasing him, or not. Shortly after he'd kissed her, she had made her excuses and vanished into the early evening air. Although it was true that it was him that had warned her that it was close to his suppertime. He had enjoyed kissing her. It all seemed so unreal. Then, sure enough, the next day, 2nd October, she appeared at his door, and whisked him out for a stroll down the quiet country lanes. This time they held hands, and opened up to each other more, talking about school, his work, holidays, and the war. She wore that same outfit, again, and told him to stop calling her Miss. Jack had to pinch himself that Victoria fancied him, but he had no worry for she doted on him, and confessed to having fancied him for weeks. He, in turn, found her refreshing, and hadn't realized the attraction until it hit him in the face.

In the half-light, Jack glanced at his watch, and declared, with a slightly worried look on his face.

"Best be getting you home, soon, don't want to be keeping you out after dark."

"Oh! There's no hurry." She swung him round playfully, in a semi-circle.

"Well, if you're sure?"

"I am."

"Don't like the look of those rain clouds, though."

They enjoyed a kiss, and made their way past a field full of cows, which were lying down. Overhead, the sky blackened, and the first few drops of rain began to fall.

Jack drew closer to Victoria, and looked around him.

"We're miles from anywhere, we'll get soaked!"

Victoria wiped the rain from her eyes, and pointed.

"Over there, there's a barn, let's go and see if we can use it for shelter…"

The pair quickened their step, climbed a gate and crossed a rapidly muddying field to a barn on a hilltop. Fortunately, the entrance was not locked, and they found themselves inside, with only towers of hay and each other for company. The floor was strewn with hay, and its smell permeated the barn.

Jack stood rather fidgety by the entrance, and Victoria rested against a block of hay. She said.

"Just think what we could get up to in here…"

Jack merely smiled back. He hoped and feared as to what she was thinking.

"Come over here, Jack," she beckoned.

He went over to her, and they kissed immediately. Then they kissed a second time, and a third.

"I'm a naughty girl, Jack," she declared, running her fingers through his hair.

Jack was distracted. Outside, faint thuds and booms signaled that an air raid was underway in the distance. The boy went to the door of the barn, and slid it back slightly. The bombing was happening a long way away, although Jack could make out frequent small flashes of red, coupled with the noise of explosion. Who was experiencing hell, tonight? He pulled the door shut, once more, for the girl inside was getting impatient. Jack was surprised to see Victoria slipping out of her dress, and he stood open mouthed.

"Victoria, what are you doing?"

"I've got to get out of these wet clothes."

"Victoria…?"

She stood before him wearing nothing but her underwear. She purposely maintained his gaze, as her arms moved slowly round her back to undo her bra. She said.

"Surely you prefer me out of my clothes?"

He opened and closed his mouth like a fish. She continued.

"I told you I was a naughty girl. I want you to make me a woman, Jack."

"Victoria, Is this…?" He shifted uneasily on the spot. His eyes were drawn to her wholesome figure.

"Come on, Jack, I'll be sixteen in a couple of months, and you can't get pregnant the first time." She urged him. "Don't you want to do it before the German bombs kill us all?"

He drew over to her. As they began to kiss, she put one hand against his face, and with the other, she undid his trousers, so that they fell down to his ankles. Together, they undid his shirt, and he threw it into a corner. They pressed their bodies tightly together, and kissed passionately, their hands crawling all over each other. She stepped away, with her back against the wall of hay, and she removed her bra, to reveal a pair of sizeable breasts. He looked at her hungrily; they both wanted each other.

"You are a naughty girl!"

Jack bent down on one knee, and began to kiss her warm chest, and caress her well-developed thighs, so that her skin prickled with sensation.

"Oh! Jack!" She sighed, and gazed up.

The rain pounded on the roof of the barn. Outside, the din grew louder, as the rain and bombing grew fiercer.

They lay down on the floor next to each other, and removed the last of their undergarments. They looked at each other's naked body in wonder for a few moments. She ran her hand over his chest that had sprouted a few hairs. Then he climbed on top of the girl, closed his arms around her, and started to slide in and out of her.

The girls at school the next day were shocked. Nancy had overheard, in disbelief, Victoria during a flying visit, bragging to her friend Betty, about her night of passion. *Victoria's done it!* She hissed to Beth, Clara and Samantha. They were good girls. Samantha profoundly declared that she would save herself for marriage; Clara regretted that she hadn't even kissed a boy. Victoria, for her part, felt that the other girls secretly looked upon her with admiration for her daring. Victoria saw Jack for another couple of weeks, and then declared that she had lost interest in him.

It was 7:45 p.m., the blackout was underway, and Mary Baker shivered in the cold night air, as she hurried home from an elderly friend's flat. Mrs. Gillett, a widow in her early seventies, lived several streets away from Mary. Mrs. Gillett had often looked after Mary when she was a child, and Mary felt duty-bound to go shopping for the widow, when the latter's rheumatism played up particularly badly, and this was happening with increasing frequency. Mrs. Gillett would repay Mary's kindness, by sharing a cup of tea with her. This, Monday 7th October, had been such evening, and, as usual, one cup of tea became two cups, followed by a third…

The old lady did so worry about the war, and now that the Germans had started to bomb London, her fears were compounded. She felt it so personally that her fellow Londoners had been forced to spend their nights underground like rodents – poor people. Then there were the homeless, and those killed and maimed. This 'Blitz' was too terrible to comprehend, but, then, what else was there for a lonely old woman to think about?

Of course, Mary did her best to reassure Mrs. Gillett, however, she often found herself saying things like *if a bomb's got your name on it then there's not much you can do about it.*

Mary pulled her coat tighter, and increased her pace. She looked skywards. Without a doubt, *they* would be over again, tonight. The Luftwaffe had targeted London relentlessly for thirty nights in a row. Hitler and his henchman Goering, believed that they could destroy the Londoner's will through terror bombing, but,

Mary was convinced that the people of London had a great deal more resilience than Herr Hitler gave them credit for.

Although the bombing was destroying many factories and warehouses, the effect on industrial production was negligible. The pessimistic had believed that in the first month of a bombing campaign against London, at least fifty thousand people would die, and half a million homes would be destroyed; such estimates were hugely wide of the mark.

Mary could recognize the engine sound of the enemy bombers. The German aircraft had a low uneven drone, whereas the British aircraft had a smooth steady purr. She would occasionally catch a glimpse of light from the down-pointed muffled torches of shadowy figures that were other pedestrians. The darkened houses all seemed lifeless and uninhabited, the road uninviting and depressing.

As Mary rounded the corner into another deserted street, the sirens sounded. Next came the familiar sound of the ack-ack guns, and the sight of the searchlights moving lazily across the sky.

The droning that signified the arrival of the German bombers became louder and louder. As Mary walked, very soon, she realized with dread, that the noise of the enemy aircraft was louder, and terrifyingly closer than ever before.

Mary was seized by fear. As the not too distant rumbling sound of the first explosions came, she broke into a sprint her eyes wide open, like those of a frightened rabbit's caught in a car's headlamps. Before long, all the explosions merged into one continuous terrifying sound.

Incendiary bombs started to descend from the sky like raindrops. One landed further back along the road down which Mary traveled. On the opposite side of the street, a couple more landed in neighbouring gardens, whilst a fourth incendiary crashed into the roof of a semi-detached house. It was like Bonfire night, except that it was the buildings, which were on fire.

The crackle of the flames frightened Mary. Almost tripping over her feet in her haste, Mary turned into the next road -she was still three streets away from home. It might as well have been a hundred miles! There came a loud screaming sound then an explosion, as a bomb fell behind some houses in the neighbouring street.

The whole world around Mary had gone mad. Howling dogs could be heard. On the other side of the street, a stick of bombs fell, one after the other, sparks shooting into the air, roofs buckling, destroying half a dozen houses in a row. Dirt, dust and rubble raining down upon her, Mary collapsed against a garden hedge, shaking like a leaf.

People began to emerge from the burning houses, their faces betraying a mixture of emotions -anger, bewilderment, despair and relief (in the sense that they had not been killed). Mary overheard one mother sobbing.

"We've nowhere to go! The children! How can we feed the children?"

Then there was the young girl of about ten, who asked her father, whose hand she held.

"Why was it us, why has our house been bombed?"

Mary dearly wished there were something she could do to help those desperate people. She sat there frozen, unable to move or think coherently, merely watching events as they developed, as an equally petrified by-stander.

In the distance, the clanging of the bell from a fire engine could be heard.

Bang! Bang! Bang! Still the bombs fell, nearby.

Mary clambered to her feet and ran. She no longer knew which was the way home, she was unable to think with any clarity, and simply headed away from the fires.

Before she got very far, Mary collided with a young boy. Mary had no idea where the boy had come from, only that he had appeared, running from the opposite direction, nor what he was doing. Winded, Mary stared at the boy for a few moments as she caught her breath.

"S-sorry." They apologized together.

The boy pointed to a semi-detached house that was three houses along, and panted.

"My house."

The boy sensed that Mary was even more frightened than he was, and he took her by the hand. Without hesitation, Mary followed this stranger through the gate, up the short garden path and into the darkened house. The front door was unlocked.

"Is that you, Jack? For Christ's sake, where have you been?" A male voice boomed from the ground floor.

"We're hiding under the table, dear," came a female voice.

Outside erupted with explosions.

Jack led Mary into a room at the rear of the house, and the pair squeezed under a sturdy wooden table. As the boy's mother and father made space available, they gazed at Mary inquisitively, as she said.

"Oh! Hello?"

"This is-" Jack began. Alas, he did not know the strange lady's name.

"Oh! Mary," smiled the intruder.

The boy's parents introduced themselves as Bill and Emma Allen. They did not seem to mind their temporary addition to the household. However, there was little time for further pleasantries, as an explosion close by shook the building. Suddenly, plaster descended from the ceiling, the curtains were torn to shreds, and the floor was peppered with broken glass. Mary was now breathing in short sharp breaths, and had her eyes clenched shut. A second explosion and Mary found that she could no longer hear anything, as if she had water in her ears.

They lost track of how long they were under there, whilst the madness continued outside. The family shared the shelter with Mary bound together by a bond of a people suffering a common peril. Bill lamented the falling bombs and firmly declared that the Germans deserved the same treatment back.

When, at last the bombing was over –or it could have just been a lull, one could never be too sure- Mary realized that she really ought to recommence her journey home. Her hearing thankfully now back to normal, Mary thanked Jack sincerely, and said that she would be forever indebted to his family. As Jack's parents surveyed the damage to the house, the boy saw Mary to the door. As Mary shut the garden gate behind her, once again, she was on her own.

In the next street, several firemen were bringing a fire under control, using a hard canvas hosepipe, which had a heavy brass nozzle at the end. Mary was alarmed as to how black and greasy their faces were, from the smoke. Across this part of London, there were innumerable fires, and the sky glowed orange and red, a whirling frenzy.

As she negotiated the fire hose, Mary's feet ended up in a puddle. There was something different about the puddle, and Mary realized how hot the water was.

More people were wandering aimlessly, blankets wrapped tightly around them. The walking wounded looked a real mess, and were invariably covered in white plaster dust, and their clothes, faces and hands were bloodied. A nurse was handing out tea and hot water bottles, and a doctor kneeling beside a crater could be heard uttering the word 'morphine'.

Mary became detached from everything that was going on around her, as if it was a bad dream from which she would awake. She felt like a passive observer, but at the same time was severely numbed and shocked by what had happened. Then, a single question dominated her thoughts –*her house*, had it survived the bombing?

Mary had no idea what time she got home, nor by what route she had taken. In an unrestrained flood of tears she fell into George's arms. After that, her recollection of events was a blur, as she succumbed to sleep. It was a tormented sleep, during which she relived her experiences of that terrible night.

The scene the next morning was one of devastation. The gas supply had gone down, the water struggled out from the taps at a slow trickle and local bus services were non-existent. Two adjoining houses further down Mary's road had been completely destroyed; a gaping hole betrayed where they should have stood. All that remained was a poignant pile of twisted brick and plaster rubble, and roof tiles that were sprinkled across the street like playing cards. A brief word with a tearful neighbour revealed to Mary that, the fate of the occupants was still unknown, but one had to fear the worst. The explosion had also blown the windows from half the houses in the street.

As Mary traversed more shattered streets, which were either running with water, littered with glass, or both, she was met with more gruesome sights.

Bits of floorboards, pieces of furniture, broken picture frames and children's' toys poked out from the dirty rubble. From the numerous bombsites came a vile smell that was a raw mixture of powdered brick dust, gas, sewers and smoke. Some dwellings were still steaming even hours after the raid. Firemen and wardens, most of them with tired, sunken eyes, silently went about the grisly task of removing the dead from the debris. There was a saloon car with a square van back, which was the auxiliary ambulance. Here and there, stood small groups of anxious relatives. Mary saw one woman tugging at a rescuer's sleeve pleading for any information alas he had no news to give her.

After seeing a bloodstained leg being removed, with nothing attached to it, Mary, feeling very sick, averted her gaze. Where yesterday, houses, shops and churches had stood, now there was nothing. Mary wandered, *where's my part of London that I have come to know and love gone?*

Then Mary saw the body. It was the dust-covered body of a little boy, no more than eight years of age. A policeman was helping a doctor carry the stretcher into the ambulance. The body was dressed in pyjamas, and had such a peaceful, cherubic look on it's face. The policeman looked searchingly at the body, unable to answer the one simple question –why?

Where yesterday, there were children playing gaily, mothers going about the daily chores and husbands working, now there was homelessness and despair, death and sorrow. Mary paused, and thought, *this is home*, how can this happen *here?* In one night, mankind seemed to have gone back from the twentieth century to the dark ages.

On Monday 7th October 1940, the Germans sent troops into Romania, with the consent and co-operation of the Romanian government, to take control of oilfields, and ensure the supply of Romanian oil to the Axis.

Out in the Atlantic, German submarines were now hunting in 'wolfpacks' of up to a dozen boats. One pack sank fifteen ships in six hours. The toll of Allied ships lost would continue to climb.

However, on 24th October, Hitler failed in a nine-hour attempt to persuade General Franco to bring Spain into the war on Germany's side. The frustrated German leader confessed to aides that he would rather have his teeth pulled out than go through such an ordeal again!

On Monday 28th October, Italy invaded Greece from occupied Albania. Hitler believed that Mussolini was making a serious strategic mistake. Whilst the Italians advanced slowly, the Greeks mobilized quickly, and over the next few weeks, the Italians would meet their match, and suffer heavy losses in Greece.

The Prime Minister, Winston Churchill, informed the House of Commons, on Tuesday 8th October 1940.

"A month has passed since Herr Hitler turned his rage and malice on to the civil population of our great cities, and particularly on London. He declared in his speech of September 4 that he would raze our cities to the ground, and since then he has been trying to carry out his fell purpose.

…There has been a considerable tailing off in the (German bombing offensive) last ten days, and all through the month that has passed since the heavy raids began on September 7 we have had a steady decline in casualties and damage."

The Prime Minister gave out some statistics, and explained that it was taking a ton of bombs to kill three-quarters of a person, and that, at the present rate, it would take ten years for the Luftwaffe to destroy half the houses in London. He concluded.

"Quite a lot of things are going to happen to Herr Hitler and the Nazi regime before even ten years are up…neither by material damage nor by slaughter will the British people be turned from their solemn and inexorable purpose."

In late October 1940, Mary wrote from London to her children.

"We are having it very bad up here -weeks and weeks of continuous bombing, without an end in sight. They (Hitler's Luftwaffe) cannot even leave us alone for just one night. Somewhere or other in London 'gets it'. The middle of the month saw the worst attacks, when there was 'Bombers' Moon', that is a full moon. Yesterday (26th October) St. Pancras and Victoria stations were both hit.

Your Father sleeps like a log in the Anderson shelter, although I myself continue to find it difficult to sleep, what with the noise and vibrations caused by bombs falling nearby. We now put some spare clothes in a case every night, and take that down to the shelter, just in case we loose all our clothes in a raid.

The A.R.P. and rescue workers are all by now tired, dirty and unshaven. The rescue workers seem to work with indifference, and sometimes show great insensitivity, as they labour over the rubble. They take little notice of the distressed relatives who stand and watch. I have known of them to be rude and aggressive to some victims. However, they must be tired, having performed this most difficult of tasks, day in, day out, for weeks on end. And when one stops and thinks about their constant race against time to free victims buried beneath the wreckages of buildings…and the hopelessness and frustration that they must feel, when the moaning and cries of victims dies out, and the important race is lost…If that were your Father or myself doing that job, then maybe we too, would try and detach or distance ourselves from the soul destroying work. We lost our warden in a raid a week ago, and an elderly gent has replaced him who is well into his seventies. I shouldn't really complain —he's an affable chap- but his eyesight and hearing are both poor. It is heartening to see in the ruins of houses graffiti that praises the A.R.P. and A.F.S…that people that have had their entire lives turned upside-down, and lost everything can still show a little appreciation of the rescue services. One feels a lump develop in one's throat at the sight of numerous Union Jack flags that stand defiantly in the rubble. It is queer to suddenly find clothing and other possessions resting unceremoniously up in trees -a cap, or child's toy thrown there by bomb blast.

Ann, who lives a few doors away, opened her bedroom curtains one morning, and was surprised to see a large piece of shrapnel from one of our own ack-ack guns firmly embedded in her garden. On reflection, Ann realized that she had had quite a lucky escape, and that if the shrapnel had fell a couple of yards nearer, it would have come crashing through the roof into her bedroom. It seems that they can almost be as much of a menace as the German's bombs!

Edna next door, has a sister from one of the slum areas, who's taken to sheltering nightly in the Underground, and from what I hear, the conditions in which they have to sleep are simply appalling. Along the front edges of the platforms, spaces two yards deep are left for passengers until 7:30 p.m. Between 7:30 p.m. and 10:30 p.m. one yard is left clear. After that, the trains' stop and the current is switched off, and people even sleep between the rails! Apparently, the first Tube station that she and her family tried was liable to flooding from the Thames, so they thought it best to find another one, elsewhere. The places are full of fleas and lice, the toilet facilities are quite inadequate, the air is stale, and there have been many cases of scabies. The smells are of dirt, sweat and urine. Invariably, there is always some person moaning or wailing, and babies crying down there. There are families of ten or even twelve, people talking feverishly, playing cards, and also those that just sit or lay there in a numbed silence. People even sleep cramped on the steps and escalators, on bedding covered with dirt and dust. I am informed that, tragically, on 14th October, Balham Underground station was hit, and dozens of people were killed. I suppose that for those central Londoners without shelters of their own a night spent in the Underground is still the lesser of two evils – just. Edna tells me that many people begin to queue for the Tube from early in the morning, to guarantee a place for the night!

I have noticed recently, that buses of various colours have arrived from other counties, to replace the many red London buses that have been destroyed by the Blitz; I personally find that they add a kind of flavour to the city.

I feel an almost overwhelming sense of joy to see friends and neighbours reappear from London's bombed-out streets, each day. Everywhere, the people of London are showing great courage. No longer are the material things in life so important, compared with one's relationships with family and friends.

I enjoyed reading about your night spent helping out the W.V.S., Hannah. It sounds as if they appreciated it and I expect that they will invite you back again, sometime soon. Maybe next time you will get to play cards with the soldiers!

I do so very much miss you both. Hannah, dear, do please make sure that you provide Richard with any assistance that he may need with his schoolwork, and try and keep that mischievous Tom on the straight and narrow!

Please don't go worrying about us; your father says that we will sleep in the shelter for years if we have to!

Love XXXX"

Another patrol passing by uneventfully. Flying his Spitfire at 18,000 feet, against the backdrop of a sky that was turning slowly a beautiful and fascinating red, Peter felt at ease with himself and the aircraft, although undeniably a little tired. All the temperatures and pressures on the instruments were as they should be. Soon be turning for home.

Three quarters of an hour ago, they were lazing around dispersal, virtually an entirely different squadron from that of 13th July, each one of the pilots consumed with their own private thoughts. Today was 29th October.

Peter glanced at the five Spitfires around him; they looked so elegant and graceful, and shone a magnificent copper colour. The ground far below, criss-crossed with roads, and pinpricked with cottages, and the occasional church, and the blue sea stretching endlessly away, was largely unseen below the late-afternoon haze.

Peter turned his head around, searching in a multitude of directions, to confirm there were no signs of any hostile aircraft. Things had begun to quieten down, now, as November approached, yet daily, planes were being shot down, and R.A.F. fighter pilots being killed. The bright days of September had given way to ground mist and clouds in October, making it difficult for the enemy raiders to take off from and return to their French bases. In October there had been times when theirs –and other squadrons- spent whole days without coming to readiness, and there had been much more time available to train new pilots, and take them on familiarization sorties. The Germans had been sending over fighter-bombers, such as the Messerschmitt 110, which could carry a smaller bomb load and ably defend itself, at higher altitudes, against less heavily defended targets. With October almost over, the Luftwaffe had lost some two hundred aircraft in the skies over Britain, that month, to the R.A.F.'s one hundred.

Peter found his thoughts wandering, to her…Hannah, that sweet girl who had a hint of cheekiness about her –*that* did seem a long time ago, now! Only two months had passed, although he appreciated that so much could happen in 'just two months'. What would Hannah be up to at this current moment –cycling, tending to farm animals, or maybe studying? Did she think about him? Did she even care about him? He had been out with a couple of girls in the past; one was more a puppy love, in the last year at school, then the other girl was the sister of a friend that he used to play tennis with. Their romance had been more serious, lasting several months, they had even discussed marriage, until they inexplicably started to grow apart and became bored of each other…then the war came. Now, Hannah captivated him –he thought of her figure; slim but not too skinny, her sense of humour…maybe third time lucky?

The pilot was bought back to reality by a voice over the RT.

"Red leader, this is Red two. Sight of 2 aircraft at eight o' clock."

Peter peered down to his left. There was a pair of aircraft haring along, a few thousand feet below. He couldn't make out what they were, though, due to the angle and glare of the sun. He began to feel that familiar sense of anticipation build up inside him. Archie, the Red leader ordered the Spitfires to alter course and follow the aircraft, which flew on, apparently unaware of the presence of the Spitfires further up.

Red leader's voice came over the RT, and confirmed what Peter suspected.

"OK, chaps, false alarm, they're just a couple of Hurricanes. Turn for home…and the bar."

One had to smile.

Sometime later, the airfield, with its green camouflaged hangers came into view. The flaps went down on Peter's Spitfire, and the speed fell to below a hundred miles per hour, as he crossed the hedge into the airfield. The plane landed with a gentle bounce. The other Spitfires descended upon the airfield, and the pilots slid back the aircrafts' hoods, as the ground crew dashed over. Peter pulled the handbrake on, and turned the engine off, which coughed a couple of times before going silent. The sky was a dark blue, streaked with red, the sun a shrinking semi-circle on the horizon, and there was a nip in the autumn air. When all the aircraft engines were switched off, it was silent, and the atmosphere still and slightly melancholy.

Peter walked over to the dispersal hut, away from the smell of oil and high-octane petrol, to return his flying kit to his locker. The only things in the sky now, were two birds gliding across the tops of distant trees. One day, all this would be history.

Although he did not know it, two days later, the Battle of Britain was officially declared over. It was the first defeat of the war for the Germans. They had mistakenly believed that the R.A.F. could be destroyed within days of the start of a bombing campaign. Goering, a vain man, had little understanding of the limitations of air warfare, relied too much upon instinct, and chopped and changed tactics too often. He was guilty of not having pressed on with attacking Britain from the air immediately after Dunkirk. Surprisingly, and crucially in 1940, German aircraft production had been insufficient to replace the heavy losses of the past few months. The Luftwaffe would now concentrate its efforts on the nightly bombing of British cities.

COVENTRY DEVASTATED!

Hannah recalled the chilling newspaper headlines of a week ago, when the Luftwaffe had switched their attacks from London to the provincial cities. On the night of 14th November 1940, aided by a full moon, the German bombers targeted Coventry in an attack, which had lasted for over ten hours. The enemy had dropped thirty thousand incendiaries and five hundred tons of high explosive bombs on the city. There were over 1,400 casualties, and a hundred acres of the city lay in ruins. The next morning, a black sooty fog clouded the sky, the air was hot, the water supply had been knocked out, six out of seven telephone lines were out, and no buses or trains ran. Only the tower, spire and charred outer walls of Coventry Cathedral remained, two hospitals, hundreds of shops and a third of the city's houses had been destroyed; thousands had been made homeless. Refugees poured out of the city, in cars and some pushing handcarts; their faces were grimy, and they had reddened eyes. People panicked, shook and fainted in the city's streets, and many were in such a state that they lost their ration books. The dead were buried in mass graves. The

German propaganda machine, invented a sickening new term for this mass destruction -'Coventrating.'

Next it was the turn of Southampton. On the night of 23rd November, the city centre was devastated, and there were heavy casualties. The city then endured a seven-hour raid on 30th November. The following night, there were insufficient water supplies, and many houses had to be left to the mercy of the flames, despite the best efforts of firemen from seventy-five other districts. As with Coventry, people fled the city in droves, and even ten days after the raids, few people were sleeping in the city. On the 20th and 22nd November, the city of Birmingham suffered heavy attacks. Seemingly, no town or city was immune from the wrath of Goering and his Luftwaffe. Whose turn would it be next?

Beth gazed at Hannah across the breakfast table that morning, concerned, at the girl that had now become her close friend. Hannah had that worried look on her face, which seemed so typical of late. The autumn had been a difficult and testing time for Hannah and the refugee 'townie' children, with the nightly bombing raids on London, the boys and girls must live in dread that each morning, the post would bring news of the death of one or both of their parents, in the capital. But, Hannah took the whole war to heart –the fates of the populations in occupied Europe, the life and death struggle of the British airmen; the severity of the raid on Coventry had deeply shocked her, when she read about it. Then there was Hannah's apparent love for Beth's cousin, Peter. Beth gave her friend an encouraging smile.

"Have you any news from Peter?"

Hannah asked Beth the question, practically daily. Beth had nothing new to say to her friend on this matter, since they had received Peter's last letter a couple of weeks ago. Beth shook her head, and said.

"You really are quite love struck, aren't you, Hannah?"

"Yes, you know that I am." Hannah conceded. "Although I mean…I'm sure that Peter must have a girlfriend." She added, shrugging her shoulders.

"Oh! I don't think that he has." Beth said reassuringly.

Hannah's attraction to Peter bordered on being obsessive. She wondered if she could be in love with someone who she doubted loved her back. What did she even know about love? She could hardly profess to be an expert on the topic.

"Yes, but he'll probably think me too young for him. A silly schoolgirl!"

Beth stretched her arm across the table, and squeezed her hand reassuringly.

"Well, you've left school now."

It was true. Her school days were over. She had never imagined the moment would come. She was sixteen, a young lady. But, now she was stuck in a rut, between leaving school and joining up. In 1941 she would choose one of the services and allow herself to go wherever fate would lead her. For the time being, she was trying to make herself useful, helping out around the farm. The Pavitts were happy with the arrangement, Hannah was a hard worker, and they treated her like a daughter.

Richard and Tom entered the room. The latter said cheekily.

"Come on sister, off to school!"

Beth rose to go.

"I'll see you this evening then, Hannah."

"Yes, have a nice day at school."

"What? Another day with Mr. Lawrence!"

Later on, seated next to her friends in the classroom, at their new school in Ashford, Beth relayed the conversation to the girls.

"She does seem quite love struck," agreed Samantha.

Clara spoke.

"I'd love to have a handsome airman as a boyfriend."

"So dashing." Samantha added, dreamily.

"I've got a cousin in the Royal Navy." Nancy declared. "He's out in the Atlantic protecting our shipping convoys from Hitler's U-boats."

"Really. What's it like out there at sea?" Enquired Beth.

"Cold, lonely and dangerous. I think he must be very brave," came the reply.

Looking around the classroom, Beth could see her brother, Richard and some of the other boys mischievously throwing paper aeroplanes around, without a care in the world. Tom threw one, which immediately nose-dived to the floor. One of the twins declared that Tom's plane must have been a Heinkel, causing much laughter. Beth smiled; boys would be boys. She returned once more to the subject of Hannah.

"So, you see, the problem at the moment is that she hasn't got a dashing airman as a boyfriend. Plus she's missing seeing all of us at school."

"Do you know what type of girl Peter likes?" Asked Nancy.

Beth sighed, and cupped her face in her hands.

"I don't know…I wish –if only there was someway I could get them together…"

At that moment, an object struck Samantha on the back of the neck. She looked around, and discovered a paper aeroplane on the floor besides her chair. A couple of rows back, several of the boys sported impish grins on their faces. Samantha glared at them.

"It was Henry!" Declared Tom not bothered about dropping his friend in it.

"I was aiming for Nancy, honest." Said Henry by means of explanation.

Nancy turned round.

"Well, that's nice!"

The girls decided to get their revenge. Samantha picked up the plane, straightened its nose a little, and launched it towards the boy's row. A cheer went up from Beth and Nancy.

Henry ducked, and the paper aeroplane flew over him, to land on the floor and finally settle by the classroom door. Seconds later, Mr. Lawrence, their teacher entered the room. A strict and austere man of fifty, he had been a no-nonsense Petty Officer in the Navy in the last war, and looking down at the floor, he frowned at the paper aeroplane.

"That's enough of that!" He sternly declared, retrieving the plane. "There is a war on. Don't you know that paper is rationed?"

The class fell silent.

By the beginning of December 1940, over twelve thousand civilians had been killed by the bombing in the London area, but there had been no mass panic amongst the population. Nevertheless, as the festive season approached, the second wartime Christmas would be harder than the first.

CHAPTER 13 – THE DANCE

Hannah had only decided to go to the dance under protest. She admitted it was quite silly, really; she dearly wanted to go, but was afraid to. She knew that Beth's cousin, Peter, would be there, and that was the crux of her dilemma. To see the airman that she worshipped, again, would be delightful, she loved him and his stories. However, Hannah feared that one of her friends might embarrass her in front of him, or that Peter might pay her little attention, or worse still that the pilot would not even remember her! Therefore, although Hannah desperately wanted to see Peter, the girl flipped logic on its head, and convinced herself that it would be best if she avoided the dance, and stayed at home. At least that way, she would not be disappointed…

Beth had convinced her otherwise. Hannah had harped on about Peter so much, to Beth, for many months, that there was no way, after all that, that Beth was going to not let Hannah accompany her to the dance in mid-December. Hannah would only mope around the farm, being melancholy, whilst everyone was out enjoying themselves. Beth had stressed the fact that Peter had specifically invited his cousins *and their friends* to the dance. Richard, Tom and Samantha were going as well. Officially, they were meant to be sixteen, the minimum age limit, so Hannah's companions had to pretend to be a year older than they were.

Both the girls, Beth and Hannah, spent an age dolling themselves up with perfume and jewellery, in preparation for the evening. It crossed Hannah's mind that maybe Beth was also trying to impress someone.

In the farmyard, Ted held open the car door, whilst Beth, Hannah, Richard and Samantha squeezed into the back seat. Tom sat next to his Father in the front. As Ted turned the key in the ignition, the children sat wide-eyed with anticipation. Richard felt like a prince surrounded by princesses, and thought that all three of the girls looked very pretty, even if their red lipstick were a little too bright.

The drive through the country lanes, in the blackout, was quite spooky, and Tom, letting his imagination run away from him, pictured hobgoblins lurking behind every tree. Beth and Samantha sat giggling most of the journey, although a pensive Hannah was decidedly mute.

Once they arrived at their destination, Ted drew the car up outside the dance hall, at the foot of the entrance steps. The five children scrambled out, and could immediately feel the warmth emitted from the building.

Hannah's heart sank. The girl paused, as two young attractive W.A.A.F.'s in uniform made their way up the steps towards the entrance doors, just in front of her group. How could she compete with them? –So confident, mature and imposing in their uniforms. And then there was Samantha, resembling Cinderella; she had turned fifteen in October, yet looked very much older. She'd even painted her legs with leg-make up, and used an eyebrow pencil to draw the seam of fake stockings, as you couldn't get real silk ones any longer.

Beth tapped her friend encouragingly on the arm, and smiled.

"Come on, Hannah, let's go!"

Hannah smoothed her dress, and took a deep breath.

Inside was heaving with people enjoying the party atmosphere. There must have been close to a hundred people in the room, mostly young, and noticeably more men than women. There were many uniformed R.A.F. personnel, a handful of sailors, a sprinkling of Women's Land Army and a number of locals from the village. The room was bedecked with balloons, and festooned with Union Jacks and flags from the Empire. There was a live band, a table that provided some nibbles and naturally a bar. Despite the large number of guests, the place felt cosy.

An anxious Hannah scanned the room. There was no sign of Peter, yet the girl still had that feeling of butterflies in her stomach.

Almost straight away, a cheeky rating in his late teens locked his arm around Beth, and pleaded with her to dance with him. The girl politely declined his request. When the young man moved away, again, as quickly as he had appeared, Beth had a look on her face that was asking of her friends, *did I do the right thing?*

Hannah nodded, and chuckled.

"That man reeked of alcohol!"

"And he had a leering half drunk look in his eyes," added a disapproving Samantha.

"You can do better than that, Beth," said Hannah reassuringly.

Richard and Tom slipped away to the table of food. Beth called after them.

"Just you two stay out of trouble!"

Led by a wary Beth, the three girls melted away to sit like wallflowers in a quiet corner of the room. They began to talk among themselves, whilst keeping a sly eye on the dance floor, to view the most desirable men.

After a short while, Beth stood up.

"Oh! Look, Peter's arrived." She announced.

"That's great." Samantha said, and grinned at Hannah.

"Oh! Dear...!" Hannah said under her breath. There was a sinking feeling in the pit of her stomach with nerves.

The pilot had spotted the girls at the same time. He strode over to the trio, and first warmly greeted his cousin, with a kiss on the cheek.

Peter turned to Hannah. That pleasant brown-haired evacuee girl that was staying with Cousin Beth at the farm -she looked slightly older and more desirable. Yes, he knew she'd come. The pilot greeted the brunette in the silk dress with a broad smile.

"I recognize this fine looking girl."

"Oh!" Hannah flushed, but maintained the pilot's gaze.

"It's Hannah, isn't it?" He asked, even though the girl's name was firmly embedded on his brain.

The girl nodded.

Peter observed.

"I do like your dress."

"Enchanted," smiled Hannah.

Samantha was beginning to feel like a spare part. The pilot came to her last.

"Now, you must be…" Peter hesitated. "…Nancy?"

It had been a good few years since Samantha had seen Peter; however, she was still not impressed at this faux pas. Samantha did not want to be mistaken for Nancy or Clara, for that matter. She was beginning to question what Peter's attraction to Hannah was.

"Er…no –Samantha," the girl forced a smile.

"Sorry, *Samantha*. No harm intended."

"No harm done."

Peter noticed the absence of glasses in the girls' hands, and offered.

"How about I get you three charming young ladies a drink?"

"Thanks, Peter," said an appreciative Beth.

"That's very kind of you," added Hannah.

Having made a mental note of the girls' requests, Peter disappeared to the bar.

Hannah sighed.

"He's so nice…"

"I can tell he likes you," said Beth.

"Do you think so?"

Beth squeezed Hannah's arm, and nodded excitedly.

"Yes!"

Peter returned from the bar. He handed the grateful girls their drinks, and announced.

"There's someone I'd like you all to meet…"

Peter signaled to somebody hidden amongst a crowd of people. Meanwhile, Beth glanced across, and raised her eyebrows, first to Hannah, then to Samantha. They both mirrored her look of expectation.

A young man in R.A.F. uniform walked across to the group.

"This is Neville. He does a splendid job as my armourer." Peter led the introductions. "Meet my Cousin, Beth, and her friends, Hannah and Samantha."

He shouldn't have been there either. The pilots didn't normally socialize with the ground crew. But, Peter had wanted to repay the help he'd given him, the hard work he'd put in day and night, keeping his Spitfire up in the air all those months. Pilots had come and gone, due to death or serious injury, but Neville had been there the entire time. Neville wasn't particularly tall; below his dark hair he had a genial face, and an enthusiasm in his eyes that became all the more apparent at the sight of the girls.

"You never told me that you knew so many nice looking girls!" Said Neville as he dug Peter in the ribs, and laughed. "You kept that very quiet!"

"Well." Samantha beamed, playing with her hair. "I can see that we're going to have to watch you R.A.F. boys!"

"They're such charmers, aren't they?" Teased Beth.

The group burst into laughter.

Not in the slightest discouraged, Neville spoke again.

"Have any of you girls been on the dance floor, yet?" He asked.

Beth shook her head.

"Poor show!" Declared Neville.

It was Samantha that he asked to dance, and the girl readily agreed. The attraction seemed to be instantaneous and mutual. The pair melted away onto the dance floor.

"Well, he certainly doesn't waste any time!" Beth remarked.

Peter had a look of incredulity on his face. He had only known Neville to be a technical expert and a keen reader! After a moment or two, he confessed.

"I'm completely surprised! Neville's one of the quietest chaps on the base — wouldn't say boo to a goose! I can only presume the quantity of alcohol he's had has made him lose all his inhibitions!" He shook his head, in disbelief. "Incredible."

The two girls did find this amusing.

"And Samantha didn't exactly put up any resistance," stated Hannah.

Beth spoke. Her tone was sincere.

"I think that if a male's interested in a female, he should make his feelings known to her. I mean, the worst she can say is no. But, he'll be glad he's asked her, if she's attracted to him, too."

"Listen to you getting all serious, Cousin Beth," noted Peter. He then surveyed the room, and enquired. "So tell me, who are *you* interested in, then?"

Beth suddenly became defensive, and folded her arms.

"No one in particular." She replied vaguely.

Beth disappeared, with the flimsy excuse that she needed to pay a visit to the ladies.

The pilot's eyes had been following Beth, as she sidestepped her way through individual groups across the room, until she became a blur amongst all the people. He declared.

"Cousin Beth likes to keep me guessing." He asked Hannah. "Have you any idea who she might like?"

"Not at all. Sorry to be no help."

It took Hannah a few moments to realize that she was now alone with Peter. After a silent pause, both began to speak at the same time. Peter gestured for Hannah to say her piece first, and she made some comment about there being a very pleasant atmosphere in the dance hall. Peter nodded in agreement. Was she imagining it, or did Hannah detect that Peter had become somewhat unsure and lost for words?

"Are you still enjoying it at the farm, then?" He enquired.

"Oh! Yes, very much. It's lovely with Beth, Tom, the village, the meadows…"

"Yes, it is."

"I see we're making good advances against the Italians in North Africa."

Peter smiled. He swallowed, and decided it was the right moment to get something off his chest.

"Hannah. Do you know why I invited all of you over here, tonight?"

Hannah shook her head.

Peter continued.

"I was keen to meet you, again. I've been doing a lot of thinking, ever since I closed that farmhouse door behind me, that balmy August night, and…now, I don't wish to offend you by saying this, but —well, from what I've seen so far, I think you're really nice." He added. "Quite sweet."

Hannah flushed.

Peter asked, with a concerned look on his face.

"I hope I haven't offended you, have I?"

"No, of course not." Hannah was quite lost for words; to have such praise heaped on her, and from someone so handsome! "What you've just said was very nice."

"Would you like to dance?"

Hannah nodded in acceptance, and accompanied Peter to the centre of the dance floor. He admitted to her that.

"I told Cousin Beth that she was to force you to come!"

Peter placed an arm very gentlemanly around Hannah's waist, and the pair began to dance. They came across Neville and Samantha, who were inseparable, and very much enjoying themselves. The former gave Peter a wink.

Hannah studied some of the other couples on the dance floor. There was an old Colonel arm in arm with a Wren, several airmen paired up with W.A.A.F.'s and a couple of Land Girls dancing together for a lark. Hannah smiled to herself, as she spied Tom unsuccessfully trying to wrestle in amongst some of the W.A.A.F.'s. Before long, Hannah had totally absorbed herself in the music and her dashing dancing partner. He spoke to her a little, his voice calm and reassuring. She closed her eyes contentedly, and wandered if this might be the start of something beautiful.

Beth had discreetly kept in the background. She frequently took sips from her drink, and smiled bashfully when she met someone's gaze. She was pleased that her cousin and Hannah appeared to be getting on so well, not to mention Samantha and her fellow. Now, where had the two mischievous boys got to? Richard appeared at Beth's side.

"I really wanted to dance with Samantha, tonight, but she's been glued to that bloomin' pilot the whole time!" The boy sulked.

"Actually, he's not a pilot," the girl informed him. She frowned. "I didn't know you liked Samantha?"

"I thought Samantha liked me, too —such beautiful blonde hair." Richard stared morosely up at the ceiling then his eyes dropped to the floor, his hopes dashed. "Well, I *did* like her."

Richard looked glum; neither did Beth feel particularly cheerful. That was typical Samantha, the princess, with all the men after her.

Beth spoke.

"I know someone who would dance with you."

"Who? Tom?" Suggested an unenthusiastic Richard.

Beth clasped her hands together in front of her, and uttered the solitary word, almost as a whimper.

"Me."

Richard saw Beth in a completely different light. Until that moment, he had only ever thought of the girl next to him as his friend's (Tom) sister, or alternatively, as his sister's friend. Deep down, he had always been aware that Beth was a pretty girl, but they were both young, and she was looked upon by Richard –indeed, all the children were- as a playmate (and Beth wouldn't disagree). However, they were all growing up, and on the threshold of becoming young adults. Richard had liked Samantha, who, in turn, had chosen the airman, although Beth, instead, intimated that she felt something for Richard. Maybe Beth was merely being friendly, for Richard reasoned that neither of them had anyone to dance with. Things in life were never simple.

"Really?" Richard's mood perked up instantly.

"Yes." Beth shrugged her shoulders. "That's if you'd be interested."

"Of course I am!" There was a definite glow on Richard's face. "I'd really like to dance with you."

"Then, let's go!"

The pair joined hands, and ran excitedly onto the dance floor.

They danced several numbers, before taking a breather near the entrance, at the same time enjoying some fresh cool air away from the heat of the dance floor.

A couple of minutes later, Tom joined them.

"Been having fun with the W.A.A.F.'s?" Enquired Beth.

"Them!" Complained a disgruntled Tom. "I asked one of them for a Christmas kiss, and she refused me."

"Oh!" Beth was not at all surprised, really.

"Her name was Josephine. Do you know what she said?"

The other two looked at Tom expectantly.

"She told me that she might reconsider my offer when I start shaving, in a couple of years! Cheek!"

"Oh dear! How old was she, then, Tom?" Probed Beth.

"Only twenty-two."

"Oh! Tom! She's far too old for you."

Richard found this highly amusing.

Beth patted her brother on the head.

"Poor old Tom…"

Tom moved hastily away.

"Stop patting me on the head like a puppy!" He shouted.

Beth made a suggestion to her brother.

"Still, there's always the Land Girls…"

Hannah had not wanted the evening to end. She had chatted and danced a great deal with Peter, and even though she (like her brother and the other children) got to bed very late, Hannah found that she was unable to sleep such was her excitement. At the end of the evening, the pilot –*her* pilot- had expressed a sincere desire to see her again. Hannah pulled the bedclothes further over her, closed her eyes, and let out a deep sigh; she feared that, when the morning of 15th came, it would all turn out to have been just a dream.

In December 1940, the British people settled down to endure a Christmas in the shelters, where small coal stoves provided warmth, wardens played Santa; people exchanged small gifts, and danced the night away to gramophone music. People compared the pros and cons of various shelters, as they embarked upon the 'shelter crawl', in a similar manner to a pub-crawl, enjoying concerts, religious services and even film shows. The national diet got as exciting as cereals, vegetables and whole-meal bread.

During a review of the war on Thursday 19th December 1940, the Prime Minister declared.

"So far we have been no more successful in stopping the German night raider than the Germans have been successful in stopping our aeroplanes that have ranged freely over Germany. We must expect a continuance of these attacks and must bear them."

Over the last half of 1940, Germany had been receiving attention from Britain's own bombers. The industrial Ruhr area, with its network of factories, docks and railways, was continually bombed, and as a result, output at Krupps armaments factory was down fifty percent. One traveler on the German railways had to change trains fifty-two times such was the damage! By the end of 1940 Berlin had been bombed thirty-five times by the R.A.F.

Bristol was bombed heavily on 2nd and 6th December. The university, many hospitals and churches were hit. Sheffield was hit twice. Birmingham, Manchester, Liverpool and Merseyside were also attacked. The next heavy attack on London by the Luftwaffe was not long in coming...

The night of Sunday 29th December, Mary had been reflecting upon a second Christmas spent without the children at home. She had been worried sick whilst John had been fighting in France, but he had made it through, only to be posted to Africa. It had been proved the right thing to do to send Hannah and Richard away into the country, away from Hitler's terrible bombs –she had read their letters telling her how they had enjoyed themselves at that dance. The house felt so empty, and Mary wandered how many more Christmases the children would be away for;

probably the next one, at least, for even the most optimistic conceded that there seemed little chance that the war would end in 1941.

In November, a British air attack by Fairey Swordfish torpedo bombers on Taranto harbour disabled three Italian battleships and severely damaged four other ships. After the raid, the balance of sea power in the Mediterranean swung in Britain's favour. On 21ˢᵗ November, the last Italian invaders fled Greek soil.

The Jews were suffering in occupied Warsaw. Around 400,000 Jews were now living six to a room in a sealed ghetto, cut off from the outside world. Inside, all wireless sets were taken, and telephone lines had been cut by the Germans.

The French were hungry, and were fighting each other whilst standing in the food queues. In Denmark, the Germans were draining the country of cattle. In Belgium and Holland, there were also food shortages, and many homes faced the winter without any heating.

Mary had heard the distant wail of the air raid sirens, and she moved unhurriedly across to the upstairs window. George was asleep, oblivious to it all. *Whose turn tonight?*

The target was the City of London and Southwark. Before long, the sky over the centre of London was lit by a crimson and yellow glare, as thousands of incendiaries rained down. Mary tried to imagine the hell that was going on over there under the fire-demon…the flames, the heat, charred timbers, loose bricks, collapsing walls, the fireman valiantly going about their job in immense danger. Her thoughts turned to the men up in the German bombers –What were *they* thinking? Did the airmen wrestle with their consciences and question whether their missions could be justified during this Christian period?

Before the night was out, the inferno would destroy eight Wren churches and the Guildhall and damage three hospitals, the Old Bailey and the Daily Telegraph building. Miraculously, St. Paul's Cathedral survived, again. At the height of the blaze, firefighters were forced to blow up buildings to create firebreaks. The event, which could be seen over thirty miles away, was called "The Second Great Fire of London."

In recognition that the voluntary fire-watching system was inadequate, two days later, the Government announced that it would make it compulsory for everyone aged between sixteen and sixty who was not already engaged in Government, Army or Civil Defence services to register for fire-watching duties.

The King had summed up the national mood on Christmas Day.

"If war brings its separations it brings new unity also, the unity which comes from common perils and common sufferings willingly shared. To be good comrades and good neighbours in trouble is one of the finest opportunities of the civilian population, and by facing hardships and discomforts cheerfully and resolutely not only do they do their own duty but they play their part in helping the fighting services to win the war. Time and again during the last few months I have seen for myself the battered towns of England, and I have seen the British people facing their ordeal. I can say to them all that they may be justly proud of their race and nation."

CHAPTER 14 – LETTERS FROM THE DESERT

In the summer of 1940, Italy maintained a powerful army in Libya, consisting of some quarter of a million men. In neighbouring Egypt, the British had less than forty thousand men. After the fall of France, in June, the British began to make daily armoured raids across the frontier, on enemy outposts. On 13th September 1940, 250,000 Italian troops crossed into Egypt, and the severely outnumbered British forces were ordered to fall back, rather than fight for useless ground. The Italians advanced sixty miles to Sidi Barrani then paused in order to set up a fresh water pipeline, extend the Libyan road and stock Sidi Barrani. They also set about constructing a number of separate large, defensive camps.

The small British force, planned to attack the Italian Army, within a few months, by penetrating the undefended fifteen mile gap that lay between the enemy army, which was deployed in two halves. The British could not afford to lose Egypt to the axis, because of the vital importance of the Suez Canal. Britain had been able, despite the threat of invasion, to feed some much-needed reinforcements to North Africa. John Baker was part of this force, and after he began to settle in the desert, towards the end of August, he wrote home.

"Dear Mother & Father.

To live in the North African Desert, is to inhabit another World. You know that, before I came out here, I thought (I suppose, on reflection naively), that the desert would be very similar to one of our Kent beaches, only a little hotter. Incredible though it may seem, there is not actually *that* much sand here! The landscape is flat and featureless, save the occasional shallow depression, and comprises hard flat rock, stones, and often bog, mud and, yes, sand. The sight of 'seifs' really is quite something. These are great dunes formed by winds, which are miles long, and higher than the tallest buildings in London. The sand, which creates such pretty views, can also be a menace. A man can sink a couple of feet deep in the pretty, yellow sand; and it also proves to be the worst surface for a vehicle to negotiate. Even the best desert tracks are bumpy. The going is usually best on a firm, pebbly surface. However, even on that terrain, one has to be careful, for, sometimes, soft sand lies beneath the apparently firm surface.

We were issued with regulation tropical kit. This includes sunhats and baggy khaki shorts, which are buttoned on each side so that at night they can be lowered to make long trousers.

The creatures, with which we share our desert home, are most vexing. The flies (green and quite big) are everywhere around. They deliberately seem to go for one's ears, mouth and nose. The wretched things make meal times difficult, and whenever one tries to enjoy a cup of tea, without fail, the flies all assemble around the rim. One is forced to put a hand over the top of the mug, and consume the tea by means of short, frequent sips. Our drivers complain that the dead flies constantly accumulate on the windscreens of their vehicles, and flies can even block the carburettor! Then there are the scorpions, and their deadly poison. Every morning we go through the ritual of shaking our army boots upside-down, to check for any undesirable visitors that may have taken up residence inside, before putting the boots on. In addition to the flies and the scorpions, there are also ants, bugs, cockroaches and lice to contend with!

At the cookhouse, meals consist of bully beef, plus tinned vegetables, rice and sweet potatoes, which are grown locally. Rarely are we given a couple of tablespoons of curry. I consider myself quite fortunate, to receive fruit from the Nile Delta. Breakfast is a queer affair, the meal comprises army biscuits (of which there is a plentiful supply), covered with a little tinned milk and some sugar. This is accompanied by a refreshing mug of tea.

Water comes distilled from the sea, and is not very pleasant to drink, being too hot and salty. But, to brew the water up into a hot cup of tea, makes the drink very refreshing –and morale boosting! Despite the best efforts, you are thirsty most of the time.

A couple of the men have had the misfortune to suffer from gippy tummy. It is a struggle to maintain hygiene, although, rest assured Mother, that your son is doing his best to stay clean. The daily water ration is approximately three-quarters of a gallon per man, for all purposes. A good proportion of this goes to the cookhouse, for the communal preparation of food. I keep my water in a can, and I have to stretch out my day's ration to clean my teeth, shave in, wash my face in and clean my clothes with. As you can appreciate, it is essential that the water be extensively recycled! Some of the men, have devised quite clever, elaborate means for water recycling, so that much of the water is used a score times, and is most likely in excess of ten days old!

Regarding sanitation, we can dig down latrines in soft sand, but on harder rock surfaces, it is necessary to transport thunder boxes to the required area. Then, every morning we create a wonderful bonfire, when petrol is poured into the latrine, and the whole lot is set alight!

Perhaps the most disagreeable thing about the desert, are the 'khamsin', or hot winds. The sandstorms that they create are awful. They go on for hour after hour, and make everyone tetchy (myself included). The sandstorm, a gigantic dark wall of cloud, roars towards you making a terrific noise. When it envelops you, one can hardly breathe for dust and sand, and it becomes incredibly hot. It is very difficult to even stand up. When, at last, the storm is over, you find that one's hair, skin and uniform have changed to a shocking orange colour. Exasperated, one is disgusted to find that the sand has even found it's way inside one's mess tin!

Understandably, navigating around the desert is no simple matter. The army has ingeniously placed numbered petrol drums at intervals of roughly ten miles square, which can be found on a map. We also rely on a sun compass (which works by where the sun's shadow falls on a central needle), in the day, and a theodolite (which we are fortunate to have obtained, as they are fairly rare, and you have to be quite an expert to use them), at night.

Whenever we come across some Arabs in the desert (which is not that often), they barter with us. For instance, they will give us local eggs in exchange for some cigarettes. The Arabs would then be quite insistent that we give them a pass so as to show their loyalty to the Allies. These people are always very polite, although one feels that you could never trust them a hundred per cent.

Your son has managed to pick up a little Arabic, on his travels. 'Saeeda' means Good Day. The word for tea is 'shai.' A woman is a 'bint'. To ask the time, you say 'Sar kam da watti?' I particularly like the saying 'alakeefic' –couldn't care less!

XXXXX – John."

John wrote home again in mid-October 1940.

"Dear Mother & Father.

We have spent four days much-welcome leave in Cairo.

I began by having a long soak in a bath. You cannot imagine how wonderful it felt, after having gone so long without a proper wash. After that, I promptly booked into a hotel.

This capital city, with its white houses, bazaars and open-fronted cafes, is where East meets West. On the streets, one will find trams with passengers hanging onto the outside for dear life, black-robed women, street traders always ready to barter and peasants roasting ears of corn over charcoal braziers. Everywhere, there is the smell of Egyptian tobacco. It truly felt, in this noisy, smelly city, that there was no war on, at all.

The bootblack boys are a real menace. You cannot avoid them. You can be sitting with your pals, drinking Turkish coffee, on a café terrace, when before you know it, there's a grubby, skinny Egyptian boy at your feet, cleaning your boots (getting a good shine on them, mind you). With an impish grin on his face, he then holds out a hand, and asks for piastres (coins).

I spent one day of my leave with Tom Walker, 'doing the sights.' A couple of natives led us around on their mules (for the obligatory number of piastres, of course), and we saw the Pyramids and the Sphinx. In Cairo itself, we saw the palace of King Farouk and many mosques, although we didn't go inside.

Although we visited the cinema once (we saw last year's film 'Goodbye Mr. Chips'), we spent all our evenings touring the local bars and cabaret, downing too many pints for our own good. Well, during one such evening of merriment, one of the local 'bints' came and put her arm around Bill Gardner, in a very friendly manner. He thought that his luck was in, however, it transpired that the Egyptian girl was only after a free drink or two! How we laughed."

John thought back and dared not mention to his parents that when they had first arrived in Egypt, during a talk, a medical officer warned them in stark terms, on the dangers of venereal diseases, which could be caught from sex with local prostitutes. In spite of this talk, one night, a couple of men couldn't resist visiting Berka red light district! Much later, they returned, looking moderately happy. Apparently, they had been obliged to join a long queue, in a dilapidated building that stank like hell. Both the men went with (in their words) some beautiful, young 'bint', who, beforehand, stressed to them that it was a very busy night, and she requested that they "be quick!"

John smiled to himself, and concluded.

"The Egyptians as a whole are an agreeable people, and very obliging. However, I feel that the Wogs are *very* different to us, and we never socialize with them, as such.

Hope that you are both 'taking it' well in war-torn England.

XXXXX – John."

On Monday 9th December 1940, John wrote home, again.

"Dear Mother & Father.

Today we went on the attack. Our targets have been Italian desert forts a number of miles south of Sidi Barrani, a coastal town on the Mediterranean Sea.

The guns of our artillery opened up with a determined burst –a wonderful moment. Then, at 7 a.m. the splendid men of an Indian division, who had daringly got up close to the enemy positions during the night, spearheaded the attack.

We British had been brought up to within half a mile of the Italian positions, by vehicles. We advanced soon after the Indians, and were met by scores of Eyeties, who couldn't seem to surrender quickly enough! It was, perhaps, for this reason that I witnessed little fighting and only then at a distance.

There were countless abandoned lorries everywhere, including ten-ton trucks and Fiat runabouts. It was strange yet morale boosting to see some Italian medium tanks, lined up in a neat row, their crew being captured whilst still warming up their engines! Overall, for little loss of our own, we took hundreds of prisoners, and captured a number of Eyetie guns.

Quite impressive long walls constructed solely from desert stones dominated the camp itself. Artillery emplacements, bastions and machine-gun nests intersected these walls. We also discovered tank traps. Amongst the scrub, we found large dumps of ammunition, and many barrels of fuel. We also claimed the prize of numerous Eyetie bicycles. Constructed into the stony ground, were tent-covered dugouts.

Was your son happy when Bill Gardner dragged him into the enemy cookhouse! Inside, was nothing less than large quantities of mineral water and Chianti. In addition to this, there were plentiful supplies of fish, olive oil, tomato and, of course, spaghetti. I couldn't resist supplementing my evening meal with the latter.

The officer's mess was palatial; inside we found perfumery and silverware alongside the elegant uniforms of –believe it or not- satin and velvet!

After our encounters with Jerry, I found the Eyeties an easy foe to beat. I almost felt sorry for those Romans, as we packed them off in lorries to prisoner of war camps.

A truly satisfying day!
XXXXX – John."

The British took the remaining camps surrounding Sidi Barrani, one by one. On 11th December 1940, British G.H.Q., Cairo, announced that Sidi Barrani itself had been captured. On 12th December the British Prime Minister addressed the House of Commons.

"While it is too soon to measure the scale of these operations, it is clear that they constitute a victory which in this African theatre of war is of the first order."

Thirty thousand Italian soldiers were taken into captivity, whilst the British pursued the remaining enemy army into Libya. From the skies above the desert, the R.A.F. persistently bombed Italian aerodromes, fuel dumps and vehicles. Bardia, just inside Libya, was the allied army's next target, and the British began to besiege the town.

On Tuesday 7th January 1941, John wrote home.

"Dear Mother & Father.

We have resumed our offensive.

On the night of 1st January, our airforce gave the Italians a right proper New Year's present, by bombing their positions in and around the port of Bardia. The R.A.F. continued the attack, the following day; it was relentless, and lasted for hours. The town lies a dozen miles inside Libya, and we had been lying in wait, surrounding the two Eyetie divisions, which had been trapped there for over a week.

The assault, proper, on Bardia, began on the 3rd January. British tanks and Australian infantry tore through the Italian perimeter defences. Throughout, the pressure was maintained by the guns of our navy (out at sea), and from the R.A.F. It all went like clockwork.

The evening of 4th January, your son was proud to be a member of a patrol, which started to infiltrate the town, and we began to mop up remaining Italian resistance, which was satisfactorily light.

The following day, the Italians in Bardia surrendered, their commanding officer, a fellow nicknamed 'Electric Whiskers', having escaped into the desert. Overall, we took tens of thousands of Eyeties prisoner, this time. Again, we captured much enemy equipment –anti-aircraft guns, tanks and literally hundreds of transport vehicles. We have written on Italian lorries 'Benito's Bus' and 'Rome next stop', and have passed signs put up by military policemen declaring 'If you lika the spaghetti keep going!' Miraculously, our own losses (British and Australian) were only in the hundreds.

Bardia was a decisive allied success. However, it was not just a simple case of the Eyeties laying down their weapons and waving the white flag! Once the battle was under way, the initial Italian artillery bombardment against our positions was intense, and we had to repeatedly take cover. I later saw a number of dead Eyeties lying next to their guns, and I realized that those brave men must have kept on firing until the end.

In the town, the Union Jack flies triumphantly over Government House, we continue to advance, and your son is in good spirits.

XXXXX – John."

Saturday 8th February 1941.

"Dear Mother & Father.

The defeated Italian Army is in full retreat! On 22nd January, we took Tobruk, along with 15,000 prisoners. After a night artillery barrage that was, I am told, as intense as those of the Great War, Australian sappers moved in, followed by our infantry and armour. Italian trenches and defensive forts were overrun and the town surrounded. An Australian hat now flies from a flagpole, as there was no Union Jack!

On 30th January, Derna fell to us. The Italians had made good use of the hilly, rugged terrain surrounding the seaport town. Our attack was met with accurate fire from 20mm guns and dive-bombing and machine-gunning from Italian planes. However, once more (in the end), British infantry and tanks proved superior.

The Italians then abandoned Benghazi, and made a desperate attempt to flee our pursuing army, by means of the Benghazi – Tripoli coastal road. Travelling in lorries, we followed a fast-moving armoured force, whose aim was to cut off the retreating Eyeties.

We set off on our 150-mile journey on the morning of 4th February, travelling along a poor quality desert road, which was strewn with boulders and slabs of rock. The speed, with which our vehicles traveled, threw up a constant cloud of dust. Icy rain and wind (incredible in the desert, you'd think) did not aid progress.

Next day, 5th February, we arrived at Beda Fomm on the Benghazi-Tripoli road. Our armoured vanguard had already got stuck into the Italian column, and we joined in by attacking the Italian flanks. For good measure, our artillery opened up, as well. I was amazed to see that the enemy column was a good ten miles long, however it was in a sorry state. It consisted of armoured cars, civilian buses, lorries, tanks etc. On reflection, the Eyeties must have had more vehicles and weaponry than we did, but we took them so much by surprise that they never really stood a chance. It was a rout. Many Italian lorries and tanks were on fire, and this caused the ammunition inside these to explode. The Italians panicked so much that they started to fire upon their own vehicles! Throughout, the noise was deafening –bullets whistling through the air, constant explosions, and injured men screaming out in pain. The air was full of dust, flames, shrapnel and smoke. Only a handful of enemy tanks managed to escape our trap. Dozens more tanks and countless other Eyetie vehicles perished as blazing wrecks along that fated coastal road.

Early afternoon, on 7th February, white handkerchiefs began to appear, as over 20,000 Italians surrendered. Everywhere was strewn with pieces of uniforms, helmets, weapons and burst open suitcases. Believe me, I saw some grisly sights around the wrecks of Italian tanks. There were dead Italians whose bodies had been burnt to cinders. Some of the enemy had been cooked inside their tanks to such an extent, that all that remained was black goo. This had been war in its most horrific sense, and I felt like being sick up on the spot. The enemy had paid a heavy price in their defeat at Beda Fomm, and many of our men now felt quite a bit of sympathy for the Eyeties. Yet again, we took a big booty of war material.

I later spoke to one of our tank commanders, and admired his magnificent vehicle. The Matilda tank has heavy armour, which, I was informed, makes it virtually invulnerable to Italian anti-tank guns. It is very reliable on the battlefield, even after days of having been on the go non-stop!

We have now advanced an incredible 500 miles since early December last year, and the whole of Cyrenaica (North-East Libya) is in our hands.

Onwards to Tripoli!

XXXXX – John."

A couple of days earlier, on Friday 6th February 1941, the Australians entered the Cyrenaican capital, Benghazi. The following day, the British arrived. As the *Daily Express* reported.

"In the grey, cold early morning light they got down from their trucks in the streets and marched into the square before the Town Hall. They were unkempt, dirty, stained head to foot in mud. They had their steel helmets down over their eyes to break the force of the wind.

…They had fought three battles and a dozen skirmishes. They had lost some of their comrades, dead and wounded, on the way. They had often been hungry, cold and wet through in these two months of campaigning in bitter weather.

…The townspeople swarming round the square had half sullenly expected brass bands and a streamlined military parade. Instead, they got this little ragged group of muddy men. They hesitated. Then a wave of clapping broke down from the housetops…"

By 9th February 1941, the British had travelled another 165 miles across the desert, to El Agheila, which would mark the furthest point of their advance. In the space of two months, 133,000 Italians had been taken prisoner.

That same day, Winston Churchill paid tribute to the allied army, which had.

"…Broken irretrievably the Italian military power on the African continent."

CHAPTER 15 - COURTSHIP

It was the last Saturday in January 1941, and Hannah and her handsome pilot friend were strolling through the fields outside the village, enjoying some time together, as he had a twenty-four hour pass. Although it was a clear day, and the sun was out, there was a chill breeze in the air that reminded them that it was still winter. Hannah rather shyly kept both her hands deep inside her trouser pockets, although she secretly desired to hold Peter's hand. The R.A.F. officer, older, more confident, was much more at ease, and when he spoke, he did so breezily. He wore his smart blue uniform, and to Hannah, this made Peter ever the dashing hero. The girl dare not pinch herself for fear that it might all turn out to be just a dream.

Hannah's mind went back to the conversation at the breakfast table, the previous day, when the other children had teased her terribly over her friendship with the young pilot. Richard and Tom had, of course, been the worst culprits, but now even Beth had ribbed Hannah a little over her 'boyfriend'. It was Hannah's firm belief that they were all envious.

The distant roar of an aeroplane broke Hannah's thoughts. It reminded her that, although the immediate threat of a German invasion had all but disappeared, for the time being, war was still very much in evidence in Britain.

The pair halted, and, for several moments, Peter was distracted from his female companion. Peter stood rigid, his hand to his forehead, his eyes scanning the sky, straining to make out the remote aircraft.

"I think...I can just make out two aircraft," the pilot informed his girlfriend.

"Looks like one of our lads is chasing Jerry home."

The plane disappeared, and, the excitement over, Peter turned round, and acknowledged Hannah with a smile.

Hannah asked the pilot earnestly.

"Do you think that we can win this war?"

After a brief pause, Peter replied.

"We won't be defeated. I believe that there's no longer any likelihood of us being invaded." He began confidently then continued, realistically. "But, to actually land our troops in France, again, and defeat Germany and Italy...it could take years. If only America or even Russia could come in on our side..." Peter looked to the skies for inspiration. "But, I don't know *how* they could enter the war." He concluded, through gritted teeth. "Britain and Germany —we'll just fight ourselves to a bloody stalemate."

"We've shown that we —Britain- can stand alone against Hitler." Hannah said resolutely. "I bet that, last year, he thought that he could just hop across the Channel and defeat us on our *silly little island!*"

"Yes, I think he did," agreed Peter.

The pilot gazed intently at the fields of brown, green and yellow, and the hills and woods that extended seemingly endlessly into the distance. He pointed at no particular spot, and declared.

"I see all this from above, and more –the little towns and villages, the country churches, our heritage- when I'm in my plane, and I think what a bloody nightmare it would be if the Nazis beat us, and laid waste to this land."

"I dearly wish we could all live in peace, again, in a World without Hitler, without having to live in fear; us, the French, the Poles…" Said Hannah.

"Hopefully one day." Peter placed a hand on Hannah's shoulder.

At that precise moment, the girl felt as if she had known the pilot for all of her life. She turned her neck, and looked directly at him. Hannah had an intense feeling of well being, as Peter slid his hand slowly down her bare arm, and took her delicate hand in his. They started walking, once more. To Hannah, it felt very, very nice; she had never imagined that a man could make her feel like this.

Peter asked Hannah about her family, and the latter now began to talk more freely.

"My parents live in London –of course you already know that!" She chuckled.

"Before she met Daddy, Mummy worked for six years as a shorthand typist. I think she used to enjoy it."

"And your Father?"

"He works in an office. He fought in the last war, for all four years from start to finish. And would you believe that he came away without as much as a scratch on him." Hannah stared down at the ground, and stated. "But, he doesn't like to talk about it…"

Peter nodded sympathetically.

"Most people of our parent's generation are like that, Hannah. You find that a number of veterans of the Great War bear mental scars."

"He was at a place called Passchendaele –so Mummy told me." Hannah recalled. "I never knew Mummy's brother, he was killed at the battle of the Somme," she lamented. "According to Mummy, the soldiers only took a hundred yards of ground at a time, and thousands died in the process."

Peter squeezed Hannah's hand tighter, and said nothing. He had heard such stories, too.

"The rationing creates ever more challenges for Mummy." Hannah began. "She says in her letters that she's encouraging my Daddy to eat potatoes instead of bread –he keeps on finding things like potato salad and potato scones on his dinner plate, not to mention sweet potato pastry!"

"Lucky Dad –I don't think!"

"Actually, we've started to feed Oscar potatoes."

"The dog." Peter smiled.

"As well as Winalot."

"Of course."

"I think that Oscar eats rather well," declared Hannah.

"One of the chap's father's a 'backyarder'," said Peter.

Hannah frowned.

"Backyarder?"

"He keeps animals –chickens and rabbits- in their backyard for food." Peter explained. "Trouble was, they grew so attached to 'Flopsy', that when they went to slaughter the animal, his sister was pleading to spare its life, in floods of tears; the father felt so rotten."

They walked along in silence, for a while, hand in hand, until Peter spoke.

"The chaps at the airbase have all been asking after you." He declared.

"Oh! No!" Hannah put her other hand to her mouth.

Peter leaned his head closer to the girl, who was now looking at him expectantly, and he said reassuringly.

"Don't worry. I assure you they're all saying nice things about you."

Hannah looking visibly relieved fanned her face with her hand, somewhat theatrically.

Peter spoke, again.

"I've told them that I've got a very pretty girlfriend. If it's ok to call you that – my *girlfriend?"*

This time it was the turn of the pilot to become unsure of himself. Hannah was trembling with excitement inside. She need no longer worry that he didn't like her - how wonderful that the most handsome man she had ever met actually reciprocated her feelings. Without hesitation, she answered.

"Yes, of course it is."

The pair came to a gate at the edge of the field. Hannah leaned against the gate and smiled radiantly, she felt so happy.

Peter held Hannah's gaze, and edged his face ever closer to hers.

Awkwardness and embarrassment almost made her move away, for she did not know how to kiss a man; but she adored him and she stayed put. He placed his arms around her, and she embraced him. Their lips met, and next moment, her tongue was moving around expertly inside his mouth. Her eyes were closed, though his remained open, as, for some time, her smooth-skinned face brushed against his handsome features, during that special first kiss.

"You know, none of the other chaps girlfriends are as pretty as you, Hannah." Peter beamed.

A gentle breeze blew Hannah's hair out of place. As she moved her hair out of her face, she smiled sweetly.

"Now you're just trying to flatter me."

"Well, it's true."

"I bet that, in the past, you've courted lots of attractive girls."

"What makes you think that? I haven't," the pilot insisted, as he climbed onto the gate.

"You must have!" Hannah accused. "You're simply pretending not to, just to make me feel better."

Before Peter was able to get a word in edgeways, Hannah continued.

"I bet there are lots of nice W.A.A.F.'s at your airfield?"

"Oh! Hannah! You are a silly little thing!" Peter helped Hannah down from the gate, and put his arm around her.

The girl burst into laughter, at herself and her paranoia.

Peter laughed, too. They were getting on fantastically, and Hannah wished that they did not have to hurry home for the evening meal.

A short while later, the farm loomed into view. The late afternoon sun was descending upon the horizon. The countryside was silent; they were very much alone. It was queer though, that Land Girls may be working beyond that hill, or an army dispatch rider speeding round a not so far off corner to deliver his urgent message. Soon it would be dark, and a frost would start to cover the fields.

"Hannah, the chaps at the airbase…" Peter began.

Hannah wandered what was coming next.

"Yes…?"

"Well, the thing is, they all want to see what you look like." The pilot continued. "And I don't have a picture of you."

First, he calls me his girlfriend, and now he wants a photograph —he must be keen! Hannah felt as if she was walking on air.

"A photograph!" She said excitedly.

"Yes, a photograph." He nodded.

"Yes, of course you may have a photograph," grinned Hannah.

As the pair walked across the dirt covered farmyard, arm in arm, laughing and joking Hannah caught a glimpse of a face at one of the upstairs windows of the farmhouse. Within a second, the image disappeared.

Emily welcomed the couple at the front door with a warm smile. Next moment Richard and Tom both hared down the stairs, two steps at a time, into the kitchen. Sporting an impish grin, the freckly-faced boy demanded to know.

"Where've you two been?" He turned to Richard, and covered his mouth as if whispering, although his words were clearly and deliberately audible. "I bet they've been kissing!"

To save further embarrassed looks from Hannah and her airman, Emily scolded her son.

"That's enough, Thomas! You scamp!"

As 1941 arrived, at home, the prices of twenty-one foodstuffs including biscuits, coffee, cocoa, honey, nuts and tinned food were pegged at the December 1940 levels. This actually led to price falls for some products. For Britain, the cost of war rose to above £11 million per day, and as tax revenues were only meeting a quarter of all expenditure, the budget deficit inevitably ballooned further.

In East Africa, the British began an offensive against Italian held Eritrea. On 25th February, after a two-week campaign, Mogadishu, the capital of Italian Somaliland fell to British and African troops. This had been the swiftest British advance of the war. During January and February the allied forces pushed ever deeper into Ethiopia, which Italy had conquered in 1936.

In mid January, Germany started to bomb the Mediterranean Island of Malta. In one day alone, eighty Stuka dive-bombers attacked Valetta (the capital's) harbour. During 1941, the island would endure over a thousand air raids.

The Luftwaffe bombed Bristol, Cardiff, Plymouth, Portsmouth, Swansea and even neutral Eire during the first month of the year. The R.A.F. hit back by dropping 20,000 incendiaries on Bremen, targeting oil refineries, shipyards and the Focke-Wulf aircraft factory.

In the Warsaw ghetto, the suffering intensified. The Germans were allowing the Jews only half the amount of food that they needed, and people were falling dead in the streets by starvation. Hans Frank, the Nazi governor of Poland believed that killing a Jew by starvation saved a valuable bullet.

Heinrich Himmler, head of the SS, announced a programme to expand a concentration camp at Auschwitz, so that it could accommodate over 100,000 prisoners. Inmates at various concentration camps were being used as slave labour, forced to carry out strenuous physical work for German industry; but worse was to come.

In the latter half of February 1941, Mary wrote from London to her children.

"The raids have become noticeably less frequent since the turn of the year. It's funny how after a couple of nights with no bombing, everyone starts to bicker over petty things, again. Edna complains about the Stephenson children climbing over her garden wall, and showing total disrespect for her flowerbed, Mrs. Woodrow grumbles about the Hewitt's dog scaring her cat, and *everyone* moans about the (food) rationing. But, when a few bombs fall on London, again, then the camaraderie returns! Do they not realize that some more tragic Mothers (and Fathers) are still losing Sons in the fighting? Walking through the bombed out areas becomes ever more distressing. I saw one elderly gentleman carrying the body of his wife out of the rubble, and the most heartbreaking part about it all, was that he was talking to the corpse as if it were alive: "Gladys dear." It left me choked for some time afterwards. The other day I queued up for ages (what's new?!), only to be informed by the shopkeeper that there was no fat, fruit or honey! On the subject of food, an aggrieved Mrs. Kent informed me that she recently bought a 'milk substitute' for five shillings a pound, which she swears was a cheap mixture of baking powder, flour and salt! You can imagine what *that* tasted like! Your father does reliably inform me, however, that there is still plenty of alcohol around!

Mrs. Kent has now got her eldest daughter (who's only thirteen) involved in domestic responsibilities and looking after the younger children, since her husband died in a raid, and her schoolwork is suffering as a result. Mr. Kent was the main breadwinner, and Mrs. Kent is now working a lot more.

Bunks have been installed in the underground stations by the government, and there are even some very novel food trains running from station to station. Some shelters provide their own entertainment such as concerts.

Did you hear Mr. Churchill's broadcast the other day (9th February 1941) – his first for months? I felt a degree of satisfaction when he spoke about Britain standing up alone against the German and Italian dictators. It seems impossible to believe how our small, outnumbered forces scored such a decisive defeat against Mussolini's forces in Libya (although your Father says that he never rated the Italians much, anyway). We both especially liked Mr. Churchill's message to America- *Give us the tools and we will finish the job!* Such encouraging words from the British Bulldog.

I am delighted to hear about 'your pilot', Hannah. Peter must be very brave and I can see how proud you are of him. Make sure that he always acts like a proper gentleman towards you. I look forward to meeting him, which I'm sure I will do before long.

Your loving Mother. XXXXXX"

The crowd spilled out from the warm bosom of the cinema, onto the blacked-out streets. People rubbed their hands together, and pulled their coats tighter, to protect themselves against the cold, that February night. Hannah and Peter, hand in hand, emerged from the hustle and bustle, and hurried past darkened shop fronts, following the barely visible white painted line that marked the edge of the pavement. They made towards the bus stop, a handful of minute's walk away.

Hannah had, as promised, sent through the post the picture that Peter had requested. Rather embarrassingly for Hannah, the most up-to-date photograph that she could lay her hands on, was one taken of her two years ago in her Girl Guides uniform, when, in Hannah's view, she looked so much younger and sillier! She dared not contemplate the reactions of the other pilots, when they saw her photograph!

The film, starring Leslie Howard, had been overtly patriotic, as was the norm. Beforehand, the newsreels informed them of continued allied advances in Africa. After the newsreels came a Mickey Mouse cartoon. Then a song sheet would appear on the screen, and the audience sung along to an organist, as a small white ball moved over each word during the duration of the song. There was also a song during the interval.

The pair discussed the film (and its message), for a few minutes. Hannah clasped Peter's hand tighter, and flashed him a smile, her face young, innocent and full of life. They passed another courting couple, a sailor and his girlfriend, arms around each other, spending more time kissing than walking. Conversation turned to the R.A.F. and Peter's early days of flying. Hannah pressed him to talk about it.

"I joined up after seeing an advertisement in the paper. I had to go through a written test and medical, and then endure some questions in front of a board of officers." The pilot smiled. "The fact that I was into rugby and tennis seemed to impress them. I started to learn to fly, at a civilian flying training school, in some dreadful two-seater biplane. Well, the instructor started to loop the loop, and I thought that I was going to bloody well fall out of the plane!" Peter gave his girlfriend a disapproving glance. "Did I say something amusing, Hannah?"

The girl put her hand to her mouth, to suppress the giggles. Peter continued.

"We had to go through twenty-two stages of instruction –aerobatics, recovering from a spin, diving, banking…You know, even the basic moves to us novices, were very disorientating, to begin with. I first went solo, after nine hours in the air."

"Nine hours; was that all?" Hannah looked at him in wander.

"That was considered average." Peter went on. "We then did a couple of weeks of drilling, physical exercise, learning a few administrative duties, etc. Do you really want to know all this?"

The girl nodded.

"I didn't want to start boring you," said the pilot.

"You're not boring me. It's very interesting."

"Where was I? Yes –we then had further instruction, learning set piece attacks against bombers, each particular attack having a number. It was only then that we had gunnery practice. There, I received my wings, which was sewn over the tunic pocket –that was a fine moment."

"You must have felt really proud."

"Yes. Then after that, I was posted to my squadron…it all seems so long ago, now."At that moment, they reached the bus stop. It was deserted. Peter checked his watch.

"Probably won't be here for another ten minutes, or so."

Hannah looked from side to side. As far as she could tell, they were very much alone.

Peter turned to face his girlfriend, and placed his arms around her lower back. She responded likewise, looking forward to what was coming next.

"You're beautiful, Hannah." He said, as he pressed his lips against hers.

Each kiss with him seemed more intense and passionate. His body felt warm against hers, and she felt cosy inside. Hannah wished that the moment could last forever.

The bus dutifully came and picked them up. The twenty minute journey (even after eighteen months of blackout) had a feel of unreality about it. In the town, and then as the vehicle moved out into the country lane, there was not the slightest chink of light anywhere. A weak blue pinpoint of light illuminated the interior of the bus. Hannah and her airman sat, his arm around her shoulder, for the most part, in silence, at peace, smiling into each other's faces. There were just a couple of other passengers on board.

A couple of war posters on the bus caught the girl's attention. One was a request to the housewives of Britain to finish traveling on the buses by four o'clock, leaving them free for war workers. The other, was rather quaint, titled 'Billy Brown of London Town', with a cartoon of a bowler-hated gentleman waiting to cross the road, accompanied by the words.

Down below the station's bright,
But here outside its black as night,
Billy Brown will wait a bit,
And let his eyes grow used to it,
Then he'll scan the road and see,
Before he crosses, if it's free,
Remembering when lights are dim,
That cars he sees may not see him.

The bus drew up at the edge of the village, and the two lovers disembarked, thanking the driver. The country air was silent and solemn. The only sound came from treetops that were stirred by the night wind, and rustled the bushes. Some distance away, an owl hooted. Stars peeped out of the dark expanse of sky. For a few moments, they stood gazing at the sky. It was a beautiful, clear night. Peter's expression changed, so that he looked dubiously at the sky. Somewhere up there, would be the hum of aircraft engines, and the dark thought crossed Peter's mind, *where would the German bombers be visiting tonight?*

Hannah beckoned to him to go. They walked past the war memorial. Peter spoke.

"The Great War, 1914-1918." He let out a mournful sigh, his breath misting the air. "And this war. 1939 to...when? 1942? 1943? 1944? 1947? 1950?"

Hannah stroked his arm; it always worried her when he got like this. But, it was better to let him vent his feelings. She was aware of the immense pressures that he faced daily. He took her hand, and was grateful of the comfort that it bought. He continued.

"We took a Hun prisoner, a few days ago. He virtually crash landed onto our airfield..."

"Really?"

"Myself and a couple of the other chaps got to see him. We wondered how he spoke English so well. Turns out that he studied at Oxford for a few years in the thirties! I actually found it hard to dislike the chap. He was grateful of our good treatment of him, and was quite non-political, certainly not like your typical arrogant Nazi...he's just batting for the wrong side." Peter concluded.

They reached the farm gate, and went through, opening and closing it quietly, so as not to awake the others.

Peter kissed Hannah on the cheek, on the front doorstep.

"Home sweet home."

Hannah thought back to that wonderful night at the end of the summer, when she had first met Peter, and immediately fallen for him. Then, she could only hope against hope that he felt the same way towards her. And here they were now, together, a couple. The girl smiled a contented smile.

They went inside, and enjoyed a final cup of tea and light conversation, before they went to their separate bedrooms. He would be getting up early the following morning to catch a train back to the airbase. They enjoyed a last passionate kiss goodnight, outside her bedroom door (he was sharing with Richard and Tom), and he declared.

"I love you Hannah."

"I love you, too."

Mary turned off the kitchen tap, walked wearily out into the back garden, and placed the burdensome metal pail full of cold water down with a thud beside the dolly tub. She caught her breath back, and regarded the weekly pile of washing with little enthusiasm. Oblivious to the sound of birds and spring flowers, she poured the last of six bucketfuls of water into the dolly tub, and then got a fire going underneath. Sometimes it was an inconvenience when the fire went out, although today, thankfully, when Mary checked the temperature by dipping her finger in the water, it had been heated. She now placed the clothes and a solid bar of soap, which was, thankfully, not yet on ration into the tub, and began to stir the contents with the wooden long handled dolly-peg.

Sometime later, with the laundry clean, Mary started to feed the clothes through the mangle with its large wooden rollers, into some rinse-water underneath. This process would have to be repeated a couple more times until the water became clear. As she turned the handle over and over, Mary's cheeks went pink with the effort. She was always hungry, and exhausted by a combination of the lack of food and housework. She was fed up of queuing outside shops, only to discover that inside, the shelves were almost empty. She was tired of bombs and tired of the war. Mary frequently felt tearful about the sheer effort required to get through every day, and at the hopelessness of the current situation, which appeared to be without end.

"They got Buckingham Palace again last night."

Mary took a few seconds to register a voice coming from across the fence. She stopped turning the handle, and looked round to see her neighbour, Edna, who was standing on tiptoe, her face just visible above the fence. Edna looked much older than her fifty-two years, her curly hair had long turned grey, and her glasses were such that they made her look like a wise old owl. The spinster wore a flowery apron over her clothes.

"Oh! Morning, Edna. Sorry, I hadn't noticed you there," said Mary apologetically.

"Not to worry, dear."

"Buckingham Palace, you say?"

"Yes," Edna nodded, "Incendiaries and high explosives. Most of the bombs fell in Green Park, although a policeman was found dead."

"How awful."

Edna nodded again. Mary enquired.

"Are those unruly Stephenson children still ruining your garden?"

"Yes. It's that football keep coming over the wall every five minutes," she shook her head resignedly, "I know they're good kids at heart, I just wish that they'd be a little more careful and mind where they're treading...away from my flowerbed."

"Yes."

After a brief silence, Edna observed.

"You look exhausted, dear."

"Oh! No different from normal," Mary then conceded, "Well, today's the hardest day of the week, laundry day."

"Come round and have a cup of tea, dear."

"I'd dearly love to Edna, but I've got all this washing to put out on the line."

"That won't take long, come round in a bit when you're ready."

Of course she'd stayed far too long next door at Edna's. They had talked about each of Mary's children respectively, and the war. When Mary returned home, she had to rush the ironing with the gas iron, and still found that she was behind time for dinner.

That was yesterday, Monday 10th March. Every day the coal fire had to be cleared out and re-laid. Today, Mary had the task of black-leading the grate with a stiff brush. She then put on a pair of rubber gloves and set about dusting and cleaning the remainder of the house with a few drops of paraffin on the duster. The chores satisfactorily performed, Mary glanced at her watch. In ten minutes it would be time for her to leave for her rug-making group to aid the war effort.

Over the past few months, Mary had seen some sights on the streets; the London bus half submerged in a crater, wrecks of trains in stations, areas cordoned off where brave bomb disposal teams were working on unexploded bombs. Along the dockside entire rows of warehouses lay in ruins, the Guildhall was bombed out, the John Lewis store had been derelict for months and the western curve of Regent Street was charred, entire residential streets were wiped out, uninhabited. In other places, buildings, which had lost their frontages or an entire top floor stood defiantly, battered and bruised. Despite these homes being at the mercy of the elements, it was evident that where a couple of rooms were still just habitable, people had taken their chances that the remaining structure was still strong enough, and stayed put. Mary admired these people, the inhabitants of bomb damaged dwellings, for they currently led a gold-fish bowl existence, their tastes in furniture, wallpaper, pictures, ornaments –their whole lives- visible to all and sundry that walked down the street. Mary wandered how she would cope, even for a day, if she were looking out from such a house, in its sorry state, instead of into it. She narrowed her eyes for a vengeful moment, and wished to bestow the same fate on the German civilian population. Then, a feeling of guilt and shame dispelled such thoughts from her mind. Was it too much to hope for an end to the suffering – *everyone's* suffering?

The street down which she walked, was like so many others; it should have been buzzing with children playing, birds on roofs, vehicles moving lazily along it, maybe even a delivery boy on his bike. Instead, it was silent, deserted, a third of the homes flattened, another third irreparably damaged, the final third fortunate enough to still boast a small (and probably dwindling) number of occupants…a shipwreck of it's former self.

Mary stopped dead. An object in the sky had caught her attention. It was a horrible, dangerous, descending object, that caused death and destruction, and on seeing it, Mary felt a sinking feeling in the pit of her stomach. A long cylinder in excess of two metres long and over half a metre wide that was a land mine bomb (actually a magnetic sea mine) was floating noiselessly down by parachute towards the far end of the street. This monster of a bomb weighed over two tons, was full of explosives, and would go off a quarter of a minute after impact. Mary had heard about these mines, although she had never seen one before. She had been told that their blast was fierce, because they did not penetrate the ground. The ensuing deadly effect involved an incredible noise, a blinding light and further successive pressure waves. She had no reason to disbelieve the stories about them, that houses half a mile away would sway on their foundations, vehicles would be thrown up in the air as if they were toys, and that a couple of the monsters could obliterate a street. Even if one did attempt to run away from the mine, one would probably not get far enough away. Not all exploded, but even so, many were booby-trapped.

The mine was only a few hundred metres above the road. With few options, and so little time, Mary hurried over to a bombed out building, to seek shelter amongst the untidy broken masonry, behind a half-ruined wall. Mary sat paralyzed with fear, hands around her knees, which were tightly drawn up to her chest, waiting for the end. Thoughts raced through her mind, she dearly wished that she could see her children for one last time. At forty-four years of age, she felt that she still had so much of her life left to live. Waiting...

Nothing. The mine must have landed, and the fuse must surely be buzzing, counting down its fifteen seconds. Mary wanted to get it over with; the waiting was awful. She checked her watch; she'd sat there for one minute, two minutes, three...

It dawned on her that, for whatever reason, the mine had failed to go off. Mary got to her feet, and tentatively crept out from the ruins. She blinked. With disbelieving eyes, she saw that further down the street, swinging perilously close to the ground, it's canopy tangled up in a sturdy tree branch, was the landmine.

A boy had wandered out of his house into the street to nose at the mine, curiosity having got the better of him. A steel-helmeted policeman appeared, wobbling up the road on his bicycle. He descended, at what he believed to be a safe distance, and scratched his face, staring inquisitively at the bomb. The boy's mother appeared out of the house like a shot, and screamed at him to get inside and take shelter. The disposal experts from the navy would have to be called, and several streets would have to be evacuated.

Fortune had smiled upon Mary. Ironically, to release the tension of the past few minutes, she laughed, and so much so that the tears streaked down her cheeks, yet it could all have turned out so different.

CHAPTER 16 – SPRING 1941

A German general (and a tank division) was sent by Hitler to take charge in Tripoli, on 12th February 1941. The general had distinguished himself in France, the year before, and his name was Erwin Rommel. He was to become respected by men on both sides, in the desert war.

The last of the German forces would not arrive in North Africa until May, and no one expected any offensive action by the Germans until then. Rommel, however, had other plans. He believed that the Allies were not particularly well prepared for a fight, and indeed, many tanks had been withdrawn from the allied front line, for maintenance. On 24th March the German forces struck.

In early April, on the Allied side of the line, John reflected upon the events of the past couple of weeks. His diary entry began.

"We are in retreat. After our successes in the winter, I feel ashamed to write these words. The German Afrika Korps, which began arriving in Libya a couple of months ago, has been on the attack (for two weeks), with their Italian allies…"

The fierce desert sun burned relentlessly down upon the cursing, swearing group of hollow eyed men trudging along the rocky road. Their limbs were tired; their skin caked in dust and their spirits at rock bottom. A number of them sported bloodstained bandages, a couple of men were suffering from gippy tummy. The yellow landscape was bare, save the occasional sprinkling of camel thorn and sighting of a bird or scorpion. They had earlier passed by a small Arab village that consisted of a number of tattered tents, without giving it a second thought. The double-crossing nomad bastards would probably declare their support for the Germans as soon as they arrived. One of the men walked over some bugs that were busying their way across the road, and trod on a couple vindictively.

"How much bloody further?" Complained one man.

Someone else muttered an incomprehensible reply.

"I said how much bloody further?" Demanded the first man, wiping a dead fly from his sweat drenched neck.

"Don't bloody know, alright" said the man behind John Baker.

Another said his piece.

"Old Albert's got a leg full of shrapnel, and he's not complaining," the man turned round to Albert. "How is your wound at the moment, Albert?"

"Bloody agony, now you mention it," winced Albert. "And less of the old, thank you! I can still keep up."

A young Sergeant from another company, the most senior rank present, spoke up.

"OK. Cut the gossip, and save your energies for the march."

It had all began as an orderly fighting retreat –the Tommies making courageous last ditch stands. The Allied artillery worked tirelessly throughout, firing off fierce barrages against Jerry. However, the counter-attacks against the advancing Germans were, regrettably poorly co-ordinated, and the Allies were too little in number, and no match for the firepower of the enemy tanks. After a few days, the panic really set in. It was a sorry state that most of the Allied troops couldn't seem to retreat fast enough! John wished that he had Bill Gardner marching besides him for support. Bill had recently been promoted to Corporal, and was further back, leading another section.

John glanced across at Charlie Lawrence with pity. In their haste, they had all neglected hygiene, a little bit, and Charlie Lawrence developed sores all over his knees and legs. Charlie's problems were only just beginning, for the sores acted like a magnet to the flies, which laid their disgusting eggs in his wounds, causing him much discomfort. In the end, the medical officer made him cover his sores with strapping, and that seemed to do the trick. It could have happened to any of them, Charlie was the unfortunate one. Him, old Albert...

Suddenly, a fawn coloured British Army lorry came haring down the road behind the marching men. As it neared the column, the driver slowed down a little. The men withdrew to the side of the road, in order to let the vehicle pass safely by. The lorry drew level with the men, throwing up clouds of dust, half choking them. The vehicle was bumping along the edge of the road, such was the driver's haste, and it seemed as if he would lose control at any moment. To cries of 'Idiot!' the vehicle drew ahead of the column, and that appeared to be the end of the matter, when it skidded dangerously, and went careering off the road, before it came to a halt.

"Christ! This is all we need!" Cursed the Sergeant.

The Sergeant trotted over to the lorry accompanied by John, and a couple of other men. It had half disappeared into a yellow haze. One of the men observed.

"With idiots like him around, who needs the Germans?"

As the dust cleared, the Sergeant tapped on the windscreen.

"Are you alright?"

A dazed figure clambered out of the vehicle; the man's legs almost gave way as he touched the ground. He had sandy hair, a sunburned face and rabbit teeth.

"Yes, thanks." He added. "Damned engine's kaput though. End of the road for this vehicle." He conceded.

The Sergeant's expression hardened into a frown.

"You're not going to leave that lorry like the rest of them are you?"

It was like May 1940, all over again. Frequently, British drivers were irresponsibly abandoning vehicles that had stalled, or broken down with minor problems, which could have easily and quickly been fixed. For many, there was a concern that Jerry was about to overtake them! It wasn't just this man, everyone was retreating, no one had been ordered to stand and fight, anymore.

"The German's overwhelmed us, destroyed all the other vehicles." The driver was trembling; a note of panic had developed in his voice. He made to leave. "We've got to get out of here!"

"Look, Corporal, I'm sorry you lost your friends, but I can't let you abandon your vehicle just like that." The Sergeant's voice was sympathetic but firm. "Calm down and set about fixing it. The lads will give you a hand." He revealed a flask of rum and handed it to the man. It seemed to steady his nerves.

"Alright," nodded the driver, and looked into the bonnet.

The Tommies found this welcome respite. The driver shared round some water that he had spare, and the men in turn helped him get his lorry onto more stable ground. They felt sorry for him, as the sole survivor of a fierce enemy attack. The few thousand Germans reinforcing the Italians were a force to contend with.

John was just beginning to relax by the roadside with a few others. Someone got out a mouth organ, and the atmosphere became more lighthearted. One man distanced himself from the rest of the group, however.

"Look at droopy mouth over there," observed a tall Londoner. "Missing your Berka bint are you?"

The other man remained silent. The Londoner continued, for the benefit of the others.

"She looks like a camel, although the size of her..."

"Shut up lofty!" Snapped the other man.

A third Tommy joined in the banter.

"Thought he was complaining yesterday that she'd given him VD!"

"Hamida told me that she'd be faithful to me."

"Yes, right!

The men's attention turned elsewhere, as a noise began to fill the air, drowning out the mouth organ. Tiny dots had appeared in the sky above. John threw himself to the earth.

Once more, he was to suffer the misfortune of being under attack by his sworn enemy, the Stuka dive-bomber. Three of the monsters came down, sirens shrieking, towards the desert road; a handful of Tommies fired their own rifles uselessly at the enemy aircraft.

"Hit the ground!" Screamed the Sergeant in desperation.

With the danger past, the shaken men removed their faces from the grit, and the Sergeant counted the grim cost. The lorry had been destroyed; only the burning remnants now remained. Five men were killed by the Stukas, amongst them the driver, he had been working on his engine right up to the end.

"Can't they leave us alone for five bloody minutes?" Despaired lofty.

Someone shouted across to the Sergeant.

"I think Paul's still alive..."

The Sergeant dashed over to a man lying prostrate. However, there was nothing that he could do for him, it was merely a matter of time. Hovering between consciousness and eternal sleep, the man looked up at the Sergeant, and with a hint of recognition, blinking once or twice, he croaked.

"Father?"

The Sergeant remained silent, and maintained his gaze sympathetically.

"Take my hand please," coughed the mortally wounded Tommy.

The Sergeant gently took the man's hand, to provide a little final comfort, and held it for the ten further minutes that it took him to pass away...

And so John's entry for that miserable fortnight concluded.

"On the night of 3rd April, the Germans captured Benghazi.

We retreated through Tobruk, and then into what one would hope to be the relative safety of Egypt…back where we started from last September. We cannot afford to lose Africa, we *must* hold onto Egypt and the vital Suez Canal."

Friday 18th April 1941, Hannah had volunteered to pay a visit to a few of the shops on the main street, for Emily and Ted. Later she planned to do some writing. She found it an outlet, and invariably found herself writing a pose about love and the war. She had even begun to dabble in a bit of poetry. Ted had read some of her work, and was impressed.

On her journey, she had first encountered Ken, who was his usual amiable self, and nodded a friendly hello. Walking past the pond, Hannah sincerely wished that she could have had some bread to offer to the dear little ducks. On reaching the cemetery, the girl took a peculiar interest in the shadows on the grass, cast by the sun on the gravestones. Then she noticed the daisies that had appeared in abundance – how perverse that skeletons lay not far beneath so much life. Hannah's morbid thoughts were quickly broken, as a songbird, perched on the cemetery gates, hit some beautiful notes.

Hannah was halted by Mrs. Woodruff, who struck up conversation with her. Mrs. Woodruff wore a grey skirt beneath her equally dreary coat. Grey was as exciting as fashion had become in wartime in 1941. Her headscarf stood out, patriotically displaying the Morse code for 'V for Victory' around the edge. After the customary exchange of *how are you's?* Mrs. Woodruff immediately quizzed the girl.

"Who's this handsome young pilot friend of yours, then, Hannah?"

In her naivety, Hannah was amazed at how fast news seemed to travel around the village. She tried quite hard not to act surprised, but she was none too convincing.

"Oh!" The girl gave a vexed laugh. "His name's Peter, and he's a cousin of Emily's –rather a cousin of *Beth* and *Tom*."

"Is he?" It was Mrs. Woodruff's turn to show a little surprise. She then declared. "I saw you walking with him, oh, some weeks ago, now. Peter looks a decent young man."

"Thank you."

"I expect that he's shot down a fair number of enemy aircraft?"

"Quite a few, I believe." Hannah would confess to having no idea of the precise number, for it got very confusing when Peter began to speak about 'probable' and 'shared' kills.

"You must be very proud of him,"

"Yes…"

Mrs. Woodruff blared.

"Young love!"

Hannah looked self-consciously around the street and flushed.

Yes, love. The concept of love was new and mystifying to the sixteen year old. Although Peter was her first boyfriend, the tingly feeling of excitement she felt at the mere mention of his name suggested that what she was experiencing definitely was love.

Mrs. Woodruff smiled a maternal smile. Satisfied with the gossip, she excused herself.

"Well, I'd better be getting on my way…"

Hannah went into the saddlers, in order to settle up on a bill for items for the horses at the farm. After the brightness of outside, it was dim and shadowy, and a smell of leather permeated the place.

Mr. Javes, the saddler, was an amiable man in his late forties. He had thinning dark hair, kindly eyes and a brow that was furrowed like one of Ted's fields. He was a total professional at his job, which he had been at since his early teens. Mr. Javes came away from his work, and dusted down his hands. He made some comment about having been overwhelmed with work for the army for the past two years. As he scratched his head, and searched around for a pen, he enquired after Emily and Ted.

"As far as I know, they're fine." Hannah went on. "Although Ted complains a lot about all the paperwork and form filling. He says that all he wants to do is to farm!"

"I'm sure he does."

Hannah continued.

"Would you believe that we've actually got more cows at the farm, now, as there's still plenty of demand for milk. Sadly, we've had to get rid of the chickens, because Ted says they're uneconomical."

"Is that so? I can see you've been learning a lot, young Hannah."

"Yes, I suppose I have. I'm helping out Emily and Ted around the farm until I'm old enough to join up."

"Really?"

"Yes. There's only so much I can do though, as I'm not very strong. Ted's lent me a couple of book on agricultural science. I like to do quite a lot of reading, and writing too, in order to keep myself busy."

Hannah handed Mr. Javes the money. The saddler asked her.

"And are they still looking after you and Richard alright?"

"Yes, of course," nodded Hannah. "We love it out here on the farm."

With a glint in his eye, the saddler asked Hannah.

"And how's your young man, at the moment?"

Hannah smiled to herself. Here we go again, another one wants to know!

"Peter's very well, thank you."

"He's a good sort, and the two of you go well together —make sure that you hang on to him," was the saddler's sound advice.

Hannah departed, and headed towards the post office (run by Edward's parents). She needed some stamps. She gave a cursory glance to a poster that advised the public to 'Save for Victory', and hastened her step, with her eyes pinned down to the pavement lest she be stopped to indulge in more conversation.

Once inside the post office, Hannah joined a short queue, and waited patiently, behind Mr. Norman, the warden. A couple of middle-aged women were engaged in lively discussion about the recent budget. Increased taxation would be paid back through Post Office Savings accounts after the war as 'post-war credits', four million new taxpayers created (bad), the standard rate of income tax at a record level of 50% (bad) and subsidies and price controls to keep down the cost of living (fair enough). The Chancellor had made no attempt to balance the books (unforgivable!).

Just as it came to Hannah's turn to be served, and a couple more people had joined the queue behind her, Clara's father, the policeman, burst into the post office. All eyes were on him, as he announced.

"Yugoslavia's fallen! I've just heard that they surrendered to the Germans late last night, and that the cease-fire comes into effect at noon, today."

The policeman's announcement was met with silence. Pointlessly, a woman behind Hannah in the queue checked her watch. Behind the counter (serving), Edward's father clenched his eyes shut, and slowly shook his head mournfully

Hannah looked down at her feet, in dismay. She thought back to twelve days ago, when Hitler's armies invaded Yugoslavia because the (mainly pro-British) Yugoslav people had overthrown their pro-Axis government. The capital, Belgrade, had been bombed mercilessly, despite having been declared an open city, and as many as thirty thousand had died. Germany had two thousand planes at her disposal; her opponents could barely muster a sixth of that figure. Within a week, Ante Pavelich, an Axis Quisling had taken control of Croatia. On 16th April, the Germans had entered Sarajevo, and today -this final, inevitable collapse. Over 300,000 men would become prisoners of war. However, some Yugoslavs would retreat to the remote areas of their country, and continue to fight a guerilla war.

Speaking a couple of months later, a Yugoslav general conceded that.

"Men died in an unequal struggle of men against guns and hand grenades, against tanks and aeroplanes."

The Nazi's could now concentrate the might of their army and Air Force on the already beleaguered Allied forces in Greece. For Britain, there was likely to be more bad news before any good.

Churchill had, for a while, been in favour of a Balkan front, and the transfer of troops from the desert to Greece had actually begun in early March 1941. The soldiers received an enthusiastic welcome from the locals. Greece appeared vulnerable to German attack, since Hitler was keen to eliminate any threat from the British in Greece to Romanian oil fields. However, even with military assistance from Turkey and Yugoslavia (which may not be forthcoming), Greece would probably still fall to the Germans, if invaded! Furthermore, there was disagreement between the allies, over which defensive line to hold, one covering Salonika, or another further south. Although the British forces were almost fully motorized, their equipment was more suited to the desert, and not the steep Greek mountain roads.

When the Germans invaded Greece and Yugoslavia on 6th April 1941, there were problems from the start, for the British in Greece. The Luftwaffe hit an ammunition ship in Piraeus harbour, on the first day of the invasion. The ensuing violent explosions, as the ship blew up, caused unimaginable destruction, to the docks and town, and the blast shattered windows ten miles away. The Greek population was severely shocked and awed.

On 15th April, one R.A.F. squadron lost *all* its aircraft to strafing Messerschmitts.

John and other weary British troops boarded the evacuation ship on 28th April 1941. Through sorrowful eyes, he took one last look at the tragic country that he had left behind. Earlier, they had trudged along dirt roads in constant fear of attack from the air, and laboured along the beach, where the thick sand made the going hard and slow. But, at last they were at the end of their ordeal. The Tommies had lived and sheltered from the Luftwaffe in lemon orchards and holes that they had hastily dug in the sides of hills. They had endured wind, rains and snows; and they thought it couldn't get any worse after the desert! They hadn't washed, shaved or changed their clothes for days. They had had to grab tins of bully beef and fruit from abandoned army stores.

They were fortunate to be taken away by a destroyer; however, men were leaving Greece in all types of boats, including barges and fishing boats. On board, John received cocoa and bully beef from the sailors. He noticed that as the ship moved away into open sea, at times water washed over the deck, due to the weight of guns and stores.

"I'd rather die quickly from a Jerry bullet than from drowning on board this overfull heap of metal," lamented one soldier.

"Any more defeatist talk from that man and I'll have him thrown overboard!" Came the voice of a jocular midshipman.

As he squeezed his way further along the deck, John reflected on the campaign that had been waged for political rather than military reasons. He had fumed in his diary earlier on in April.

"Landed in Greece on 9th April 1941. What a total farce the campaign has been - one retreat after another bloody retreat! In my mind a definite trend is emerging that, when we fight the Eyeties, we are more than a match for them, but when we're confronted by Jerry, we (and by that, I mean the British Army as a whole) seem to fall apart. I wonder if it is down to tactics, being poorly equipped, or simply being outnumbered. We got off to a bad start, when we were under constant air attack from German aircraft as soon as we landed at port at Piraeus."

The German land assault came from Yugoslavia and Bulgaria (they were now willing allies of the Nazis). Despite initial set backs, caused by demolitions, minefields and muddy roads, they advanced over fifty miles in a mere three days to take the Greek port of Salonika. German commanders of battle groups consisting of self-propelled assault guns, engineers and motorized infantry, led from the front, assessing the terrain and enemy strength for themselves. The Allied initial defensive line was quickly broken, and...

"We 're-deployed' a good hundred miles back into the Vermion mountainous area. The going was treacherous, as on occasions, our vehicles were only a foot away from the edge of mountain roads. *A hundred miles voluntarily given up just like that!* I recall Churchill saying that wars are not won by retreats."

The Tommies had insufficient time to prepare further defences, and within a few days withdrew, once more, along primitive roads towards the southern beaches and ports. John, like many others, personally felt ashamed to pass by the hill shepherds (and their flocks), abandoning them to an uncertain fate. He had spoken to one Greek patriot, who recalled how, in the mountains in the depths of winter, the Greeks, armed with little more than courage, had kept Mussolini's invading troops at bay for months. In November, they had destroyed the crack Italian Alpini division, and even pushed into Albania.

"The worst thing was that, even as we retreated, the villagers gave us oranges and water. They even greeted us with cheers –*cheers!*"

The German air attacks had seemed endless. It felt as if the British spent the majority of the time cowering in ditches, as the Luftwaffe bombed and strafed at will. Often they could see the faces of the pilots. Then Bill Gardner was killed in one such raid; the whole platoon deeply felt his passing. Another of the 'old guard' had gone. Only a couple of nights before, he'd been happily drinking a Greek pub dry, he didn't want the Bloody Germans to get their hands on the beer. John now had only the memories of an army career together, which had seemed a lifetime with Builder Gardner. John knew Bill's parents would be devastated.

The Greeks had blown up railways and roads at key places, sometimes using explosives to create rock-falls on narrow mountain roads. Such actions only held up, rather than halted the German advance, and on the 23rd April the heroic Greek allies surrendered. At the start of the battle, the Greek King George had uttered the stirring words. 'We shall win with the help of God...the country does not waver, does not submit, does not surrender. Forward, children of Hellas, for the supreme struggle, for your altars and your hearths.' That day John felt the tears welling in his eyes.

On 24th April, the first British withdrew from mainland Greece, and three days later, Athens, the Greek capital fell to the German invader.

"The entire Greek venture had been over at the blink of an eye; we hadn't even spent three weeks in the country. I can't help feeling what a waste it was, that many good men were left behind, dead or as prisoners, and also that much of our material was lost –aircraft, guns, trucks. Railway engines and rolling stock had also been destroyed in Greece. All the lads feel fed up, and the poor Greeks now face a bleak future under the Nazi conqueror. But we were a beaten Army, and there was little else for us to do than to evacuate, faced with (especially after the fall of Yugoslavia), overwhelming German forces.

Armed with few possessions, we now head for Crete, and place our trust in God that, we fare better there, if, as seems likely, Jerry invades that island."

The Allies had been heavily outnumbered, and on 30th April 1941, the Prime Minister provided parliament with a summary of the campaign.

"The conduct of our troops…merits the highest praise." Mr. Churchill spoke of British "Marching columns, who, besides being assailed from the air, were pursued by no less than three German armoured divisions, as well as by the whole strength of the German mechanized forces which could be brought to bear." He mentioned heavy enemy casualties, and that the Germans "On several occasions, sometimes for two days at a time, were brought to a standstill by forces one-fifth of their number."

Although the Greek campaign was a strategic error, and resulted in British losses of some twelve thousand, to have refused to help the Greeks would, according to Churchill.

"Have been fatal to the honour of the British Empire."

By spring 1941, Britain was hit hard, on land, at sea and from the air. The German *Afrika Korps* under their brilliant leader, Erwin Rommel, had attacked the allied forces in Libya, recapturing first El Agheila, then Benghazi, followed by Derna and Bardia. When Derna fell, the British General Richard O' Connor was taken prisoner. The port of Tobruk had been surrounded, and a long siege lay ahead. The swift advance had taken the Axis forces five hundred miles to the Egyptian border, which they crossed on 26th April. The next day, Winston Churchill threatened to "shoot the generals" if Egypt fell. The British commander in chief in North Africa, General Wavell, complained about the quality of British tanks against German tanks and anti-tank weapons. The Eritrean capital, Asmara, had fallen to the British on 1st April, but that was a mere sideshow.

At sea, Allied shipping losses were becoming more severe. The U-boat menace increased, as new long-range U-boats made their appearance. In mid-April 1941, realizing that the weekly figures for allied shipping losses were becoming demoralizing, Churchill ordered the ministry of information to stop publishing them. In March, over 500,000 tons of allied shipping was sunk, and in April, the figure was even higher.

The Blitz intensified, as the Luftwaffe hammered London and other cities. In March, Birmingham, Bristol, Merseyside, Portsmouth and Plymouth were all bombed. On the night 13th/14th March, in Scotland's worst air raid yet, only seven houses in the shipbuilding town of Clydebank were left undamaged, and the population retreated to the moors. By mid March only around a quarter of the population remained in Portsmouth, so frequent and so severe was the bombing. Civilian casualties across Britain for that month stood close to ten thousand (including 4,200 deaths), double the figure for the previous month. In April, London endured its heaviest raid since December 1940, and three consecutive nights of raids tore the heart out of Plymouth, many homes being hit more than once in the devastation, leaving thirty thousand homeless. Tens of thousands of people deserted the town to spend the nights in barns, rural churches, quarry tunnels and on Dartmoor.

For a whole week, from Thursday 1st May, Liverpool and Merseyside were targeted. The raids destroyed the city's Corn Exchange, Museum and station. The Malakand, an ammunition ship, and an ammunition train were hit. A bomb landed on a school shelter, resulting in 160 deaths. Fires raged in the docks, and the docks worked at only a quarter of their usual capacity, for a while afterwards. Liverpool was temporarily 'cut off', with anxious relatives unable to contact their families, because the telephone network was put out of action. Close to 1,500 people were killed in seven days, and rumours quickly spread of civil unrest and martial law (which proved to be untrue) although more anger was seen in Merseyside than elsewhere.

However, despite the raids on all these cities, war production was little affected. Even so, at home, the British people had to endure more and more hardship. On 17th March, jam and marmalade were rationed to 8oz per person per month, and the April war budget raised income tax to the record level of 50%. There had been an increase since the outbreak of war, in the number of young people under the age of seventeen found guilty of breaking the law. In early March, Ernest Bevin, the Minister of Labour, asked for a hundred thousand female volunteers to sign up for factory work, due to the shortage of manpower.

There were some British successes. On 4th March 1941, Britain's new raiding force, the commandos, staged a raid on the Norwegian Lofoten Islands. Some 800,000 gallons of oil and petrol were burnt, and 225 Germans taken prisoner. On 29th March, the Royal Navy won a victory off Cape Matapan in the Mediterranean, when three Italian cruisers and two destroyers were sunk. On 6th April, Addis Ababa, the Ethiopian capital, fell to the Allies. A month later, Haile Selassie, the emperor of Ethiopia returned to the capital, welcomed with a twenty-one-gun salute.

In Berlin, Hitler said that Churchill had the knack of making glorious victories out of defeats. The German leader boasted that.

"The National Socialist state stands out as a solid monument to common sense. It will last for a thousand years."

Hannah keenly anticipated her too few weekends spent with Peter, for days (and often weeks) in advance. The precious time they spent together went by way too quickly. She found it impossible to think of life without him.

With the warmer weather that came with Spring Hannah and Peter had taken the opportunity to go for a picnic. Assisted by Emily, Hannah had carefully organized the picnic hamper that contained bread, a jar of homemade jam, a tub of salad, a homemade cake, cutlery, cotton serviettes and a flask of tea. Despite their best efforts, restrictions imposed by rationing meant that the menu could be no more exciting.

Richard and Tom had threatened to sneakily follow the couple to their picnic spot, however, a stern warning from Emily put paid to that idea. The boys remained at the farm, and re-enacted the recent battles in the desert with toy soldiers, and using stones to represent tanks.

It was a glorious day, the first weekend in May, and Hannah marveled that, for a change, starlings, swallows and other bird species, rather than aircraft dominated the sky. The river water was so still and calm, and ducks glided in and out of the reeds, whilst the hedgerows buzzed with swarms of insects. The pair walked contentedly along the riverbank, hand in hand, in search of a picnic spot, Hannah in a green dress and Peter in his R.A.F. uniform (minus jacket and cap), gallantly carrying the hamper. They laughed as a couple of pre-teenage boys dressed in long shorts and pullovers (!), skipped past, waving their butterfly nets wildly, and catching nothing in the process.

"I used to come and play out here often as a small boy, along with Beth, Tom and my sister." Peter declared.

Hannah gazed dreamily at the water.

"It's so beautiful."

"Yes, it is." Peter agreed, adding. "As near to paradise as one can get –I'd say."

Hannah nodded.

The pilot continued.

"I remember once, about seven years ago, Tom boasting that he was the best swimmer, certainly far better than the girls. Beth and Charlotte (my sister), asked him to prove it, by swimming across to the far bank of the river, and back again."

"And could he?" Enquired Hannah.

"Could he heck! He couldn't swim at all. Almost immediately, I had to jump into the water, to save the stupid fool from drowning! Worse still, he'd entered the water fully clothed."

Hannah could not suppress a grin.

"That sounds like our Tom."

"That's not all. When we got back home, we looked like a pair of drowned rats, and we didn't half get a telling off from Aunt Emily, for getting our clothes soaked," explained Peter.

"Oh dear! Did you get the blame?"

"No. Aunt Emily's always known that her son's a mischievous devil. In fact, he'd probably make a damned good pilot!" Added the airman half-jokingly.

Hannah dug Peter in the ribs.

"Oh! You surely can't be serious?"

"If you heard the stories of what some of the chaps at the squadron have got up to in their youth…"

"I think I'd rather not know," said Hannah discouragingly.

"You'd be amazed how we were ever capable of winning the Battle of Britain!"

Hannah frowned.

"Samantha did tell me once something along the lines of the R.A.F. pilots being delirious from drink most of the time. I strongly disapprove of that sort of behaviour."

"I'm sorry, I shouldn't tease you, darling Hannah," chuckled Peter. He then placed his arm around the girl's lower back.

The young couple crossed into a meadow, and settled down where it gently sloped, so that they could gaze at the water some fifty yards away, down below. They caught a glimpse of the blue-green of a kingfisher as it flashed over the river before it disappeared behind a hedgerow. Hannah realized that there was something she had neglected to bring.

"Darn! I've forgotten to bring a blanket!"

Peter felt the ground with his hand.

"Not to worry, the grass is dry." He smiled.

Hannah unpacked the contents of the hamper, and placed them neatly on the grass. She handed the flask to the pilot, and he poured the hot brown liquid, first into her cup, then into his. Before long, both of them were tucking into their sandwiches.

Hannah spoke.

"I received a letter from Mummy, yesterday."

Peter turned his attention away from his meal, and looked at his girlfriend, squinting in the bright sun. Hannah continued.

"She says that yellow ragwort and something she calls 'fireweed' –whatever that is- are growing in abundance on the bomb sites in London."

The pilot raised his eyebrows.

"Fireweed?"

"Yes." Hannah nodded. "Mummy went on to say that the black redstart bird is now nesting in the city, for the first time ever."

This was all news to Peter.

"Fireweed and black redstart…fascinating."

Hannah grinned proud of her bit of knowledge.

"How's your older brother, John?" Asked Peter.

"I'm not sure if he's in Greece or Crete, now," answered Hannah.

"If he is still in Greece, then he's a prisoner," stated Peter. "Sorry, that's not being very helpful." He quickly added.

Hannah sighed.

"No, you're quite right. I know that the German occupation of Greece was completed last month."

"Yes…" Peter bit his lip and nodded.

"I just think…" The girl began. "It seems to me that, we've (Britain) got a wonderful Air Force and useless army. Our army is beaten in France, then the R.A.F. saves us in the Battle of Britain…only for the army to mess it up once more, this time in Greece."

"It's not all black and white though, Hannah." Declared the pilot. "Take Africa, for example. Rommel's taken ground from us in the north, but, on the other hand, we're being successful against the Italians, further south, in Ethiopia. And we both know that we were heavily outnumbered in Greece." He added. "I'm certain that the British soldier is very courageous."

"Yes, I know John is." Declared Hannah. The girl took a few moments reflection, as she munched a couple of bites on her sandwich then said. "There's John fighting for his life in the Mediterranean, you risking your life daily up in the air, Mummy and Daddy suffering the nightmare of Hitler's bombs in London…and me safe out here in the country, contributing nothing to the war at all. I feel so useless!"

"That's not true, you help out around the farm."

"Yes, but its not exactly proper war work is it?"

"Do you feel that you should be out there driving a Matilda tank across foreign fields, then?"

"No, of course not."

"Look, you're only young, Hannah." Peter said reassuringly. "And it's only right that you should be out here, looking after your younger brother. Besides, you're helping the war effort more than you think, by keeping the spirits up of a certain young pilot, and providing him with a pretty little face to think about during the lonely dark nights."

Hannah flushed.

"Am I just being silly?"

"Yes." The pilot nodded.

Self-consciously, Hannah turned her back on Peter, and fiddled with nothing in particular in the hamper. When she turned round again, she half expected to see Peter staring at her with a smug grin on his face. However, the airman was now lying lazily on the ground, with his arms cradling his head, and his half-open eyes looking up at the sky.

Hannah went to lie next to him. She found herself lying on her side, playing nonchalantly with the grass.

"So, what are your hopes and plans for the future, Hannah?" The pilot enquired, without making the effort to turn his head, and look at the girl at all.

"I would like to join the A.T.S."

Peter turned to face Hannah. He suggested.

"I say, why not join up now?"

"But I can't, I'm not seventeen until mid- September."

"You could always try going along to the recruiting office and fibbing about your age."

Hannah thought about this for a moment or two.

"I'd dearly like to join tomorrow, and do something useful," she paused, "Oh! But…it would never work!"

"It's got to be worth a try," he encouraged her, "Just think what a wheeze it would be if you succeeded! You'd look good in that khaki uniform."

"Yes," she grinned in agreement.

"I think you could pass for seventeen years of age."

"Are you saying that I look old for my age?" She prodded him playfully in the chest.

"No. Seriously though, think about giving the idea a go, Hannah."

"Yes, I think I will."

"So, that's the A.T.S. sorted. What other plans have you got, darling Hannah?"

"One day, I'd like to marry, and have children."

"Who are you planning on marrying, then? Do you have anyone particular in mind?"

"Maybe I was thinking of Tom." Hannah jested.

"Hmmm…a cradle snatcher?" Peter stroked his chin.

Hannah chewed on a couple of strands of her hair, and looked direct into Peter's eyes. She removed her hair from her mouth, which spread into a grin, as she uttered the single word, almost as a question.

"You?"

The pilot gave her a lingering look, put his hand gently to her cheek and kissed her.

Mary really had had enough, this time. As she emerged red-eyed from the shelter, she knew immediately that London had had it bad –*very* bad, the previous night. There was an acrid smell in the air, and a large cloud of brown smoke, which partly blocked out the sun, covered much of the city. The sound of bells clanging from ambulances and fire engines could be heard, and Mary's first thought was, *how many dead this time?*

Out in the streets, the indomitable spirit of the Londoners seemed to have at last been broken. People wept openly at the hopelessness of their plight. Lots of them had given up; they knew that the Luftwaffe would return, again, so what was the point in cleaning up the city? The raid caused over two thousand fires classed as "serious", covering a massive area between Hammersmith and Romford. Westminster Abbey, the Houses of Parliament, Lambeth Palace, St. James's Palace, Scotland Yard, the War Office, the Law Courts, the British Museum, the Tower of London and fifteen hospitals were all hit, and every main line railway terminus was put out of action. The pumps would not be withdrawn from the last fires until eleven days after the raid. Thirty miles away from the capital, charred pieces of paper appeared, having been carried by the wind. Over five thousand homes were destroyed, and the figures for human casualties (1,436 killed) were a record for one night's bombing.

The May 10th / 11th raid was, according to Germany *a reprisal for the methodical bombing of the residential quarters of German towns, including Berlin.*

But, for the people of London it had been one raid too many.

Mary was grateful for one thing – Thank God the children were away from this hell, safe in the country.

A rather curious incident occurred that same night. Rudolf Hess, Hitler's deputy, took off from an airfield in Germany, in a Messerschmitt fighter, and later parachuted down from the plane, to land on farmland near Glasgow. On his capture, Hess claimed that he had flown to Scotland, to bring about peace between

Britain and Germany. Hitler apparently had no prior knowledge of the flight, and described his deputy as being insane. Hess would spend almost half a century as a prisoner, until his death at the age of ninety-three. To this day, the mystery of his flight, and how much the British really knew about it beforehand, remains a matter of speculation.

CHAPTER 17 – THE HELL OF CRETE

On Tuesday 20th May 1941, Winston Churchill informed Parliament of a German attack on the Mediterranean Island of Crete.

"An air-borne attack in great strength has begun this morning, and what cannot fail to be a serious battle has begun and is developing. Our troops there –British, New Zealanders and Greek forces- are under the command of General Freyberg, and we feel confident that most stern and resolute resistance will be offered to the enemy."

They had been a disheveled bunch when they arrived on the island, at the end of April, as part of an allied force of 25,000 men. Half the men in John's platoon were missing blankets or entrenching tools. However, they considered themselves quite lucky, for some men in other companies, only possessed the uniforms that they wore. No blankets, no mess tins, no rifles, no nothing. Generally, there was a shortage of mortars. To cap the lot there had also been an unpleasant outbreak of lice.

However, equipment shortages aside, the first couple of weeks spent in Crete had been enjoyable. The Tommies were able to unwind, after the disastrous campaign in Greece. They found 'tavernas' offering egg and chips, drowned themselves in local wine, and held parties on the golden beaches.

However, in mid-May, the German air offensive began so to soften up the island's defences. The Luftwaffe willingly attacked anything that moved bombing and strafing airfields, anti-aircraft guns and the harbour at Suda Bay. On 14th May, a tanker was hit in Suda Bay, sending a huge plume of oily smoke up into the sky. The toll of allied shipping sunk in the harbour would creep inexorably upwards. The German planes had even attacked bathing parties!

To make matters worse, the R.A.F. had been bled dry (in Greece, and further still over a few days in Crete, by bombing of airfields and dogfights against superior numbers of enemy aircraft). On 19th May, there only remained five fighters in Crete, and these left the island that day, with the aim of operating from bases in Egypt.

The island of Crete, 160 miles long by 40 miles wide, is characterized by steep mountains in the south, and the northern coastal plain where the terrain is more habitable, and the majority of the towns, including Chania, the capital are located. In 1941, there was only one metalled road on Crete, which ran along the north coast, otherwise there were only rough tracks. The mountainous geography of Crete divided the island into a number of self-contained battlefields. Two of these areas, were Heraklion, half way along the north coast, and Maleme-Suda Bay, further west. Both areas, with their airfields, would be key targets for the Germans, and due to a shortage of transport, each sector would have to defend itself. The Heraklion area was defended by the British and Greeks, whilst Maleme was guarded by Greeks and

New Zealanders, there were also Australians on the island. A third of these defending troops were positioned on the perimeters of airfields, with two-thirds hidden outside, under camouflage. There was also artillery support, from guns near to airfields and possible landing beaches. When the Germans landed, the plan was to launch swift counter-attacks from the concealed positions.

The allied commander on Crete, General Freyberg, had won the Victoria Cross in the First World War, he was fearless and popular with his men, but he could also be obstinate and obtuse. Publicly optimistic, to maintain the morale of his men, he was, from the outset, privately pessimistic about the battle for Crete, believing that the island would fall to the Germans without air support from the R.A.F...

The British defensive positions at Heraklion formed a u-shape, around the perimeter of the airfield, town and harbour, with the Greeks deployed inside the town. The German attack of 20th May began with the usual bombardment by the Luftwaffe, to soften up the allied defenders, and the area thundered to the sound of explosions. However, camouflage had done the trick, and when the German transport aircraft appeared, they received a very hot reception from the anti-aircraft guns. Before long, many enemy planes were on fire, or had even blown up, destined never to reach the ground. Worse was to follow, as German *Fallschirmjaeger* (parachute troops) –hundreds of them- descended like cotton wool from countless Junkers Ju52 transport aircraft. Many of the paratroopers that did manage to land were killed shortly afterwards. John thought the enemy were sitting targets, as they eradicated a number of Germans who came down in an open field. He almost felt sorry for them –*almost*. The bodies would rapidly decompose due to the extreme heat, and large number of ravens on the island. Some paratroopers did, however, manage to get a foothold in the town's southern suburbs.

John thought back to the events of that fateful day, 20th May, now a week ago, when the battle for Crete began –a day of bloody mayhem. The Germans had landed seemingly all over the island in gliders. The Luftwaffe had attacked the aerodrome of Maleme, and destroyed most of the defending aircraft and anti-aircraft guns. The Germans had also attacked Suda Bay, where the Royal Navy was based.

You had to see it to believe it at Maleme, and John was quite glad that he *couldn't* see what was going on. Word had it that the Germans held the balance of control over the airfield, however, their hold on the airfield was so tentative, that the Ju52's could not land fast enough. In rushed panicky descents, planes landed violently on the runway, and slid along on smashed undercarriages, pieces of aeroplane falling off all over the place! The enemy soldiers would disembark before the planes had stopped moving, and then go straight into battle! Throughout, the allied artillery and machine-guns bombarded the runway. They took their toll, for scattered around the edge of the airfield were a staggering amount* of battered, blazing, smoking aircraft. Yet, nothing would seem to deter the Germans.

---

* Over 100.

By the evening of 21st May, the Germans had taken control of the aerodrome at Maleme, despite determined counter attacks by the Allies. At one stage, German troop-carrying aircraft were landing in Crete at the frightening rate of one per minute, and thousands of Nazi troops were now on the island. However, German casualties were high —over one third of the invaders had been killed, wounded or taken prisoner; but, still they came.

John had witnessed with his own eyes, a German glider crash into some rocks, killing all its occupants. He had heard how Cretan villagers, who had armed themselves with axes, scythes, shotguns, spades, and even weapons captured from the Germans had killed other Germans. Then there were sinister tales of how desperate Germans, had despicably moved forward behind a screen of allied prisoners. There were seemingly no depths to which the Nazis would not stoop.

On the night 21st – 22nd May, the Germans had tried to bring reinforcements to Crete by sea; however, the enemy convoy was intercepted by the Royal Navy, and never reached the island. As the British guns opened up, the sound of distant explosions coming from across the water, woke John from his sleep. From afar (tens of miles away) John watched in wonder, as distant flashes of white light were visible, followed by the orange-red glow of fires from the enemy ships. It appeared that Jerry was getting a right battering.

Knowing that if the Germans could be denied an airfield before they built up sufficient forces, then the allies would most likely hold Crete, General Freyberg decided to counter-attack, and recapture Maleme airfield, using the New Zealanders. Unfortunately, the attack of 22nd May commenced hours later than the planned start time of 1 a.m. (which would have permitted a few hours under the cover of darkness). Despite being supported by tanks, the New Zealanders ran into trouble straight away, and the attack bogged down in the face of fierce German resistance. Worse was to come at dawn, as German fighter aircraft joined in the battle, strafing the New Zealander's positions at low level. Although the soldiers fought bravely, the allied attack failed, and it was the turn of the Germans to go on the offensive.

There was constant activity after dark. The Germans were continuing to land parachutists, and the searchlights, which were desperately probing for descending paratroops, illuminated the night sky. There was the frequent sound of the Allied guns, and tracer and flames provided a real fireworks display.

The officers, the strain telling on their faces, deliberated as to whether to attack, again, stay put or even to retreat! It was decided that, with the forces at their disposal, further attack would achieve little, since the Germans now had too firm a foothold.

The pattern over the next few days at Heraklion was that the Germans were reinforced, but still failed to achieve a decisive breakthrough. For their part, the British overestimated the strength of the Germans, and simply sat still. There was going to be a week's frustrating stalemate. There were all-to-brief moments of celebration, such as when some British passed through with around a dozen dazed German prisoners. The captives were all very young, under twenty years of age.

One of the guards informed John that they had put up little resistance, and had not seemed too bothered to have been captured. A number of the Germans wore looted khaki shorts, because it had become oppressively hot in their own kit. However, the acuteness of the island defender's position soon became clear, when some Stukas appeared, and proceeded to attack the British positions. There would be no respite from the air. Low flying ME 109's would suddenly appear, guns blazing. And, because the bullets ricocheted from rock to rock, the Tommies could be struck as one rebounded. The R.A.F. was nowhere to be seen. "Ruddy Absent F***ers" Sergeant White called them.

Two days ago (24th May), the Luftwaffe heavily bombed Heraklion. The Tommies, with John amongst them, moved out, and had left behind a town that was a shell of its former self. The streets were littered with rubble, fires burned, and dogs ran on the loose. Sewers had broken, and the stench from that and decomposing bodies was overwhelming. John was only too glad to leave the place.

Under cover of darkness, early on 27th May, John and thirty others of number one platoon took up a defensive line three quarters of the way up a hill, behind the cover of some trees and hedges, along the Chania-Alikianos road. Rather than being a continuous line, it consisted, in reality, of small groups of two to three men, with gaps of twenty yards or so in between. John found himself next to a couple of Tommies manning a Bren gun, who were methodically checking their ammunition. Away to the right, were a couple more men, and next to them, the road that meandered its way up the hill. Some distance below, number three platoon was positioned, which represented the first line of defences. Now all the British could do was to watch and wait. Unfortunately, no one had informed them that their Australian allies had withdrawn from the left flank.

Black gave way to white, as a ground mist heralded the arrival of a new day. The mist dissipated, as the powerful rays of the sun broke through, and the familiar heat haze developed. Another scorcher of a day! From his position, John could see the German troop carriers amassed on the beaches and fields adjacent to Maleme and its aerodrome. Yet more of the planes with the little black crosses on them arrived, and the contrast between the opposing sides disheartened him –the Germans were being steadily reinforced, the British were not. John had a grandstand view of the fields up which the Germans must attack. As the wind swept through the crops, it exuded a heady perfume; John reflected upon what madness it was to bring war to the island. But, the Germans, under their opportunistic (madman) leader Hitler, had broken the peace, and John, as a professional soldier would unquestionably do his duty and uttermost to defend Crete.

Several fields below, the Germans fanned out, and advanced, half-crouching, in large numbers. The same paratroopers that had helped Germany win such stunning victories in Belgium and Holland; these were well-trained men, some of them would undoubtedly be holders of the Knights Cross, and may have even been personally decorated by Hitler. Their manner was slightly cautious, most probably because of the unexpectedly high casualties of the previous few days. What concerned John, though, was that there were too many to count. As they neared, the Germans would disappear and then reappear, as they quietly slipped in and out of hedges and trees in the olive groves, like snakes along the floor of the jungle.

The familiar noise of battle commenced, as bombs and shells descended on the defender's positions, and small arms fire opened up. John felt his mouth go dry, as the front line of Tommies started to engage the enemy in battle.

Countless grey-clad figures fell, but there were such overwhelming numbers of them, that they were quickly able to puncture the first line of British men. The Germans seemed to be making the best progress, over to the left, and John could see the men on that side, in the second defensive line fighting fiercely, hitting Jerry with all the firepower they possessed.

A couple of British wounded staggered up the hillside. Their faces were ashen. One had sustained severe injuries (from at least two enemy bullets), to an arm, which was barely attached to his shoulder. The other, half-dazed, sported a very bloodstained bandage around his head, and was mumbling incoherently -a depressing sight.

Before long, John and the rest of the men around him came under direct fire. The crack of bullets through the air came worryingly close to John. A few determined bursts from the Bren gun sent a group of Germans scurrying back a little distance down the hill for cover. The immediate threat was over. However the British had won only a brief breathing space.

A lull in the battle signified that the Germans were consolidating the positions that they had gained, and were reassessing the situation. A voice from one of the British N.C.O's doggedly urged everyone to stand firm.

As John wriggled into a more comfortable position, his attention turned to a solitary figure in the road, some seventy to eighty yards away. A helmet-less Tommy, evidently seriously injured, was crawling up the stony road, at a pitifully slow pace. John noticed that the lower half of the man's trouser was badly torn, and that his lower leg and ankle was bleeding profusely. The Tommy groaned, and paused for, perhaps, quarter of a minute, before his muddied hands edged him forward, once more, that little bit closer to the British line. The wounded man embodied a spirit of defiance and hope. John thought that he glimpsed a smile on the man's face, or it might have been a grimace. He looked as if he was in his thirties, probably a family man with a wife and two young children at home.

One of the medics had scrambled past John, eager to step out onto the road, to go and provide the suffering Tommy with some succour. However, an N.C.O. ordered the medic to stay put, since the man on the road was too exposed, and the Germans could not be trusted to respect the Red Cross on the medic's helmet.

The pair was still remonstrating, when a single shot rung out. The Tommy became motionless, and a red stain appeared in his side, which steadily grew in size. His tortoise-like advance had bought him to within thirty yards of the Allied positions. It seemed at that moment that hopes for the remaining Tommies was fading fast.

The order came to retreat. The Germans had broken through half a mile away on the left flank, and there was a real danger that the British positions might be attacked from the rear. Ammunition, or lack of it, was becoming a problem for the remnants of number one platoon. Captain Smith confirmed that there was no likelihood of any reinforcements arriving (only the Germans were being reinforced), since the Allies were being put under pressure all along a thirty-plus mile front. The British withdrew through the ditches along the edges of the fields, like small mammals scuttling for shelter, as swift as they could.

Once at a safe distance, and drastically reduced in number, the Tommies, sweating in the spring heat, many without helmets, rejoined the dirt road, and marched as two ungainly columns. Later that same day (27th), Chania, the Cretan capital fell to the Germans.

Ten minutes later, they reached a village. The officer in charge announced that they would make their next stand here; the way things were going it might also be their last. The men dispersed to take up positions in and amongst the chalk white (stone) houses. The plan was to draw the Germans in, and eradicate them in the street fighting, which should favour the defenders.

The village consisted of about thirty to forty houses. There was the one road leading into the village, which branched off into two directions, at the centre of the village. Fearing the worst, most of its inhabitants, had fled the past couple of days. One raven-haired woman in her thirties emerged from her house, with two children in tow, and asked the Captain as to what she should do. The Captain told her in simple terms, that she and her children should leave immediately –The Germans were coming, and the British would only be able to delay their advance for so long. Less than two minutes later, the woman, with a bag slung across her shoulder full of just a few meagre possessions, and sobbing, departed form the village with her children.

The first Germans to make their appearance were clearly only a patrol, fewer than ten in number, to probe for weaknesses. They advanced up the road, keeping close to the walls of buildings, to present a harder target. At the first hint of gunfire from the British positioned inside the buildings, the Germans beat a hasty retreat, just one of their number sustaining a minor injury. John, occupying the sixth house inside the village, never even got a shot at them.

The fighting proper commenced, as enemy mortar bombs began to fall –a steady succession of thuds and screams from the buildings opposite John, signified that these weapons were meeting their targets with deadly accuracy. Next, came the sound of German voices. Small arms fire could be heard around the first few houses in the village.

John heard a faint whisper, then a loud 'crump', as a mortar bomb announced its arrival in the street outside, which sent a shower of broken glass flying into the room. John quickly gathered his senses, and rested his head against the wall, before carefully leaning through where the pane of glass should have been, and looking out into the chaotic street.

John spotted a solitary grey-clad figure running into the village towards a house, but he was too slow, and by the time he took aim, the German had gone. He was searching for an unseen enemy, for the Germans were obviously all around, but he had a limited field of fire from the building, and was also likely to receive a mortar bomb through the roof, at any moment!

Having checked the back of the building, and noticing that rocks largely obscured it, John opted to sneak out of a rear window. Moments later, he was haring along, past the backs of houses, and scrambling over stone walls, whilst throughout, guns cracked, bombs exploded, and the agonized screams of men came from inside the village. As he came to the road junction at the centre of the village, he was dismayed to discover that the only British that he could see were dead. Equally appalling, was the sight of a boy lying lifeless in the street. Evidently, not all of the inhabitants had got out of the village to safety.

No sooner had he halted, than John was alerted by a sound of movement from within the rocks behind him. John spun round, rifle at the ready. He spied a German helmet, and that was all he needed. The German never even had the chance to spot John, as the bullet hit him in the face.

The German had not been alone, and a determined burst of small arms fire came from amongst the rocks. John scrambled to his feet, and sprinted like mad, the bullets whistling past his head, the entire time. He dodged and weaved into the centre of the road, and threw himself down, diving for cover, behind an old well.

Panting for breath, he turned round, and was surprised to see some faces peering out at him from a couple of the buildings. As he squinted in the sunlight, John recognized a few of the bemused faces. A concerned voice, which he recognized as that of Sergeant White, called out to him.

"John Baker! What on earth are you doing down there, lad?"

There was no time to reply. The Germans were drawing closer, house by house. Furthermore, there was however many of them who had relentlessly pursued John from the rocks. That persistent group, were now taking frequent potshots at the well. John felt that the entire German Army was shooting at him, and he had but one thought —to survive!

From the relative safety of buildings, those few British provided John with some covering fire. One German that had got a little too brave, exposed himself to the British, and fell.

Throughout, small pieces of stone were being chipped away from the well, and falling besides John. Meanwhile, German bullets created a pattern of chips and holes in the front of buildings.

A German was hit, and then a Tommy would receive a bullet, too. Both sides were firing blind at each other, like two drunk boxers sparring in the dark, and there was poor John caught right in the crossfire. He simply *had* to get away from there.

A grenade thrown from an unseen British hand exploded near the German positions. This provided the enemy with a timely distraction from the British soldier pinned down by the well. John sprung up, and began to sprint for the cover of the nearest building on the British held side of the village. The respite was all to brief, as the sound of gunfire meant that the enemy had started shooting at John, again.   Instead of running in a straight line, John weaved from side to side, to provide the Germans with a more difficult target.

Then his luck finally ran out. John felt an excruciating pain in his lower leg that was like a severe bee sting and he found himself rolling the last handful of yards into the doorway of a building, almost losing his rifle in the process. He had been shot, and the blood was coming out of the hole in his trousers that the bullet had made. Grimacing, he crawled on his hands and knees deeper inside the house, in search of something with which to bind his leg, to prevent further blood loss. Fortunately, we was able to find a clean looking table cloth, and he tore this in half, and tied it tightly around his wounded leg; although it checked the blood flow, the pain was not lessening.

Outside, the battle was still raging intensely. The Germans set their mortars to work on the remaining British positions, once more, and it appeared that they were slowly flushing the Tommies out from the buildings one by one.

John found himself climbing out of a rear window of another house, although this time, with his wound, the task became more difficult. He was pleased to discover a couple of Tommies defending the very next house, however, they informed him that they were each down to their last round of ammunition, and that they were vacating the premises.

A short while later, the trio had reached the last house in the village. Approximately a score British were assembled there in all and the looks on their faces betrayed the fact that their situation was hopeless. There was a sense of urgency around the place, and a medical officer (seemingly the only one left) only briefly quizzed John about his injured leg. John replied that that his leg hurt, but he could still walk reasonably well, and that he would soldier on as best he could. An officer announced what they all knew was inevitable – they were pulling out.

They began to head south, towards the southern coast, where they hoped that the Royal Navy would evacuate them. The march would be an imposing one, for they had a distance of thirty miles to cover, and every man was hungry, thirsty and had been fatigued by battle. The road was a tip, littered with discarded helmets and rifles. There was also the miserable sight of bombed out and torched vehicles. It was all too reminiscent of the retreat to Dunkirk…Except it was if anything worse, for there was the tortuous heat of the sun, and the nuisance of flies the whole time.

They met more men on the way –remnants, stragglers from other battered units, whatever you liked to call them; Australians, New Zealanders, British, most of them leaderless. Discipline had broken down. At one stage, an Australian private passed awkwardly by them, on an army motorbike, which he was struggling to control, evidently a deserter, and the vehicle stolen. The allied troops were without air cover, and faced the danger of being bombed and machine gunned by the Luftwaffe. They had to leave the road, and take a harsher track that was stony and cruel to the feet. Behind them, the Germans –far superior in number, and better equipped, were pursuing them relentlessly.

John's spirits sank ever deeper, as he surveyed the tall mountains that the route obliged them to pass through. The road was anything but straight, consisting of numerous hairpin bends that went up and up over two thousand feet. He had already crossed two brooks, and was having to walk with wet feet, -not particularly pleasant. He had been struggling to keep up, and he knew that the air would be thinner in the mountains, making things even more difficult for him.

The weather worsened, and during a pause, the officers arranged for a small group of men to form a rearguard, to delay the German advance. John decided that he could continue the difficult trek no longer, and so volunteered to stay behind. As the column of retreating men disappeared into the distance, into the barren uplands, he was naturally pensive. Now, perhaps more than ever, his fate would rely on the luck of the Gods.

In the end, there was no heroic last stand. The Germans appeared, and after the briefest exchange of gunfire, the most sensible option for the outnumbered British was to raise the white flag in surrender; at least their lives would be spared that way. With the exception of one haughty officer, the Germans treated the British well, and even went as far as providing the prisoners with cigarettes. For the Germans, it had been a tough battle too, and they gave their enemy some grudging respect.

As John was led away into captivity, he thought of his parents, brother and sister, everyone except himself. He felt that he had let them down, now that he had abandoned the fight. It truly marked the lowest point of his life. But, he had not asked to be shot, indeed, he had struggled on to the limits of his endurance, and done everything that was asked of him, during the course of this war, in Belgium, France, Africa, then lastly Greece and Crete. Now, as John sat out the remainder of the war, it would be down to others to continue the struggle, for however long it would take to defeat the evils of Nazism.

After retracing his route back down the harsh mountain road, John found himself in a large, stinking prison near to Chania. Initially, there were no proper latrines, and as for food he had to survive on a pitiful daily ration of three biscuits and a little porridge. Outside, the dead lay unburied. Within a couple of months, John would be transferred to a prison camp in Poland.

On Sunday 1st June it was announced that all allied forces had been withdrawn from Crete. Ironically, it had been a year since Dunkirk. Nine days later, the Prime Minister was obliged to defend his record to M.P.'s. Winston Churchill told an angry Parliament.

"I have not heard that Herr Hitler had to attend the *Reichstag* and say why he sent the *Bismarck* on her disastrous cruise. I have not heard that Signor Mussolini has made a statement about losing the greater part of his African Empire."

The Prime Minister went on.

"I do not consider that we should regret the battle of Crete. The fighting there attained a severity and fierceness, which the Germans had not previously encountered in their walk through Europe. In killed, wounded, missing and prisoners we lost about 15,000 men. This takes no account of the losses of the Greeks and Cretans, who fought with the utmost bravery and suffered heavily. On the other hand, about 5,000 Germans were drowned in trying to cross the sea and at least 12,000 were killed or wounded on the island. The German Air Force suffered extraordinary losses. Above 180 fighter and bomber aircraft were destroyed, and at least 250 troop-carrying aeroplanes, and this, at a time when our own strength is overtaking the enemy's, is important."

It was true that the British had extracted a high price from the Germans for taking Crete, however the *Fallschirmjaeger* returned to Germany as conquering heroes, and Hitler now ruled an empire that stretched from the Atlantic coast, across to the Balkans. The whole of continental Europe with the exception of the neutrals (Portugal, Spain, Sweden and Switzerland), was either occupied by the Nazis, or ruled by puppet governments. Hitler's armies seemed unstoppable, only Britain, which he had not been able to subdue, remained a thorn in his side...but, given time, the British should yield. Egypt, Russia and Turkey were all under threat; to which of these countries would the German dictator set his sights next?

CHAPTER 18 – FATE PLAYS A HAND

Hannah thought back to that decisive day in late May. It had began as usual at the breakfast table, her sitting there all pensive, fiddling nervously with her spoon, before her visit to the recruiting office, the other three, Beth, Richard and Tom talking excitedly before departing to school. She had deliberately dragged her feet getting ready, and Emily, who was fully supportive behind Hannah in her venture, gently told her that it was time she better got going.

As she climbed the steps to the headquarters building, she felt butterflies in her stomach, and feelings of doubt crept in –would she appear too young? Once inside, a lieutenant who didn't seem that much older than herself, took her under his wing, asked her a few questions, vital statistics, schooling etc., and together, they completed a few forms.

There was a wait for the medical, a humiliating ordeal. Half a dozen recruits were obliged to stand in their underwear whilst a female Medical Officer who was built like a battleship went along the line inspecting them like pieces of meat, prodding them here and there. It could only have been worse if a man had been inspecting the girls.

The Auxiliary Territorial Service, or A.T.S. was the women's branch of the army. The A.T.S. had been launched in September 1938 as an attachment to the Territorial Army, and the women received two-thirds of the men's pay. Women aged between seventeen and forty-three were allowed to join the A.T.S. They were not allowed to fight in battle, so worked as clerks, cooks, drivers, postal workers, storekeepers amongst other things. In 1940, A.T.S. telephonists were some of the last to be evacuated from Dunkirk. The uniform worn by the A.T.S. consisted of a khaki shirt and tie, serge khaki tunic with four pockets on the front and a mid-calf skirt. Brown epaulettes bore the letters A.T.S.

Hannah had got friendly with a girl called Iris, who was eighteen. Boredom was the main reason why Iris had joined up, plus a niggling sense that in some small way she should do her patriotic duty. She confided in Hannah that on the bus on the way to the recruiting office, she had almost felt like getting off and going back home, wandering if she had really thought it over properly, and done the right thing! Her friends had even tried to discourage her from joining.

Later on, over tea, Hannah had enlightened her brother and the Pavitts with events during her day at the recruiting office.

"So you're a fully signed up A.T.S. girl, then?" Asked Beth.

"Yes," replied a proud Hannah.

"You're really leaving us?" Asked Tom.

"Yes," nodded Hannah.

"It won't be the same without you," said Richard.

"Hannah's been spending more and more time with Peter than with us, anyway," reasoned Beth.

"But you'll see me some weekends," there was a tinge of guilt in Hannah's voice. "What will you be doing there, Hannah?" Enquired Emily, as keenly interested as the others.

"Well, I wanted to be a courier, and learn to ride a motorcycle. I would like to ride my own little bike. However, they've decided to made me a cook, instead."

"You might fall off a motorbike," observed her brother.

"I'm sure you'll be a very good cook," said Beth reassuringly.

Tom spoke.

"Can you cook, then, Hannah?" He asked.

"Yes, cheeky!" Replied the girl.

The group laughed.

Hannah continued.

"When we were there –at the recruiting office- after having signed up, one of the army men gave us a little speech about how our period of service would make us 'better wives, mothers and citizens' and so on."

Tom addressed his sister.

"You'll have to join up next year, then, Beth!"

The girl thumped the grinning boy playfully on the arm.

"I'm not planning on marrying anyone yet!"

They had laughed some more with Hannah that evening, as she recalled more stories of the A.T.S. They finished their meal, and the atmosphere became more subdued. Hannah looked at the young faces around the table. They were all growing up so fast. The group of four friends was slowly being broken up. She wondered *how soon before Richard and Tom got sucked into the fighting?* Hannah would now learn how to salute an officer, stand to attention, and spend many hours marching around a barrack square. She gave out a heartfelt sigh and declared.

"I'll miss you all."

The village of Oak Green was holding a fete to raise funds for the war effort. Nearly everyone in the village had rallied round to assist the fete, by helping out at stalls, providing prizes or showing support merely by being in attendance. The weather was scorching, this first Saturday in June the village green had been transformed by an army of tents and stalls, and Union Jacks in abundance. There were numerous trestle tables, on which were displayed bric-a-brac, books, plants, toys and more –some neatly arranged, some jumbled. There was the opportunity to win prizes at a coconut shy, hoop-la, raffle, hooking a duck, and a strength tester. If one was so inclined, there was a fortuneteller to visit, and for the children, there were donkey rides and a Punch 'n' Judy. Later on, there would be a chance to participate in some (silly) races, or to enter an animal in a pet show.

The Vicar, Mr. Bailey, with Mr. Hamilton dutifully at his side, formally declared the fete open, with a mercifully succinct speech, in which he spoke about the war. The conflict had now been going on for twenty-one months, and although the

British Nation was not anywhere near the mortal danger that she faced the previous summer, recent war news (with the 11th May Blitz, and loss of Greece and Crete), was poor. In keeping with the spirit of the day, the Vicar concluded his speech in an upbeat mood. Having endured so much already, the country, aided by the Empire, would continue the struggle for years, if necessary. Only eleven days ago, the British had tasted victory at sea, when the mighty German battleship, the *Bismarck* was sunk. This was welcome, since the *Bismarck* had sunk H.M.S. *Hood*, the World's biggest battle cruiser on 24th May. There had been only three survivors out of a crew of 1,416. Over two thousand had perished on the *Bismarck*. The vicar's speech was greeted with warm applause by the villagers, the ladies in their gay summer outfits, many of the men in their Sunday best, and the children wearing shorts and skirts.

The Baker children were attending the fete with Beth, Tom and their mother. Ted was not with the group, since he was assisting on one of the stalls. It would do him good, and take his mind off the farm. There was the constant balancing act between livestock and crops. Trying to feed more cattle on less grazing land, ploughing grassland for crops, restoring old tired soil on arable land with temporary grasses (leys), increased problems from diseases, pests and weeds –the list of anxieties was endless. The twins soon managed to catch Richard and Tom, and they disappeared in the direction of the coconut shy. Beth and Hannah felt duty bound to stay with Beth's mother, and the girls found themselves barely managing to feign interest, whilst Emily searched endlessly through a table of ornaments.

Clara's father David walked up to the group.

"Afternoon, ladies," he greeted the two girls with a smile.

It took Emily, engrossed in her ornaments, a moment or two to acknowledge the Constable's presence. She turned round from the table.

"Oh! Hello David. How are you?"

"I'm fine thank you." Came the reply. "How about yourself, Emily?"

"Busy. It's ever since the war started…"

"*Ploughing* for victory, I suppose?"

"Yes," sighed Emily.

The policeman turned to the girls.

"How about you two? Are you still enjoying yourselves, going on your cycle rides around all the villages?"

Beth answered.

"No, we haven't been, recently." She laughed. "Not since Hannah's had her boyfriend! She spends most of her weekends with him, and forgets about the rest of us!"

Hannah flushed.

"I'm sorry. But, you see I don't get to see Peter that much, only at weekends, with him being in the R.A.F. and me now in the A.T.S. You must believe me –you are still my best friend, Beth." She added emphatically.

Beth placed a reassuring hand on Hannah's shoulder.

"I know that, Hannah. I'm only pulling your leg!"

The policeman winked at Hannah.

"I know what it's like, young love. Although you'll find it hard to believe, I was young, once –a long while ago, now." He continued, through mist-filled eyes. "I remember when I was courting Clara's mother, I couldn't bear to be apart from her."

Emily smiled at the old romantic; she recalled that it was much the same for her, when she and Ted first met.

Clara and Samantha appeared. After the December dance, Samantha had courted Neville for a couple of months then discreetly dropped him, citing to Beth that she didn't want to be tied down, which was a bit of a shame as the airman was very fond of her. Clara announced with pride, that she had won a small toy cat as a prize on the coconut shy.

Beth remarked that she had seen her brother and Richard near there, a while ago. Samantha spoke.

"They were having a go at the coconut shy."

"-Or ten!" Chuckled Clara.

"Tom had used up almost all of his money, trying to knock down a coconut for Victoria," explained a grinning Samantha, "without success."

"Why would he want to do that?" Enquired Hannah confused.

"To win her a prize, because he fancies her," stated Clara.

Hannah gasped, and Emily shook her head, despairingly.

The Constable gestured to Beth and Hannah.

"You girls should go off and have some fun."

The girls hurried away, leaving Emily behind in conversation with David. They were quite taken aback to discover a man at one stall criticizing Churchill and his conduct of the war, stating that the Greek campaign was sheer folly and that Crete was little better. A couple of others nodded in quiet agreement. The girls hurried past. The four youngsters were debating whether to have their portraits drawn by an artist, when Richard appeared, hands in his pockets, with a dejected look on his face. He explained.

"Tom got a present for Victoria, he didn't even win it himself. Then he told me to clear off, because he wanted to be alone with her. He and Victoria have disappeared somewhere, together."

Beth raised her eyebrows.

"Really?"

"I feel really browned off!" Richard kicked the ground with his shoe.

Samantha, her manner stroppy said.

"That Victoria –she's such a flirt!"

Hannah made some remark along the lines that Tom should know better than to get involved with Victoria. Beth shrugged her shoulders –that was his lookout. They discussed the subject no further.

"Never mind, we'll look after you, Richard," said Beth.

The girls, with Richard in tow, opted to try the donkey rides. There were only two of the animals, whose bright red nametags revealed them as Ben and Bob. They had such adoring faces, that the girls would willingly have taken the donkeys home with them. After paying the required eight shillings, they rode the donkeys in pairs, first Clara and Samantha, then Beth and Richard (Hannah did not fancy a ride).

Hannah and Samantha liked the idea of having their portraits sketched. The artist, a handsome man in his late twenties, who had somehow managed to avoid the call-up, probably on medical grounds, asked to draw Hannah first. The girl sat down on a stool, tidied her skirt, and posed unnaturally stiff, with a regal air about her.

"Relax, Hannah!" Shouted Clara.

Realizing that the artist would take some time to draw his two models, Richard suggested to Beth that they nip home to collect Oscar for the pet show. The pair departed. Meanwhile, Clara could no longer resist temptation, and so the girl slipped quietly inside the fortuneteller's tent.

Twenty minutes earlier David, the French refugee, had been having problems of his own. He had managed to win a Dinky toy sports car by successfully throwing a ring onto a yellow plastic duck's head, and was now in danger of losing the prize. A couple of ruffians from the next village, who were in another class at the school in Ashford had turned up at the fete. They had rapidly been getting bored, reduced to kicking the turf disinterestedly, when they recognized David, and saw him and his car as easy prey.

"I won't ask you again, David, give it to us, or else!" Began the first, a big tall square-jawed boy called Tim; his tone was menacing.

His sidekick, Stan, a shorter lad, with a pockmarked face, pushed the French boy, who stumbled a couple of steps backwards. Still, he held the toy car firmly tight with both hands, as if it were gold.

"No!"

Whilst his tall friend stood by grinning, Stan grabbed hold of his victim's arm, and the French boy's face betrayed a look of worry.

"Get off Stan."

"I want the car, give it to me, you Jew!"

David let go of the toy; his expression was now one of shock. Stan's words had surprised, shaken and upset him as much as his aggressive actions. Tears were welling in David's eyes.

Three more boys appeared, and closed ranks around Stan, much to his surprise. David looked at the boy nearest to him with a glint of hope in his eye.

"Tom?"

Tom had taken upon it himself to become David's protector since their rather bizarre first encounter the previous summer. Initially, people suspected this was due to feelings of guilt about Tom's poor start with his new acquaintance. However, he had got to know and like the French boy -at school rather than outside school, where he still hung around with Harry, Henry and the Bakers- where David educated Tom about France, and encouraged him academically. Tom, in turn, seemed proud to act as David's chaperon, and help him develop at sport. This afternoon, Tom, accompanied by Harry and Henry (Richard was still at the coconuts) had arrived on the scene just in time for David.

Stan became worried himself, now that the tables were turned. It had not gone unnoticed to him that his tall accomplice had started to back away, and for good reason –David's group outnumbered them two to one. Tom looked at the boy with the poor complexion clutching the toy albeit with a looser grip. He reckoned he'd make a good Nazi; he was certainly as racist as one.

"Are you going to hand that car back over?" Tom demanded, looking the other boy straight in the eye.

There would be no tense stand off. Tim had already turned on his heels, and the policeman was fast approaching. Stan opened his palm and dejectedly dropped the Dinky car on the ground, before departing.

"We'll get you for this, Pavitt!" Threatened Stan, once he was a safe distance away.

"Coward!" Tom shouted back.

David thanked Tom and the twins. Tom was surprisingly modest, and said that he was merely helping a friend out. He detested Stan and Tim –always throwing their weight around when together, but –like most bullies- vulnerable when alone. He picked up the toy car and went to hand it back to David; however, the grateful French boy shook his head, and insisted.

"No, you keep it, Tom."

Thus Tom 'won' his car.

Tom could not believe how his luck was in with Victoria –*posh* Victoria who lived with her rich parents in the largest house in the village. Plus, at sixteen, she was an older, maturer girl than those in his school year. Harry and Henry would be so jealous, when they found out! The pair had left the fete in order to take Victoria's toy sports car 'prize' (which she found a little odd, but still liked) back to her home, but had made it no further than the churchyard.

Leading Tom by the hand, and professing how grateful she was to him (for her trophy), Victoria took the boy midway up the gravel path, before she sat down, with her back disrespectfully resting on a nineteenth century gravestone. She beckoned Tom to sit next to her, and the latter obeyed.

"Thanks for the prize, Tom," she playfully flicked a ladybird off his arm, and looked at him intently.

"That's OK. It was nothing."

Tom stared at Victoria. He had never seen her this close up before, and he thought that the posh girl had a slight piggy face, although in an attractive sort of way, and her enticing eyes shone like emeralds, saying *come and get me*. Before he knew what was happening, Victoria had placed a hand on Tom's bare knee and her tongue inside his mouth. Then he responded likewise.

When, at last, the posh girl pulled away, again, Tom felt as if he had kissed a wet fish, and he did not know exactly how to proceed next. However, he was excited, and this excitement intensified, when he saw Victoria pull her dress down a little from one shoulder, to reveal some flesh.

The girl smiled enticingly, and drew his head into the softness of her chest.

Next moment – footsteps! The pair quickly scrambled to their feet. The Vicar loomed into view and the boy and girl, red-faced, hurried past him, back down the path. Mr. Bailey responded with a disapproving look.

Clara had reappeared from the fortuneteller's tent. At the same time, the artist completed Hannah's portrait. The girl liked the drawing; she felt it made her look mature and pretty. Samantha, in turn, took Hannah's place on the stool.

Clara spoke feverishly.

"She –the fortuneteller- told me that, in the future I was going to marry a rich man, and have four children." Clara grabbed Hannah by the arm, and her eyes lit up, as she added virtually delirious with excitement, "*And* I shall go to university!"

Hannah tried to calm her friend down, for she felt that Clara had got very carried away with the predictions.

"I'm very pleased for you, Clara. Now, didn't we want to have a go at hooking a duck?"

"But, it's your turn, now, Hannah." Declared the policeman's daughter.

"Oh! No, no, I couldn't." Hannah dismissed the idea. She had an inkling that it was Miss Townsend dressed up in that tent.

"Why not?"

"She'll probably just say the same stuff to me, as she did to you."

"Hannah, I insist you give it a try," encouraged Clara. "Go on –it's only a bit of fun!"

"Oh! Alright then…"

It was a totally different Hannah that emerged from the fortuneteller's tent, some minutes later. The girl had a disturbed look on her face, and walked straight past Clara, as if the latter did not exist.

A concerned Clara called after her.

"Hannah?"

Hannah did not alter her course, or even turn her head; instead she reacted by breaking into a run. Clara gave chase.

Hannah reached the road, and when she saw Beth and Richard appear with Oscar, she broke down by the kerbside, burying her head in her hands.

Beth dashed over to Hannah, and enquired.

"Hannah, what is it, dear?"

Beth was still awaiting a reply from the sobbing Hannah, when Clara and Richard joined them.

"It…it's that fortuneteller." Hannah was breathing rapidly, and could only talk in short bursts. "I knew I should never…" The girl wiped a tear away from her eye. "…Never have gone to see her!" After a pause, Hannah continued. "She told me that a…" Hannah shut her eyes, she could barely bring herself to say the words that she would utter next, and so pained her. "…That she could foresee death in the near future, for a male close to me."

Beth put her arm around Hannah, and asked in disbelief.

"She said *that*? Are you sure?"

Hannah nodded, her lip trembling.

"Yes." With a haunted look on her pale face, she declared. "This means that Peter's going to die!"

Beth gently stroked Hannah's hair, and considered the fortuneteller's words. It could conceivably mean that any one of a number of people could be the subject of her prophecy –Peter, Richard, Tom, Hannah's father, or even Ted. However, it would not aid the current situation, to draw Hannah's attention to that fact.

Hannah looked searchingly at Beth, who was now fighting back the tears, herself, and cried.

"Peter's so young, and we've only known each other for a few months. I don't want to lose him –I love him, I love him!" Hannah gripped Beth on the arms. "Peter's going to die, isn't he?"

It had put a lid on things really. After Hannah's encounter with the fortuneteller, none of them were in the mood for fun anymore. Oscar would have to forgo the pet show. The Baker children and Beth said their goodbyes to Clara and Samantha, and made their way, downcast, back to the farm. Beth reasoned that Hannah was overreacting, but then what if the fortuneteller's prediction *was* right?

Ted was fuming. He had joined them later, after packing up his stall. He declared, in a raised voice, that the fortuneteller was speaking a load of "Superstitious mumbo-jumbo," and Emily had to restrain the farmer from going to "Sort the woman out for frightening the poor girl!" The subject was declared taboo in the farmhouse.

The girl turned the corner of the road and headed down the main street towards the war memorial. She walked tall and purposely with her chest sticking out, the sun was hot on her bare arms. She had put gravy browning over her legs and used an eyebrow pencil to create the illusion of stockings beneath her short skirt. She had eaten some red liquorice sweets to give the impression of lipstick, and as a finishing touch, dappled some soot on her face to look like eyeshadow.

Two boys cycled past on their bikes. One turned to the girl and shouted out.

"Hey! Look at Oxo legs!"

Victoria narrowed her eyes, and kept on walking.

A minute later, she reached the road junction, and halted besides the war memorial. She glanced up at the clock on the tower of the church, and smiled to herself, for he'd be there any moment.

She turned her head, and began to look expectantly down the road in anticipation of the motorcycle. She'd first met him exactly a week ago. The meeting was pure chance and the attraction instantaneous. He'd just pulled over at the side of the road in this far corner of the village, to check his bearings. Victoria had appeared, and approached the uniformed figure scratching his head. The girl had confirmed his route, and the pair had got talking some more. He was almost twenty years of age, thickset, an army dispatch rider, and the Corporal's stripe on his arm seemed to impress the girl. He'd set off on his way, once more, and promised to stop off at Oak Green to see her for a little while on the return journey.

The sounds of a motorcycle engine made Victoria take her attention away from a couple of ducks that had been gliding through the water in the pond. The motorcycle rounded a tree-lined bend, and came tearing up the road, startling the birds in nearby trees.

He came to a halt between the pond and war memorial, and took off his pulp fibre helmet.

"Hello, Victor," she smiled.

"Hi, gorgeous," he grinned.

He wore a three-quarter length waterproof coat, leggings, high leg boots, and leather gauntlets; on his helmet was the blue and white flash of the Royal Corps of Signals. Above a squashed nose, his piggy eyes viewed the girl with hunger. To him she was a young nubile available woman, nothing serious, a bit of fun. Something to take his mind off the long hours spent on the road. It was evident she had dressed up for him.

She looked at him with a mixture of adoration and lust. She was falling for him, and what she had felt for Jack the previous autumn paled into insignificance in comparison. Victor was a real man, a charmer, whereas Jack was hopeless, and had been an embarrassment, which had served his purpose. Victor said he'd take her out in London sometime. He joked that he'd forgotten to bring her flowers. The pair embraced.

"Have you ever been on one of these before?" he asked, gesturing towards the motorcycle.

Victoria shook her head.

"Hop on the back, then, and I'll take you into town."

He put on his helmet again, climbed onto the motorcycle, and started it up. She got on behind him.

"Remember to hold on tight," he shouted above the roar of the engine.

They took off down the street at speed, past the church hall, and sleepy outlying homes, where plumes of smoke rose lazily from chimneys. Her arms were tightly around him, and her hair flailing in the wind, whilst he leaned low over the handlebars and stared fixedly at the road ahead.

They passed by Beth and Hannah. Beth turned to her companion and asked.

"Was that Victoria just gone by on the back of that motorbike?"

He took her all the way into town, dropped her off a little distance from the army building where he delivered the necessary message to a well-spoken Captain, to return to her within minutes, and then raced back to Oak Green. She invited him back to her house. As they entered the long driveway, he removed his helmet, and slowed to a more sedate pace, and she grinned.

"My parents aren't in at the moment."

They came to a stop, and he leaned the motorcycle against a large tree.

"Nice place you've got here," he observed.

"It is, isn't it?" She agreed, and started to kiss him hungrily.

"I haven't got long," he warned, "Don't want the Lieutenant wandering where I've got to."

"No," her face dropped for a moment, then, with a glint in her eye, she said, "We'd better go inside."

Within a minute, she'd whisked him through the palatial hallway, passing a number of ancestral portraits, up the stairs, and into her bedroom. She shut the door behind them. She pulled him onto the bed, and before long, their arms were all over each other in a torrent of unrestrained passion.

Three weeks later, Victoria's world fell apart.

She had seen Victor twice more, when an unexpected and unfortunate chain of events occurred. She had missed her period, and an awkward visit to the doctors revealed that she was pregnant. After the shock, she accepted this need not necessarily be disastrous, since she believed herself to be in love with Victor. Then, the day that she intended to announce her big news to the approaching dispatch rider, her plans went awry. As he entered Oak Green, it didn't look as if the motorcyclist was going to stop, and Victoria had to signal to him to do so. She was even more surprised to find that when he removed his helmet, it was not Victor under the Signal Corps' uniform! All was apparently not lost, for the rider knew Victor, and informed the girl that Victor had been taken off that particular route. He promised to get a message to his colleague from her. With slight embarrassment, Victoria stressed that he must inform Victor that she was expecting his child. After seven anxious days, the familiar sight of the motorcycle loomed into view, and the girl by the war memorial pressed her hands together in expectation. The soldier dismounted, and walked across to Victoria with a look of indifference on his face. Next, came perhaps, the biggest shock of them all.

"What did you say your name was, love?" He asked her.

She was momentarily taken aback.

"Victoria."

He'd denied all knowledge of the girl. He'd never clasped eyes on her, let alone slept with her. She protested to the man standing in front of her that that was ridiculous, she was carrying Victor's baby. But, even when his colleague pressed Victor about his alleged relationship with the girl and mentioned the pregnancy he was met with denials and lies. The dispatch rider regretted that there was nothing more that he could do, and that he had to get going. Victoria, tearful, tugged pleadingly at his coat; he *must* help her somehow.

"I'm sorry, love."

With that, the man got on his motorcycle, gave Victoria a last pitiful glance, then went on his way, leaving the girl very much alone.

Victoria collapsed down against the memorial. Deep down, she realized that Victor didn't want to know her, or her baby. As the tears streamed down her face, she called him a serpent, a coward, she felt totally used by him, and regretted that she had fallen for his charm. It was all just a game to him, another notch on the bedpost. She knew that she would have to tell her parents soon, and that she would be ostracized. The light was fading, as rain clouds moved in, and the wind stirred the leaves on trees. The hairs pricked on her arms. A dark and judgmental cloud now hung over her life and future. In desperation, she would try and get Jack back, get him to help support her and the baby, alas to no avail.

CHAPTER 19 - RUSSIA

The 22nd June 1941.

Hannah repeated the words in her head, once more, like a mantra. 22nd June 1941 – A truly momentous day, one that would go down in history, and perhaps even mark *the* turning point in this awful war. As the girl watched the slowly setting sun, she noticed a cat slink its way across the fields at the back of the farm. I suppose to you, thought Hannah, it's just been like any other day, no cares in the world, save getting the necessary three or four meals in a day. To be a cat, or (like Oscar) a dog, even, oblivious to mankinds troubles…Hannah half closed her eyes, and tried to imagine the scene hundreds of miles away to the East, the Stukas diving, the relentless drive of the panzers, the destruction, the suffering, and the terror. She quickly opened her eyes, again; no, she did not want to imagine what was going on in the Soviet Union, as over three million men of the Wehrmacht advanced, ignorance probably was bliss. Hannah recalled Ted's words -*My enemy's enemy is my friend,* and reflected upon the events of Sunday 22nd June 1941…

There they all were, the four children that were, doing nothing in particular, in one of the outlying fields, whilst Ted, assisted by a farmhand toiled on his tractor. The two boys were messing around in the grass, and as usual, it was Tom's voice that could be heard most of the time. Beth had been keeping herself busy, sitting at the edge of the field, by some bluebells, sketching the scene, and from the serene look on her face, she seemed to be totally at peace with herself. There appeared to be some merit in this hobby of Beth's, reasoned Hannah, she sat crossed legged, playing with her hands, edgily. The two girls had been silent for a while, when Beth spoke.

"I can tell that you're missing a certain airman, Hannah."

"Is it that obvious?" Relied the other girl, sheepishly.

"Yes." Beth smiled. "You always go all morose, the weekends Peter isn't here."

"Do I?"

"Yes. And look at you now, all tense, as if you don't know what to do with yourself." Beth sighed. "Being in love…"

"I do worry about Peter, what with him risking his life almost daily. I suppose that's why I feel so uptight. What with that fortuneteller saying…"

Beth interrupted her friend.

"You mustn't believe what that fortuneteller said, Hannah. You've got to put it out of your mind. Peter's a very good pilot, and the Germans aren't even attacking Britain so much, now."

Hannah remained unconvinced. She felt that her friend's confidence was misplaced, and that she was in fact making matters worse. She was petrified that Beth's confidence was tempting fate, and that she would receive a phone call in the next twenty-four hours from the airbase that would confirm her worst fears. Truth was, the fortuneteller had made her paranoid. To avoid further discussion of the issue, Hannah changed the subject.

"I think that we're going to have to keep an eye on your brother –and Victoria!"

That Hannah had deliberately changed the subject was quite evident to Beth. The latter conceded defeat regarding the issue of Peter, for the time being, and replied, nonchalantly.

"Oh! It's nothing serious between those two. If you know Victoria as well as I do, then this time next week, she'll have long forgotten our Tom."

"Yes, she is a bit of a flirt."

"A bit!" Beth laughed, "That's an understatement!"

Over in the centre of the field, Tom would have begged to differ with his sister.

"It was lovely kissing Victoria, you know? When we're both older, she's going to be my wife."

A disbelieving Richard retorted.

"I thought you told Henry that kissing her was like kissing a wet fish?"

"Did not!" Tom added. "I wouldn't have kissed her ten times otherwise, would I?"

"You told Henry that you only kissed Victoria once, because the vicar came along, and disturbed you both." Said Richard accusingly.

"Well, Henry's a liar!"

"Is she better than Vera Lynn, then?" Sneered Richard.

"Tsshh! Vera Lynn? That plumber's daughter!" Scoffed Tom.

"I remember you telling me the other week, that you fancied Vera Lynn more than anyone else in the world–Gracie Fields, even."

Tom shrugged his shoulders.

"That was then. I'm going to go all the way with Victoria…"

"How do you know that?"

"Because she told me."

"Well, that's not what I heard! She told Clara and Nancy that of all the boys she's kissed, you were one of the worst!"

"Clara and Nancy? I don't believe you!" Tom turned his back on Richard, and folded his arms in a huff.

Moments later, Emily appeared in the field. She dashed over to Ted, with a purposeful look on her face, and gestured to her husband to turn the tractor's engine off. Before she even spoke, everyone in that field sensed that Emily had something important to say, and the children gathered around her.

"Germany's attacked Russia!" The farmer's wife paused to catch her breath. "They began the attack in the early hours of this morning." She said to no one in particular, "You now realize what this means?"

Emily was met with blank faces.

"I don't like the Russians, they stabbed little Poland in the back in 1939!" Declared Beth.

"Aren't the Russians our enemy?" Asked a confused Richard.

"So, the Russians are now fighting the Nazis," pondered Ted. "Presumably my enemy's enemy is my friend...?"

"Yes." Nodded Emily feverishly. "The Russians have become our allies. Isn't it wonderful news?" She grinned at the children.

Richard turned to Hannah and enquired.

"Hasn't Stalin got a moustache just like Hitler's?"

Ted had not missed Richard's words. He snapped.

"That's enough! They're on our side, now."

Hitler was staunchly anti-Communist, and he also feared that Russia might intervene in the war on Britain's side. Therefore, Russia had to be knocked out. 'Operation Barbarossa', the attack on the Soviet Union, would be waged with deliberate medieval cruelty. It was an ideological crusade, to eradicate the Slavs, who Hitler regarded as subhuman. The German dictator believed that Russia could be defeated within a few months. However, if conflict in the East dragged on for longer, then Hitler risked war on two fronts, as Britain became stronger, with arms supplied by the U.S.A.

That night, Churchill broadcast to the country, and pledged to collaborate militarily with the Soviet Union. He declared.

"Any man or state who fights against Nazidom will have our aid. Any man or state who marches with Hitler is our foe."

The Prime Minister went on.

"We have but one aim and one irrevocable purpose. We are resolved to destroy Hitler and every vestige of the Nazi regime...The Russian danger is therefore our danger..."

As Hannah gazed out of the window, at the end of that historic day, she may well have liked to contribute to the excited debate that was taking place in the local, between Ted and a few of his farming friends.

"I personally feel uneasy being allied to the Russians," declared the twin's father, Joe. He surveyed the room, and added with a look of disgust. "They're Communists!"

The man next to him chirped up.

"They killed their own Royal Family!"

Ted folded his arms, and listened in respectful silence.

The last, a younger man, his spirits clearly buoyed by the attack, said.

"I think it's the best news I've heard for ages. It will give our country some respite." He paused. "With a bit of luck the Nazis and Communists will bleed each other to death..."

The twin's father spoke again.

"I only give the Reds a few weeks, anyway."

"No, no, it'll take longer than that –it's a big country." Disagreed the man next to him. "Remember, Napoleon failed in his attempt to take Russia."

Ted emptied his beer glass, and moved his tongue across his lips, to prolong the enjoyment of his drink just that little bit longer. However, it was not only the alcohol that had satisfied him. He declared.

"I admit I'm no lover of the Communists. Though whatever you say about Stalin and the Russians, what matters most is now that the Russians have joined in on our side, we're no longer fighting this war alone."

War made strange bedfellows. But if Churchill believed that it was right to ally Britain to Russia, then Ted would back him all the way. Millions more fighting men had overnight come into the war to fight alongside Britain against the hated Nazis.

The other men quietly nodded in mutual agreement.

Ted made a silent toast in his head.

To Russia!

Saturday 5th July 1941 had been as near to a perfect day as it could be. The hot summer sun burned down; the fields were alive with the sound of insects and the crops swayed in a gentle breeze. The country lane was lined with bluebells and snowdrops. Hannah walked with her airman, with his arm around her shoulders; frequently they looked amorously into each other's eyes. A little distance in front of them, were Beth and Richard, and at the front of the group, ever impatient that the couple bringing up the rear was content to amble along, was Tom. Earlier in the day, the five of them had gone strawberry picking, and then Peter had treated them to a snack in the tearooms in one of the neighbouring villages. All the children enjoyed having Peter around; he fitted in well with the group, and was not so many more years older than them, although secretly, every one of them looked up to him.

"Come on you two, stop kissing!" Came Tom's voice, again.

The banter with Tom amused Peter. His younger cousin had already mimicked an enemy aircraft; waving his arms around enthusiastically and substituting bombs for berries, which he pelted at Hannah and Peter, causing much hilarity. He'd teased Hannah over her Tangee lipstick, an orange-red shade that was common in the A.T.S.

"Just because you're missing Victoria!" Shouted back the pilot.

Tom went silent.

Peter continued.

"Hannah's filled me in on all the details…"

"I'm not missing her! I'm not even interested in Victoria, anymore!" Tom's body language, however, suggested otherwise.

Beth turned to her brother.

"Who are you after now, then, Tom?" She asked.

"Is it Clara?" Suggested Hannah.

Tom pulled a face, and muttered something incomprehensible. He halted, waiting for the two lovers to catch up then let go of an unseen branch so that it recoiled and struck an unsuspecting Peter in the face.

"Oh! You tyke!" Peter wiped his brow.

Hannah laughed. She had only narrowly avoided receiving a mouthful of leaves, herself, the branch missing hitting her because she was shorter.

As the group continued gaily up the country lane, the war was farthest from their thoughts. The Soviets had been ill prepared for the attack by the efficient German fighting machine. The Germans had powered over two hundred miles into Russia, the city of Minsk had been surrounded by two German *panzer* groups, the Soviets had within two weeks lost thousands of aircraft, and over 150,000 taken prisoner by the Germans. Many prisoners taken by the Germans were left to starve. Special killing squads of SS *Einsatzgruppen* were murdering Jews with machineguns, and hanging Soviet officials from gallows. Finland, Hungary and Romania had also joined the war against Russia. All in all the news from the Eastern Front was bleak, and the Soviets still had further dreadful military reverses to come.

Resistance was beginning to occur in occupied France. One hundred thousand French coalminers went on strike and cost the Germans 500,000 tons of coal. Small groups had started to carry out acts of sabotage, or distribute clandestine newspapers, or assist Jewish prisoners to escape. However people offering resistance ran a high risk of arrest and torture.

But Britain was safe for the immediate future. Now the only attacks by the Luftwaffe were nuisance raids, typically just by one or two aircraft. Coastal towns and villages were targeted (as indeed they had been all throughout the Blitz), and sometimes even trains were attacked.

"Any more cheek from you, Cousin Tom, and I'll throw you in the river!" Peter warned jokingly.

Tom skipped merrily along, at the head of the group, once more. He delved into his pocket and took out a sweet.

"Are you going to share any of those sweets with the rest of us?" Beth asked her brother.

Peter had bought them the sweets, and it was amazing the transformation in the confectioner, how helpful he was to the hero in pilot's uniform.

"Now, what's that song you were trying to teach me, darling Hannah?" Peter asked.

Hannah started to sing.

"When the A.T.S. go marching by,
There's a look of pride in ev'ry eye,
Oh, the world knows they won't give in,
Women with the will to win."

Beth turned round.

"Oh! You're not singing that damned 'March of the A.T.S.' again, are you Hannah?"

Peter squeezed Hannah's arm.

"Please, do go on."

Hannah chuckled, and she continued.

'When the A.T.S. go on parade,

Ev'ry mother's heart goes on parade…"

A beautiful red squirrel scurried in front of Hannah, and momentarily paused to glance inquisitively at the girl, before it darted off, going about its business, again. Hannah leaned her head against Peter's shoulder half closed her eyes, and sighed.

"This is wonderful."

Something had disturbed the birds, which flew out of the trees bordering the road some distance behind the group. For a few moments longer, they kept walking, unconcerned, until Peter was alerted by the sound of bigger bird, an angrier bird, one made of metal, that was swooping in low, and flying at a terrific speed above the road.

Peter had seen such birds many times before, he screamed frantically.

"It's a German aircraft…!"

He did not even have time to shout *look out!* None of them saw the aircraft until it was almost on top of them. Peter threw Hannah along with himself into the ditch, and prayed that the others had followed suit, and moved swiftly.

The plane roared past, almost touching the treetops, its machine guns blazing away. During those terrifying moments in the ditch, under Peter's protective arm, Hannah dared not raise her head a fraction, although she could sense the bullets skim past dangerously close on the road.

The sky cleared, and a trail of lingering white smoke was the only reminder of the nasty shock that they had just received. Hannah's pulse rate slowly descended to normal, and she began to breathe more steadily. Peter assisted the girl to her feet, and she winced on noticing a friction burn on her knee.

Peter had not even noticed what type of aircraft it was.

Suddenly, the blood drained away from Hannah's face and her head felt as if it was spinning; she really thought that she was going to faint. There was a body in the road. And it showed no sign of life.

"TOM!!!"

For a split second, the nightmare was not happening to them, but to someone else. It was not Tom lying there —you couldn't kill him, not mischievous freckly-faced Tom. He was full of life. He wasn't dead he was only sleeping.

The agonized scream had come from Beth. Beth ran over to her dead brother, and collapsed next to him, in an unrestrained flood of tears. Several bullets had fatally struck him. The reactions of the others varied. Richard, not knowing what to do, stood staring in a state of shock, whilst his sister who had began to weep, went over to provide comfort for Beth.

The most intense display of emotion came from Peter. Hannah had never before seen the pilot get anywhere near being this angry.

"This f***ing war!" He shouted at the road, rather than any of the other three with him.

Beth remained kneeling beside her brother's body, though Hannah and Richard turned their attention to Peter.

Peter continued, still shouting, shaking with anger.

"Why Tom? He hasn't done any harm to anyone. He's not a soldier or airman! I should be dead, not him!" He turned to face Hannah, whose face was streaming with tears. "Out of twelve men when I joined the squadron, do you know how many are still alive?"

Hannah did not –*could* not- reply; she merely shook her head.

"Two of us!" Peter bellowed. "Two out of *twelve* –and the other one's crippled. I gave up making friends long ago. Do you know something, Hannah?"

The girl bit her lip so hard that she almost drew blood. She desperately wanted Peter to stop, his ranting was not making the situation any easier, and none of this would bring Tom back. She mustered a faint.

"What?"

Peter went on.

"My best friend, Percy Green, he survived an aircraft collision at twenty thousand feet, only to be killed by the bastard German pilots as he parachuted down to earth. When they found his body, it was ridden with bullets, the cowards had shot a defenceless man…" He clenched his fist, and his voice cracked, as he ended. "…Just like Cousin Tom, here."

The pilot went over, and tenderly rested an arm on Tom's body. He sobbed.

"F***ing Chamberlain! F***ing Germans! F***ing war!"

The death of his cousin had been the final straw that had broken Peter. He had been through so much, seen so many good men die, attended too many young men's funerals –maintained the stiff upper lip (British resolve) for far too long. He had had no time to grieve properly, and felt intensely guilty that he had survived. What kind of law in nature decreed that, randomly one man should live and another should die? He could picture the German pilot returning home, and reporting on another successful mission –an English teenage boy killed.

Across the boy's body, the two grieving cousins joined hands. The bottom had fallen out of both their worlds. There would be no more climbing trees, poaching fish, building snowmen, patrolling the village, or throwing paper aeroplanes at the girls, no more clowning about or intimate moments with Victoria -no more Tom. Tom would never grow old; he would always be remembered as a very young person.

Naturally, the next few days had been extremely difficult, characterized by a silence, as if the whole farm was conscious of Tom's passing. All of them felt numb to the core and unenthusiastic to do anything. Peter had calmed down, although Emily had taken it very badly, being in a semi-permanent state of tears. None of them were able to think very straight, and various friends and relatives had dropped in to help the family in their own small way, sometimes by just being there. Peter's mother had been especially helpful, assisting Emily in the cooking of meals, and Clara's father had also been a rock.

Mr. Bailey had been excellent in leading a compassionate funeral service, which was packed with villagers. The twins, Edward, Victoria and all the other youngsters were in attendance. Ted read a piece, and broke down only at the end, when he was overcome by his emotions. He later admitted that it was the hardest thing he had ever done.

Outside, after the service, as the mourners dispersed, Peter retreated to a far corner of the churchyard. Hannah instinctively followed him. Peter took a cigarette out of his jacket pocket, and lit up. Hannah was taken aback –she had never seen the pilot smoke before. After one slow puff of the cigarette, Peter held it out in front of him, with a hand that was slightly trembling. The strain was evident on his face, and there were shadows of weariness under his eyes.

Hannah sensed the anger, bitterness and guilt that were resurfacing inside her lover.

"Please don't start swearing, again, Peter." She requested.

"What's it all about, Hannah?"

Hannah had not anticipated a question –this question. She stared blankly at Peter.

He continued.

"Everything, life, the war…"

He'd lost all his R.A.F. friends, although many pilots that had fought in Britain and France the previous year were still alive.

"Well…"

"I mean, what's life come to that we're all trying to destroy each other, British, German, Italian, Russian? How long can this madness go on for?"

He desperately yearned for a time when it could all be over. A decade or so into the future, when matters such as whether to buy the latest kitchen appliances, or where to go on a family holiday would be all they had to worry about. To come home from work, whatever that might be, and to find dear sweet Hannah waiting there for him.

Hannah would, for the moment, have to be the strong one, and be a pillar of support for her pilot. She replied.

"I don't know. No one can answer that. But, what really matters is…well, we've just got to enjoy every day we have."

"Yes." Peter nodded, managing a faint smile. "Very well put."

Hannah touched Peter's cheek with her hand. She dearly wanted him to be at peace with himself again. Together they would set him free from his chains of anger and bitterness. Hannah would help him conquer his fears, open his mind and listen to his darkest secrets, starting with the death of Percy.

"Please stop feeling guilty. You're the one who's done the most against the Germans. If it hadn't been for you and the other pilots defending our island, then…"

For a second or two, the pair of them silently contemplated life in a Britain occupied by the Nazis. No, the scenario –concentration camps, slavery, and the destruction of British institutions- was too grim to imagine.

Hannah went on.

"We owe you a big debt." The tears welled in the girl's eyes. "You saved our country."

"Now don't go overboard, Hannah."

"You'll always be my hero," she said.

There was a pause -a complete change in both their moods.

"Will you marry me?"

The girl looked at the airman in disbelief.

"Marry you?"

"Yes. Why not?"

"Peter, I'm flattered, but I'm only sixteen!"

He had to be with her.

"You know I love you, darling Hannah. I love you deeply. Dash it! You're a girl with a good heart. You make me feel good about myself, and to forget all my problems. You're the person I want to spend the rest of my life with. But, if you've got any doubts, if you don't feel the same way…"

"I love you, too."

"Well, then?"

She wanted to be there with him for as many hours of every day as she reasonably could, to tend to him, cook for him, fall asleep next to him, especially during this vulnerable phase. She dearly missed him when he was away –his voice, the touch of his hand on her cheek, his lips against hers, his everything. She wanted to indulge in love and passion with her pilot, offer him her heart and make him happy.

"Yes, I will marry you, but let's wait a year or so, when I'm eighteen."

She took his hand soothingly.

Back at the farm, Richard found himself comforting Beth. He had seen her crying in her bedroom, all alone, desolate, and felt deeply sympathetic for her –how could one get over the death of one's sibling at such a young age, and in such tragic circumstances? How could Tom be so easily and cruelly taken away from her?

Sobbing, Beth asked if Tom's death was to be their reward for having spent the first couple of years of the war in a rural idyll. Richard told Beth that she must not allow herself to think like that. The truth was, and it was an unpleasant truth, that unlike in the last war, this time the killing was totally indiscriminate. In the Second World War, according to Hitler's terms of warfare, civilians had been directly in the front line as well, and would continue to be.

Beth stared across the empty room.

"If I close my eyes, I can still see Tom standing in front of me, laughing and joking, and fooling around..."

Richard put a comforting arm around the girl that had become his close friend.

"That's it, try and hang onto the good memories of Tom."

"I don't suppose that he would have wanted us to sit around being miserable over him, forever." The girl conceded.

"No. And we won't ever forget him. None of us, not even when we're old and grey," said Richard encouragingly.

"You and Hannah, you will both stay on here?"

She really wanted them to.

"Yes. I'll be here for you."

Richard said those last words with the utmost sincerity. His face touched the girl's, and the tears streamed down their reddened cheeks together, for a while.

When Richard leaned back, he did so only slightly, and with a degree of hesitation. He felt that a unique bond had developed between the pair; something that transcended the conscious, each could read the other's mind. They were now brother and sister – Beth and Richard. Their minds flew back to the dance the previous December, and now, in July, as they gazed into each other's eyes, both knew that what they would do next would somehow be right.

As one, they edged their faces closer, and their lips pressed together. The kiss was long and passionate. It was as if they had always meant to be, that the attraction had been instantaneous from day one, and that their mutual sorrow had at last bought them together. If any good could come from Tom's death, that it could act as a catalyst, and lead to something beautiful between his sister and best friend, it may be read as a sign that they (and the others) could start believing in the future.

Now the fight against the Nazis had become so much more personal, and important. In just under two years since that fateful announcement from Chamberlain on 3rd September 1939, the war had bought suffering upon both families, with the capture of John, and the premature death of Tom. They would all have to help and support each other through the difficult summer of 1941, no matter what lay ahead.

THE END

"Dear Mummy & Daddy,

It has been a horrible week. It is the middle of summer, the sun is out, and we should be happy, but instead we are sad. This war of Hitler's has caused the death of dear Tom, and caused everyone at the farm great sorrow. All of a sudden, the farm feels a colder and darker place; it's the memories, I suppose. Sometimes I wander if life will ever be the same again, although deep down I know that we all have to overcome our grief, and move on.

I wander if it is too much to ask (or to pray), that this awful war can soon end, and that we can live without daily fear of bombing and killing. I feel that I have really grown up, and become more responsible, the past few months, and being the oldest, I know that I must be strong for Beth and Richard. I also realize that material things are of no significance compared to friends and family. Until the war, I had never really gone anywhere outside London, but now I have met all kinds of new people, and shared many new experiences with them, for that I am grateful. To help those nearest and dearest to each other is what *really* matters. Without the war, I would never have met my pilot. I love Peter with all my heart, and want to be with him for all eternity, through the good times and the bad. I would give anything in the world to have Tom back.

XXXX Hannah."

EPLIOGUE

As 1941 wore on, life in Britain became dull, drab and restricted. Parts of London, such as Silvertown became deserted, and were taken over by stray cats and rats. People became bored and depressed, and in the absence of bombing their thoughts turned to food, or rather, the lack of it, as rationing continued to bite. People were always tired, and more prone to coughs and colds; spirits were further dampened by the harsh winter of 1941/42. The public's opinion of Churchill had gone down, he was viewed as constantly promising more than he could deliver, and fewer people listened to his speeches, but, then, there was no one else to blame. As 1941 turned to 1942, many Britons wanted an Allied landing in France, or elsewhere against the Germans.

The story will continue again a couple of years later in (mid) 1943. The war has truly become global, with the involvement of Japan and the U.S.A. The allies are slowly winning the war, and the story concentrates on the soldier Richard, as he advances through Europe, and on his romance with Beth, with whom he is deeply in love. On the German side, an SS officer battles with fanaticism for his Fuhrer, the madman Hitler, who becomes increasingly deluded in his bunker.

BIBLIOGRAPHY

A great deal of the work on this story was the research involved, which was aided by each and every one of the following listed below:

Binns, S. & Carter, L. & Wood, A., *Britain at War in Colour* (Carlton Books, 2000)

Binns, S. & Wood, A., *The Second World War in Colour* (Pavilion Books, 1999)

Bishop, P., *Fighter Boys Saving Britain 1940* (Harper Collins, 2003)

Boyle, D., *World War Two in Photographs* (Rebo Productions, 1998)

Brayley, M., *The British Army 1939-45 (1) North-West Europe* (Osprey Publishing, 2001)

Brown, M., *Evacuees Evacuation in Wartime Britain 1939-1945* (Sutton Publishing Ltd, 2000)

Brown, M., and Harris, C., *The Wartime House: Home Life in Wartime Britain 1939-1945* (Sutton Publishing Ltd, 2001)

Calder, A., *The People's War: Britain 1939-1945* (Pimlico, 1992)

Campbell, J., *The Experience of World War Two* (Greenwich Editions, 2001)

Clayton, T. & Craig, P., *Finest Hour* (Hodder & Stoughton, 1999)

Croall, J., *Don't You Know There's a War on? The People's Voice 1939-45* (Hutchinson, 1988)

Cross, R., *World at War* (Parragon, 1998)

Gilbert, A., *The Imperial War Museum Book of the Desert War: 1940-1942* (Sidgwick & Jackson Ltd, 1992)

Harris, C., *Women at War in Uniform 1939-1945* (Sutton Publishing Ltd, 2003)

Hart, P., *At the Sharp End: From le Paradis to Kohima, 2nd Battalion the Royal Norfolk Regiment* (Pen & Sword Books Ltd, 1998)

H.M.S.O., *Roof Over Britain: The Official Story of the A.A. Defences 1939-1942* (H.M.S.O., 1943)

Herridge, C., *Pictorial History of World War Two* (Treasure Press, 1989)

Lake, J., *The Battle of Britain* (Silverdale Books, 2000)

Lord, W., *The Miracle of Dunkirk* (Wordsworth, 1998)

MacDonald, C., *The Lost Battle of Crete 1941* (Macmillan, 1993)

Matanle, I., *World War Two* (CLB International, 1989)

Mosley, L., *Backs to the Wall: London Under Fire 1940-1945* (Book Club Associates, 1974)

Nesbit, R, C., *The Battle of Britain* (Sutton Publishing Ltd, 2000)

Reader's Digest Yesterday's Britain (The Reader's Digest Association Ltd, 1998)

Shulman, M., *Defeat in the West* (Masquerade, 1995)

The Second Great War, volumes 1-4 (The Waverley Book Company Ltd, 1939)

The War Years (1) 1939 The Day War Broke Out (Marshall Cavendish Partworks Ltd, 1990)

The War Years (3) 1941 The World on Fire (Marshall Cavendish Partworks Ltd, 1991)

Tonge, N., *A World in Flames: Civilians* (Macmillan, 2001)

Turnbull, P., *Dunkirk Anatomy of Disaster* (B.T. Batsford Ltd, 1978)

Wellum, G., *First Light* (Penguin Books, 2003)

World War Two Day by Day (Dorling Kindersley, 2001)

Printed in the United Kingdom
by Lightning Source UK Ltd.
124753UK00001B/22/A

9 781845 492274